THE FIFTH COLUMN

JOHN FENZEL AND TOM RENDALL

BREATHE PRESS

Published by BREATHE Press

BREATHE is a registered trademark of BREATHE, Inc.

This is a work of fiction. Names, characters, places, and incidents either are the product of the author's imagination or are used fictitiously, and any resemblance to actual persons, living or dead, business establishments, events, or locales is entirely coincidental.

Printed in the United States of America

Library of Congress Cataloging-in-Publication Data
Fenzel, John
Rendall, Tom
The Fifth Column / John Fenzel.—ed.
I. Title

ISBN 978-0-9822379-2-2 (acid-free paper)
1. President—Fiction. 2. Congress—Fiction. 3. Supreme Court—Fiction. 4. Government—Fiction.
6. CIA—Fiction. 7. Assassination—Fiction
8. Military—Fiction. 9. Maine—Fiction.
10 9 8 7 6 5 4 3 2 1

First Edition

Dust jacket design by Kate Handling Creative

For our Fallen Comrades and their Families

Acknowledgements

The Fifth Column is, in every way, a collaboration. Many people have encouraged and supported this effort, and have stood by our sides from the outset. Foremost, are the men and women who we have both served alongside in times of peace and war--at home and abroad. You know who you are. Your extraordinary service, and your stories were the inspiration for this novel. While this is a work of fiction, the men and women who have inspired our characters are as genuine as they are selfless and heroic.

We are very grateful to all of those who have provided their ideas and support in crafting this novel from the very beginning. This is the collaboration—because no (good) novel is possible without it.

Ciri Fenzel's tireless efforts on our behalf have been crucial to *The Fifth Column* throughout—from beginning to end. Without her hard work and commitment to seeing this project through, this novel simply would not have materialized. From weaving together the initial story idea to the process of writing, revising and publishing—Ciri's constant support and belief in this as a story of value are evident in virtually every page of this novel.

As always, Dr. Joan Murnane's world-class medical and veterinary expertise set the stage for *The Fifth Column*. Joan's unwavering support to this effort, every stop of the way, has been essential to a story that is at once realistic, plausible and compelling. Joan's support is nothing new, of course—she played an important role in crafting the story for *The Lazarus Covenant* as well!

We are very grateful to Tammy Thorp for her discerning eye and enthusiastic support. As an early editor, international security expert, and good friend, Tammy's clarity of vision and deep understanding of the Department of Defense, the interagency, and our world were instrumental in ensuring we were crafting a convincing and cogent story. Tammy's critical eye is evident throughout these pages, and for that—as well as her friendship—we could not be more fortunate.

Thank you to Knute Turgidson—a patriot, warrior, leader and operator. A great friend who provided vital operational insights that could only come from someone who has long traveled the warrior's path. Knute's tireless efforts and amazing eye toward detail and discerning vision were crucial to the success of *The Fifth Column*—from beginning to end.

Muriel Fenzel—who has been listening to John's stories for over a half century, and who has never hesitated to tell him when he was completely "off the reservation"—a valued editor, voracious reader, and passionate supporter, and incredible mom, always inspiring others toward a higher standard.

We could not be more grateful to Pete Clarke who led us on a full "insider's tour" of the United States Naval Academy. Pete's insights were not only eye opening, but also startling in their implications for the long-term safety and security of the installation. While the scenario described in The Fifth Column is fictitious and frightening, it is all-too conceivable. It's also likely that we can thank Pete for the inordinately long Department of Defense Security Review for this novel!

Sincere thanks to Emil Praslick, a legend in the long-range competitive shooting community, extraordinary service rifle coach the U.S. Army Marksmanship Unit (AMU), and the finest shooter we know.

Many thanks to LTC Dave Clore (USA, Ret.), a great Soldier, leader and friend—for his tremendous insights into installation security, and who helped us recall our days in 5th Special Forces Group (Airborne) at Fort Campbell.

Sincere thanks to Kate Handling—an amazing designer—for creatively bringing *The Fifth Column* to life on these pages, and for her steadfast patience and attention to detail.

Each of these magnificent people read and worked on *The Fifth Column*'s manuscript as it evolved, and could not be more grateful for their guidance, ideas, enthusiasm, and support. Because of their help, we know *The Fifth Column* is a better, more relevant, cogent, and enduring story.

"A nation can survive its fools, and even the ambitious. But it cannot survive treason from within. An enemy at the gates is less formidable, for he is known and carries his banner openly. But the traitor moves amongst those within the gates freely, his sly whispers rustling through all the alleys, heard in the very halls of government itself. For the traitor appears not a traitor; he speaks in accents familiar to his victims, and he wears their face and their arguments, he appeals to the baseness that lies deep in the hearts of all men. He rots the soul of a nation, he works secretly and unknown in the night to undermine the pillars of the city, he infects the body politic so that it can no longer resist. A murderer is less to fear."

Marcus Tullius Cicero

Prologue

LUKE ARCHER HAD COME TO EXPECT the unexpected. That's what he attributed his survival to throughout all the years. But as familiar as the sound of incoming rotor blades was to him from years past, he never expected to hear them pounding directly outside his bedroom window at 3:07 in the morning.

Not any more at least. After twenty years in the most secretive corners of the Special Operations community, and another decade and a half in the CIA, he thought those days were over. After a turbulent career in and out of uniform, building a cabin on a remote lake in midcoast Maine, and teaching fifth graders at a local elementary school was his way of sealing that deal to himself. And yet, through the years, he'd come to understand that for every promise made, they usually came with a price attached, and this would be no exception.

Beau, Archer's German Shepherd, began whining intermittently at the foot of his bed at first. And then as the pounding intensified, he started barking wildly at the front door. Archer felt a familiar sensation in the pit of his stomach. He rose quickly, put on a pair of coveralls and boots, and grabbed one of the semi-automatic rifles standing inside his closet—this one, a 7.62mm DPMS carbine, equipped with a night vision sight. He stepped outside his side door into the frigid winter air— made colder by the helicopter's rotor wash blasting snow as it landed. An extended whiteout descended on the house, sending drifting snow, a fierce wind, and frigid air in a ubiquitous cloud around him.

It was bitter cold, even by Maine standards. Standing behind a tree, shivering—Archer's heart was beating like a bass drum. He could dimly make out the outline of the helicopter only yards in front of him.

Brown-haired, with broad, well-formed shoulders, and a former weightlifter's build, Archer was barely provided cover by the tree. The powerful wind from the helicopter rotor wash blew snow into his shoulder-length hair. His face was weathered and unshaven, with skin taut along high cheekbones, a strong jawline, and crow's-foot eyes that looked as if they had seen too much in a single lifetime.

He'd purchased the property ten years ago from a friend, sight unseen—but he'd never expected his front yard would someday serve as a helicopter landing zone.

Squinting his eyes and shielding them until the rotor wash diminished, he recognized the black helicopter to be a UH-72A Lakota—a Light Utility helicopter that he knew was used by both the Army and the "three letter agencies"— including the CIA—principally for VIP transport.

Archer swore under his breath—the Army wouldn't be paying him a visit at this late hour and after all these years, so that left only one other possibility—and the realization gave him an even greater feeling of foreboding.

A crewman exited the helicopter and as the rotors slowed, he opened the passenger door. A tall man stepped out—ducking his head and walking quickly toward the front door, wearing what appeared to be jeans, boots and a leather aviator's coat. As he drew closer, Archer recognized the man well before he reached the porch as Chris Stockman— the Chief of the CIA's Special Activities Division, or "SAD." Only a year ago, Stockman had worked for Archer when Archer was the SAD Chief.

"Chris?" Archer shouted above the helicopter's whine. "Why are you here?"

Stockman extended his hand to Archer, but it was not reciprocated. "Can we go inside?"

Archer nodded and opened the door, giving Beau a command in German, to which he laid down, just inside the doorway. Maintaining an intermittent, low growl, he never took his eyes off Stockman.

"He's well-trained," Stockman said, removing his jacket. "But I'm not sure he likes me."

"He doesn't like anyone at 3 o'clock in the morning." Archer said, placing the carbine on "Safe," and setting it back in the closet. "Normally I'd say it was good to see you, but at this hour, even a rabbit knows a weasel's track same as a hound does."

Stockman shook his head, confused by Archer's southern colloquialism. Stockman was an imposing figure. Six and a half feet.

Thick legs, like a Russian power lifter's, and a barrel chest. Archer recalled that he would not hesitate to use his stature to his advantage—to intimidate, or to threaten, if necessary. He wiped the snow free from his cowboy boots in the entry before walking over to the stone fireplace in the center of the cabin. "Well, if you have to know, the most obvious reason is that your phone number isn't listed, and you only list a post office box for your pension. Some folks in the office remembered your plans to relocate here. We would've called, but we had no other way of getting hold of you."

"I prefer it that way," Archer replied quietly, motioning Stockman to the sofa opposite him.

As he sat down, Stockman pointed at a photo on the mantle beside a wooden box. "A good photo of you and Becky."

Becky had been Archer's wife, murdered under mysterious circumstances years before. Stockman had met her several times in social settings at Fort Campbell, Kentucky, when he'd been assigned to as an advisor to 5th Special Forces Group.

Archer nodded, looking up at the picture. "It was the last photo of us together."

Stockman nodded his understanding. "What are you doing with yourself these days?" Stockman asked conversationally.

"Teaching fifth graders," Archer replied. "Hardest job I've ever had." Anxious to change the subject, he asked pointedly. "Now, maybe you can tell me—what's the real reason you just landed in my front yard?"

"We have eyes on a funeral in Peshawar," Stockman answered directly.

"I'm done with all of that," Archer interrupted. "You, more than most, should know that."

Stockman nodded, paused, and continued. "They're all noncombatants—civilians—but the funeral is for the cousin of Omar Mehsud Shah, and we have two sources who say he's attending."

"How reliable are they?" Archer asked. "...Your sources?"

"Very," Stockman nodded. "Confirmed and corroborated. Listen, you're the only one who knows what Shah looks like—his mannerisms

4

— who's seen him up close. We need positive identification before we can act."

"Where are you conducting this from? CTC?"

Stockman shook his head. "Too sensitive. We're doing it all in-house, at Langley."

Archer stood up and walked to the window, fighting back a whole host of visceral responses that involved completely losing his composure. Just the mention of that name—*Omar Mehsud Shah*—was enough to bring a series of long-suppressed memories flooding back. In Technicolor. Traumatic, painful memories he preferred to forget.

Archer nodded his understanding, feeling his adrenaline beginning to surge. He looked down at Beau. "Okay, if I'm going to do this, I need someone to watch my dog." He inhaled deeply to calm himself. "And I'll need a substitute to teach for me today. Let me send a few emails, and we can go."

As Archer typed an email to the principal at his school, and then to Beau's Veterinarian, Dr. Elena Campbell, he contemplated the reason for such a dramatic interruption in routine...for being pulled back into a world that was all-too-familiar, yet one he had desperately been trying to escape for good.

Omar Mehsud Shah.

By any measure, Omar Mehsud Shah was a ghost. He seemed to exist in name and deed alone—no one in Western intelligence or military circles had ever seen his face, until Luke Archer had viewed him through the scope of a sniper rifle in Pakistan's Northwest Frontier Province more than a decade ago. After his escape from captivity under Shah, Archer never thought he'd see him again. And yet, he realized there were few other people who would create quite as irresistible an incentive to return to Langley and its dark underbelly of clandestine operations.

After sending a few emails, Archer stepped away from his desk, and picked up the black tactical style pack lying next to the front door. "Okay, let's go."

"Were you *expecting* to go somewhere?" Stockman asked, visibly surprised. "You're already packed?"

"My 'A' Bag," Archer replied, slinging the backpack over his shoulder. "Old habits die hard."

Boarding the helicopter, Chris Stockman pulled out the dossier on Omar Shah and handed it to Archer as they lifted off. "You're familiar with most of this," Stockman shouted over the rotor noise. "But it's been updated since you left Langley."

Archer took the file and kept it on his lap before opening it, recalling the events of that day long ago in the Frontier Province, and those that followed.

It wasn't a routine mission. Both USSOCOM and the CIA had classified it as "Extreme High Risk," with several layers of "Top Secret" Code-Word Special Category/"SPECAT" information classifications assigned. The mission required that he, alone, link up with a local CIA asset in Peshawar, and infiltrate into Northern Afghanistan by any available indigenous means to conduct a reconnaissance of a planned meeting of Taliban and Al Qaida leaders.

It was the most dangerous "Singleton" mission he'd ever conducted in his career, and it didn't end well.

Shah's identity was confirmed by the local Pakistani CIA asset—a physician based out of Peshawar—accompanying Archer. Even when Archer called the identification of Shah into Langley, they wouldn't approve the Predator strike, despite Archer's repeated requests. He was about to pull the trigger himself when a group of young Pakistani boys stumbled upon his position. Archer could have killed the boys as they were approaching, and no one would have faulted him for it. But he didn't. As a consequence, they began shouting, and Archer and his asset were both captured by Omar Shah's militia. The asset from Peshawar was executed on the spot, in front of Archer.

Archer had been taken prisoner—shackled, tortured, and interrogated continuously for two weeks. As terrible as the physical punishment was—the electrical shocks, the beatings, a broken arm, and branding to his back, the worst part of his ordeal was the sleep deprivation. During that time, he began hallucinating, and could feel himself gradually losing his sanity. Oddly enough, the pain he sustained from the other methods of torture, however excruciating, brought him temporary moments of lucidity. After many of those sessions, Omar Shah would appear in his cell, speaking to Archer as if they were good friends. Shah had done his research, and somehow knew Archer had been a Special Mission Unit (SMU) Operator. He correctly surmised that Archer was now working for the CIA, leaving Archer no real space to counter or equivocate, only to resist as best he could. Ultimately, he broke under the torture he sustained—something that still haunted him.

Over the course of those two weeks, when he wasn't being observed, Archer was able to gradually loosen the fixture holding his chains to the concrete wall. The day before his birthday, he learned from one of his guards that they were planning to execute him, by beheading— and were planning to videotape all of it for propaganda purposes.

"Do me a favor, and come with a sharp blade," he replied to the perplexed guard, and added, *"Hogs like us don't know what a pen's for...."*

Had the guard been proficient in English, they would have noticed Archer working feverishly to loosen his chains further. Or they would have found the metal spoon he'd stolen.

Thanks to some very shoddy Southwest Asian masonry work, Archer successfully freed himself late that night, and climbed through the basement window under the cover of darkness. During the harrowing three hours before the sun came up over Peshawar, he plunged through alleyways and even over rooftops at one point, stealing clothes that were left air-drying at night enroute to the Austrian Consulate—the closest western diplomatic outpost he could find. After an extended, emotional conversation with the security guards at the consulate gates, he was admitted and returned to U.S. control.

Because Omar Shah was so elusive, he'd become known in CIA circles as "The Ghost." Archer was the only Westerner who could conclusively identify him. Understanding his vulnerability in the aftermath of Archer's escape, Shah remained very much a "ghost" in every sense of the word, evading numerous direct action raids, ambushes and assassination attempts through the years by constantly changing his appearance, disappearing for extended periods, allowing rumors of his death to persist, and never following a set routine.

Archer provided Langley with a detailed physical description of Shah; but the truth was, The Ghost was as nondescript as any other ordinary forty-something male in the Southwest Asia. From Shah's experience in fighting the Soviets as a young man in Afghanistan, he'd learned how to seamlessly blend in with any crowd no matter where he was—whether in Islamabad, Kabul, Berlin, or London.

Archer wondered if he would be able to still identify Omar Shah—it had been nearly fifteen years since he'd seen him. But he knew that he would instantly recognize Shah's calm, deceptively soothing voice if he heard it; and his broad, smile that widened before he laughed...if he saw it. Both the smile and laugh were unmistakable, and were indelibly imprinted into the recesses of Archer's memory.

Landing at an airfield in Portland, a business jet awaited Stockman and Archer, engines running.

Less than two hours later, they landed at Reagan International Airport, and were met by a security detail in a black Denali that drove them down the George Washington Parkway to Langley.

Turning around enroute, one of the men handed Archer a color-coded CIA visitor's badge with his old official photo and orange stripe designating his authorization, security clearance and level of access. "This is for you, Sir," the man said. "It's good for today, and can be extended if needed. The security protective officers will be waving us through the external security facility and main gate, onto the compound."

Parking in the executive parking garage under the Old Headquarters Building, commonly referred to simply as the "OHB," Archer looked up at the camera overhead and smiled, recognizing it as the same location where a very senior Agency officer was once captured on a security video in the front seat of his car in a compromising position with a young female employee. With Archer's intervention on his behalf, the official, fearing termination, received only a gentle reprimand, and the story soon faded away.

"Archer, this way," Stockman called out, directing him to the Director's private elevator.

The CIA's Operations Center is on the 7th floor of the OHB, in close proximity to the offices of the CIA's senior leadership so seniors and watch officers can quickly assemble when needed. After signing several documents reading him on to a Top Secret Special Access Program (SAP) codenamed "GHOSTLINE," Chris Stockman led him through a series of thick doors and a battery of guards inspecting IDs prior to entry.

From his prior experience, Archer knew the CIA Operations Center was far from the elaborate "Star Chamber" described by many authors and screenwriters. Instead, the Center consisted mostly of a "cubicle farm" that was divided into activities that encompassed everything from geographic operational regions to functional issue areas ranging from global economies and uranium production to compiling the President's Daily Brief, commonly referred to as the "PDB." Archer had spent hundreds of hours with intelligence analysts who lived in the Ops Center and he'd come to rely upon the handful of those who were assigned to his own programs.

Returning here, Archer felt the familiar surge of adrenaline return, along with the full awareness that he'd left it all behind for a reason.

Chris Stockman guided Archer to another glass doorway leading to a back room where only specially cleared people were permitted entry. Inside, the computer screens beyond all the glass walls glowed and flared. Archer saw two others he recognized in the room—Laura Chicone and Dan Thorne—viewing a large-screen Predator feed. Archer knew both of them well from a long past, working on countless operations together. The recognition and expressions of surprise between all three friends was instantaneous.

"I honestly never expected to see you back here again," Laura said, stepping back from their hug, smiling with white teeth and bright translucent red lips. Her face was as finely formed as he'd recalled, and her intellect was matched only by her quick wit.

"Neither did I," Archer replied. Looking around he realized he stood out in his work jeans and red flannel shirt, amidst all others who were in business attire.

"They say once you step into all of this, you can never really leave," Dan said, shaking his hand.

Archer shook his head. "Well then, we'll have to pretend I'm not really here, because after this, I'm leaving. Again." He looked up at the Predator feed on display. "What've we got?"

Chris Stockman flipped a switch and the "smart" glass walls instantaneously switched from clear to opaque, providing additional privacy inside the room.

"We have a Predator on station over the funeral for Tahir Shah, Chief Surgeon of the Frontier Children's Academy in Peshawar. Tahir was the cousin to Omar Mehsud Shah, and in the late '80s supported him and his *Mujahidin* fighters during the Afghan War against the Soviets, earning him an immense amount of prestige. His reputation and achievements are expected to bring dozens of former *Mujahidin* and current Taliban to his funeral. We've heard from his family doctor that Omar Mehsud Shah is attending."

"All the buzzards come to the mule's funeral," Archer commented absently, then pointed to the screen. "Is this the best view we've got?"

Laura shook her head. "No, we have ISR eyes-on—two unarmed Predators with enhanced optics."

She switched the monitor to a close-up image of the funeral prayers being led by an elderly man wearing a white cap and a gray embroidered jacket, leading the funeral prayers over a simple wooden casket that was covered in red flowers. The digital image was so close and so clear that the pores of the man's skin were visible.

"That's Sirajul Haq, head of the Islamic political party, 'Jamat-e-Islami'," Laura commented.

"Quite a close-up," Archer replied.

Laura nodded. "Canon built three of these lenses. We bought two for these Predators and *Sports Illustrated* got the other."

"There are a hundred or more people there, and it looks like more are joining them," Archer said. "Can we zoom out to the crowd?"

Dan Thorne drew Archer's attention to another screen in front of them.

"That's ISR too?" Archer asked.

Stockman looked directly at Archer. "That's from a sniper scope."

"Who's behind it?"

Both Laura and Dan looked over at Stockman, deferring to him to answer, or not. "One of your old teammates—Machla Peretz."

"Max?" Archer exclaimed incredulously, using Machla's acquired masculine nickname.

Machla "Max" Peretz was a former Israeli Mossad member whom he had personally recruited to the CIA just seven years ago—at first as a reports officer in order to take advantage of her fluency in Hebrew, Urdu, Farsi and Arabic and her immersion on important operational areas. With every operation, it became clear that she possessed a unique set of additional operational skills that were exceedingly rare to find in any operative or analyst.

Stockman nodded. "That's her."

Archer shook his head, visibly angry. He turned to Stockman. "You put her out there alone? An Israeli woman in the middle of Peshawar? What the hell were you thinking?"

Stockman held out his hand to placate Archer. "She's got a whole network over there supporting her behind the scenes, probably even has access to assets from her former employer... Vehicles, Predator coverage, a full QRF and we have folks in position all around her, standing by to assist, if needed…." He paused. "And she volunteered for this."

Archer continued to shake his head. "She's as talented as they come. But why risk her life for this? With all that gear she's carrying, she'll be lucky to get out alive—you know that."

"It's too late to change anything now," Stockman said evenly. "You're coming into this midstream. She's going to be fine."

"It's never too late to abort when the risk is unacceptable," Archer countered. "Now I remember why I left this outfit."

Laura Chicone turned around in her seat and pointed at the screen. "Can I interrupt?" She asked impatiently. "Max wouldn't be very happy we're having this conversation right now—if there's one thing we all know about her it's that she'd want us to focus on the target in front of us."

Archer nodded slightly, looked up at the screen and stared intently at the gathering prayer assembly 7000 miles away. "Pan out to view the men in the front row."

Laura typed a message to Max, and after a few seconds the image drew back. Archer studied the image of each male visible on the screen—all were wearing traditional Pakistani attire, standing behind Sirajul Haq, bowing and appearing to chant a series of prayers.

Archer stepped closer to the screen, and studied one middle-aged man dressed completely in white. During his capture, Archer had only seen Omar Mehsud Shah with a moustache. This man in white had a long, full beard—but the resemblance to Shah was unmistakable. He pointed at the man. "That's him—can we zoom in on his face?"

After a flurry of typing from Laura, the view of the man became so close, it surprised all four assembled around the screen. After a few minutes of waiting, the man began to take part in one of the funeral prayers and Archer could see the wide gap between his front teeth. "Now his hands," he directed.

Within seconds, the camera panned in on the man's right hand, and that was all Archer needed to see. The man was missing part of his right index finger. Shah had told Archer that it had been amputated after he was shot in the hand in a gunfight with Pakistan's Special Services Group—a raid that he'd narrowly escaped.

"That's him," Archer said decisively, and looked over at Stockman.

"Okay, got it," Stockman said. Laura Chicone typed furiously. "We'll track him with an armed Predator, and strike his vehicle when he's in transit."

"Watch him closely then," Archer said quietly. "He's slicker'n goose grease."

At once, the image of Omar Mehsud Shah changed as the crowd stepped back in noticeable shock and surprise. Suddenly a blotch of red bloomed in the center of the chest of Shah's white *shalwar kameez*, a stain that quickly grew in circumference as he crumpled to the ground.

"What just happened?" Stockman asked Laura insistently.

"Max just messaged that she's leaving her hide-spot, and—" Laura stopped mid-sentence.

"And what?" Archer asked.

Laura turned to Archer. "She said, 'Tell Archer that was for him.'" Laura said. "She fired the shot."

"Goddamn it!" Stockman frowned. "This wasn't the plan!"

"Can you get her out of there?" Archer asked calmly. Insistently.

"She's in a taxi, headed to the Pearl Continental Hotel," Laura reported directly, reading her monitor.

"Okay. Activating her E&E plan now," Dan Thorne said calmly, using the universal abbreviation for "Evasion and Escape." "We have her joining a scheduled British Airways flight as one of their flight attendants."

"What other support do we have on the ground for her?" Archer asked.

"Our team at the consulate in Peshawar will keep a look out for her—there's really nothing else we can do until she checks back in. Next contact will be in four hours when she's at the airport."

Archer walked over to Stockman. "Chris, the price of me helping you identify and eliminate Shah is that you take care of Max—understand?"

Stockman didn't say a word, visibly incensed that he'd lost control of the entire operation so unexpectedly, to his own team on the ground. It was clear that he held not only Max Peretz, but also Archer, responsible for the sudden turn in events because of his past working relationship with her in Israel and throughout the Middle East.

Archer walked out of the room. He turned to see another former SMU Operator and CIA colleague approaching him down the hall who he recognized as Jack Condon, from his hunched-forward, lumbering gait.

Condon always had a bearlike face with the freckled skin of an Irishman. That hadn't changed. What had changed were his thick horn-rimmed glasses that covered eyes Archer always knew were wide, alert and discerning.

"Jack?" Archer exclaimed. "Is that you?"

"In the flesh, Lucas!" Jack answered smiling. "Older, wiser, and a bit wider."

Archer nodded, smiling. He'd known Jack Condon for decades. They had followed one another from assignment to assignment in both the United States Special Operations Command, and in the CIA. Archer always admired his grit and intellect, and regarded him as one of the true good guys. He'd always carried more than most ever could on his wide, round shoulders. "Were you involved in this op, Jack?"

Condon nodded. "On the periphery. I found out about the funeral and recommended they find you to identify Shah."

Archer smiled slightly. "So I have you to thank for the 3AM wake-up?"

Condon laughed. "Yeah, I guess you do."

"Should've known an Irishman was behind this," Archer replied lightheartedly. "You doing well?"

Condon shrugged. "Divorced, kids out of the house, broken down. Borderline diabetic. But I still have the dogs."

Archer nodded and looked around them, down the hall. "What about this place?"

"Yeah, that's a different story altogether. And a longer one," Condon replied. "Let's grab a beer sometime, and we can talk."

"I'd like that," Archer said. "Listen, will you make sure they take care of Max?"

Condon nodded back in Stockman's direction. "He's pretty furious right now, but I'll make sure, and let you know." He paused, and his tone noticeable changed. "Did you hear about John Lee?"

Archer inhaled. John Lee was his senior weapons sergeant on his Army Special Forces "A-Team" three decades ago when he was a young Captain—an African American with the charm and good looks of Denzel Washington, and the quiet courage and grit of any John Wayne character. "What about John? I just talked to him a several weeks ago." Archer asked. "Is he okay?"

Condon shook his head. "I'm sorry to be the one to tell you— he's dying of bone cancer. A rare form, from what I understand. They've got him in the UNC-Chapel Hill Cancer Center. They're only giving him a few days to live."

Archer's smile disappeared and he pursed his lips. His heart sank. John hadn't told him about his cancer. "Okay. Thanks. I'll go down to see him," he said solemnly. Looking up at his old friend and shaking his hand, Archer said, "Keep me informed about Max, okay?"

Chapter 1

LUKE ARCHER WAS ABLE TO CONVINCE Langley Flight Ops to make an eleventh hour change to their flight plan back to Maine, and instead fly him to UNC-Chapel Hill. The flight was less than an hour, but gave Archer time to reflect on everything that had just transpired—suddenly thrusting him back into a world he'd done his best to leave—forever. It had worked, up to now. But now looking down at the landscape from 30,000 feet, he also realized that his decision had kept him from the close friendships that had sustained him during the most difficult times of his life—the tragic news about John Lee was only one example of an ever-widening gap.

Somewhere over Richmond, the co-pilot handed Archer a handwritten note he'd transcribed:

Max safe at U.S. Consulate in Peshawar. Sends her regards—JC.

Archer inhaled deeply with relief, but also understood clearly that Machla Peretz had countermanded the intent and directives surrounding her Special Reconnaissance role, by killing Omar Shah herself, rather than leave it to chance and the vagaries of obtaining political approval in Washington. She would likely be flown directly back to Langley and face a disciplinary review that would determine her future in the Central Intelligence Agency. A review that would likely result in her termination. The fact that she'd taken that shot for him didn't surprise Archer, knowing Max as he did.

After graduating from the University of Cape Town in South Africa, and then teaching English in Tel Aviv, Max had been approached for a job in the Mossad. Her language abilities, her Level Six Black Belt ranking in Krav Maga, combined with her tactical skills contributed to her meteoric rise through the ranks of the agency, where she achieved the rank of commander—the youngest man or woman who had ever held the rank.

During her time in Mossad, she was involved in some of their most daring and important operations. In her final operation, she was assigned to track down a physicist at one of their nuclear plants who sold Israeli fissile material to North Korea. She found him in Hong Kong and followed him to Bangkok.

She successfully lured the scientist to her hotel room and drugged him. As she and her team were in the process of smuggling him back to Israel on a ship to face trial, the scientist struggled with Max and suffered a heart attack. Despite forensic evidence to the contrary, Max's team blamed her for overdosing him.

The entire affair caused Max to lose faith in many of her Mossad colleagues and superiors. Max's immediate superior, however, still believed in her, and quietly asked Archer if he could keep her gainfully employed in the CIA as a dual U.S.-Israeli citizen.

Once Max left Israel, she never returned. By all accounts, her case was rare. Israelis who leave Israel are called "yordim", meaning those who go down [from Israel]. When people do emigrate from Israel, it's usually for financial reasons and career opportunities—not to be kept on clandestine ice.

While Omar Shah's elimination as a threat was not unwelcome, Archer viewed taking Max out of the game as an unacceptable cost to pay. She was that talented, and that good. And yet, with his own awareness of "the System" that had developed within the intelligence community, he knew Max's days were now numbered with the CIA through her apparent insubordination.

Ten minutes later, the co-pilot passed Archer another note from Jack Condon:

Shen meeting you at the hospital. Will escort you. —JC.

Shen Lu was Archer's old Special Forces Communications Sergeant. He had been one of the quietest soldiers, with one of the most brilliant minds, Archer had ever encountered. Long retired, Shen was a free agent on the military contract scene. After he retired, he'd become a multi-millionaire due to his patents on communications software and hardware. Both were now being used by the special operations and intelligence communities—technology that introduced revolutionary new capabilities from leveraging Intelligence, Surveillance and Reconnaissance platforms to intercepting and decrypting encrypted cell phone calls, to listening to conversations through enclosed buildings using the vibrations of window glass.

Archer knew Shen lived alone in Durham, North Carolina—and had served with John Lee in multiple assignments, on countless wartime deployments. It had been a few years since he'd seen Shen, but he was like a brother to John—and to Archer. Both men had become like family to him.

As a soldier in the Taiwanese Army, Shen's trainers recognized his analytical and intellectual skills almost immediately, and he was assigned to Taiwan's 862 Special Operation Group. When a neighbor and friend of his family was abducted by Abu Sayyaf militants in the Philippines, Shen learned of the kidnapping, and took it upon himself to find and rescue her.

With a small group of fellow Soldiers, Shen took leave and began planning his friend's rescue, despite warning from their chain of command to not get involved. The orders were ignored. Posing as a Chinese-speaking doctor, Shen was able to open communications with the kidnappers, and locate the Abu Sayyaf jungle base camp where his neighbor was being held prisoner—in the Southern Philippine island province of Sulu. With only limited help from his friends, and an abundance of improvised munitions, Shen launched an early morning raid on the camp that resulted in seven Abu Sayyaf members killed, and his neighbor's rescue—20 days after her ordeal began.

Despite the dramatic success of the operation, Shen was disciplined for conducting an unsanctioned raid on foreign soil, and separated from the Army as a result.

Archer had known the family of the woman Shen had rescued in the Philippines, and learning about Shen's predicament, agreed to meet him. Over dinner in Tainan, Archer was impressed by Shen's courage and independent approach, and agreed to fast track his U.S. Citizenship and recruit him into the Army to attend the Special Forces Qualification

Course. Shen had been the "Honor Graduate" for his Special Forces Communications Sergeant Class, and along with John Lee, had followed Archer throughout the remainder of his days in Special Forces. When Archer retired, Shen left the Army to start his own military contracting company.

Archer looked down at the expansive complex of buildings that comprised UNC's Healthcare Campus. With the helicopter's descent onto the hospital's helipad, knowing he was about to see a friend in his last days, Archer felt a familiar sense of sadness that approached despair. Standing off the far side of the helipad, he saw Shen standing straight, ignoring the force of the rotor wash.

As Archer stepped outside, Shen walked rapidly toward him, and extended his hand. Archer grasped it firmly and drew Shen to him in a tight hug. He hadn't changed much in the four years since he'd last seen him—light, olive skin, and large eyes made larger with his wired circle "John Lennon" glasses that complemented his fine, well-formed features. What had changed was his now long, black hair that he'd grown out since his Special Forces days.

"Thanks for coming," Shen shouted over the helicopter's engines. "It'll mean a lot to John that you came all this way."

"I wish I'd known," Archer replied. "I'd have come a lot sooner."

A hospital administrator led Shen and Archer down a set of stairs to an elevator that took them to the third floor.

"How is he?" Archer asked.

Shen shook his head. "Not good. But you know him. He's as tough as they come."

After walking through several sets of double doors and nurses' stations, they turned a corner into a critical care room filled with a single empty hospital bed, bordered by computer monitors, respirators, lights and a television mounted to the ceiling. Sitting in a chair to the right of the bed, John Lee was dressed in a hospital gown and holding a red pillow on his lap. His face was drawn. When Archer and Shen entered the room, his eyes lit up and he broke into a wide smile.

"Archer, ya' came all this way!" Lee exclaimed in a very hoarse voice. He began coughing hard, almost uncontrollably—holding the pillow tight to his stomach. "The pillow helps," Lee finally said breathlessly when the coughing attack concluded. He motioned to the set of chairs beside him. "Have a seat."

Archer shook Lee's hand and put his arm around John in a close hug.

"It's good to see you, Brother," Archer said, sitting down beside him.

"Sorry it had to be like this," Lee replied. "It's really good to see you."

"I would've come sooner—"

Lee waved him off. "No worries," he said almost gasping. "I hear you got The Ghost."

Archer's brows furrowed. "How'd you know?"

Both Shen and Lee smiled knowingly. In the dimly lit world of Special Operations and Intelligence, news about sensitive SMU ops traveled fast through what long ago became known as "The Jungle Telegraph."

"Max got him," Archer said. "He never had a chance with her."

Lee shook his head. "You both got him. She didn't know what he looked like—she needed you to identify him."

Archer shook his head. "You know Max—I never want to be at odds with her."

"Anyone who tries to cage a wildcat ain't crowded with brains," Lee replied in kind. It was an old tradition for them both. "Give her my best when you see her. Still remember the first time you introduced us to her, right after you got her to the U.S.."

Archer nodded. "I'll do that," he paused and looked over at Shen, then back at Lee. "When did all this begin?"

Lee shrugged. "A few months ago. At first I thought it was bad arthritis, and payback from all the airplanes we jumped out of. Until—" Lee stopped and looked over at Shen.

"Until when?" Archer asked, looking at both men.

Lee nodded slightly. "You heard about the cabin I built in the Blue Ridge Mountains, west of here?"

Archer nodded, recalling a conversation they'd had about land he was purchasing several years ago. "On Cold Mountain—in the Pisgah?"

Lee nodded. "It took me a few years, but I finished it. Sits on 65 acres, bordering National Forest land—so it was the best possible—" Another coughing attack started, and less than a minute later ended. Lee spit red-colored phlegm in a cup. "It was the best possible place to build—or so I thought."

"So you thought?" Archer asked.

Lee nodded slowly. "Yeah," he said. "At night, I'd be awakened by all sorts of tremors shaking the cabin—I thought they were earthquakes and aftershocks. Drove the dogs nuts." He looked over at Shen—who nodded silently. "Turns out the National Forest land adjacent to mine wasn't National Forest at all, but belonged to the Department of Energy."

"On your mountain?" Archer asked, suddenly intrigued.

Lee took a sip of water, and struggled to swallow. "Then these "suits" showed up and offered to buy my land, and wrote a check for triple what it appraised for."

"Triple?" Archer replied, surprised. "That never happens."

"Yeah, my thoughts exactly," Lee said. "I told 'em it wasn't for sale, and to stop frackin' or whatever it was they were doin' that was causin' all the shakin'."

"It didn't stop?"

Lee shook his head, and leaned over his pillow. "It got worse. And suddenly all of my well water went from clear to dark brown, and you could actually light it on fire right outa' the tap! Killed both my Labs. The water had apparently been toxic before it turned color. I probably survived because I drank bottled water only. Too bad I hadn't shared it with Gumbo and Gunner. They'd still be alive."

"Jesus, I'm sorry, John," Archer said, knowing well how much John had loved his two dogs.

Lee shook his head. "No matter. I'll be joining 'em soon."

"Were they fracking?"

"That was my theory," Lee answered, sipping water through the hospital cup's straw. "I finally went over to check. But they had an eight foot fence and double-strand concertina surrounding the entire damn sid'a the mountain, and you couldn't get in there if your life depended

21

on it."

Archer shook his head and smiled, knowing his friend all-too-well. "So, of course, you broke in?"

Lee nodded and spit into his cup. "Ya' know, I never did have the sense God gave a goose, and this was one a' them occasions, I suppose. That night I buried my dogs and I was mad as hell. I cut through their fence, and found the entrance to the tunnel into the mountain. It had a hidden single lane road and a railroad that aren't on any map—Google Earth, TerraServer, Waze, or anything else for that matter."

"What are they doing up there?" Archer asked.

"It wasn't fracking, that's for sure—because there weren't any drilling rigs, hydration units, roustabouts or roughnecks anywhere in sight. But what was there were plenty of black HMMWVs and dismounted private security contractors all around the mountain, emplacing sensors of all kinds—break wires, seismic, magnetic, passive and active IR break beams—you name it, they got 'em there."

"For what?" Archer asked. "What purpose?"

"Well, there's the big question," Lee answered, and motioned over to Shen to hand him the blue handheld meter in front of him. "But this isn't."

"What's that?" Archer asked, looking at the wired aluminum probe attached.

"It's a digital radiation detector," Shen answered. "An SEI Inspector EXP, specifically. Used mostly to survey leaks—an improvement to the old Geiger Counter. This responds to radiation exposure in real time."

Lee turned it on, and a slow, gradual beep could be heard emanating from the device. He pressed the probe against his chest as if it were a stethoscope; and at that moment, a sudden, pulsating rattle erupted.

Lee turned the meter off and looked up at Archer. "I was fine until I moved to Cold Mountain. Now I feel like I have some kinda animal inside me."

Archer brows drew together in thought—this revelation was as sobering as he could ever conceive—and left far more questions than answers.

A *FOX News* report on the Presidential election and transition flashed on the television, broadcasting the image of the Vice President-Elect, who they all knew well. Zachary Hastings was formerly a Special Forces and SMU commander, who ultimately commanded 5th Special Forces Group, and had risen through the General Officer ranks, all the way to four stars—commanding the entire Afghan theater of operations. Now, after two years as the Commander of U.S. Special Operations Command (USSOCOM), he was the next Vice President of the United States, running mate to William "Wild Bill" Stone, the former Governor of Maryland.

In an historic election, they had opened with a wide lead, and were finished with both a popular and electoral landslide. All of the media, pollsters and political analyses confirmed that Hastings had brought *"gravitas"* and military experience to the ticket, making the wide margins of the Stone-Hastings election possible.

"You ever hear from Zack Hastings?" Lee asked between coughs.

Archer shook his head. "Only for a campaign donation. He's in a whole different stratosphere now."

Lee nodded. "Well, he always could talk a squirrel out of a tree."

"The proverbial ten-gallon mouth, " Archer agreed in kind.

Shen handed Archer a file of papers. "Maybe he could help with this?"

"With what?"

Shen pointed at the stack of papers. "Two days ago John was served this Federal Notice of Eminent Domain for his cabin and property, right here in the hospital!"

"Is anyone at the cabin now?" Archer asked, "I'd like to go back there and check it out."

Lee shook his head. "Dogs are gone, and I'm stuck here, so it's vacant. You're welcome to everything that's there—there's plenty if you need it. But I'd be damned careful if you do go." He turned to Shen. "Give him my set of keys."

"When do they expect to occupy your place?" Archer asked.

"Two weeks...less now." Lee replied, coughing. "Bastards'll take up with any hound that'll hunt."

Shen handed Archer a D-Ring with a wad of keys attached.

"I'll check it out," Archer said to both men, getting up to leave. He pointed at the radiacmeter on the table in front of Lee. "Can I take that?"

Lee handed it to him. "Don't have much use for it anymore. You can have it. And if you do go to the cabin, you can take anything that's useful—I don't want the Feds to get it." Lee paused. "There's one thing I want you to make damn sure to find in there, 'cause I meant to given it to you next time we saw each other. Needless to say, I didn't expect to be in here, and don't expect to be goin' back."

Archer nodded. "Tell me what it is, and I'll make sure I look for it, John."

"Well, I recall you tellin' me how much more you liked the feel of the Browning Hi-Power than the Beretta or even the SIG. So I built you a custom Hi Power—you won't be able to miss it. It's a two-tone model in .40 Smith and Wesson so you could actually stop somethin'." And then after a brief pause, he added offhandedly, "Made some other mods I think you'll like too."

Archer felt himself suddenly choke up, remembering well how Lee had been fond of doctoring the team's weapons—he was the best gunsmith he knew—a real craftsman.

"Thanks, Johnny," Archer managed through his tightening throat, and the tears welling up and preventing him from seeing clearly in the room.

"No need for that," Lee dismissed hoarsely. "You came all this way—that's thanks enough. Hope you can use some of it...."

As Lee's voice trailed off, Archer asked a nurse to take a photo of the three of them sitting next to one another.

"Arch?" Lee called out to him as he began to walk out. "Don't forget to check behind the trees... and cut the goddamned cards."

Archer nodded and his lips compressed momentarily. He walked back to John and hugged him tightly, smiling at the reference to another infamous "Lee'ism" he'd heard all-too-often while they were deployed—many of which he subsequently adopted himself: *Trust everybody. But cut the cards.*

"In other words, while it may not be healthy to believe everyone is dishonest," John had counseled him in years past, *"If you have a simple way to protect yourself against dishonesty, do it."*

"See you in Valhalla, you old war horse," Archer whispered as he walked out of the hospital.

Archer looked over at Shen. Tears were streaming down both of their faces. Archer knew it was likely the last time he'd see his friend again in this world.

Chapter 2

DURING HIS DRIVE TO ASHEVILLE, North Carolina, Archer called Elena Campbell, Beau's veterinarian, to tell her his return home had been delayed. He passed a similar message to his Assistant Principal at school.

"We love Beau!" Elena replied immediately. "I'm taking him home with me, and bringing him to the office. Take as long as you need."

Archer's relief was palpable. Beau was the only real responsibility he had left, and Elena's willingness to take care of him with no advance notice was above and beyond. Elena had dismissed his heartfelt thanks and his sense of relief replying simply, "That's what we do in Maine, Luke Archer."

Elena lived just down the road from Archer. Strikingly beautiful— brunette, petite, and an avid runner and skier. Eight years out of the University of Maine's Veterinary School, she had set up shop in her home in Camden before building an actual office. Both she and Archer had arrived in Camden within a few weeks of one another, and had since developed a friendship that had grown steadily since.

In Camden, Elena was the only one in the area who knew about his wife's death, but he still hadn't told her about the exact circumstances. She was also the only one who knew about his 20 year Army career. Still, he hadn't yet told her of his past with the CIA, and wasn't in a rush to do so.

Archer continued his drive in the steady Asheville drizzle, following his Jeep's GPS directions to Canton, and winding his way along NC Highway 215.

Listening to NPR, Archer was surprised to hear a detailed report on the killing of Shah, and how it was being described so differently than the way it had actually occurred.

This is John Rasmussen in Islamabad, reporting for National Public Radio.
The Taliban leader in Pakistan and Afghanistan has

been killed by a US drone strike in an area of Pakistan that has previously been off-limits for remote-controlled aircraft, sources confirmed on Sunday.

Both the Pakistani government and members of Taliban in Afghanistan reported that Omar Mehsud Shah had been killed by an attack in Peshawar, Pakistan in an operation involving multiple drones. Earlier, the US Department of Defense said Omar Mehsud Shah had been targeted while attending a funeral for a family member.

The killing of the Taliban leader is likely to have major ramifications both for efforts to kick start peace talks and for the often stormy relationship between the US and Pakistan.

US Secretary of State, Charlotte Keaton, had this to say about the strike: "Omar Mehsud Shah posed a continuing imminent threat to US personnel in Afghanistan, Afghan civilians, Afghan security forces and members of the US and NATO coalition. The airstrike on Shah sends a clear message to the world that we will continue to stand with our Pakistani and Afghan partners."

Mullah Abdul, a senior commander of the militant group, said that Shah had died in the strike. The office of Abdul-Baser Khan, the Afghan Prime Minister, also confirmed the death, saying Shah had "refused to answer repeated calls" to end the war in the country.

Saturday's strike, at an Islamic funeral at 3.45pm local time, was the first known strike in Peshawar, the Pakistani Khyber Pakhtunkwa Province gateway that is home to many senior Taliban leaders. Islamabad has staunchly resisted Afghan demands for action against insurgent sanctuaries on Pakistani soil.

A few moments later, after punching a button on the vehicle's radio, Archer heard a nearly verbatim report on a local station.

Archer was more than familiar with the spin and adjustments that were often made in reporting on CIA sponsored operations. What was surprising about this report, however, was the speed and consistency with which it was reported. With the factual elements altered, and identical script on multiple stations.

"Well, that was quick," Archer remarked out loud.

As he continued to drive, Archer noticed that the GPS directions no longer showed any of the roadways up the mountain. He switched to the hand-drawn directions Shen had given him to show the way up to John's cabin. The gravel drive up the mountain was steep, with frequent switchbacks that made no allowance whatsoever for an oncoming vehicle. Slipping the Jeep into 4-Wheel Drive, Archer maneuvered up the gravel driveway that he knew John had cut into the mountain himself using rented machinery.

Archer thought about John Lee and the countless deployments they'd been on together—to some of the darkest ends of the earth. When circumstances were at their bleakest, John had always been the unbridled optimist, making everyone laugh. It was a rare ability, and one that he had come to realize only the best leaders possessed—to make everyone around them forget their seemingly dire surroundings. John possessed that unique ability in spades—and he already missed him. It was also just like John to give his friends one final "mission" on his way out the door; and while Archer didn't know where it would lead exactly, he owed John that, and much more.

In more ways than one, John had been a mentor to him, conveying a full range of lessons over time—from how to move in the woods, to the care and operation of hundreds of foreign weapons, to observing details most people overlooked, to viewing problems differently and addressing them in the most innovative and asymmetric ways.

Once nearly to the top of the mountain, he came to a heavy chain that had been stretched across the drive with a red, white and blue sign in the shape of a shield that read:

UNITED STATES
MARSHALS SERVICE
NO
TRESPASSING

"This is the sign you get when our government doesn't get their way. And they are two weeks early...," Archer said to himself, out loud. The chain was too heavy to drive through it, and at that moment he remembered John's last words: *Don't forget to look behind the trees....*

Stepping out of the vehicle, Archer shook his head and pulled on a full - head covering "Scent-Lok" face mask and adjusted his lightweight gloves. Combined with his over garments, these would minimize the traces of his visit.

Looking behind the large oak tree about thirty yards to the left of his Jeep's front tire, he smiled. Under a pile of brush, there was a tarp that covered a box of pneumatic bolt cutters, designed to cut through carbon steel at the push of a button.

"Ordinary bolt cutters would've been fine, Johnny...," Archer uttered, applying the device to the chain. He'd used the pneumatic variety plenty of times to gain entry in close combat scenarios, but didn't expect to see them behind a tree in the woods. Gripping the handle, he pushed the top button and with a *THWUMP*, the chain was severed instantly, falling full length to the ground in a heap.

He could practically, hear John's response, as if he were standing there with him, citing the "golden rule" of demolitions:

" 'P' is for Plenty, Archer! Even a bull without horns can still do some right sharp pushing, c'ain't they?"

After a few more switchbacks, Archer found himself at the cabin. He'd been here years ago, before. John, Shen, Max and a few other teammates had begun work on the cabin together. The logs were white and massive, chinked together in a classic trapper's design. A large porch overlooked the valley and the surrounding Great Balsam Mountain range.

Archer found the set of keys to the house under a large planter on the porch, unlocked the front door and walked inside. Turning the corner, he found himself eye-to-eye with a mounted full-sized wildebeest, seemingly at a full charge. Looking around the living room crowded with big game mounts on the walls, above the fireplace, and on pedestals on the floor, Archer had the sudden sensation of being surrounded and being chased in the wild. He knew how much John loved hunting, and remembered the times when they were together, killing some of these same trophies in Kenya, Alaska and New Zealand. Framed photos of those hunts stood beside each mounted animal. Archer smiled, seeing the ones with all of them together, each representing a unique time and place. Archer picked up one of the photos of John wearing a Santa Claus outfit. Becky was on his lap, kissing him. As a "Black Santa," John was smiling broadly in response.

He stared through the window at the snow that was beginning to fall outside. In an odd way, it served to remind him of his purpose in coming all this way. He found the office and the key to the basement door taped to the top of the drawer, where Shen told him it would be. It wasn't an ordinary door by any stretch— a secret, reinforced trapdoor that John had constructed in front of the desk, further hidden by an oriental carpet.

Archer unlocked the hatch and lifted it to the side, revealing a stairway down to a large circular vault. Looking around, he shook his head in surprise. By any measure, it was an arsenal—with weapons systems on full display that ranged from military-style carbines in various calibers to shotguns, handguns, sniper rifles, grenade launchers and machine guns, as well as night vision systems, scopes, suppressors and silencers—all lining the walls and sitting atop tables and cases that contained a wide variety of combat knives and hatchets. At the far end, a gunsmith shop had been set up, complete with work benches, mills, lathes, precision grinders, heat treat ovens, tooling machines, and reloaders.

Archer knew John had a Class 3 Federal Firearms License that allowed him to stock and sell the vast majority of the weapons in this vault, but was reasonably certain not all of them were covered. Some of the more exotic and hard-to-find systems, he knew, had been brought back from battlefields abroad, and could never be domestically licensed. Archer shook his head, but neither was he entirely surprised.

On one of the benches, in a separate display case, his eye found the custom Browning Hi-Power John had crafted for him in a separate display case. He gently opened the cover and removed the Browning, examining it, shocked to see a second, much smaller, but closely matching pistol nestled beneath it.

Not only had John Lee checkered all the necessary surfaces of both weapons, but also on each he had installed a set of Tritium Night Sights, a light rail that would accommodate a tactical light and laser and threaded the barrels in order to accommodate a compensator or suppressor. A metal protector was screwed in place over the threaded portion of each barrel. Looking closer, he saw that the finish of both weapons was two tone—the top slide done in a flat black, slick-to-the-touch finish. The lower half and light rail were a luxurious smooth bronze.

But it was the grips that shocked him further as he stared at the ancient Greek helmet facing him above the words, "Molon Labe."

Archer knew the phrase, as well as the story behind it.

"Molon Labe - Come take them," the Spartan King, Leonidas had replied when the Persian King, Xerxes, had asked, through a messenger, that the Spartans lay down their weapons and surrender during the battle of Thermopylae in 480 B.C.

Though Leonidas and his 300 Spartans chose death over surrender, their sacrifice slowed the Persian advance to Athens and facilitated the preservation and translation of the Ancient Greek ethos into what would become known as "Western Civilization."

Archer picked up a long, black suppressor next to the Brownings and placed the small pistol in his jacket pocket. He attached a Streamlight TLR-2 Laser/Light on the larger Browning's light rail. Flicking on the light and laser, he checked the laser dot against the iron sights on a distant wall—ensuring they were completely aligned out to 20 yards.

Archer slid the Browning into a leather paddle holster he found next to the case. It fit the pistol and light/laser snugly, but the weapon could be withdrawn without a sound.

He selected an M4 Carbine from a rack on the wall. Stacks of magazines, fully loaded with ammunition, lay beside and beneath each weapon. He grabbed several magazines for each of the weapons he had selected and inserted them into a black nylon chest rig. In one of the drawers filled with combat knives, he recognized a Spartan Harsey Hunter Knife still stored in its sheath and attached it to his belt. At another counter, he picked up a night vision monocular, a set of the latest night vision goggles, a powerful infrared handheld laser, and a tactical flashlight with a flip-up, infrared lens. He checked to ensure the batteries were fully charged in each before attaching them to his bandolier and belt. Spotting a small tactical rucksack in the corner of the room, he loaded it with ammunition and extra items and slung it over one shoulder.

Archer wasn't sure what to expect in his venture across the mountain, but he also didn't want to be caught unprepared. He was grateful for the full complement of equipment John had made available to him.

Climbing the staircase, Archer locked the hatchway and suddenly felt faint, realizing only then that he hadn't eaten anything all day. He searched the kitchen cabinets and found some soup and venison jerky. As a precaution, he pulled out the radiation detector that John had given to him at the hospital. When he turned it on the reading was negligible.

On a hunch, he turned on the water faucet, and as the water rushed out, the beeping became loud, successive and angry, indicating that the water supply was irradiated.

Standing at the kitchen counter, eating the jerky and soup from a paper bowl, Archer looked outside at the beautiful post-and-beam half-timbered stone-infill barn John had constructed across from the cabin.

He contemplated the implications the radiation detector's readings.

John used this water to bathe, cook and drink from—and it's what killed him.

Looking down at the key ring for the house, he saw another key for the barn door. Walking outside, he unlocked the barn door. Stepping inside, he let out an audible gasp as the light filtered inside. Two different types of light tactical vehicles, armored, one painted in OD green, and the other in flat black, took center stage in the barn, and were bordered by countless cases of ammunition of all kinds—C4, blasting caps, several varieties of smoke and fragmentation grenades, A TOW launcher and Bunker Buster Missiles, Claymore Mines, and Light Anti-Tank Weapons—all on full display.

Jesus, why in the world did you think you'd need all this...?

In the adjacent barn bay, Archer saw what appeared to be a

makeshift office, equipped with a reclaimed wood table. A large map of the area was laying on the table, with John's hand-written annotations that appeared to show ingress and egress routes to and from the cabin, and the Department of Energy complex on the far side of the mountain. A steel box beside the map contained a stack of reconnaissance photos enlarged to 8x10 size, depicting an array of images that included photos of the sensors that had been emplaced in the compound, the regular perimeter patrols, and the many semi-trucks and tactical vehicles that were driving in and out of the tunnel day and night. All of the guards were carrying automatic weapons.

Don't speculate about a target area's purpose... just rely on facts that guide you toward real conclusions....

It was an early lesson at "The Farm" – the CIA's training facility. There were things here, however, that didn't yet add up, and he sensed it would take a concerted effort to learn what was happening on the other side of the mountain.

Archer studied the photos, and looked over the wall separating the bays.

An electric Lightweight Tactical All Terrain Vehicle was parked beside him and fully charged. Manufactured by Polaris, it was a close, updated cousin to the kind he had used in the Middle East on countless occasions to move around quickly and silently. He placed his M4 Carbine in the rack beside the driver's seat where it would be readily accessible, along with the radiation detector and pneumatic bolt cutters he'd used on the entry chain less than an hour ago.

He looked outside the barn doors. Dusk was approaching, and the snow was descending in large, thick flakes.

After studying the map further, and satisfied he knew the route, Archer folded it up and placed it in his front coat pocket for quick reference.

He made one last equipment check, and started the Polaris. It was remarkably quiet, and must have been John's choice for a low visibility reconnaissance. It had the advantage of a small, yet powerful onboard (and removable) GPS system. Driving the Polaris out of the barn and into the falling snow, he switched the GPS to the "Satellite Photo" view in order to get a clear view of the terrain.

Chapter 3

LUKE ARCHER DROVE THE ATV SILENTLY up the mountain along a trail that had been well worn with use. Through the eerie green view of the night vision goggles, he could see that for most of its distance, the trail was wide enough to accommodate a small pick-up truck, and as he went higher in elevation, it gradually evolved into a rugged footpath. Along the way, he was struck by the number of small animals, mostly dead rabbits, squirrels and raccoons near the trail—and wondered if it was the cold winter weather that had killed them, or something else.

He parked the Polaris at the trail's end point and quietly wrapped the M4 Carbine and ammunition magazines in a piece of camouflage burlap he'd found in the barn. He proceeded on foot towards a vantage point that offered views of the mountain's western side. After a short distance, he placed the wrapped weapon and ammo next to a tree and covered them with snow, brush and leaves—leaving them there in reserve, separate from the vehicle. In the wrong circumstances, there was no substitute for a long-barrel weapon.

A few minutes later, lying prone behind a large rock outcropping, Archer removed the map inscribed with John Lee's annotations, oriented himself, and unpacked the night vision monocular. Surveying the mountainside, visibility was limited by the now heavy snowfall, but through the monocular he could make out a sea of glaring light less than a kilometer below and to his right. He picked himself up and descended through the dense forest, grabbing hold of trees and saplings to maintain his balance until he came to a clearing with a tall galvanized and concertina razor wire fence extending as far as he could see in both directions. Viewing the compound behind the fence through night vision goggles, Archer could clearly see the of IR motion sensors. He counted six of them in the immediate vicinity. Carefully searching the area for the telltale glint of a camera, he pulled out the powerful Infrared Laser. Aiming it at each of the motion sensors for several seconds, he watched as the IR light sources of all six shut down, effectively disabling them without raising any alarms in the network.

He followed the route outlined on John Lee's map, along a ridgeline that ultimately opened to another large clearing. In the distance, he saw what appeared to be railroad tracks with a road leading toward the mountain—both without gaining in altitude. At first, he thought it was an optical illusion generated by the night snowfall and lights, but quickly realized it was a dual roadway and railroad leading into a tunnel dug into the mountainside. Descending the small cliff, he nearly slipped, but managed to grab hold of a group of saplings to arrest his fall. Lowering himself, and progressing toward the road and the tunnel's entrance, he encountered another fence, this one even more formidable than the outer perimeter—constructed out of triple-strand concertina and razor "barbed wire."

Archer hesitated only momentarily when he saw the red and yellow signs featuring the universal radiation symbol that read:

DANGER
NUCLEAR MATERIALS
HIGH RADIATION PRESENT
PROTECTIVE GEAR REQUIRED
UNITED STATES DEPARTMENT OF ENERGY

and:

DANGER
RADIATION AREA
US DoE

The signs were posted at regular intervals across the expanse of the fence line. At one point, he found what he immediately recognized as a sensor bolted to a concrete base—the tri-axial seismic variety he'd seen on several other occasions—used to detect motion and vibrations in the fence. Using the bolt cutter, he cut the single wire of the sensor, and proceeded to pull away pieces of concertina to create a hole large enough in the fence for him to pass through.

Walking along the ridgeline, Archer checked his detector, and saw only a slight increase in the reading—indicating the radiation levels to still be safe and fully within normal limits. With the ambient light, his NVG provided a fully illuminated view of the surrounding area. Scanning the horizon with the NVG, the lights at the entrance to the tunnel were amplified like spotlights, providing Archer a beacon to guide his path.

Searching for a position that would offer him the best possible concealment as well as an overwatch to the road and rail network, Archer realized that there was not just one entrance, but two—a separate one for vehicle traffic, and another for rail traffic. Shifting his gaze upward, he saw a ledge above both entrances that would provide a good vantage point to observe and take photos. Moving closer, he heard the lumbering roar of trucks both entering and departing the tunnel. Once he was atop the ledge, he could hear voices below. A full barrier and entry system was in place, monitoring and controlling all traffic, incoming and outgoing.

After only a few minutes, a semi-truck approached with SUV security escorts in lead and trail. As the convoy drew closer, Archer could see two massive steel canisters secured with iron load binders on the truck's flatbed trailer. Both SUVs cut away at apparently assigned spots near the entrance, allowing the truck's driver to stop under the floodlights. Archer switched the setting on his NVG and surveyed the steel canisters. On both, he saw the black and yellow trefoil symbol indicating radiation hazard—but no other markings. Archer silently snapped several photos.

The truck driver handed his paperwork to the guard.

"Origination?" The guard asked.

"South River Plant," the driver answered. The only plant Archer knew that was located in South River, North Carolina was Duke Energy's

Nuclear Power Plant. His instincts were confirmed with the driver's response.

"Enriched Uranium. Mixed with fly ash and concrete."

The guard made a few annotations on his iPad, reviewed the report generated by the Radio-frequency Identification (RFID) reader, under-vehicle survey, and the multiple cameras that were surveilling the entrance. Once he was satisfied that all requirements had been met, the underground traffic spikes retracted and the boom barrier lifted, allowing the truck to proceed inside the mountain.

Archer withdrew from his position on the ledge and sat beside a large pine tree analyzing John Lee's map. He knew that in order to gain a full understanding of the mountain complex and its purpose, he had to get inside. This would likely be his only chance to do so, and given the tight security, it wouldn't be an easy task. He considered the full array of high security measures in place outside the entrances, as well as the configuration of the mountain.

He laid the bolt cutters by the tree, keeping his pistols, camera and NVGs with him. Descending the mountain quickly and quietly, he stayed inside the woodline while paralleling the road. After a short distance, the road quickly reverted to wide switchbacks and pull-off lanes to allow any approaching trucks to slow and yield to oncoming traffic. Looking again at the map, Archer chose the tightest of those switchbacks to position himself. An hour passed before he heard any additional trucks approaching. The one approaching had a lead and trail security vehicle, and on its bed there were three giant canisters of the same type he'd just seen at the entrance with the same radiation hazard markings—but these were sealed by special white steel "casks."

Because the truck's flatbed was elongated to fit the additional canister and casks, it had particular difficulty negotiating the switchback midway up the mountain—and that slowdown provided exactly the opportunity he was seeking.

The truck had practically jackknifed itself at the turn, creating a blind spot for the black HMMWV in trail. The trail HMMWV was forced to back up, temporarily out of sight.

Exiting the woodline at a sprint, Archer mounted the cargo bed and positioned himself prone and face-down between two of the casks, allowing himself to hide in a makeshift defilade. Struggling to catch his breath, and positioned as he was, Archer felt particularly vulnerable.

"I'm getting...way...too old for this," Archer muttered, hoping that the security guard and vehicle drivers would follow exactly the same set of procedures he'd previously observed.

The floodlights of the tunnel entrance seemed to create virtual daylight, and Archer's initial sensation of vulnerability quickly transitioned to a feeling of outright exposure. That reaction, compounded by the almost complete lack of planning that got him to this point, caused caused Archer to begin to question his own judgment, yet he also understood he had passed the point of no return the moment he jumped on the bed of the truck.

The truck came to a full stop, and Archer could hear the driver's exchange with the guard.

"Cargo?"

The answer that came back froze Archer to his marrow.

"Encased Vitrified Plutonium."

Jesus—I'm laying under a cask of plutonium?

"Origination?"

"New Brunswick Power Point, Lepreau," the driver replied.

Canada? Archer second-guessed whether he heard the driver's response correctly. The potential implications of a Plutonium importation scheme were obvious, but he still didn't know the actual purpose of the complex.

After a prolonged wait, Archer could feel the truck move forward.

Inside the tunnel, he carefully raised his head and looked around just as the truck passed a sign that read:

COLD MOUNTAIN

HIGH LEVEL WASTE

MULTINATIONAL DEEP GEOLOGICAL REPOSITORY

VMAX STORAGE FACILITY

UNITED STATES DEPARTMENT OF ENERGY

Chapter 4

ARCHER JUMPED OFF THE TRUCK as it turned a bend inside the tunnel. A large ventilation duct on the ceiling of the tunnel extended as far as he could see. Four specialized fire and emergency utility tactical vehicles were parked at the ready, in a parking area cut out into the tunnel wall. Beside the emergency vehicles, there was a container office with a sign that read:

PERSONAL PROTECTIVE EQUIPMENT (PPE)

Inside, he found an equipment room with extra hard hats, protective masks, radiac meters, and dosimeters—along with uniform T-Shirts, tool belts, radios, and reflective utility vests. In one locker, he found the identification card for one of the on-site managers on a lanyard hanging on the wall:

Paul J. Haufbrau, PE, CSP
Safety Engineer

Archer quickly changed into one of the tan T-Shirts and put on a black nylon tool belt, reflective vest, and white hardhat. He untucked his shirt to conceal his holstered Browning Hi-Power and slung the Canon around his neck and shoulder. He placed his remaining equipment in an open wall locker, locked the lock and pocketed the key. Trading out John's radiation detector with one of the radiac meters on the shelf, he placed the lanyard around his neck and repeated the name and position to himself: *"Paul Hofbrau, Safety Engineer."*

Stepping into the driver's seat of one of the parked UTVs, Archer drove through the tunnel complex, unsure where the tunnel would lead, or whom he would encounter along the way—but reasonably certain that the security detail was positioned *outside* the tunnel, not inside.

After a short distance, Archer could see that the semi-truck carrying the plutonium in the two shipping casks had stopped ahead in a massive circular assembly area, where the two tunnels—both road and railway—converged. Driving closer, it was obvious that the purpose of the assembly area was to open and transload the containers onto specialized rail cars. A group of men were standing beside the flatbed and a specialized crane that was lifting the top off of one of the casks.

Dressed almost identically to each of the other men—blue jeans, T-shirt, yellow reflective vest and hardhat, Archer decided his best option was to "hide in plain sight." Parking the UTV, he grabbed a clipboard, and drew a deep breath before walking over to observe the operation up close. As he approached the work area, he was satisfied in his ability to blend in with the group. Several men glanced his way, but continued to work on transloading the contents from the containers to the rail cars.

Archer's mind raced to the several operations he had conducted in SAD when he and his team had been tasked by the CIA's Nonproliferation Center to pose as members of an International Atomic Energy Agency (IAEA) team, tasked to inspect the Bushehr Nuclear Power Plant and the Anarak Nuclear Waste Disposal Site in Iran. Several weeks in advance of the operation, they were given a crash course on all things nuclear—from an immersion in the technical language, to reactor design, indicators of weaponization, and basic radiological detection. However, that was over a decade ago. He hoped he could remember at least some of those lessons—at least enough to be conversant, if necessary.

After the first shipping cask was opened, a man who appeared to be a shift supervisor walked over to him and extended his hand.

"Dave Hamilton," the man said, introducing himself.

"Paul Haufbrau, Safety," Archer replied, meeting his handshake.

Hamilton nodded. "This is the last shipment for tonight," he said absently. "All the way from Canada."

"Convenient for the Canucks, eh?" Archer replied.

Hamilton shook his head, one eye narrowing. "Don't get me started. You here for an inspection?"

Archer shook his head. "I'm brand new here. Just a familiarization tour."

"Pretty standard process," Hamilton replied, pointing at the storage casks and then at the containers on the rail cars. "We open 'em, remove the inner tubes with the waste, and put 'em in those containers for eternity."

"Steel?" Archer asked.

Hamilton nodded. "Multi-layered."

"Impressive," Archer said. Removing his camera, he snapped several photos of the uncasking operation in front of them.

"And from here?" Archer inquired. "Where do they go?"

"The system's fully automated from here. Those containers you see there are all the dry storage variety. Once we fill 'em here, they're sent to the tunnels five hundred meters below. The really hot stuff, like this," Hamilton said, pointing at the casks, "will be crammed into bore holes in the tunnel walls, packed in bentonite. We're also doing some rock melting trials in one of the newest shafts."

"Rock melting?" Archer asked, completely unaware of the term. "We're actually doing that now?"

"Still experimental, but it shows promise," Hamilton answered. "Melting this kind of waste in the adjacent rock just from the heat it generates alone is a pretty radical idea—never been done before outside the laboratories—but if we prove it can produce a stable, solid mass that encases the waste, it could solve a lot of issues for the entire industry. Would be a hell of a lot better than Direct Injection."

"What if it doesn't work?"

Hamilton shrugged. "If it doesn't generate enough heat and leaches into the ground water, or if it's transported back to the surface in some way... well then, we have an even bigger problem."

"Doubt the public or the politicians would go for it," Archer said.

"Well, that's what shut down Yucca Mountain in Nevada, and it's why this place exists—completely off the grid," Hamilton replied. "To do it all as far away from the politicians and the public as possible."

Archer nodded, silently seething at Hamilton's comment because of the obvious fatal effects it ultimately had on John Lee. "Didn't think DoE would ever have the guts to follow through with this," he said, taking a wild guess that the Department of Energy had to have the lead on a project of this scale.

"DoE?" Hamilton laughed. "This is all V-Tec's doing—now, DoE sanctioned it and gave us the mountain, but it never would've happened without V-Tec leading the charge—namely Dr. Craine. We all have our jobs thanks to him."

"V-Tec?" Archer asked with genuine ignorance.

"They're the largest nuclear energy conglomerate in the world," Hamilton replied. "Hardly anyone knows about them. They're worth billions, but have somehow managed to keep themselves off the Fortune 500 list, just to keep a low profile, I suppose."

Archer nodded, careful not to push too hard and raise suspicions. "Keeps the protesters away, I guess." He looked at his watch. It was 4:30am. "You guys get off soon?"

Hamilton nodded. "Yep, we're about a half hour out. Long night."

"Be safe," Archer replied. "Good to meet you."

"You too, Boss," Hamilton said. "Welcome to Cold Mountain."

Under the guise of "Safety Engineer," Archer snapped as many photos as possible with his Canon and with his iPhone throughout his drive back up the tunnel before parking the UTV back in its original parking place. He re-entered the container office and secured his equipment from the wall locker. When the workers began filtering toward the entrance, he joined them exiting the complex to find several inches of new snow. Archer boarded one of the buses to a secure parking lot at the base of the mountain. He hitched a ride to the other side of the mountain, located his equipment where he had mounted the truck and hiked back up to retrieve the Polaris and M4 Carbine he'd left at the end of the trail.

Leave no traces...

Archer speed-dialed Shen Lu, hearing him answer on the first ring.

"I'm at the cabin," Archer said. "And have some answers, but we need to move John's belongings out of here while we still can."

"Got it. I'll get some help and a U-Haul. We'll be over in a few hours. I'll use a company card for the U-Haul rental."

Archer thanked him, not wanting to reveal too much over an open phone line, and understanding "company card" to be the non-traceable variety.

"Arch?" Shen asked quietly. "John passed away early this morning—I was here with him. He kept asking me if he was in heaven yet, and I kept telling him 'Not yet.' Finally, at around 4:30am, he was."

Chapter 5

WHILE LUKE ARCHER WAITED FOR Shen and his crew to arrive at John Lee's cabin, he thought about his old friend and all the good that his life had stood for, in the most remote and deadly corners of the earth. John had been more than a great NCO—he was one of his closest friends and mentors from the outset of his Special Forces career. He'd been the best man at his wedding, and had refused to leave his side after Becky was killed in their home fifteen years ago. John also played a key role in convincing the CIA to bring Archer on nine months later.

Archer found the graves of John's dogs. Walking into the cabin, he found an abundance of framed team photos on nearly every continent in the world. Looking at each of them, the memories flooded back, and so did the tears. In an effort to use his time effectively—but primarily to keep his mind off the loss of his good friend—Archer logged on to the computer in John's office to conduct some preliminary open source research on *V-Tec International* and its CEO, Dr. Robert Craine.

A Google search revealed multiple results for V-Tec, including its corporate website that made clear its status as a "Fortune 50 diversified energy development and security company based in Arlington, Virginia—with offices worldwide." Boasting an "unblemished safety record" and the ability to "produce power safely and in harmony with the environment," Archer saw that the company was founded in 1914 by Texas Oil Magnate Les Craine, and since remained a private, family-held corporation.

From the company's description, he was able to determine that Robert Craine was Les Craine's grandson, representing the third generation of family ownership—that started with oil production in Houston, and since expanded into natural gas production and nuclear power. Now, claiming 15 separate product service lines, 70,000 employees, 100 nationalities, in over 85 countries, V-Tec's claim was that today they were widely recognized as the global leader in natural gas and nuclear plant production.

Archer could not find any photograph or bio for Dr. Robert Craine on the website, but did find something that had been pieced together from multiple sources on Wikipedia, with a brief summary:

Robert Craine, PhD

Born: February 10, 1956
    Houston, TX

Residence: Potomac, MD
Alma Mater: 1978 Graduate, United States Military
    Academy (BS)
    1990 Graduate, MIT (MA / PhD, Nuclear
    Science & Engineering).

Occupation: Businessman
    Chairman, CEO, President, V-Tec
    International

Salary: Unknown
Achievements: 70 U.S. and Foreign Patents Granted

One footnote caught Archer's attention:

WSJ, November 2015: Robert Craine criticized over his hostile bid to take over Raines-Riley, Inc., a smaller nuclear energy rival, in an email from Eric Raines to Dr. Craine, described V-Tec's actions as "madness, aggressive, and borderline illegal."

Archer shook his head at the description of Dr. Robert Craine and V-Tec International. It was all he really needed to begin to understand what he was up against. He switched his Google search to the topic of "Rock Melting" and he clicked on the top result:

Rock melting. Deep Rock Melting is a nuclear waste disposal concept that involves melting radioactive waste into the adjacent rock. The concept involves producing a stable, solid mass that encases the waste in a diluted form, dispersed throughout a large volume of rock, that cannot easily be leached back to the surface. The radioactive waste could be placed in an excavated cavity or a deep borehole. The heat generated by the wastes would then accumulate resulting in temperatures great enough to melt the surrounding rock and dissolve the radionuclides in a growing sphere of molten material. As the rock cools it would crystallize and incorporate the radionuclides in the rock matrix, thus dispersing the waste throughout a larger volume of rock. Rock melting has not yet been implemented anywhere for radioactive waste. There have been no practical demonstrations of the feasibility of this option, apart from laboratory studies, and environmentalists have widely warned of its dire implications and effects on the environment.

That explains all the dead animals near the trail, Archer thought to himself.

His cell phone rang as he continued to research online. Shen's voice was noticeably stressed and agitated—and, Archer knew, completely unlike him. Shen Lu was one of the calmest, most understated operators he'd seen. "They killed him, Arch!" Shen yelled. *"They Goddamned killed him!"*

"What?" Archer exclaimed. "Shen, calm down, Brother. What are you talking about?"

"Arch, listen to me—they fucking killed John!" Shen exclaimed. "Not accidentally, but deliberately. Because of the circumstances of his death, UNC just did an expedited, preliminary autopsy, ran a few tests that confirm he was poisoned with a high concentration of polonium."

"Polonium?" Archer repeated. "Not plutonium?"

"No!" Shen shouted. "It was goddamned polonium—the same shit Putin used to kill Litvinenko ten years ago!"

Archer nodded. Shen was referring to the case of Alexander Litvinenko, an ex-KGB agent who had defected to the UK's MI-6, and poisoned by a dose of polonium administered through a cup of tea in 2006. He felt his heart race as Shen continued talking excitedly over the phone. "Listen—where are you now?"

"About twenty miles out," Shen replied. "I have Jack with me."

"Condon's with you?"

"Yep," he answered simply. "Long story."

"Okay, let's get off this line for now. See you soon."

After the line disconnected, Archer felt his own rage building as he considered what Shen had just told him. Polonium was one of the most rare, highly controlled, and lethal substances on earth. Its use or release in any form would be sure to raise red alerts throughout the Federal government, and he knew the cavalry would be arriving on this side of the mountain soon. They'd need to act very quickly. But something tugged at the back of his mind... polonium was hard to come by and is not normally released to the market by sources in NATO countries. It was mostly available from sources associated with the old Soviet Union.

Archer looked down at his phone and saw the app he'd been searching for. By indicating the alternate communications system, Archer had told Shen to move all communications onto the end-to-end encrypted program *WhatsApp*.

Archer clicked back to the Wikipedia page on Robert Craine, and considered the footnote he'd just read about V-Tec's attempted hostile takeover of what was obviously a much smaller company.

"Dr. Robert Craine, you are about to find out what 'aggressive madness and borderline illegal' can really mean..."

Shen Lu and Jack Condon arrived at the cabin in a full size U-Haul Truck. Before they could step out, Archer had Shen back the truck up to the cellar door that connected to John's basement arsenal.

"I had to come," Jack said to Archer, as he stepped out of the truck. "Once I found out what they did to John. I had some leave coming - so here I am. I created a cover as best I could"

"We're certain he was poisoned with polonium?" Archer asked.

Shen nodded, and handed him the coroner's report. They said they'd never seen so much radiation in one body before, ran all sorts of tests and he came up hot for trace amounts of plutonium, and a massive dose of polonium—around 30 micrograms. They don't normally test for polonium...it's that rare. But in this case it was about the only logical explanation for his symptoms and rapid onset of death."

"Polonium-210 is 250,000 times more toxic than Hydrogen Cyanide," Jack interjected. "John never had a chance."

"I thought only the Russians had access to it?" Archer said. "The FSB used it to kill Litvinenko—and they gave him a twenty-six and a half microgram dose."

Jack nodded. "Putin gave his personal stamp of approval on the Litvinenko assassination," he said. "That's an indicator of how hard it is to obtain. But the truth is, as difficult as it is to get, anyone who has access to a nuclear reactor can create it. It just requires the right skill set, deliberate intent, and an abundance of caution."

"And once you have it, it's easy to transport and hide from detection," Shen added.

Archer quickly briefed both of them on what he had seen and heard at the Cold Mountain nuclear storage site, much to their own surprise, and growing anger. He checked his watch. "Okay. Doubt we have much time before the Feds come and all hell breaks loose around here."

"We *are* the Feds," Condon said wryly.

"It doesn't much matter who we are—we'll all likely end up dead or in a Federal prison if we're here when they arrive. The signs around this place range from the U.S. Marshalls Service to DoE," Archer replied, pointing at the cellar door and the barn. "Everything John collected needs to be loaded on the truck."

Archer had found a box of Tyvek coveralls in the barn and had brought the box outside. "Here," he said, "Put these on. Masks and gloves too. This place will be swept eventually and we can't leave anything behind."

Working together, it took slightly less than an hour to load the truck up with every equipment item and piece of ammunition from both locations. "The NRA would probably kill to have all of this in their museum," Condon commented, out of breath.

"Once we're done with it, they're welcome to it," Archer replied.

Shen Lu came out of the house carrying John's Mac Desktop and Canon, and placed them in a box on the back of the truck. "That's it."

Jack Condon followed, carrying a single bottle of Scotch and placing it in the same box. "1926 MacAllan's," he commented. "Rarest and best Scotch on the planet. I'll be damned if the Feds are getting any of it."

They took off the protective suits and rolled them up in a garbage bag. Archer handed them several addresses of storage lockers along their route. "Here are a few stops we'll make along the way. Alternate commo plan from here on out."

Shen and Jack nodded.

"Okay," Archer said, glancing back at the cabin, then back at Shen and Jack. "Let's go."

Chapter 6

ARCHER DECIDED THAT THE BEST location to set up a temporary headquarters and storage site for much of John's equipment and ammunition would be at his farm in Camden, Maine. He had a large renovated antique New World Dutch Barn on the property with guest quarters above that provided more than enough storage space and accommodations for his friends. The risk was the distance they would need to travel without being detected—or arrested—along the way with a truckload full of Class III weapons and ammunition. They would set up several other stashes in remote self-storage units along their route to Maine.

Archer had taken precautions to ensure the property was not traceable to him, but he was concerned that his security and that of his team was in jeopardy.

As the covered CIA helicopter landing on his front lawn demonstrated, his "clean break" with his past had not been as clean and neat as he'd preferred, or assumed. He knew it could only be a temporary arrangement, but it was all he had. For now, as long as time and circumstances would permit, he'd use his home as a base to prepare for what was yet to come. With a fledgling team of friends he knew well, who had gathered around to assist, he was hopeful that their activities would go unnoticed, at least for a time.

It was a marathon 24 hour drive to Maine, made slower still by the need to drive on secondary roads to avoid the automatic license plate readers stationed along the interstates. As a further measure, they changed out the jeep's license plates with an auxiliary set allocated by the CIA— "on loan," as Laura Chicone described them.

Jack Condon drove the Jeep as the trail vehicle, and Archer drove John's old Dodge Pickup as the lead, with the U-Haul in between driven by Shen. Maintaining separation between vehicles to avoid the appearance of a convoy, they employed well-practiced tradecraft using the "Waze" app to detect police and traffic delays along their route, with each vehicle in secure communication throughout.

They arrived at Archer's farm the next evening without incident, and to Archer's surprise, Laura Chicone and Dan Thorne were standing by a Jeep Grand Cherokee, waiting for them, and teasing them with barbs about Archer's overly careful driving habits, and interspersed taunts of *"What took you so long?"*

Archer smiled and motioned for everyone to gather around just inside the barn's front door.

"Look, I know you want to help," Archer said quietly, looking at each of them in the eyes. "We're all hurting about John's death, and we're goddamned angry. But if John were here, he'd tell us to not think about what happened to him, and to focus instead on preventing anyone else from getting hurt." He spat out a thick wad of chewing tobacco to the ground. "And then, he'd tell us to keep our day jobs, at least for the time being."

The group smiled collectively and sympathetically, knowing that's *exactly* what John Lee would say to them, and *exactly* how he'd say it.

"And he'd want us to watch out for one another," Archer continued, pausing for a moment. "So, to honor him, that's what we'll do. We'll take the long view on this, pick our own timing, and follow our own methods. All of us need to ensure any absences from work don't attract attention. Whoever killed John is well resourced and probably sponsored by some government—ours or someone else's. So, if ya'll agree, the first thing we'll do is find out what the hell's going on, and then we'll stop it." He paused. "We're far more effective staying in our jobs, and using *their* resources wherever possible." Archer waved his hand around the barn. "In the meantime, this can be our headquarters. Come and go as you please, on your own schedule. Plenty of rooms upstairs for you to stay in—and I have a guest room in my cabin too. My guess is we'll have about a week before this place is compromised, so we'll have to split the effort into other covered and decentralized facilities."

Laura looked up at the group. "Archer, I have quite a bit of leave built up—if you don't mind, I'll take some of it, as needed."

"Me too," Jack added.

Archer nodded. "Okay, coordinate your leaves so they're don't draw suspicion."

Dan motioned to the Jeep. "We can't safely return that rental here—it'd draw too much attention to us. I'll drive it to D.C. and return it at Reagan Airport."

Archer nodded. "We'll need to do the same with the U-Haul."

"I can drop it off in Newark," Jack offered. "That should be far enough away. I'll check back in at Langley, and conduct a low viz, classified search on V-Tec, Dr. Robert Craine, and the nuclear storage facility at Cold Mountain."

Laura nodded. "Make sure you cover it with another search effort so it doesn't attract immediate attention."

Shen held up his phone. "One last thing, *everyone*—remove the sim cards from your phones now." He pulled out a Ziploc bag and handed out small black cards. "Here are some new ones."

Dan looked down at a text he'd just received on his iPhone.

"Max Peretz just arrived at Andrews," he said. "I told her about John, and she wants to help. In fact, she insisted."

"Okay." Archer said, visibly gratified. "Now, if it's okay with y'all, I'm gonna go pick up my dog just down the road."

Chapter 7

LUKE ARCHER WASN'T FULLY PREPARED for Beau's full weight when he charged into Dr. Elena Campbell's office waiting area, and jumped on top of Archer, nearly pinning him to the wall.

"He missed you," Elena said. She was wearing surgeon scrubs, and laughing. "Sorry, he got away from me—he must've known you were here."

Archer smiled, petting Beau with obvious effort, and doing his best to calm him down. "I missed him. Thank you."

Elena shook her head. Her eyes were dark-lashed and kind. "Not at all—Beau's always welcome. Glad to have him, anytime."

"I'll likely be taking you up on that offer."

She looked at him with a slight smile. "You should, Luke Archer."

"I have some old friends visiting over the next couple weeks," he said, rubbing Beau, and looking up at her. "Maybe you could come over and join us for dinner one of these nights?"

Elena nodded and grinned. "I'd enjoy that."

"How much do I owe you for boarding?"

She shook her head. "It's on the house."

Archer nodded his gratitude. "Okay. Barbecue—tomorrow night then."

"Wake up, Luke Archer…you are not trying to sleep again are you? We must have another chat," Omar Shah announced conversationally. "But first, I need your undivided attention, I believe…."

There is another person behind me, and he pulls a rope from a pulley system that is attached to the ceiling—a standard block & tackle. I know it's there because I am forced to look straight up, and I can see it. At the end of the rope, there's a hook. The hook is cold against my skin, massive, blackened and scratched from use…made from iron—probably handcrafted by a blacksmith. When the man pulls up on the rope, the hook forces my hands into an unnatural, vertical direction.

The searing hot pain radiates upward from my arms to my skull. I hear myself screaming. But Shah...he seems to be amused, laughing.

There is always a choice for the man behind the rope—to go slow, gradually pulling upward, or to pull up quickly, all at once. Later, I learn it is best to have it all done at once, in one motion. The pain is no less severe, but it is of a shorter duration.

Regardless how the man with the rope chooses to maneuver it, the effect is instantaneous. Both shoulders dislocate in unison, circulation shut off, and all bodily functions are released. Mercifully, the human body is programmed to pass out when pain becomes too intense. An adept torturer understands that, and can keep his subject awake and alert.

My senses go completely black. Darkness rushes over me.

The man with the rope is not skilled in the finer art of torture, though. They cannot awaken me, and for a brief moment, believe I am dead.

The shock of ice water hitting my body with force awakens me with a start, and I realize my feet are off the floor. My own weight feels like hot knives against my limbs and joints splitting me apart. I scream again in agony...begging to be let down.

"Ah, you are awake now, Colonel Archer," Omar Shah says smiling broadly in his soothing tone. "You were snoring—did you know that?" His laugh resonates in the small room. I smell my own urine and shit.

I'm released and fall to the ground in the middle of it.

God, what do you want from me?

"What do you want from me? Or from your God? It is no matter! You will soon have both. You are CIA, are you not? Sent to kill me?

Fuck you...

Omar Shah nods silently at the Rope Man, and my arms go straight up and I am lifted off my feet. This time, I do not pass out, and experience the excruciating pain. Pain shoots through my head like heat lightning. I hear myself gasp soundlessly.

So this is what it feels like to be crucified...Please God...

"Are you CIA?"

"Yes, Goddamn it! I fucking am! I'll be the fucking United Nations if you want me to be! Now let me down!"

"You were sent to kill me, were you not?"

"Yes...absolutely! Let me down from here, so I can complete my goddamned mission! Or just kill me...I don't care. Just get it over with."

The man with the rope releases me, and I fall into a heap onto the floor once again. One of my shoulders slips back into its socket and I lose consciousness again.

I see myself from above. Prone, face up, in ragged Pakistani garb. Omar Mehsud Shah is standing over me, laughing. My eyes are open.

Am I dead? Is this heaven or hell?

"Tomorrow, Luke Archer, we will create a video for the entire world to see. For your cooperation, you will have clean clothes and a good dinner ..."

Archer awoke drenched in sweat, joints aching. His eyes shut in reflex, now well accustomed to the recurrent nightmare that had plagued him for years. No matter how hard he tried, he had no ability to stop it, or even control it.

He slipped on his jeans, cowboy boots and a winter coat, and summoned Beau to follow him out to the barn.

Jack Condon was waiting for him in front of the barn with an anxious expression. Inside the barn, the group had set up a makeshift operations center, with tables pulled together—and John's computer and equipment that had been pulled off the U-Haul.

"You all ever heard of sleep?" Archer said, looking at this watch. "It's damn early."

"V-Tec isn't operating alone," Jack said without preamble, not giving Archer an opportunity to comment. "They have a massive $1.2 billion Department of Energy contract, along with government grants to the "Craine Foundation" for "Nuclear and Radiological Safety.""

"That's interesting," Archer replied. "But not illegal."

Laura entered the barn, and stood beside Archer, listening.

"Right," Jack answered. "But here's where it gets more interesting. According to the IRS, the Craine Foundation has been receiving regular seven figure deposits from the Consumer Finance Protection Bureau's Civil Penalty Fund, for 'Consumer Education Programs' and 'Financial Literacy.'"

"What does that mean, exactly?"

"Well," Jack replied. "First you have to know the CFPB. They're a relatively obscure agency—but also a very powerful one. They write their own regulations and enforce them by fining companies and people for violating them. That money's supposed to go back to the victims, but because they aren't congressionally funded, they also need the fines to pay the salaries of their own attorneys and staff."

"So it's the Treasury Department's own self-licking ice cream cone," Archer commented.

Jack nodded. "The gift that keeps on giving."

"And they're funding V-Tec?" Archer asked.

"It's just another one of their funding sources," Jack said. "No doubt there are many more. For instance, there's also quite a bit of money coming in from the 'Canadian-American Trust Bank,' whatever that is—based on Bermuda. It has all the classic signs of a trade-based money laundering scheme."

"And that polonium they used to kill John Lee—" Laura commented.

"What about it?" Archer asked, intensely interested.

"That strain, with that concentration," Laura replied. "It had to come from Russia."

Archer shook his head slowly.

"What's wrong?" Jack asked, his brow furrowed.

"You found out all of that overnight?"

"We're just getting started," Laura said.

Using a well-practiced code, Luke Archer texted Sam Owen—

the one freelance journalist he'd come to trust during his career in the Central Intelligence Agency. From past experience, he knew Sam could be trusted to get the story right. Within five minutes, Owen replied via text:

CU @ lunch 2morrow. Same place.

That place, Archer knew, was Rí Rá Irish Pub in Portland, Maine—an hour and a half drive, due South from Archer's cabin.

Archer knew that talking to Sam Owen was a risk—but considering all options available—from contacting the FBI to taking matters in their own hands, Archer and team agreed Owen was currently their best option. And certainly the best to begin the effort.

Chapter 8

FROM HIS VANTAGE POINT ON THE LEATHER sofa by the old potbelly stove, Luke Archer saw Sam Owen as he walked into the back entrance of the Pub. He was the only bald-headed man in sight, obviously in his mid-fifties, wearing a trademark brown tweed jacket.

"I hear they got that stove from Spike Island Prison, in County Cork," Owen said.

"Apropos, I'd say," Archer replied, shaking Owen's hand. "I ordered you a Guinness."

Sam Owen was not your typical journalist. In fact, ten years ago, he wasn't a journalist at all—but a New York City detective investigating white-collar crime. With a Master's Degree in Finance and Accounting from New York College, Owen knew how to read the most complex corporate balance sheets and detect money-laundering schemes where no one else could. When his cases were being passed over for trial for "lack of sufficient evidence," Owen saw his opportunity to make a difference by exposing his findings in a series of prominent *ProPublica* articles that brought down one of the largest hedge funds in the country. The day the article ran, Owen submitted his resignation to the NYPD and began writing more articles for newspapers, journals and E-zines.

During his dual careers in the Army and CIA, Archer had learned that taking the time to consider all options, and progressing forward with the "right" first step was often the difference between success and failure in any operation—however simple or complex. Once the issue was presented to the FBI, there would be few other options left to pursue.

Owen pointed at Archer's glass half-full. "What are you drinking?"

"Woodford Reserve," Luke answered, inviting him to sit down.

"Drinking Bourbon in an Irish Pub?" He chided, shaking his head. "Blasphemy."

"Yeah, and this isn't the first."

"That bad, eh?"

"I'm gonna give you a chance to bail out on this before I even say a word," Archer said in a subdued voice. "It's already killed one of my friends."

Owen took a swig of the Guinness and shook his head. "What've you got?"

Archer wasn't surprised by the quick dismissal—an old war correspondent who never depended on stringers for his stories, Sam Owen was as fearless a journalist as he'd ever encountered. He pushed an envelope full of his surveillance photos from Cold Mountain, the IRS documents Jack had found on V-Tec and the Craine Foundation, the Department of Energy record of contracted appropriated funds to V-Tec, income statements and balance sheets from the Canadian-American Trust Bank, and the CFPB's disbursements from the Civil Penalty Fund to the Craine Foundation.

None of this, Archer knew, constituted any real proof of illegal activity though. At least nothing that would stand up in court. He needed more.

Owen pulled the papers partially out of the envelope, glanced through them and looked up at Archer with eyes wide open. "Christ, we're not talking mere millions here, but *billions*!"

Archer nodded. He pulled up a photo of John Lee and him together in Afghanistan, both dressed in civilian field gear, holding M4 Carbines arm-in-arm, smiling. "This is John Lee," Archer said. "When we were fighting in Helmand Province. And this—" He flipped to the photo taken at the hospital of them both. "This is John the day before he died at UNC-Chapel Hill."

Archer paused, and handed another 8x10 envelop to Owen. "John was deliberately poisoned with polonium."

"Polonium?" Owen asked with skepticism and surprise. "Are you sure about that?"

Archer pointed at the envelope. "That's the coroner's report and the autopsy," Archer replied. "The well water on his property was also contaminated with plutonium."

"John's property?" Owen replied. "Is that anywhere near Cold Mountain?"

"His cabin is on the mountain," Archer answered. "And they're experimenting with a procedure called "Rock Melting'—injecting nuclear waste into holes they bore into the mountain, melting the surrounding rock until it actually becomes part of the mountain."

"How do you know all this, may I ask?"

"I got in there, and checked it out myself," Archer replied. "Those are my photos."

"How'd you get in?"

"Don't ask."

"Jesus," Owen muttered, reviewing the documents and photos. "A virtual 'nuclear mountain'."

"Tread carefully," Archer said, leaning toward Owen. "The resources that have been invested in this, the involvement of multiple agencies—it all points to something much larger than just a rogue department—far more dangerous and entrenched."

Owen nodded. "Then what is it exactly?"

Archer shrugged. "It's either a covert, synchronized, interagency operation on a pretty massive scale, or…" His voice trailed off, and he took a gulp of his bourbon—finishing off the glass.

"Or?" Owen asked, intrigued.

"Or, I'd rather not speculate right now."

"Okay. Let me look into this a bit. I'll be in DC in a couple days," Owen nodded. "Let's meet there, if possible."

Chapter 9

DURING THE DRIVE HOME, Archer wondered whether he was overreacting —whether there was a simple explanation for everything that he'd seen over the past two days.

Am I too close to see anything clearly right now?

In contacting Sam Owen, Archer hoped to inject daylight into what he saw as a very opaque, and increasingly dangerous situation. Archer respected Owen, and knew that if there was anyone with the integrity and drive to get to the bottom of everything, it would be him.

Sam Owen's reports extended from remote battlefields to natural disasters and Wall Street scandals. He was always one of the first on the scene. As an investigative reporter, he was smart; and, as a former war reporter, he was fearless. Seeing Owen's initial reaction during their brief meeting was enough confirmation for Archer to know he wasn't overreacting.

Archer's phone vibrated, and he heard Shen's voice through his Bluetooth headset.

"Max arrived—just got finished briefing her," Shen said. "She's up to speed on everything."

"Good. I'm about an hour away," Archer said. "I invited a friend over for BBQ with us. My vet—she looks after Beau. You'll like her—it'll give us a good reason not to talk shop."

"I'll let Laura and Max know," Shen answered. "It'll be a good break from all this."

Archer smiled broadly in the barn's doorway, seeing Max Peretz behind a computer screen. Seeing Archer, she immediately stood and hugged Archer more tightly than he could ever recall.

"Whoa!" Archer exclaimed, laughing. "Hey! I'm unarmed!"

After an extended embrace, Max drew back and looked into his eyes with genuine excitement. "Archer, it's been too long."

"It has," Archer answered. "I was worried about you."

Max nodded. "I know a lot of people aren't too happy with me for taking that shot, but I didn't have much choice."

Archer shrugged and smiled. "Well, you did the world a favor, and you're a welcome sight. I thought we'd have a barbecue tonight. I have a friend coming over—she watches Beau when I'm away."

"Ah, *only* the dog sitter!" Max laughed. "Why do men always use their dogs for cover? Such courage."

"Ya, ya..." Archer droned, slightly embarrassed. "Listen, she doesn't know about any of what's been happening. Use our covers for tonight. We can talk about John, and remember him—but nothing operational, for her sake."

"For her sake, or for yours?" Max retorted.

"Yeah—mine too," Archer said. "I still have to live here."

Chapter 10

LUKE ARCHER WELCOMED ELENA CAMPBELL as she exited her jeep. She held on to his arm as he led her to the barn, and he experienced a sensation of genuine warmth as they walked. Inside, a full table was set, alongside a large outdoor grill, billowing with smoke. The smoke combined with Camden's sea air to create a unique air of "Down East" comfort and relaxation, that he hadn't experienced elsewhere. That, and the relative solitude in this place were the reasons he moved here. Now, having this group of friends—men and women who he deeply respected and enjoyed being around, was as emotionally gratifying as it was rare.

Archer introduced Elena to his friends as "Beau's favorite doctor."

"Any friend of Beau's is a friend of ours," Laura said, shaking Elena's hand.

"What about Luke Archer's?" Elena laughed. "He doesn't count?"

"We trust Beau more," Max joked.

"Luke said you've all known one another for quite awhile," Elena said, smiling.

"When you're in jail, it's helpful to have good friends who'll bail you out," Jack said, raising his glass.

Max nodded and laughed. "And your best friends will be in the cell beside you saying, 'Damn, that was fun!'"

"You've been in adjacent cells then, I take it?" Elena replied warmly.

"No," Shen answered in a serious tone. "We're just Archer's friends of last resort—the ones who've been willing to bail him out...."

"Okay, enough," Archer protested, over the howls of laughter. "Food's ready."

"I'm impressed," Elena said. "This is quite a spread."

"All you gotta say to motivate this group," Archer replied. "Is 'Barbeque' and suddenly you have all the cooks in the kitchen trying to outdo one another."

"Barbecue's more complicated than anyone thinks," Laura laughed. "Even more complicated when you have a Chinese guy and an Israeli chick telling you what to do, and how to do it."

"Barbecue's the closest thing Americans have to Europe's wine, or Japan's Saké," Shen replied. "You're so lucky you have us to lend a hand."

Archer remained standing as everyone sat down at the table and poured from the Magnum of 1959 Château Lafite Rothschild he'd been saving. Once finished, Archer held up his glass and announced, "A toast...to John Lee—a great warrior, Soldier, and friend."

The chorus came back, "To John."

"Luke told me what a great friend John was to each of you," Elena said to the group. "I'm very sorry."

"He was one of the very best," Max agreed. "And if he were here right now, he'd say something like, 'I beat you to Valhalla—but take your time anyway."

"'And he'd tell us all to get back to work'," Archer chimed in, passing a plate of barbecue to Elena.

Everyone laughed, and traded their own stories about John.

Elena was sitting beside Max, and across from Archer. "Max is your nickname?"

Max nodded. "Machla was the name that my grandmother was known by. I was named after her, and she was the first to call me 'Max.'"

"Your grandmother was Israeli?"

"She was an Auschwitz survivor," Max replied, serving grilled vegetables to each their plates. "But her entire family was killed in the Holocaust. She died when I was ten years old."

"You remember her well, it seems?"

Max nodded and smiled, and finished her first bite. "She was tall, slender, had a perfect unlined face. Her cheekbones were high, and her eyes were beautiful and dark. Looking at her when I was young, I could see where my mother had gotten her olive skin and white teeth."

"You have those same features," Elena observed sincerely.

"You are very kind," Max answered. "The one feature I most

admired was her ability to feign courage in the face of terror."

"You do that pretty well too," Archer interjected, causing everyone at the table to laugh.

At one point, Shen looked down at his iPhone and left the table. When he returned, he asked Archer to step outside.

When the door shut, Shen handed Archer his iPhone displaying a black & white photograph of a dark-colored SUV and its license plate.

"What's this?" Archer asked.

Laura stepped out of the barn and joined them.

"Just for the hell of it, I set up an alert in the DHS's ANPR system to notify me of any vehicles with DC-based Federal Government plates within 50 kilometers of our location. These two SUVs just popped up."

Archer understood Shen's reference to "Automatic Number Plate Recognition," widely used by law enforcement for electronic toll collection and to search for vehicles with active alerts tied to them. Laura joined them outside.

"Who are they?" Archer asked. "Do we know?"

"They're registered to The Department of Energy," Shen answered. "Specifically, their Office of Intelligence and Counterintelligence."

"I didn't know DoE had an intelligence agency," Archer said.

Laura nodded. "It is one of the 'Seventeen Intelligence Agencies' we've heard so much about. If you believe their official story, they gather intel on foreign nuclear weapons, so their front is on technical intelligence— nuclear weapons and nonproliferation, nuclear energy, energy security—that kind of thing."

"So, what are they doing in Bangor?" Archer asked.

"Probably not here for the *lobstah*," Laura said off-hand, in a contrived Maine accent.

"They're driving to Camden—toward us," Shen answered. "I don't like it, Arch."

Archer exhaled, and tapped the barn door with his foot. "Okay, I don't want to overreact, but we should take some precautions. You, Max and Laura take shifts out here and set up an O.P. in the woods near the entrance. Unless we're facing a real threat, I don't want to raise any alarms, or send Elena home."

"We'll use the back door." Laura replied. "You won't see or hear a thing."

Archer pursed his lips and nodded silently before walking back inside the barn.

Archer did his best to keep the conversation flowing while Shen, Laura and Max took turns coming and going from the barn. Using codes long established, and "WhatsApp", the first text message Archer received from Shen read simply, "IP"—for *"In Position."* Then "AC"—for *"All Clear."* All well-practiced shorthand that was now like a second language for them.

Max was positioned in an observation post near the driveway entrance, Shen and Laura were in the barn participating in the conversation with Elena and Archer.

Archer was hopeful Shen's information would amount to nothing, but the two DoE vehicles were distinctly out of place when the only nuclear reactor in Maine—the Maine Yankee Atomic Yankee Power Plant, now out of operation—was an hour southwest of Camden between Wiscasset and Boothbay. Out of place enough to raise a red flag.

It was Max's text that quietly and instantly caused Shen and Laura to look up at Archer.

ART: 2SUVs 4PAX/ADEPtl—KTM

Alarm Response Team: 2 SUVs with 4 Passengers/Armed Dismounted Enemy Patrol—Kill Team

The key was that the team was moving directly toward its target with no apparent attempt to serve a warrant. They might be in vehicles that appeared to be official DoE vehicles, but were likely not on official DoE business.

Archer looked at his watch and back at Shen and Laura. "You

both need to hop on that conference call now don't you?"

Shen and Laura nodded, and then politely but quickly excused themselves before leaving the table.

Archer debated telling Elena of the imminent danger that was approaching, but weighed the odds, and decided against it. Another text message came from Max.

```
AA: P2 DVWY, ETA: 5 MIN, WPNS: S-M4/M9
```

Avenue of Approach: Parallel to Driveway, Estimated Time of Arrival: 5 Minutes, Weapons: Suppressed M4 Carbines and M9 Pistols.

"Is everything okay?" Elena asked. "Seems like everyone left in a big hurry."

Archer nodded hesitantly. "They'll be right back. We'd forgotten about a call we had with John Lee's family. We're doing our best to coordinate his burial at Arlington National Cemetery." He picked up the bottle of Château Lafite Rothschild. "More wine?"

Elena nodded and smiled, while Archer refilled both of their glasses—regretting the need to lie.

A muffled racket erupted not far from the front of the barn that sounded like a series of bats hitting baseballs, in quick succession. Beau suddenly jumped up and began barking uncontrollably at the closed door.

Elena got up to try to calm him down.

As Archer stood, leaving his Browning Hi-Power strapped under the table, he saw Max's text message:

```
TIC - 4EKIA
```

Archer was able to immediately translate Max's operational code: *Team in Contact, 4 Enemy Killed.*

Archer read Max's message and quickly typed a response:

BZ/RTB

Well done. Return to Base

Archer joined Elena in calming Beau down. "Not sure what's gotten into the old boy."

"Well, something caught his attention out there," Elena answered. "He can be a little hypersensitive sometimes."

Elena looked at Archer with a slight smile, and what seemed to be a knowing expression. "No, not Beau...."

Luke Archer returned to the cabin after driving Elena home, giving his team the time they needed to recover the bodies of their attackers, photograph them, survey their equipment, search for identification, and then transport and bury them in a remote area of Camden Hills State Park.

"They were obviously professionals. Between 30 and 35 years old. Males." Max said. "We have their iPhones. We can use their thumb prints to break into them while we still have them here."

"Who do we know at NSA?" Archer asked. "Somehow they tracked us here. We're gonna need some help intercepting their communications and determine who's intercepting ours."

"Dag Thorsen," Laura answered. "He's been there for five or so years now."

Archer nodded. Dag Thorsen was a former Norwegian *Forsvarets Spesialkommando*, or "FSK," commando who, with Archer's assistance, immigrated to the United States to pursue a career in cyber security, and ultimately went to work at the NSA. Just under six and a half feet, Dag was a virtual giant—in stature as well as intellect. Dag Thorsen owed his American citizenship to Archer for pulling every stop and every string—from Visa to Green Card to employment in the U.S. intelligence community, citing his computer and language proficiency. "Okay, let's get hold of him."

"How did they know we were here?" Shen asked.

"I don't know," Archer answered. "But once whomever they

were working for finds out their kill team isn't coming back, they'll come back in force. So we're gonna need to relocate."

Chapter 11

ARCHER ARRIVED AT BALTIMORE-WASHINGTON International (BWI) Airport and caught an Uber ride to Cafe Milano in Georgetown. Enroute, he called Camden Middle School to request an extended leave of absence based on a family emergency. Conveying her understanding, the school principal told Archer his job would be waiting for him when he returned.

Entering the restaurant amidst the gathering evening crowd, he scanned the bar. On the television set above the bar, Zachary Hastings was arguing with one of the CNN reporters about perceived problems with the transition of presidential administrations. Watching it, Archer had a brief flashback to the heated arguments they shared in Kabul over a full range of issues—from operations to logistics. Seeing Hastings, as the future Vice President, was more than a little surreal for Archer to fully grasp.

Looking around, he saw Sam Owen already seated at a large, round table against the glass doorway. Several high-profile personalities were seated at different tables close to Owen's—a former Secretary of State, a billionaire media magnate, and an all-but-forgotten celebrity model and movie star who had still retained her natural beauty.

Owen stood, and Archer shook his hand. "We're in good company, I see," Archer commented, sitting down beside him.

"The crowd's interesting here," Owen replied. "*The New York Times* called it a place 'where some of the world's most powerful people go to be noticed, but not approached.'"

"That would be nice," Archer said quietly. "We had an interesting crowd approach us in Camden last night."

"How'd that go?"

Archer shook his head. "I don't think they were expecting a welcome committee."

The sommelier poured a red wine into their glasses, and then displayed the bottle. "Peter Michael Au Paradis 2012," he announced. "An exceptional Napa Cabernet."

72

Owen held up his glass. "Glad you're okay."

Archer met his toast, clinking glasses, and took a sip. "It says a lot about who we're up against."

Owen opened up an email on his iPhone, and passed it to Archer. "Turns out we're up against a lot more than just the Department of Energy and some rogue company."

Archer put his glasses on and read the email.

```
Sam - here are the fund transfers from DoE
and the CFPB to private individuals and
sole source contract awards over the past
two years. As requested, I've included an
extract summarizing those payments relating
to V-Tec, Dr. Robert Craine, the Craine
Foundation, and Cold Mountain, NC.
Best,
Jack
Jack Owen
Program Examiner
OMB
```

"Your brother?" Archer asked, looking up at Owen.

"Cousin," Owen replied. "Now, scroll down."

Archer scanned the document and stopped at the list of sole source contracts that the Department of Energy alone had awarded during the past year.

U.S. Department of Energy and CFPB Sole Source Contracts

Vendor Description	Amount	Agency
V-Tec, Inc.	$7.8M	DOE
Craine Foundation	$798,000	CFPB
V-Tec, Inc.	$9.1M	DOE
Dr. Robert Craine	$4.5M	DOE

```
Heidi Bend              $1.5M        CFPB
Cindy McCormick         $1.5M        CFPB
Susan McKaren           $1.5M        DOE
Jack Bernan             $7.6M        OMB
```

"Who are these three women?" Archer asked, pointing at the last three entries.

Owen nodded, taking his iPhone back. "Well, this is where it gets even more interesting—Heidi Bend is the wife of Senator Horace Bend, Chairman of the Senate Energy Committee. Cindy McCormick is the wife of Congressman Ted McCormick, Chairman of the House Committee on Energy and Commerce."

"And Susan McKaren?" Archer asked.

"Wife of Governor Mike McKaren," Owen replied. "Governor of the Great State of North Carolina."

"Can you forward that to me?" Archer asked.

Owen nodded, and pointed toward the menu as the waiter poured the wine. "I've ordered some antipasti for us—but highly recommend the risotto and the veal chop for the main course."

Chapter 12

AFTER COMPLETING THEIR DINNER, Luke Archer followed Sam Owen out the front door of Cafe Milano, and saw him suddenly collapse to the ground.

The blotch of blood darkening the front of Owen's shirt was all that Archer needed to know to understand they were under attack. The glass window in front of the restaurant suddenly shattered - a second shot, and then another in quick succession. The chaos of women screaming, men yelling, tables falling, and glass shattering all around them was further aggravated by people running both in and out of the restaurant seeking cover.

In the midst of the growing pandemonium, Archer pulled Owen's body inside, in front of the cloakroom. He checked for a pulse on Owen, but found none.

He knew Owen had been killed by a sniper's bullet—a sniper who most likely had been positioned on a rooftop directly in front of the entrance to the restaurant. The sound of the crashing window that followed, he realized, was from a bullet most likely meant for him.

Archer looked over at the *maître d'*, also seeking cover behind his dais, and in a quiet, but firm tone, advised him to call the police.

Staying low to the ground, Archer waded through the panicked crowd to the sliding glass doors behind the table where they'd just been sitting, and slipped outside.

Running from the restaurant to the main thoroughfare that ran through Georgetown, he turned and entered a Mexican restaurant. Climbing the stairs quickly, he pulled a baseball cap out of the pocket and placed it on his head. Breathing heavily, he found the hatch to the roof, and unholstered his Browning Hi-Power as he ascended the steps.

The roof was unoccupied, but provided a good view of the surrounding streets. He was looking for a specific silhouette...a unique profile that fit someone with the capability to kill from a distance, and escape undetected.

When that image came into view, he did a double take— a

woman—fit, petite and inconspicuous, carrying what appeared to be a yoga mat case slung to her shoulder. He watched as she moved through the crowd on the street, nimble and catlike, boarding a waiting black SUV. Pulling a small cylindrical monocular from his pocket, he sighted in on the rear of the SUV—the license plates were the standard Federal Government variety.

Archer pulled up WhatsApp, and called Laura Chicone "They just killed Sam Owen—the reporter who was working for us," he whispered. "Government vehicle. Meet me at our usual spot."

Archer knew Laura would understand that place to be the Lincoln Memorial.

"My God." Laura stopped on the steps of the Lincoln Memorial and looked at Archer. "What the hell's happening?"

Archer shook his head, looking down at the reflecting pool, the Washington Monument, and Capitol Building in the distance. "Over dinner, Sam showed me an OMB email that indicated Senators, Congressmen and Governors are on payroll through their spouses. The only explanation that makes any sense is that we're up against our own government or some entity that operates within our own government, almost like a parasite."

"Who are they? Laura asked. "Do we know?"

"As far as I can tell, these people aren't accountable to anyone, and they're self-funded through government contracts, among other devices," Archer said softly, walking along the marble colonnade.

"And obviously, they're willing to eliminate anyone who stands in their way."

Laura pulled out an iPad from her backpack. "It doesn't end there," she said, turning the iPad on. "As I thought about it, it seemed like too much of a coincidence that a team was suddenly dispatched to find us all the way in Maine." She located the screenshot, and passed it to Archer. "So I did some searching of the SUV license plates, and found this on the MPD Surveillance feed at DoE headquarters."

The image was a close-up taken forty-eight hours ago, of four men and a woman standing beside a black government SUV."

Laura pointed at the photo. "These three men were members of the kill team," she said. "I'm not sure who the woman is—but we know the fourth man."

Archer recognized the woman as the assassin he'd observed from the rooftop, and inhaled the cold winter air. The fourth man in the photo was Dan Thorne.

Chapter 13

"OKAY," LUKE ARCHER WHISPERED, clearly flabbergasted. "That's about the last thing I was expecting."

Walking into the interior of the memorial, Archer tried to come to terms with Laura's revelation and Dan Thorne's betrayal. He couldn't find the right words.

Looking up, he pointed at the statue of Lincoln. "You know, they say Lincoln's hands are positioned in a way to show him using sign language to communicate his initials— with his left hand shaped to form an 'A', and his right hand to form an 'L'."

"Is that true?" Laura asked.

"Some say it's an urban legend, but as it turns out, the sculptor had a son who was deaf, and also knew sign language. Lincoln was also the President who signed the law creating Gallaudet University."

"Coincidence?" Laura asked.

"Yeah," Archer shrugged absently. "I don't much believe in 'em."

The doorman opened the door for Luke Archer and Laura Chicone, welcoming them to The Jefferson—one of Washington, D.C.'s best hotels, and a kind of "safe house" that Archer had used in the past to meet assets in a low-key, but comfortable setting.

The manager of Plume restaurant greeted Archer by name, and led them inside to an isolated corner table that Archer had requested in advance. The manager seated Laura, and welcomed them back.

The sommelier showed Archer a bottle of 1986 Château Gruaud Larose.

"A stunning Bordeaux," the sommelier commented. "The Chateau Gruaud Larose vineyard hasn't changed since it was created in the 1700s. It was first owned by a knight named Joseph Stanislas Gruaud. Today it's one of the few Bordeaux estates to use a 'hail reduction cannon.' It's triggered by radar, so when the radar detects hail, the cannon fires shock waves that break the hail stones into bits to protect the vines and the grapes."

Archer thanked her, and they watched her uncork and decant the wine. She poured a sample for Archer, who followed the standard tasting procedure.

"We had this wine at Fort Campbell didn't we?"

Archer nodded. "It was one of Becky's favorites."

"I miss her," Laura said.

Archer nodded. "So do I."

"I think about her often," Laura said. "That job as political advisor to the 5th Group Commander was one of the most memorable assignments I've had. Had it not been for that job, I wouldn't have met you and Becky. She was a good friend."

"She's still with us," Archer said softly. "I really believe that."

"They still have no idea who killed her?" Laura asked after a few moments of silence.

Archer shook his head, and pursed his lips tightly. "Not yet—it's a cold case, but the say they're still investigating."

"So they say."

Archer nodded. "Yeah."

She held up her glass. "To Becky," she offered.

Archer touched glasses solemnly. "To Becky." He tasted the wine, and held it for a moment before swallowing.

"How do you keep going?"

Archer shrugged. "You just do," he replied. "You focus on what's right in front of you. Like now."

"You know we can't fight them alone," Laura said directly. "We're totally outgunned and out-resourced." She paused, looking uncertain. "Why us?"

"If we don't do it, who will?" Archer asked, rhetorically, returning to her comment about fighting alone.

"If we're going to make this our fight, we're going to need help."

"Well, at this point," Archer said nodding. "I only want the kind we can trust."

Laura nodded, savoring the wine. "Any ideas?"

"A few," Archer answered. "But I was hoping I wouldn't have to go there."

"Max wants to pay Dan a visit," Laura said. "You know what that means. She's in a killing rage."

"Can't say that I blame her," Archer answered. "But tell her not to do anything just yet,"

"Could we try to infiltrate their organization?"

"Two of my friends are dead because of this group," Archer said. "I don't want to see any more of you end up the same way."

"Our friends…."

"Pardon me?"

"Two of *our* friends are dead," Laura mildly corrected. "We all have skin in this game, Archer, and we all have a pretty good idea of what we're up against. And now they are hunting us. The best defense is always a great offense—and we have little time until they can locate us again."

Archer nodded, sufficiently chastened—knowing well she was right.

Archer's cell phone rang. Recognizing Jack Condon's cell phone number, he stepped away to take the call, out of earshot.

"They were able to trace the polonium to Argonne National Laboratory," Jack said, without preamble.

"Where's that?"

"It's a National Research Lab just outside Chicago," Jack replied.

"How did they figure that out?"

"By analyzing trace radioisotopes found during John's autopsy," Jack explained. "They were able to figure out it was produced by Argonne."

"I have no idea what you just said," Archer replied.

"It's very difficult to identify the source if the polonium is pure," Jack continued. "But this wasn't. Every reactor in the world has its own signature. In addition to the Polonium-210 they found in John's body, there were unique trace amounts of Thallium-206, Radium-226, and Bismuth-210—in concentrations and type that were unique to what Argonne produces."

"I thought polonium only came from Russia?" Archer said.

"Russia does export about ten grams of polonium to the United States each month, so that would be a logical conclusion," Jack explained. "But different types of radioactive materials pick up different characteristics when they're produced, so if you have samples of the material, like we did in this case, you can do the forensics to analyze their trace constituents. This definitely came from Argonne."

"What do we know about Argonne?"

"I'm on their website now...it's run by the University of Chicago for DoE," Jack answered. "Looks like a very competent team. Wait—Arch?"

Jack stopped, and for a moment Archer thought he'd lost the connection.

"What?"

"So, Argonne is operated by University of Chicago together in a corporate partnership with V-Tec, Inc., and Dr. Robert Craine is Chairman of their Board of Governors."

"Send me whatever documentation we have on all of this," Archer said. "I just met with Sam Owen, and he was on board - until they killed him. He was concerned, and agreed we were well beyond the realm of logical—or legal—explanation."

"That's cause for us to be doubly concerned."

"And doubly careful," Archer added.

Chapter 14

LUKE ARCHER SAT IN HIS HOTEL suite at The Jefferson, watching a *60 Minutes* interview with Zachary Hastings. Watching him in his role as the Vice President-Elect made him realize how the degrees of separation had become increasingly compressed over time.

Zack Hastings had been Archer's company commander when he was a team leader in 5th Special Forces Group. At the time, Hastings was single, and consistently took full advantage of his position, rank and his "Gentleman's Quarterly" good looks in order to date a full range of fashion models, beautiful White House staffers, and even Hollywood actresses, enhancing his public image. The TED talk he gave five years ago to great acclaim on the topic of national defense led to his selection as Secretary of State, which in turn led to his nomination as Vice President. Articulate, smooth, with a refined appearance, Hastings' rise through the Army's ranks had been meteoric.

Archer watched the *60 Minutes* profile with a measure of bewildered fascination.

> *Promoted early at virtually every rank, early selection for every position he achieved. He even skipped from one to three stars, just before he was selected to be the President's National Security Advisor. Zack Hastings was then promoted to four stars, making him the youngest full general in the nation's history at 52 years of age. He was selected to command the Resolute Support Mission and all U.S. Forces in Afghanistan, and then selected by President Williamson to be his Secretary of State. Now, two years later, William Stone, the former Governor of Maryland, selected General Hastings to be Stone's Vice President and running mate. With Stone' election, Hastings has taken on a lead role in the presidential transition.*

As he normally did, Zack Hastings performed flawlessly in the interview, deftly handling the most challenging questions, no matter how predisposed the bias or agenda. When asked,

"General, you have never held elective office—what makes you qualified to be a heartbeat away from the highest office in our nation?"

Hastings' response was brilliant and incisive:

"Well, the American people have made it clear in an historic landslide election, that they are fully confident in my qualifications to be Vice President. You know, we've had five Presidents in our history who never held elective office—Zachary Taylor, Ulysses S. Grant, and Dwight Eisenhower among them. I was asked by Governor Stone to be his running mate precisely because I wasn't a political firebrand, and because I've served our country in other ways."

Despite their three decade-long professional association, the relationship between Archer and Hastings had always been strained at best.

During one of their combat deployments in Afghanistan, Hastings refused Archer's request to launch one of his teams to rescue a SEAL team that had been ambushed on the border with Pakistan because of the "undue risk to men and aircraft." As a result, Taliban forces had killed every member of the SEAL team.

On another occasion, earlier, in the mid '90s as then, an Army Special Forces Major, Archer had returned from a Middle Eastern deployment to learn from his wife that his Group Commander, then-*Colonel* Hastings had made a point of knocking on their door several times during the previous weeks to "check in" on her in Archer's absence. On each occasion, she politely informed him she was just fine, thanked him, and bid him goodnight.

It seemed like strange behavior, but after questioning him about the odd nature of these visits to Colonel Hastings, Archer quickly learned that Hastings viewed his "Command Check-Ins" as a "leadership responsibility" to every one of his deployed officers, and directed all of his subordinate commanders to do the same for the families in their units. Archer also learned that most of the spouses were flattered by his visits and calls, and did not see them as out of line.

The Special Operations community is small and insular—and it came as little surprise to Archer that he had followed Hastings to the same units, and often on the same missions. On one occasion, Archer saved then-Brigadier General Hastings' life, when a suicide bomber attempted to detonate his vest beside him. Archer had been keeping a close eye on the Afghan officer, and shot him in the head with an M4 carbine at 25 meters when he exposed the detonator in his hand. Hastings thanked Archer, but was noticeably shaken by the experience. Oddly, Hastings never conveyed any further sign of gratitude or other positive sentiment for Archer, after he'd saved his life. Rather, Hastings actually seemed embarrassed by the incident, and began to actively oppose him whenever possible.

Now, as unlikely as the possibility could ever have seemed to Archer, Zachary Hastings was going to be the next Vice President of the United States, regularly appearing on television, on the internet, and in newspapers—and widely regarded as the savior of the Afghanistan campaign. A ubiquitous presence always seemed to be what Hastings had sought, and now he was achieving just that.

Archer's phone vibrated, and he heard Laura's voice on the other end of the secure WhatsApp call. "Justice Anthony Hill just died," she said. "They're saying 'natural causes.'"

What are the odds?" Archer answered.

"The family's refusing to allow an autopsy. Seems like too much of a coincidence."

Archer inhaled, thinking of all the implications a newly tipped Supreme Court would hold for the country. The report wasn't yet on Cable News or on the internet.

"He was 80 years old, wasn't he?" Archer added.

And further, "This could upset the balance of the court in a major way." For the last several years, The Court had been regularly disposed towards 5 to 4 rulings.

"They won't allow a replacement to be voted on until after Inauguration Day," Laura responded. "What are the odds his death wasn't accidental?"

Archer paused before posting. "We can try to find out."

Chapter 15

LUKE ARCHER TOOK A SEAT across from Dan Thorne and Max Peretz in Del Frisco's restaurant in Washington, DC. Thorne did his best to conceal his anxiety throughout their lunch meeting—communicating his shock about their close brush with his kill team in Maine, and Sam Owen's murder at Cafe Milano. The encounter was well orchestrated, representing their best opportunity to draw information from Thorne—betting on a natural tendency toward overcompensating to conceal his betrayal.

"Justice Anthony Hill was poisoned with polonium," Thorne said quietly. "With a pretty massive dose."Archer nodded, and leaned back in his seat. "Who knows about that?"

"Only a few people," Thorne replied, sipping his tea. "It's all being very closely held—they're looking for a Kremlin connection."

Archer looked down at the menu, and shook his head. "The lunch special—Red Herring, served cold. I don't recommend it, actually."

"Pardon me?" Thorne said.

Archer nodded at Max, who placed copies of Bermuda-based bank statements in front of him. All the statements were in his name.

"Didn't realize the CIA was paying its analysts so well these days, Dan," Archer said. "$1.5 Million in deposits over the past year. Business must be good, eh?"

Thorne shifted uncomfortably in his seat. "Look, there's a simple explanation here—"

Max placed the Metropolitan Police Department surveillance photo in front of him, showing him clearly conversing with the members of the kill team who had visited them in Maine.

"We know," Archer said quietly. "Now, it shouldn't come as any surprise that Max has her own plans for you.

"What kind of plans?"

"The kind that don't involve you walking out of this restaurant on your two feet," Archer replied. "Honestly, I don't blame her, because

I feel the same way."

"Arch...Max...," Thorne stuttered nervously, doing his best to keep his voice low. "How long have we been friends? How many operations have we conducted together? Let me explain!"

Archer held his hand out, palm forward. "We'd like an explanation, but not the bullshit version you're about to hand us. Instead, we thought we'd give you a choice. You give us the unvarnished truth—all of it, right now—and we won't report your Bermuda bank account to the IRS, so at least Angela and your kids will be taken care of. Anything else, and they'll be on the street."

Thorne looked down, breathing deeply and now sweating profusely.

Why did you kill Justice Hill?" Archer asked. "Let's start with that."

Thorne looked up at Archer with an expression of capitulation and resignation. "He was in the way."

"How so?"

"An impending court case that would allow V-Tec to sell nuclear reactors abroad. He and Dr. Craine hadn't had a good history together."

"Why don't you tell us how you killed John Lee?" Max said.

Archer could see Thorne was about to object again, but the shock of their quiet confrontation in a public setting, had its desired effect.

"Okay, Okay," Thorne began, taking a deep breath—hands out to placate. "Angela doesn't know anything, okay? Just promise me nothing will happen to her or the kids!"

"You should have thought about them a long time ago," Max replied, seething contempt.

"They'll be fine, Dan," Archer assured. "But only if you start talking to us, now."

Thorne sat for a moment, seeming to collect himself. After another sip of tea, he swallowed, and began his confession. "The organization is called 'Soldiers of the Union'— 'SU' is the acronym used. It originated in the Civil War days to protect Abraham Lincoln. Winfield Scott, George McClellan, Henry Halleck—all of the Union generals...they were all members."

"But not Grant," Archer replied under his breath.

"With the direction the country's going, all of us could see we're heading toward a civil war...the racial tensions...the crime...the federal debt. Everything," Thorne said. "Stopping a civil war before it engulfs us all—that's all the justification I needed.

"And your low government salary too, I'll bet," Archer commented. "How are you organized?"

"It's all highly compartmented, with a very select Bigot list" Thorne explained. "You have cells—no one knows who's in any of the other cells, and each cell recruits its own members."

"Who's in your cell?" Archer asked.

"You killed most of them at your farm. But including me, there are three of us left—Soledad D'Escoto, an FBI agent based in Baltimore," he said pointing at the woman assassin in the surveillance photo. "And Chris Stockman."

Max. "Stockman?" Archer exclaimed, incredulous, looking over at

Thorne nodded. "He's the cell lead," he said hoarsely.

"If he finds out I told you any of this, he'll kill me."

asked. "Are either of them aware that Laura's working with us?" Archer

Thorne shook his head. "No, they only know about you, Shen and Max, and all of the equipment."

Archer inhaled deeply, controlling himself with effort. "Okay Dan, here's what we're going to do. You're going to recruit Laura Chicone into your cell, and you're going to go back to Langley right now to do it. She's at the office waiting for you. Understand?"

"Okay," Thorne nodded, and swallowed.

"You know, Dan," Archer said coldly. "One thing about John is that he'd only allow people he knew very well onto his property, let alone into his cabin. You were the only person he saw for months." Archer paused. "And so, when you showed up on his doorstep, that's when you poisoned him with the polonium. I'm guessing you put it in his bourbon, as you toasted the 'good old days' with him."

"I didn't have a choice...," Thorne cried. "You don't understand what these people are capable of!"

Archer and Max stood up to leave. Max placed a single glove on and grabbed Thorne's empty teacup, placing it in a heavy, black pouch.

"What's happening?" Thorne asked feebly, noticeably frightened.

"You left the vial with the remainder of polonium in the trunk of your car. Recommend you get over to Langley now while you're still feeling up to it," Archer answered, not without sympathy. "If anything goes south, and you don't honor your side of our bargain, all bets are off with regard to your family."

Dan Thorne sat, frozen to his marrow. In complete disbelief. Eyes glazed.

"John Lee sends his regards—from heaven to hell," Max added firmly, zipping up the pouch. "Your dose of polonium is about 3 grams, five or six times more than you used to kill John. So, you might want to get moving. You don't have much time."

Chapter 16

ARCHER KNEW INFILTRATING LAURA CHICONE undercover—as a member of "Soldiers of the Union"—was dangerous, and would place her life at even greater risk. And yet, he also knew she was one of the very best in that capacity, having been undercover on many other occasions abroad. She was the most disciplined operator he knew, and her field craft was impeccable.

SU's apparent assassination of Supreme Court Justice Anthony Hill, following the murder of Sam Owen, had convinced Archer that they had no other choice, and that they had to act quickly. Laura's professional association and good relationship with Chris Stockman represented a prime opportunity to gain an inside view of the organization if he accepted her into its ranks.

"I'll be fine, Archer," Laura said over the phone. "This is the only way."

"If you feel at all threatened," Archer said. "I need you to get out of there."

"Deal," Laura replied. "For now, though, this is just another day at the office, okay?"

"Why doesn't that make me feel better?" Archer quipped before hanging up. He looked over at Shen, Jack and Max, sitting beside him in Lafayette Square, across from the White House.

"You know, this square has been used as a racetrack, graveyard, zoo, slave market, and a Soldier's encampment," Archer commented. "Now we're looking across the street at a house that's being infiltrated by a fifth column."

"Well, we need to make sure that situation doesn't persist," Shen said.

Archer shook his head, and handed Shen his rolled up copy of the *New York Times*, headlining the death of a Supreme Court Justice. "Getting you your Green Card may have been the smartest thing I've ever done." He pointed at Jack Condon. "And thanks to Jack for helping with that."

"Honored to do it," Jack replied. "It's the only way I can get friends, by importing them."

Shen smiled and Max laughed, pointing toward the statue of Lafayette. "Here comes another foreigner you managed to naturalize."

Dag Thorsen's massive silhouette against the backdrop of a completely illuminated White House was impossible to miss. His cheekbones were raised in a broad grin that has infectious to those who worked alongside him. Blonde haired, with piercing blue eyes, Thorsen was a natural leader and widely respected throughout the intelligence and special operations community as a Global Exploitation Manager, Engineer, and Special Forces Medic—a rare combination—but all jobs he'd held during a varied and accomplished career spanning over two decades, from Norway's FSK to 10th Special Forces Group, to the NSA.

"Get out of the way you big oaf!" Max shouted. "You're blocking our view!"

"Ha! My good friends!" Dag shouted in a deep, accented baritone. "So good to see you!"

Dag's athletic physique was on full display as he gave bear hugs to Archer, Shen, Jack, and then threw Max into the air, to a scream of delightful protest.

"I missed you Machla, my dear friend!" Dag exclaimed.

"Okay, now that we're all reunited, let's get to work." Archer began walking toward H Street. "This way—we have rooms reserved for us at the Hay Adams."

"I'd like you all to meet some good friends of mine," Archer said, closing the door to the suite. "This is Congressman Daniel Tory. You may already know his wife, Robin—formerly Robin Nielsen—who served in the Special Activities Division a few years back."

"Yes! Of course!" Dag Thorsen exclaimed. "Dear Lady, your actions in Europe and Russia are well-known. It's our honor to meet you!"

Robin shook her head—pointing toward Congressman Tory. "My husband had more to do with that than me. I just went along for the ride."

Daniel Tory shook his head and smiled. "Any friends of Luke Archer's are friends of ours.'"

"You may have also heard that the Congressman is running for Governor in the State of Illinois," Archer added. "So far, he's doing well in the polls."

"Good luck, Congressman!" Jack exclaimed. "Illinois could use your help right now."

"It's still early," Daniel Tory laughed. "I'm not sure the polls mean much at this point."

"I briefed Congressman Tory and Robin yesterday on what's transpired over the past week,' Archer explained, motioning everyone toward the long dining room table. "And they wanted to meet each of you. I trust them completely, and so should you."

Sitting down, Archer continued. "It was my friends, Danno and Robin Tory, who discovered the Kremlin's plans to launch an invasion of the Baltic States, and who stopped them in the face of massive resistance—not only from Moscow, but here in Washington. Their Foundation has significant resources, and it's played a significant role in promoting and defending democracy around the world."

"We're very sorry for the loss of your compatriots," Danno said. "And we're as concerned as you are."

"We could use your help," Shen said.

Danno nodded. "You have it. Hearing from Archer helped us put some other reports we've received in better context."

"What kind of reports?" Max asked.

"Last week, our Foundation received a report that the Supreme Court would be attacked," Robin said.

"And then Justice Hill passed away a few days later."

"He was poisoned," Jack said. "That was confirmed for us yesterday."

Danno nodded. "Archer told us," he said.

"The question, now, is who else is being targeted?"

"We're facing a real threat within our government," Robin answered.

"One that represents a clear and present danger to our democracy."

"They call themselves the 'Soldiers of the Union' or 'SU' for short," Jack said.

"We've heard the term before," Robin replied.

"I understand you're in need of an operating base," Danno said. "Victoria's Jewelry in Tyson's Corner at 8000 Leesburg Pike. Go there. Ask for Victoria, the owner, and tell her you are there for 'The Moussaieff Red'." He handed a signed business card to Archer. "Then give her this card—everything else will follow."

Luke Archer read the coded text on his disposable cell phone, from Laura Chicone's disposable cell.

In\Mtf\24

Successful Infiltration. More details to follow in twenty-four hours.

He responded with a simple:

K/Thx

He pulled out the battery to his phone and replaced the sim card with another. Laura's cryptic message was the best possible news he could have hoped for in the midst of the chaos and tragedy of the last several days. A new "WhatsApp" message instantly came through from Elena Campbell, with a photo of Beau looking up at the camera with one of her dogs:

Missing U, but I'm
fine, Archer

Thx. Needed that. Miss him

A minute passed, and Elena sent another message:

        Many   black   SUVs
        and sedans in town
        today

                Y?

        "Federal
        Investigation"

        Gone now

Elena's last text assured him, and yet also confirmed that he and his team were the sole focus of the Feds' manhunt. After completely sanitizing the cabin, barn and ranch prior to their departure, he also knew they would find nothing of real value, were they to search there.

Even from a distance, he felt his relationship with Elena deepening; but he was conflicted. This clearly wasn't a good time for him to be in a relationship with anyone, for their own sake, let alone his. It had been nearly fourteen years since Becky had been taken from him, but in many ways, it still seemed like yesterday. Reconciling that wasn't something he'd yet done for himself.

He pulled the curtain open, and looked down from his Presidential suite—offering a direct view of the White House and the Washington Monument. It was a breathtaking panorama that captured the significance of the office and the country's rich history. And yet, despite the veneer of beauty and appearance of routine below, Archer could see an ominous bank of storm clouds gathering in the distance...rapidly approaching.

Chapter 17

FOR NO APPARENT REASON—a car door shutting...voices outside...he wasn't sure, Luke Archer awoke at 3:29AM, with a familiar twinge of foreboding. After so many years abroad, recognizing that sixth sense was what had kept him alive. Over time, he'd learned to always act on it, no matter how safe things outwardly appeared.

Listen to your instincts...

It was a mantra he'd learned from John Lee, over time. And those whispered words were what caused him to swiftly rise out of bed, reach for his suppressed Browning Hi-Power, and ensure it was locked and loaded.

Dressed only in his underwear, he glanced through the curtain and saw the Black SUVs parked on the street, engines running, with drivers inside—otherwise a familiar sight in Washington, DC. *But at 3:30 in the morning? Not so much....*

Archer stopped. Listened. After a moment, he heard shuffling outside the front door of the suite, and looked through the peephole. Two men and one woman in dark suits were standing outside the door with handguns at the ready. His heart raced. With the thought they would expect to find him an easy target, fast asleep, in bed. He ducked into the coat closet, and left it cracked open.

The outer door's locking mechanism clicked, and the door slowly opened. Looking toward the window, he could see the reflection of three figures entering the suite and approaching the master bedroom.

Archer swung the door open, and in a well-practiced maneuver, fired three muffled shots. All three intruders collapsed to the floor, in rapid succession each with a single gunshot to their heads.

He placed a small headlamp on his head with an elastic belt, and quickly searched the three assailants. The two men wore crew cuts with transparent earpieces and push-to-talk wrist mikes. Reaching inside the woman's suit jacket, he pulled out what appeared to be an FBI flip badge. He also found a piece of paper with hand-written annotations that read:

SMS intrcpt with ME contact—Luke Archer @ Hay Adams—2145hrs.

Knowing that their drivers were waiting for them on the street below, Archer called Shen in the adjacent suite and was relieved to hear him answer.

"Get Dag and Max—come to my suite," Archer said simply. *"Now."*

Archer opened the door, Browning Hi-Power still in hand. Shen, Dag and Max stepped in and Archer pointed toward the three bodies.

"They appear to be FBI," Archer said. "This one's Soledad D'Escoto—remember her? She's the sniper who killed Sam Owen."

"Part of Dan Thorne's SU cell," Max replied. "That leaves Chris Stockman."

"He won't be happy." Archer replied peaking out the window. "Two SUVs with drivers are on the street waiting."

Shen nodded. "How did they find us?"

Archer handed them the scrap of paper he'd found on one of the agents. "They intercepted text messages—and traced them here to the hotel," Archer replied. "So they obviously have the full cooperation of the NSA."

"And the FBI," Max added.

"Give me a minute," Dag said, holstering his pistol, and removing a suppressor from his pocket for future use. "I'll take care of the drivers. That will give us some more time. And I have contacted a group of my friends from a former employer. They specialize in disaster response such as you have created here. They will leave no trace."

Archer nodded. "Switch their radios off. Take photos of the scene. We're leaving now."

Chapter 18

LUKE ARCHER AND THE TEAM LOOKED at Victoria's Jewelers from the parking lot in Tyson's Corner, grateful but also incredulous about Congressman Danno Tory's referral.

"Archer, I'm only going in there if Dag buys me that diamond necklace and earring set," Max deadpanned.

"Machla, my love!" Dag exclaimed, struggling to get his massive frame out of the back seat of the car. "You know I buy you anything!"

"I trust Danno and Robin Tory implicitly," Archer said, ignoring the banter. "But we're obviously walking into this cold. I'm not entirely sure what to expect here."

"No necklace then?" Max replied in mock disappointment.

"Just stay alert," Archer said.

Victoria's Jewelers stood alone as a commercial space, dwarfed beside several Tyson's Corner high rises, including *USA Today's* corporate headquarters. Its distinct architectural design stood out with a geometric array of triangulated glass windows, tilted inward and contained by contemporary stone and concrete walls.

Inside, the store had a geometric design. The far wall was adorned with light blue de Gournay wallpaper with birds in flight. Vintage round tables, contemporary white oak wall units and elegant glass and bronze-fronted cabinets were illuminated by ambient and accented light. The case and shelf lighting highlighted the brilliance of the diamonds, gemstones and precious metals on display. The floor and steps that led up and downstairs were made of white Carrara marble.

Archer looked around and could see the robust security system that had been fully integrated into the store's elegant layout, including alarms, surveillance cameras, safes, two-way electronic mirrors, and vault systems——much of it out of sight, but enough in plain view to act as a deterrent to the criminally minded. He approached an elderly woman who seemed to be welcoming customers, and asked for Victoria.

The woman nodded, and cheerfully replied, "I am Victoria!"

"Congressman Tory sent us, with a recommendation to see 'The Moussaieff Red'," Archer replied politely.

Victoria studied the card, flipped it over to see Danno Tory's signature, and turned to Archer's assembled group. "Yes. Please, follow me, Mr. Archer."

Archer realized he hadn't introduced himself, but that she had known his identity.

"The Moussaieff Red!" Victoria exclaimed as she led them down a flight of stairs. "It's the world's largest red diamond, you know— discovered by a Brazilian farmer in the Abaetezinho river in 1990."

Arriving at an armored door, Victoria punched in a series of numbers on a keypad and placed her hand on the platen of a hand geometry scanner. Once the scan was complete, the door clicked open.

"You see, all colored diamonds are rare," Victoria continued, leading the group down a hallway. She stopped at a round table displaying a group of seven red diamonds surrounding a larger one. Lights were positioned overhead. "But none are more so than the red diamond. We find them mostly in Africa, Australia and Brazil. Only around thirty true red diamonds are known to exist. Most are less than half a carat in size. But this…."

Lighting several candles surrounding the display, she then pointed at the center red diamond— it was triangular in shape, and noticeably larger than the others. Turning off the lights, each of the diamonds reflected the candlelight against the black velvet base in a beautiful star-like formation. "The Moussaieff Red is more than five carats. Trilliant-cut, with flawless quality."

"It is beautiful," Max replied. "All are extraordinary."

"Congressman Tory knew you would enjoy seeing them," Victoria said. The lights turned back on, and she faced a wall-mounted retinal scanner beside an elevator door. When the scan was complete, the elevator opened and she motioned the group to step inside. "And although he could not be here, his wife, Robin, is expecting you."

Their descent was rapid and steep. The thick, armored doors

opened to reveal a dramatic blue-gray Carrara marble and stainless steel staircase, leading down to a bustling integrated operations center surrounded by teak and stone walls.

Archer thanked Victoria, and proceeded down the staircase to find Robin Tory waiting for them. Robin gave Archer a hug, and smiled at the assembled team, who were dressed informally, in jeans and T-Shirts.

"Welcome to the Tory Foundation's North American Headquarters," Robin said, and turned to Archer. "You are all safe here."

Luke Archer looked around at the array of workstations, video wall displays with large plasma TV screens, and video teleconferencing systems. A conference room enclosed in glass was strategically situated in the middle of the workstations, overseeing the watch floor.

"Very impressive," Archer said to Robin. "I had no idea."

Robin nodded and smiled. "The capabilities of the Center are even more impressive," she said confidently. "The fiber optics are state-of-the-art, with full secure SATCOM capability. The workstations can call up information instantly from anywhere in the world—everything's fully automated, and all of our operators can access multiple networks simultaneously—so they can reach out to a head of state just as easily as a local sheriff in a small town. Now, what can we do for you right now?"

"Can we order breakfast?" Shen asked. "Archer wouldn't let us stop on the way over here."

"He's a very cruel slave driver," Max added.

"Yes, we can do that too!" Robin laughed. "Let me guess, *'Think in the morning. Act in the noon. Eat in the evening. Sleep in the night.'?*"

"Yes!" Shen, Max and Dag said in near-unison. *"That's exactly what he says to us!"*

Robin smiled and turned to Archer. "You haven't changed a bit have you?"

"William Blake," Archer replied, grinning sheepishly. "Hardly original, but I still like his logic."

"Colonel Archer was a mentor to many of us when we were first starting out in the Company," Robin explained. "I was one of those fortunate enough to have him as a mentor."

"Well, I'm not sure who mentored whom," Archer replied simply.

Chapter 19

ROBIN TORY LED THE TEAM to a massive transparent screen that suddenly lit up to reveal an assemblage of colored tiles that Archer recognized as a link analysis—a method of intelligence analysis that the police and military organizations use to understand their opposition.

The diagram showed the participants of the SU cells and their links to each other and suspected links to others. The sci-fi-like display allowed his team to view the established and emerging linkages on the screen while still being able to see through it at other images and videos.

"While this system won't be anything new to you," Robin began, "the information we've already been able to collect will be enlightening."

"Ahem," Jack Condon pointed at the high-tech display. "Langley doesn't have *anything* like *this*."

Robin nodded. "This does represent an upgrade. We've found the Planar screen helps us better visualize the information. But at the end of the day, the data we collect and the thought we put into the analysis are no substitute for a good strategy."

"Or good execution," Archer added.

The glass door to the conference room opened, with Victoria and two young women, carrying bags of breakfast croissants, fruit, juices and coffee.

Everyone helped themselves to the continental breakfast and sat down. Robin stood in front, and pointed at the screen. A variety of digital photos of people, facilities and locations—many of which Archer, Jack, and Laura had supplied—were overlaid to an organized template. "This is just a first step to map out the networks at play, correlate them, and identify patterns in real time."

"You've obviously invested some work into this already," Archer commented.

Robin nodded. "Both Daniel and I were very concerned after speaking to you last night," she said. "And the fact that they sent in another team early this morning was concerning, on many levels."

"Wait—you knew about that?" Max asked, surprised.

"I told her," Archer replied. "They had a right to know before we pulled in here."

"We were relieved to hear you were safe," Robin said, and motioned to the lit screen. "So, this is a working session for all of us," she continued. "Let me show you what we've been able to come up with so far, and we can build on it from there."

In this column, the players we've been able to identify to date," She said, pointing at the photos on the screen. "Dr. Robert Craine, Christopher Stockman, Soledad D'Escoto (Deceased), Dan Thorne— and then we have Senator Horace Bend, Congressman Ted McCormick, Governor Mike McKaren, and each of their spouses...."

"Here are the organizations that have been identified as participants in some way, shape, or form," she said, displaying multiple cells encased in variedly colored circles—for personalities, rectangles-for government organizations, and triangles—for corporations and civilian organizations.

Photos of the agency and department accompanied each name: the Craine Foundation, Cold Mountain VMAX Storage Facility, V-Tec International, the Consumer Finance Protection Bureau (CFPB), Department of Energy (Kill Team), Central Intelligence Agency, Federal Bureau of Investigation (Kill Team), Office of Management and Budget, Argonne National Laboratory, Soldiers of the Union (SU)..."

"Congress," Dag offered. "Elements of both the Senate and House."

Robin nodded, and wrote *Congress* on the screen by hand. Underneath she wrote: S*enate Energy Committee, House Committee on Energy and Commerce.*

"Here are photos of the Kill Teams," Archer said, texting Robin the surveillance photos and iPhone photos they had taken of the teams in Camden and in Washington, D.C., to include the photos of the bodies at the Hay Adams, taken only several hours prior.

"And their victims?" Shen asked.

Robin nodded, and the names appeared on the screen, with

their photos and map locations of their deaths. "Justice Anthony Hill (Kalorama, Washington, D.C.), John Lee (Cold Mountain, NC), Sam Owen (Cafe Milano, Washington, D.C.)…"

"Targets?" Jack Condon asked, with a white-knuckled hold on his computer mouse.

Team Archer...Supreme Court...

"Methods?" Shen asked.

Polonium poisoning, Snipers, Interagency Kill Teams…

As Robin wrote each entry, more text, digital images, and video content populated the screen, prompted by her written words alone. Using the touch screen, she quickly arranged and connected the assembled digital images with lines and arrows, organizing them in trees and radial arrays.

"Motive?" Dag asked.

"*That's* one of the most important questions we can ask ourselves right now," Robin agreed. With the swipe of a hand, she moved the bundle of assembled data to another adjacent screen. A separate screen popped up that provided a rough map of known financial transactions and communications networks.

"What makes SU different?" Robin asked the group. "And what makes it similar to other organizations we've seen in the past?"

"It's early, but they seem to have infiltrated nearly every component of government," Jack said, his brows furrowed in concentration. "Federal, State Houses...probably local governments too. Congress, Executive departments, and agencies—and they're intrinsically connected to, if not partnered with, private corporations."

"Their planning and execution is responsive and sophisticated," Shen said. "Their operators on the ground are competent—likely former law enforcement, three-letter agencies, and Special Operators."

"Their defenses are extremely advanced," Dag added. "They've obviously taken a long view in creating the Cold Mountain VMAX facility to build international revenue for themselves, and they've employed government and private security forces to defend it."

"Along with technical, layered security," Jack replied. "Sensors, ground surveillance radar, internal and external security cameras, state-of-the-art communications equipment—they've got it all, except for one thing. Their concept for storage of the material that brings them their revenue doesn't work, and poses an existential threat to the environment. Word has to get out eventually."

Robin nodded, and listed under the heading, "Vulnerabilities":

"Nuclear Waste Storage-Unsustainable."

Continuing, she gestured toward Jack Condon. "A great point—they may not know their concept doesn't work, so what happens if word of the Cold Mountain Storage Facility's existence gets out?"

"And the potential environmental effects?" Archer asked, watching the screen.

"Other methods of financing?" Robin asked.

"Our preliminary research shows that they have a full-scale criminal hacking syndicate in place out of eastern Ukraine," Jack continued. "They're adept at everything from siphoning off credit cards to corporate bank accounts, and blackmailing the entertainment industry.

"They've got the financial resources to get whatever access or resources they need, and they have people with specific expertise who quickly move on threats they identify," Robin added. "Right now, that's you."

"Lucky us," Max replied. "And now it is you and Danno as well. In other words, we have an organized crime syndicate operating within our government and it wants to remove all of us."

"It looks a lot like a 'Shadow Government' to me," Shen suggested. "A sort of 'Deep State' that won't stop digging."

Robin nodded at Shen. "You mentioned motive. Most organized crime groups are motivated by financial gain—is that what motivates SU? Or something else?"

"Money is what motivated Dan Thorne, but my guess is that they're after something else," Archer replied. "Government control. Power."

Robin returned to the screen and listed:

Motive: USG Control, Financial Gain

"Organized crime syndicates typically have a hierarchical structure," Robin said. "Is that the case here?"

"They appear to be decentralized, diffuse, non-partisan, and compartmented," Shen replied. "Not at all hierarchical."

"Another key characteristic of organized crime groups is their attempt to corrupt government officials." Robin said. "Does that apply to SU?"

"They're embedded within the government," Dag replied. "Along with some pretty powerful corporations. Every government contract V-TEC has been awarded has been sole-sourced."

"That means all of this has transcended administrations, as well as partisanship," Jack concluded.

"I did some research last night," Max said. "And learned that V-TEC also hasn't paid any taxes in over a decade."

Robin turned and wrote on the screen:

Method: Federal-Corporate Tax-Free Partnerships & Sole Source Contracts

VTEC - DoE - Treasury - IRS - Legislative Adds - ANL Board Membership

Craine Foundation - CFPB - IRS - UST

"If we conclude control of the United States Government is SU's motive," Robin asked, pointing at her annotations on the screen. "What's next?"

"Obviously, they see us as an obstacle," Archer said. "So they have to believe eliminating our group will be key to their survival."

"They haven't made any attempt to mask their operations," Max added. "Several of the assassinations have taken place in the open with no concealment of method. That implies they're not concerned about the investigative efforts of the police, the FBI, or other law enforcement agencies."

"Survival is always a motive," Robin replied, writing on the screen. Next she wrote, "Law Enforcement Organizations are complicit or cooperating.

"Expansion," Shen said. "What are their international linkages?"

"They *need* to grow," Robin added. "Exactly. And if they were to be unrestrained in their quest for U.S. Government control, how do they achieve that?"

"They've got to make a profit in order to survive," Max answered. "So greed will dictate a lot of their decisions."

"They're receiving material from Canada," Archer added. "So there's an international dimension to their operation.

"Power," Robin wrote in another tile on the screen. "How do they keep it?

"If they want absolute power, they need to be able to control all three branches of the U.S. Government," Dag answered. "So—Congress, the Supreme Court, and the White House."

"Where does all of this lead?" Archer asked. "How do we effectively respond?

"If you cannot see the full picture you can't effectively respond," Robin answered. She touched several command keys. "But with all of the information we've compiled, that picture is gradually coming into focus."

In an instant, all of the data they had collected appeared condensed on the transparent Planar screen. A large printer began spitting out color copies of the screen.

"This system allows us to take vast quantities of data from unrelated sources so we can analyze and visualize it in a rich format," Robin continued, handing out the copies. "It tells us where we have patterns, and where we have gaps in information—and that gives us an opportunity to identify, detect and disrupt threats before they occur."

"What does it tell us?" Shen asked.

"When you overlay the financial and communications data to this, it gives us a good idea of SU's agenda and target sets going forward," Robin said, pointing toward three red boxes highlighted in the center of the screen. "So it becomes predictive in that sense."

"What do we think it predicts exactly?" Archer asked.

"The one branch of government it seems they haven't yet infiltrated is the Judicial Branch," Robin answered. Another screen with photos of the Supreme Court justices popped up, with a red box indicating the vacancy left by Justice Anthony Hill, and two other light red boxes below.

"Disrupting the current balance of the Supreme Court is likely their next step. It'll require replacing two additional justices," Robin replied. "What we don't know are which ones would be likely targets."

"Anthony Hill was nominated by a Republican President," Archer said.

"But he was a moderate Justice who regularly voted on both sides, and wasn't at all predictable in the way he voted," Jack explained. "So that leaves eight potential Justices who are targets."

"Using this model, who's the third target?" Archer asked.

"Right now, it's nonspecific," Robin replied.

"With one justice eliminated, and two other potential targets, it seems obvious, doesn't it?" Archer said pointing at the screen.

"Ah, you're several steps ahead of us, as always!" Max laughed. "Maybe you could enlighten us mere mortals?"

"Who nominates Supreme Court Justices?" Archer asked rhetorically.

"In this case, it'll be the next President," Robin answered. "That means—"

Archer nodded, finishing for her. "The Vice President-Elect would be central to that decision, and their plot. He's running the transition of administrations right now."

"Well, if that's the case, they aren't wasting any time are they?" Robin asked.

Archer continued to study Robin's depiction of linkages and relationships between each of the identified players in SU. "Let's get a list of every mid-to-senior level personality involved in the Presidential transition."

Robin nodded. "We'll work on refining this, but it's a good start."

As they stood to leave, Robin handed each of the team members a biometric identification card.

"The Center is at your complete disposal," she said. "We'll register you in our system for hand geometry, iris scan, voice authentication, and facial recognition, and you'll be set to come and go freely, 24/7—including any of our vehicles, aircraft and safe houses. We also have new identities for each of you. We do routine electronic sweeps, here. Treat this place as a safe house if you like. We can provide additional locations as needed, but only on demand, so they cannot be compromised in advance."

"We're grateful for all your help," Archer replied.

Robin nodded and smiled. "I do have one question."

Archer looked up at her expectantly.

"You've been attacked several times, but there's no evidence of active law enforcement pursuing either you *or* your assailants, why is that?"

Archer thought for a moment. "Since these people are essentially rogues within their organizations, they apparently communicate with each other, but not with their superiors. We disposed of the first ones ourselves, and we have a cleaning crew that efficiently follows up. But eventually, there'll be a reckoning—and we should prepare ourselves."

"The Tory Foundation can help with that," Robin answered.

"To maintain good OPSEC, we'll need to use different safe locations and vary our routines as much as possible," Archer replied. "Limit direct phone interaction. Rotate sim cards, use WhatsApp. Pick up a new phone every other day. In the end, good operational security and being smart about our execution are what will give us a fighting chance, if not an advantage."

Chapter 20

LUKE ARCHER HAD NOT EXPECTED the level of commitment they had received from the Tory Foundation. It was extraordinary—and he knew how much Danno and Robin Tory were risking through all of their support. The Tory Foundation's Operations Center was as impressive as any he'd seen, in or out of the intelligence community—and its capabilities exceeded all of them. No expense had been spared. As a final gesture, Robin handed Archer the keys for a black Range Rover Autobiography.

The team walked out of the jewelry store in silence. They didn't speak until they were driving down the road.

"Can anyone please tell me what just happened in there?" Dag said, finally, from the driver's seat.

"All I can say is that I'm glad we're on their side," Shen replied.

"They're on *our* side," Archer corrected, turning around in the passenger's seat. "Going there and calling on them was a major blue chip we just expended—we all need to know and understand that."

"We won't screw it up," Max said.

"We can't," Archer replied. "They just put everything on the table for us, and put themselves at just as much risk."

"Now what?" Shen asked.

"I just received a text from Laura," Archer replied. "I'm gonna see what she has to say. In the meantime, we need eyes on the SU leaders we know about—Dr. Robert Craine, Senator Horace Bend, Congressman Ted McCormick, and Governor Mike McKaren."

"The politicians," Dag said. "They're mine."

"Max and I will take the good Dr. Craine," Shen added.

"Use the Tory Foundation identity documents and backstops from here on out," Archer said. "Commercial cover using countries of origin—your passports have Israel for Max, China for Shen, Canadian for Jack, and Norway for Dag."

"How creative," Max replied, offhanded.

"We're like a band of pirates," Dag laughed.

"Aye," Shen replied, staring at his iPhone. "No cause is lost if there's but one fool to fight for it."

"Love that," Max howled.

"Pirates are cool."

"Pirates," Dag laughed. "It's more fun that joining the Navy."

"What about you, Archer?" Shen asked. "Which pirate identity are you taking?"

"Me?" Archer answered, stopping the Range Rover at the Tyson's Corner Metro Station. "I'm a concerned citizen from Las Vegas, Nevada who doesn't much like foreigners," he said with a glint in his eye. "And this is where all you seadogs get off."

Chapter 21

WALKING DOWN THE PORTICO surrounding Washington, D.C.'s Franciscan Monastery, Luke Archer recalled attending Laura Chicone's Catholic confirmation in the same place, over a decade ago. She had asked him if he would be her sponsor in converting to Catholicism. Initially, Archer had declined, insisting that she could find a much better Catholic to sponsor her, but she insisted, telling him, "I'm not looking for a good Catholic, Archer, I'm looking for a good friend."

Archer turned a corner inside the portico, and found Laura standing there alone.

"The Rosary Portico, of the Memorial Church of the Holy Sepulchre, of the Franciscan Monastery of the Holy Land in America," Archer recited. "Now, I know why we have Episcopalians."

"Shhh!" Laura said, hitting Archer's shoulder. She hugged him and whispered. "The monks'll hear you!"

Archer walked beside her through the portico, grateful for the momentary distraction of light conversation. "One of these days, people will figure out how much you like this place," he said. "And you'll be compromised."

"I'll take that risk," Laura replied. "This is one of the few places in this city where everything seems to make sense."

"You okay?" Archer asked concerned.

Laura stopped and turned to Archer. Her eyes were soft and dark in the moonlight. "I'm scared, Archer. I heard what happened at the Hay Adams last night."

"Not my preferred wakeup call," Archer replied. "But everyone's okay."

Laura shook her head and continued to walk down the portico toward the church. She gestured upwards. "You know these symbols on the façade are early Christian symbols from the Catacombs?"

Archer nodded, looking up at them.

She pointed out into the courtyard. "Out there, everything's finely manicured, and they even have some original shrines from the Holy Land," she said. "But in the early days of the monastery, all of this was a small farm—barn, grain silo, sheds too—the works."

"Hard to imagine, looking at it now," Archer said. "Funny how everything can change so quickly, and so completely."

"That's the point," Laura interjected. "I walked back into Langley, and Thorne did everything he was told to do. Stockman asked me to come into his office and told me I was being 'read into the most sensitive, high risk—but nationally critical special access program in our government.' He called it 'Deep Black.'"

"What an honor," Archer said, shaking his head, his voice thick with sarcasm.

"It's completely cloaked under all of the official legal and security parameters as a Waived and Numbered *Unacknowledged* Special Access Program.

"A USAP?" Archer asked with genuine surprise.

Laura nodded. "Even the existence of the program is classified at the highest levels, and everyone who's to be read-on needs an SSBI Full Scope Poly—just for *that* program."

"Christ…," Archer whispered. "They made it a Waived USAP, of course they'd do that…."

"So I signed all of their documents, and did the poly without asking any questions."

"They actually had you do a separate polygraph for this?"

"Yeah," Laura answered. "Scared the daylights out of me. They brought in one of the most senior and skilled examiners to administer the test. I got through it 'NDI.'"

Archer nodded, understanding "NDI" to mean with "No Deception Indicated," and that she passed without exception. "Then what?"

"Nothing," Laura replied. "I just went back to my desk and continued to work. But then this morning, Stockman calls me in and briefs me on how a group of domestic far right terrorists have infiltrated all three branches of government at the highest levels, and were planning attacks."

"Well, that's a novel concept."

"He included you as part of their organization."

"I guess I should be flattered."

"He also said the President himself requested the operation, codenamed 'Sons of Liberty.'"

"That was a secret society leading up to the Revolutionary War, as I recall," Archer replied. "Adams, Hancock, Revere...they were all part of it."

"So was Benedict Arnold," Laura replied wryly.

"It briefs well at least," Archer replied.

"There's more," Laura continued. "He knows you and I are old friends, and asked me if I knew anything about your involvement in the conspiracy, or had any qualms about stopping you."

"How did you handle that?"

Laura shrugged. "I acted completely shocked, but told him I was on board."

"So I'm a *homegrown terrorist*?" Archer asked. "Is that it?"

"There's something else—but...I—"

Archer stopped. "What?"

"Stockman told me you murdered Becky," Laura said, clearing her throat. "And he says they have proof."

Archer stood paralyzed in the Rosary Portico, looking blankly at Laura, unnerved— the world suddenly spinning around him.

Laura led him to a bench, and forced him to sit. "I hesitated to tell you," she said softly, sitting down beside him.

Archer shook his head. "You had to tell me," he sighed. "Pretty brilliant, actually. Framing me for killing my own wife will mobilize every law enforcement agency in the country. And there's no statute of limitations on murder."

"He's going to have the FBI issue a warrant tomorrow morning, and you're being placed on the 'Most Wanted" list,"

Laura said. "'Armed. Extremely Dangerous.' The works."

"One thing I can say about Stockman, he doesn't believe in half measures."

"You act like you don't care," Laura replied. "What will you do?"

"Grow a beard," Archer answered. "Go see my dog, and try to convince Elena not to believe what she sees on the news."

"How did we get here?" Laura asked plaintively. "I've never seen anything like this...the crime, the corruption...except in the third world countries we used to operate in."

"Dictatorship naturally arises out of democracy," Archer answered. "Plato said that twenty-four hundred years ago, when Athens was under attack by Sparta. While this may seem new to us, it's as old as history. That doesn't mean we have to accept it, though."

"Why us?" Laura asked. "Why haven't others figured this out? Could we be wrong about all of this?"

Archer shrugged. "There've always been plenty of smart folks who couldn't tell a rotten rail without sitting on it."

"What if we do nothing?" Laura asked reflectively. "Will it even matter?"

"To make democracy work, requires a nation of participants."

"Is that Plato too?" Laura asked.

"Louis L'Amour," Archer answered. "Read all of his westerns growing up. None of his characters ran away from a fight, and in his stories the most dangerous threats always came from within."

"Yeah, but this isn't a two-buck western, is it?" Laura asked with a tone of desperation. "What's next?"

"We think their next target is the Supreme Court," Archer replied, after a long moment of consideration. "We just don't know which justices are on their list."

"Stands to reason it's the conservative justices if they're using the neo-cons as an internal cover for their program."

"They're a good scapegoat for the media, but I don't think political philosophies have anything to do with who they are, or what they stand for."

"What *is* in their interest then?"

"Further polarization of the country," Archer answered. "Pushing people further to the left, and further to the right. Inciting violence. Division and fear."

"What does that achieve?"

"Change," Archer answered simply. "It's classic Neo-Marxist strategy: 'Push a negative hard and deep enough, and it'll break through into its counter side.... Pick the target, freeze it, personalize it, and polarize it.' Alinsky's rules. For him and them, they're the quickest, most efficient way to push forward their agendas, and consolidate power."

So taking out Supreme Court justices are their way of achieving that?"

Archer nodded. "We need to find out which ones."

"I'll see what I can find out," Laura replied. "It seems they can bring the full weight of our government to bear in eliminating whoever they want. Hard to fight that."

"We have our own support system in place," Archer replied.

"Who?" Laura asked. "What?"

"The Tory Foundation."

"Robin Nielsen and Congressman Tory?" Laura asked. "Weren't they the ones who stopped Russia's invasion of the Baltics?"

"Without any help from the White House," Archer said. "They're married now."

"Saving the world has a way of binding people together, doesn't it?"

Archer nodded, as they approached the monastery's parking lot. "The alternative is significant—"

"—And the gap is large," Laura finished his sentence, reciting an oft-used catchphrase recited by the CIA hierarchy.

Digging into his coat pocket, he handed Laura an envelope with credit cards and a passport. "Listen, if you need to get out of there for any reason, use these. They're completely backstopped."

"I'm staying for now," Laura replied, taking the envelope.

"Just be safe," Archer said.

"Me?" Laura laughed. "You're the one with the hefty price on his head." Archer hugged her.

"Wait—hold on for a second," Laura exclaimed. She reached inside her car's trunk and pulled out a small rucksack, handing it to him. "Here."

"What's this?"

"iPhones," she replied simply. "I picked a bunch up on eBay over the last few months. Each from a separate identity and separate seller. They're all unlocked. There are 40 sim cards in there too. It's a way for all of us to switch phones by switching sims. Apple's security means that the texts can't be intercepted—even by the NSA."

"Brilliant," Archer said, smiling.

"Where are you going now?" Laura asked.

Archer shrugged. "Up north maybe. Lie low. See my dog. I miss the old boy.

"Not just Beau, I'm sure," Laura smiled.

Chapter 22

LUKE ARCHER STEPPED OUT of the Range Rover and knocked on Elena Campbell's door. Inside, he heard Beau's distinctive deep bark.

Despite Elena's command to "Sit" and "Stay," once Beau saw Archer, he charged at full speed through the doorway.

"Beau!" Elena shouted, before realizing the reason for his lapse in discipline. "Archer! You're here!"

"Quick trip," Archer replied, holding and rubbing Beau's head, while trying to avoid the abundent slobber.

"You're dog's a mess," Elena said endearingly. "What a great surprise. Come in!"

Beau followed Archer inside and laid down at his feet beside the kitchen table, panting.

"I was just about to open a bottle of wine," Elena said. "Want some?"

Archer smiled and nodded.

"The black SUVs are gone," Elena said, pouring the wine. "Life's returned to normal here."

"That's why I came up," Archer said. "To warn you about some false rumors you're going to hear."

Elena nodded. "Laura already called me."

"She did?" Archer asked incredulously.

Elena sat down at the table, opposite Archer. "She didn't tell me everything—I know that. Just what she thought I needed to know."

"What exactly?" Archer asked.

"The short version?" Elena said. "That you're one of the most respected Green Berets alive today. That you worked with her, Shen and Max in some terrible places with the CIA, and that they're trying to find you."

"And—" Archer interjected.

"And," Elena said. "She told me about your wife's death—how they're trying to frame you for it. And she told me not to believe what I hear from the media or FBI."

Archer nodded. "Makes me curious about the long version...."

Elena smiled. "Just girl talk—mostly how much she respects and admires you. She told me she knew your wife very well, and she also knew how much you loved one another."

"I'm sorry I got you mixed up in all this," Archer said. "I can take Beau back...."

Elena shook her head. She looked at him for a long time, searching his face. "I've got Beau. You've got enough to worry about. Both of us will be here waiting for you."

She stood. "I was just about to get dinner started—I'd imagine you're hungry."

Chapter 23

IN A RARE MOMENT OF SELF-REFLECTION, Luke Archer realized that all his time spent with Elena Campbell was as effortless as it was comfortable. And again, throughout dinner, he was impressed that she listened to him and never probed or pressed for additional details. As a result, he found himself telling Elena more than he'd typically relate to anyone else about his ordeal in captivity, and the loss of his wife. At that point Elena had taken his hand to console him.

"I always prepared her for my own death," Archer said. "But I wasn't prepared to lose her."

"Someone told me once, 'God pours life into death and death into life without a drop being spilled,'" Elena said quietly. "I believe that."

Archer nodded. "I've come to realize, at least in my case, that happiness is transitory."

"Try not to be so skeptical," Elena said, shaking her head slightly. Her tone was kind. "My own belief is that happiness is a choice we all make, no matter what our circumstances."

Over dinner, Archer told Elena more about John Lee—about his optimism and strength, and how his final visit with him had started his current path.

"But I never expected to be fighting against my own government," Archer confessed.

"I realize there's a lot I don't know," Elena said quietly. But I do trust you, Luke Archer. I sense—" She stopped for a moment.

Archer looked up at her expectantly.

"That this...it's a way of life for you."

Archer shrugged and looked beyond her, deep in thought, then down at his plate. "Maybe it is. No matter how much I try to escape from it. I've tried to put some bad memories behind me, but sometimes they don't wanna stay put."

"Why can't you?" Elena asked softly. "Escape?"

"Three and a half decades ago, I took an oath," Archer answered. "To 'support and defend the Constitution of the United States against all enemies, foreign and domestic.' Maybe it's naïve, but I still believe in it."

Elena nodded her understanding. Her dinner was on par with any gourmet meal he'd ever had, and his time with her had turned out to be exactly the respite he needed.

"Your cooking reminds me of my grandmother's," Archer said. "Not only the taste, but the scent. I've never experienced it since she left us."

"Well, that's high praise then," Elena answered. "I'm not sure I'm worthy. But I did learn to cook from my grandmother."

"You see?" Archer replied. "How did you end up here?

Elena smiled and shrugged. "My parents and generations before them were farmers. The men fought in the Revolutionary War and for the Union in the Civil War. My Dad fought in Vietnam and then went back to farming when he came home. I grew up on his farm in Connecticut, taking care of the livestock. That's what got me interested in being a vet, I think. Seemed like the natural progression."

"Why Maine?"

"Life seemed simpler here, I guess. And I like being near the ocean."

"Well, I'm not sure I've made your life any simpler."

"You're not boring, Luke Archer," Elena said with a wry smile. "I'll give you that."

After dinner, Archer excused himself, telling Elena he needed to go back to his cabin to check on a few things. Elena nodded her understanding, with a smile to fight back tears. He hugged Beau, and then kissed Elena, thanking her for dinner, as well as for having faith in him.

"We all believe in you," Elena answered. You should know that.

Archer spent a full hour skirting the perimeter of his Maine property to ensure it was not being observed or occupied. Once satisfied that there was no surveillance present, he approached the barn, pistol drawn and at the ready.

The barn doors had been left open, and there were old tire tracks in the snow, but he was relieved to find the barn vacant. He reminded himself of the sound decision he'd made some years ago to separate the barn from the rest of his property so he could use it as a clandestine storage site for just such an eventuality.

He returned to where he'd parked the Range Rover, and backed it up to the rear barn door. As he was exiting the SUV, he felt the vibration of Laura Chicone's text message come through on his cell phone. Her message was simple—and from the link alone, he could easily identify the subject.

```
As discussed. C link below:

fbi.gov/mostwantedterrorist
```

The link brought up a transcript from a news conference held at the FBI headquarters in Washington, D.C. that morning:

New Most Wanted Terrorist Announced

Michael Steinberg
Assistant Director, Counterterrorism Division
Federal Bureau of Investigation
Press Conference on Addition to Most Wanted Terrorist List
FBI Headquarters
Washington, D.C.

Good morning. Today, we are announcing the addition of Luke Beckett Archer to the FBI's Most Wanted Terrorist List.

Archer is the first domestic terrorist to be included on the Most Wanted Terrorist List, a list that has historically been reserved for international terrorists indicted for various acts of terrorism against U.S. interests.

Archer's criminal acts of violence include the premeditated murder of his wife. He is also a person of interest in the disappearance of five FBI agents in Washington, DC two days ago, an act of domestic terror, deliberately planned and executed.

The FBI is announcing today a reward of up to $450,000 for information leading to the location and arrest of Luke Archer.

Archer is a retired Green Beret and special mission unit operative who leads a known anti-government extremist terror cell of an organization known as the Sons of Liberty, or "SOL."

Archer is a U.S. citizen living in Camden, Maine. As a Special Forces Battalion Commander at Fort Campbell, Kentucky, Archer murdered his wife in the evening hours fifteen years ago at their on-base home. Claiming to have returned home to find her body in a pool of blood, Archer's indictment has only been recently secured on the basis of proven inconsistencies in his statements, surveillance footage, and DNA evidence found at the scene.

Archer and four other SOL extremists are alleged to have plotted to attack FBI Field Offices around the country. These extremists are self-recruited, self-trained, and self-executing.

SOL was formed initially by a group of extremists in Oregon.

Their singular goal was to seek retribution for the killing of rancher Norman Huggins and his family members in 2001 after they had resisted arrest on charges of illegal weapons possession and criminal trespassing on Federal lands.

SOL extremists have grown in number across the United States, and have engaged in various levels of lawful and unlawful activity. Many SOL extremists are former members of the military who have stockpiled weapons and ammunition.

Archer is also wanted for the disappearance of three federal agents in Maine last week, and three FBI agents at the Hay Adams Hotel in Washington, DC three days ago.

Archer has been on the run for two days, after a federal arrest warrant was issued for him. Search warrants executed on Archer's residence in Camden, Maine revealed that Archer was in possession of fully automatic weapons, armor piercing ammunition, and high explosives in furtherance of crimes of extreme violence.

Archer has eluded capture and we need the public's assistance to locate and apprehend this violent domestic terrorism fugitive and bring him to justice.

The FBI is working extensively with local, state, and foreign law enforcement agencies, including authorities in Germany, the United Kingdom, Canada, France, Switzerland, Denmark, Austria, Italy, the Czech Republic, Mexico, Argentina, the Philippines, and Saudi Arabia.

Archer has ties to Camden, Maine, Fort Bragg, North Carolina Ireland, and Germany. He may have moved outside the United States, possibly living in Canada.

Archer has the full ability to blend into his surroundings, and can be expected to alter his appearance to elude authorities.

Archer has very distinct and numerous scars located on his chest and back from wounds sustained while incarcerated in a foreign prison.

The FBI has distributed recent photographs of Archer. These images are included on the Most Wanted Terrorist posters.

We strongly encourage the public to take the time to review these posters, as well as detailed descriptive information on Luke Archer, which is available on the FBI's website, www.fbi.gov.

Please remember, Archer is considered armed and extremely dangerous.

If you have information concerning Archer, please do not take independent action. We ask anyone with information on this individual or his location contact your local FBI office or the nearest American Embassy or Consulate.

We have added Luke Archer to the Most Wanted Terrorist List to increase public awareness about this domestic terrorist fugitive and aid in his location and arrest.

We will not relent until Archer is apprehended and his potential for future acts of violence is eliminated. All resources of the Bureau and Federal Law Enforcement agencies have been devoted to this manhunt.

Now I will be happy to take your questions.

Archer finished reading the transcript, and with the realization that he was now officially a fugitive with a half million dollar price on his head, he removed the sim card from his phone, cut it into pieces with the scissors on his Leatherman tool, and threw the pieces into a nearby barrel of rainwater.

Archer's mind raced. The accusation that he'd murdered his wife was infuriating and painful—not only because it was patently false, but because it had been obviously backstopped with false evidence—the kind he could only speculate about at this point. Ruining reputations and framing people for crimes was nothing more than advanced "black ops" tradecraft coupled with the other black art; propaganda. Archer knew he could easily disprove the allegations if given the opportunity in an open and fair forum.

But receiving a fair hearing at this point, he knew, was extremely unlikely.

They would never give him the opportunity to prove his innocence, or to expose the real story of what was now transpiring within the government. Archer knew Steinberg from several different operations they had conducted together in Dubai and Yemen in past years, and he never much liked him. Despite the disadvantage Archer incurred in being declared a domestic terrorist and fugitive, Steinberg's statement also provided some crucial insights: first, that Steinberg was a member of their organization; second, that SU's objective was to kill him, not capture him. Finally, it indicated to him that SU's leadership was now on the defensive, and Archer and his team were on exactly the right track.

"The dictators are never as strong as they tell you they are," Archer recalled his father telling him, "And early on, the people are never as weak as they think they are."

Archer leaned over on the horse stall, and pressed a button that was hidden from view. The floor slowly retracted to reveal a ramp leading into an underground garage with a large customized Airstream Land Yacht——a 30 foot travel trailer he'd purchased before finding the land where he'd built the cabin, customized to hold all of his personal weapons and equipment. With plenty of space left over to include John

Lee's arsenal as well.

He backed the Range Rover down the ramp, and hooked up the Airstream. Before pulling away, Archer stepped back out of the vehicle and walked over to the single shelf on the cinderblock wall, holding a dark wooden case twice the size of a cigar box. Lifting it reverently from the shelf, Archer returned to the Land Rover. Sitting in the driver's seat, with the clear night sky above the ramp, he passed his fingers over the engraved name on the case:

Becky Louise Archer

Carefully driving into the park on the little used trail, Archer had chosen the campground carefully. It was secluded and not manned by any staff at this time of year. On an earlier reconnaissance, he'd found an alternate entry point to the campground.

Taking the time, he wiped his tracks back to the main road and set up a clandestine camp, minimizing use of heat and light—the trailer's insulation, he knew, would reduce any heat source inside.

Walking around the area to ensure the area was indeed isolated, he placed several anti-intrusion and surveillance devices to give him advance warning of anyone approaching.

In a short period of time, he'd created a safe house where none had previously existed.

Chapter 24

WIPING OFF THE SWEAT. Check your watch. Twelve miles... an hour and a half. The long run for the week—a good routine no matter where you are in the world. Just do it. I'm getting too old for this...joints aching. Far more winded than usual.

Shirt off. Soaked from the oppressive heat and humidity.

The door to the house is ajar.

Calling for Becky. She doesn't answer. Dog is in the basement, scratching on the door. Barking. Out of control.

Climbing the staircase, and turning the corner to the bedroom... you're there, on the bed, staring up at the ceiling. Something's not right... Your clothes are torn, and you're surrounded in crimson. The walls are splattered.

Oh Jesus...Becky! What happened?

Silence. You aren't moving...don't respond.

No! Oh God! I'm here, Becky! Can you hear me? I'm here!

Who did this to you?

Christ...what happened?

Apply pressure! Stop the bleeding!

Calling 911!

The phone's not working!

What happened, Becky? God! What happened?

Your hands are tied behind your back! Electrical wire ....

Becky! Stay with me! Don't leave me! Please! Oh God, Sweetheart! Please!

My cell phone? Where is it?

Where I left it, in the kitchen....

Rushing to grab it...

Screaming into the phone for an ambulance, knowing it's too late to save you.

Limp. Unresponsive. Not breathing. No pulse....

Oh, please... No! ...Come back....

"Someone killed her! ...My wife! ...Goddamn it, I need help! Someone murdered her!"

A door slamming shut.... My head snaps back.

He's still in the house?

Rushing to the bedroom drawer. Grabbing the Browning Hi Power.

Searching ...upstairs ...downstairs.

No one. The sound of sirens in the distance, from all directions... louder and louder...sirens everywhere.

Rushing back to the master bedroom, holding onto Becky until the police and paramedics arrive. They charge through the door and separate me from her.

"Sir, please step away! ...Sir, move away! Now!"

Blood everywhere. Oh Jesus....Jesus...Oh Why? Why God?

Sitting in the kitchen covered in your blood.

Police, detectives, people dressed in white coveralls taking photos.

Think clearly, Goddammit!

Who would do this to you? Who could possibly do this?

The detective places an evidence bag on the kitchen table. Inside, a knife ...the serrated duct knife I purchased at the same time as the electrical wire. I tell him it's all mine, they used it to restrain and kill you.

The lamppost has been broken...I was going to fix it. The supplies—they were all right there on the kitchen counter.

The detective turns the back of a digital camera toward me and asks if I recognize the knots around your ankles and wrists.

I nod. It's a Taut-Line Hitch..... Used to secure the lines of a tent...or to restrain detainees....

"We'll need to bring you down to the station to get a statement, Colonel. Please come with me."

Looking down the hallway, Your body is being placed in a black rubber zippered back: one of the technicians stepped away from the still opened back, and I see your face staring at me, eyes open.

I look again...but it's not you ...not anymore.

It's Elena.

Archer awoke with a start, soaked in sweat and still wearing his street clothes. His vision swam and the room seemed to be revolving slowly around him. Sitting up, he realized he'd fallen asleep on the

Airstream's lounge. On his chest, he was holding the box containing Becky's ashes.

It was a recurrent nightmare—one that he'd relived countless times since his wife's murder—the images and sounds were as vivid as the night he'd found her, and the terror always more intense than the time before. This time, however, it was different. It came with the actual smell of blood. And rather than Becky staring back at him, it was Elena.

Often, in these episodes, he felt like his own sanity was slipping away. Now that feeling had intensified even further. Thoughts of Elena being hurt because of him, possessed him.

Archer went to the bathroom of the trailer and splashed cold water on his face to escape the grip of memory.

Looking in the mirror, his eyes were bloodshot and tired.

He blinked several times. Something, he wasn't sure what, caught his attention outside the window in the surrounding woods of the Acadia Park campground.

He grabbed a nearby pair of Swarovski 10X42 binoculars, and looking closer through the gathering mist, he could make out the glint of red lights against the fallen snow, darting around like fireflies, well beyond the arc of the devices he'd placed.

At once, the intrusion devices began to report in unison.

Chapter 25

LUKE ARCHER LIFTED THE FLOOR HATCH he'd installed in the Airstream's galley, and withdrew the weapons and ammunition he'd set aside for quick access. Placing the tactical vest on, he felt its weight from the ammunition magazines and grenades he'd already loaded into its pouches. Archer inserted his Hi-Power into the vest's cross-draw holster. Removing the suppressed HK MR556A1-SD from the hatch, he slung it over his neck and confirmed that it was locked and loaded. He quickly lifted the Assault Shotgun—an AA-12 Atchisson—checked it, and slung it over his back as an alternate weapon.

The final item in the compartment was a Night Vision Goggle—the AN/PSQ-20 model he'd relied upon in countless other scenarios where visibility was at a premium.

Archer opened the Airstream's rear hatch and stepped outside. Turning the NVG on, he surveyed the campsite and forest around him. Satisfied the approach was clear, he ran into the forest, up a hilltop, and positioned himself behind a stone wall, beside a balsam fir. From his position, Archer had good visibility below. With the AN/PSQ-20, Archer could now see a group of six men slowly approaching the trailer at a crouch. Quietly extending the bipod, Archer set up the HK MR556A1-SD and with the attached D-750 night vision scope, he took aim at the lead man and fired.

The gun's suppressor muffled the sound of the shot, and Archer watched the man drop silently to the ground. He quickly took aim at the man beside him and fired another shot, killing him.

Archer watched as the other four men, now realizing their position was compromised, ran at full speed toward the Airstream. Automatic rifle fire echoed through the forest. In an effort to outflank them, Archer moved along a ridgeline that skirted the tree line.

They were simple fundamentals he'd learned from John Lee as a young Captain during Desert Storm: *Shoot then move. Move then shoot. ...Hesitation kills.* But he'd been able to hone these skills to a much higher level during his time "behind the fence," and the same techniques to his own people in SAD, developing them further, and training and rehearsing them for hours on end. Over the years, Archer had become infinitely more lethal than John Lee could have expected. But John had been the one who had ingrained those fundamentals well before he ever had to actually use them in combat.

From his position behind a granite boulder, he spotted one of the men kneeling behind a large tree, rifle at the ready, actively searching for a target.

Archer lowered himself to a prone position, and searched until the man became clearly visible in his thermal sight. Melted snow ran down his back, and his shirt was soaked through. He took aim and fired. The shot hit the man in the head, and his body collapsed to the ground.

The uncanny echo of John Lee's voice came back to him... urgently, insistently... jolting him with a dose of adrenaline: *Move to gain a tactical advantage—Don't sacrifice your safety...Distance is your friend!*

Seeing no one else between him and the Land Rover and Airstream, Archer transitioned quickly to the AA-12 Automatic Shotgun and rushed forward. Glancing around the corner of the trailer, he saw two of the other men skirting the dirt road to the clearing where Archer had been positioned. A stealthy movement in the brush distracted him, yielding the slight form of another man crouching...unaware of his presence, and yet approaching from the opposite direction, to his right flank.

Silently pulling the *Harsey Hunter* from its sheath, Archer pivoted toward the shooter, gripped his forehead tightly and slit his throat. The man, dressed in a black SWAT tactical uniform, armed with an M4 Carbine and a sidearm, collapsed in front of him.

Before he saw the other two men, Archer heard them on the gravel drive running in his direction. Looking carefully around for others who could be on his flank, he threw two M67 fragmentation grenades down the dirt road, and heard them exploding in rapid succession. Archer followed, walking and firing the AA-12's drum of 12 Gauge rounds toward the shadows moving inside the tree line. As he drew closer, he watched each of them fall to the ground.

Archer stopped and listened, his gaze flicking briefly around. Satisfied there were no others, he checked the intruders' bodies for identification.

They were dressed in tactical gear, and wearing black camouflage paint—professionals. But they hadn't counted on facing an opponent who was both more prepared, adept—and luckier— than they. One of the men's uniforms had been badly torn. His hands and legs were scratched and bloody, covered with smears of mud, stuck full of branches leaves. He had an ID badge from Maine Yankee Atomic Power Company—a nuclear power plant in Wiscasset, Maine. Archer collected their cell phones and used their thumbs to unlock each of their respective smartphones so he could access them later.

How had they found him? With the full resources of the government supporting their search for him, Archer knew satellite surveillance was the likely answer, but he couldn't be certain how. With his location now compromised, he knew he had to leave the area while still under the cover of darkness. Although this was an isolated corner of Acadia, it was possible that Park Rangers from a manned administration center ten miles away would eventually respond to reports of shots fired.

Most unsettling to Archer was the recurrent nightmare that had again awakened him, this time just before the kill team had a chance to attack—as if it had been a subliminal message from Becky warning him...protecting him.

He tried to shake the anxiety away, but found himself wondering what it all could mean—whether it was just random weirdness typical of dreams, if it was his instincts screaming out to him, or if it was an omen...a portent of events yet to come?

As he placed the weapons back in the compartments of the trailer, he looked up to see the framed photo Elena had given him—a selfie of Archer and her together, kneeling in front of the water, with both of their hands around Beau as a six-week old puppy, laughing.

Not Elena. He could not...would not... let the same thing happen to her.

Starting the truck's ignition, the Browning Hi Power at his side, John Lee's voice echoed in the back of his head.

Always trust your instincts....

He texted the location of the campsite to Dag Thorsen over WhatsApp, asking if it would be possible for them to "clean" the location before any authorities could arrive after daylight.

Chapter 26

LUKE ARCHER DROVE DUE SOUTH along Maine's back roads, trailer in tow, toward Vermont, New Hampshire and New York. The box containing Becky's ashes sat beside him in the passenger seat.

The long drive through Maine's scenic countryside gave him time to think about events—both recent and long past.

Placing everything into proper perspective was far more difficult now, as his turbulent, violent past had been forced to merge into present circumstances.

Now, under what seemed to be a constant state of siege, he struggled to maintain an outwardly calm demeanor through the mounting stress. That quality...resilience...had always defined him, but he knew he was approaching a boiling point he'd not experienced since Becky's murder.

Archer understood the implications—not only for himself, but for others around him.

Your own worst enemy is the one within, Becky had once told him. Always the psychiatrist—at the time, widely recognized to be one of the best in her profession. She had known him better than anyone else. She could decipher him, calm him and encourage him, seeing through his Sphinx-like composure that mystified others.

He looked over at the passenger seat and saw her talking to him now, as she always did. *If you don't conquer yourself, Archer, all other victories are meaningless....*

He looked again, and she was gone.

Archer pulled into the remote lakeside spot in White Mountain National Forest that Becky had once found while researching one of their first vacations to Maine over twenty years ago.

Setting up the Airstream on the water's edge, Archer extended the trailer's awning, unfolded a table and chair, and carefully cleaned the guns he'd just been forced to use—the MR556A1-SD first, followed by the AA-12. After cleaning and reloading the guns, he placed them inside the trailer beside the tactical vest, within easy reach.

135

He placed a Coleman stove and space heater on a picnic table in front of the Airstream. Looking for additional clues, and trying to make sense of how his location had been discovered, and who was trying to kill him, he laid out all of the cell phones, wallets, documents and identification he'd obtained from the bodies of the team he'd fought only hours before.

Searching through emails, address books and calendar events, Archer was able to piece together a collage of the team's activities leading up to their attack on him. Combing through each of the iPhone's emails, there was one common denominator to many of the messages that had been sent and received: *Tony Anderson, Chief of Staff, Department of Energy*. One email from Tony Anderson particularly caught Archer's eye:

> Maine Yankee scheduled to begin rehabilitation & modernization in 9 months by ATEC. Est. Cost: $1 Billion. Includes replacement of equipment, maintenance of power plant, and construction of 30 horizontal storage modules (HSMs) for spent nuclear fuel. Moscow contributing $500M to re-commissioning of Maine Yankee in 24 months. To begin, all Camden obstacles—as briefed—must be eliminated.
> Tony
> ***Anthony Anderson***
> ***Chief of Staff***

Based on the contents of the email and this man as the recipient, Archer assumed he'd been the kill team leader— who seemed to be incentivized to find and eliminate Archer and his team.

Okay, you have my attention... Archer muttered to himself.

The mention of Moscow was enough to set all alarm bells off in unison. SU indeed appeared to be "international," and in a very sinister way.

He began scrolling through the iPhone's photos. As he reached the last of the photos, Archer stopped and enlarged a photo with the kill team leader smiling broadly in front of the Maine Yankee Nuclear Power Plant, wearing a tactical vest over black SWAT fatigues, and carrying an M4 Carbine slung to his front, muzzle down. He was standing between two men in business suits who Archer immediately recognized as Dr. Robert Craine and Vice President-Elect Zachary Hastings.

Chapter 27

LUKE ARCHER KNEW THE PHOTO of Dr. Craine and Zack Hastings alone proved nothing, but it was an indicator of a possible association, nonetheless. As a Vice Presidential Candidate, Hastings could have been campaigning in Maine—but for him to be at the Maine Yankee Nuclear Power Plant, years after it had been decommissioned, seemed too much of a coincidence after its security team had just tried to kill him.

Archer sent Shen a copy of the photo and text through a WhatsApp message:

```
Zack    Hastings    involved.    Confirm
connection to Robert Craine. Possible
Kremlin connection.
```

Shen's response was immediate.

```
WILCO. 3 Supreme Court justices being
targeted  in  SU  raid  made  to  appear
as  Islamic  terror.  Kill  team  to  be
composed of 6 Middle Eastern appearing
men, untraceable to SU or USG, under SU
payroll/direction. Launching tonight @
0300.
```

Archer knew he had to get back to Washington immediately if the attacks were to be prevented or intercepted.

```
Will be in DC tonight. MTF…
```

The next message he sent was to Jack Condon, requesting a Tory Foundation jet to pick him up:

Need jet p/u 1430hrs today @ BML (NH)

Archer found a Challenger 350 waiting for him on the tarmac of the Berlin Regional Airport in New Hampshire. In less than an hour after "wheels-up," he was touching down at Reagan National Airport in Crystal City, Virginia to find Shen, Max and Dag waiting for him beside a grey Lexus SUV.

Dag drove with Max in the passenger seat, armed with a Mini-Uzi.

Shen handed Archer a large envelope. "From Laura," he said simply.

Archer opened the envelope to find a stack of copied emails with an orange cover sheet marked:

**TOP SECRET/SI/ORCON/NOFORN/GAMMA/HCS/SAR/SAMI
"EYES ONLY"**

TO: PRESIDENT OF THE UNITED STATES
    CHIEF OF STAFF TO THE PRESIDENT
FM: DIRECTOR, FEDERAL BUREAU OF
    INVESTIGATION
SUBJECT: Islamic State (ISIS) Threat to Congressional Leadership

1. (TS/SI) Active Islamic State (ISIS) threat identified against Speaker of the House and Senate Majority Leader.
2. (TS/SCI) <u>Time of anticipated attack</u>: Imminent.
3. (TS/SI) <u>Source</u>: BlackStone.
   0. <u>Source Reliability Rating</u>: A.
   a. <u>Information Reliability Rating</u>: 1.
   b. <u>Overall Rating</u>: A1+ (Specific-Credible-Corroborated).

4. (TS/SI) <u>Recommendation</u>: Immediate assignment of United States Secret Service (USSS) Protective Detail to named Congressional leadership targets.

Archer flipped to the next page—a screenshot of an intercepted secure text message:

```
Decoy traffic sent to WH. Confirmed
Primary Targets: Supreme Court
Justices Angela Wainwright, Harold
Thompson, and Victoria Stein. 0300
@ Personal residences— addresses
provided separately.
```

"Do we have the addresses of all three residences?" Archer asked.

Shen nodded and handed Archer a MapQuest printout, pinpointing each address. "Kalorama subdivision in DC, Potomac, MD, and Capitol Hill," he said, pointing at each location.

"Can we get the personal phone numbers for all three Justices?" Archer asked.

"The Tory Foundation is working on that now," Dag answered.

"Send an encrypted message to Jack. Have him meet us at their ops center," Archer said. "We need to move quickly."

Chapter 28

THE THREE MEN ENTERING the home of Supreme Court Justice Angela Wainwright deactivated the home alarm using the installer code. Their point of entry was a basement window in the back of the Kalorama townhome that had been unlocked from the inside by a cleaning crew the previous afternoon. They knew, from an advance visit to the home, that the master bedroom was one floor down, and two doors to the right.

The men also knew Justice Wainwright's husband kept a Glock 21 .45 Automatic in his bedside drawer. During a penetration reconnaissance of the home four days ago, they had removed the firing pin from the Glock to prevent its use.

Silently entering Wainwright's bedroom, weapons covering all points of the room, they fired four muffled shots into the bed—two on each side.

They had no way of knowing their mission had been compromised. In the coordinated crossfire that followed, three additional, higher pitched shots followed in rapid succession, and all three assassins fell to the ground almost simultaneously—two in the bedroom, and one in the hallway. Max stepped out of the adjacent room, and Dag emerged from the master bedroom's walk-in closet.

Dag checked for a pulse on each of the bodies, confirming they were dead—and proceeded to pull whatever papers and identification he could find in their pockets.

Using a wireless whisper throat mic, and speaking in clipped tones, Max called into the safe house, where Robin Tory was standing by with the three targeted Supreme Court Justices and their spouses. *"Wainwright Residence Secure, Three EKIA, Bahrain passports. Over."*

"Roger, Copy," Robin answered. *"Wainwright Residence Secure, Kalorama. Three EKIA."*

Two more calls followed, first from Shen: *"Thompson Residence Secure in Potomac, Three EKIA."*

Archer's transmission came soon thereafter. *"Stein Residence*

Secure on Capitol Hill. Three EKIA. Positive ID. Bahraini nationals."

Robin acknowledged each report, and then made a net call to all three locations. *"Transporting all six family members to MPD's Special Operations Division. They've got a lot of questions. I'll handle that on my end."*

"Roger. Please thank the Justices for their cooperation," Archer replied. *"Glad everyone's safe."*

"They thank you," Robin answered. *"Very much."*

"Tell 'em we'll probably call in the favor sooner rather than later," Archer replied, and turned to Dag. *"Let's get cleaning teams over to their homes now."*

At 2:45am, following a motorized track along the banks of the Severn River, three black Zodiac Outboard Military Boats slipped soundlessly—unnoticed and unchallenged—into the United States Naval Academy's Santee Basin, concealing themselves behind the fleet of twelve Naval 44 Cruiser/Racer sailboats. Another crew, similarly equipped, pulled their Zodiac into a small beach at Hospital Point, across from Dorsey Creek, and hid the craft beside a fence overgrown with vegetation. Two additional Zodiacs proceeded around the corner to Spa Creek and tied themselves off along the rock sea wall and around the corner, between the City Dock and the Visitor's Center, at the end of Prince George Street. Both teams dismounted, dressed in dark tactical police uniforms, and conducted quick equipment checks of their AK-47 and FN FAL assault rifles. A member of each contingent carried RBG-6 40mm Multiple Grenade Launchers.

The first tactical team moved in a linear formation toward Bancroft Hall—billed as the largest dormitory in the United States. Approaching Bancroft Hall's 7th Wing, the group stacked together at the entrance, and entered using a numeric code and ID obtained from a woman who had ingratiated herself to an unsuspecting Midshipman at a local bar only days before.

Inside Bancroft Hall, the first group moved from "Zero Deck" to the "First Deck." One of the terrorists dressed in a Naval Academy PT uniform walked down the hallway, and approached the "Mate of the Deck" and killed her instantly with a suppressed shot to her forehead. The rest of the group moved quickly, quietly, and efficiently— placing pre-made explosive charges on the doors of the dormitory rooms.

Once the group was in position, they did not hesitate—detonating the charges simultaneously to gain entry.

Moving systematically through each room on the first deck, they caught many midshipmen in their beds and executed them in place. Those who entered the hallway, even for a moment, were shot in a hail of automatic AK 47 fire. Bodies piled up in the hallway amidst a widening sea of blood. Sustained screaming and shouting erupted out of the rooms, followed by shots, then dead; eerie silence.

What the terrorists had not figured into their calculus, however, were four nationally ranked Navy wrestlers who, having observed the carnage on their floor, had hastily set their own trap for the gunmen. Scaling the corners of the walls, they hugged the ceiling tightly, and then dropping on top of the terrorists when they entered the room—disarming and killing them by hand. The wrestlers then turned the AK-47s on the other attackers, killing one, and forcing the remainder of the gunmen to retreat from the dormitory.

The second tactical team simultaneously dismounted their Zodiacs, and assembled at Farragut Field—the Naval Academy Football team's outdoor practice field. Moving stealthily across the field, they entered the grounds of Buchanan House on the corner of Porter and Cooper Roads in synchronized movements. Moving around to the southwest side, and to the rear of the house, the team bounded to the top of the stairway of the mansion's sun porch.

Soundlessly cutting the glass on the entry to the first floor dining room, they moved into the entry hallway. Half the team positioned themselves at the front and rear entrances to provide security, while the remainder of the team moved quietly and deliberately up the two-flight stairway. As they moved forward, the shadow of a man—tall in stature—stepped out of the master bedroom. The lead team member fired two shots in quick succession, and confirmed the identity of the man as Vice Admiral Thomas Joyce, Superintendent of the United States Naval Academy.

The Supe's wife screamed in horror, and rushed toward her husband. The lead team member turned his FN FAL toward her, and firing a single shot, watched her fall face-first to the floor, inside the doorway.

The third group of gunmen, who hid in place by the Naval Academy hospital, ran up the hill to the old Nurses' Quarters building, and walked inside—killing the six security guards on duty that night, at precisely 3:00AM—the same time the other attacks were launched— effectively ensuring no police assistance would arrive to Bancroft Hall or to Buchanan House in the wake of the attacks.

In a brief, yet horrific period of time, 54 Midshipmen, six security guards, the Superintendent of the Naval Academy and his wife were killed, and 22 others were severely wounded.

At Least 62 Dead in Terror Attack at Naval Academy

By JANA BRADY JAN. 10, 2017

Annapolis, MD — Coordinated terrorist attacks struck the heart of the United States Naval Academy, on Wednesday night, killing Superintendent Vice Admiral Tom Joyce and his wife, and at least fifty midshipmen in machine-gun assaults at Bancroft Hall.

The assaults were particularly brazen in scale and execution. The attackers used boats to reach the shore of the academy where they launched what terror experts have described as a "Mumbai-style attack."

The Annapolis city police said Thursday that the attacks killed at least 60 people and wounded at least 22. Midshipmen who had escaped told police that the attackers were not taking hostages, but seeking out more Midshipmen to execute on site.

The Islamic State claimed responsibility one hour after the attacks, but it remained unclear whether there was any link to outside terrorist groups.

Gunfire and explosions rang out into the early morning.

Hours after the assaults began, Bancroft Hall was in flames.

Many Midshipmen remained in hiding in the Naval Academy dormitories, making desperate cellphone calls to parents and friends, some of them to television stations, describing their ordeal.

Jacob Jensen, 21, a Naval Academy senior, told CNN: "A middle eastern guy was shouting in Arabic. He just stood there spraying bullets around, some of them impacting right next to me."

Before his phone went dead, Jensen added: "I managed to break away and escape through the first floor window. I'm now outside Bancroft Hall in the quadrangle. I think the gunmen are gone, but it's very bad here."

Attackers had also entered the private quarters of Naval Academy Superintendent Vice Admiral Thomas Joyce, according to an anonymous police source reports, and killed Admiral Joyce and his wife, Rebecca.

The Annapolis City Police Department's Special Emergency Team, NCIS, and the FBI's Critical Incident Response Group were quickly called in to assist the Military Police, who were crippled in a separate attack on their headquarters over a mile away across Hill Bridge.

An hour after the attacks, a group calling itself *Jabhat an-Nuṣrah li-Ahli ash-Shām* said it had carried out the attacks.

The gunmen, some dressed in official Naval Academy PT uniform, were thought to have gained entry by jumping over the wall behind the Naval Academy chapel. Other gunmen were dressed in black tactical gear, and used Zodiac tactical boats for access to the several miles of Naval Academy shoreline.

Four Midshipmen are reported to have offered up hand-to-hand resistance in Bancroft Hall, killing at least two of the gunmen.

"A man in a hood with an AK-47 came running down the hall," shooting and throwing four grenades, Midshipman Jensen said. "I beat it back to my room and double-locked it, and put the bureau up against the door before escaping from my window."

The Williamson administration condemned the attacks, as did President-elect Stone's transition team. The White House said it was still "assessing the situation."

Archer finished reading the early edition of the *New York Times*, and handed it to Shen. All five team members sat around the conference table, inside the Tory Foundation Operations Center. "Where did we go wrong?" he asked quietly. "What did we miss?"

"There was no indication of any additional targets," Laura answered. "*None*. Least of all the Naval Academy, for God's sake."

"No—their decision making is obviously compartmented," Dag injected, shaking his head. "It's no one's fault, and no one's omission. Not only do they have compartmented cells, they have redundancy too—to ensure total coverage and maximum effect."

"Well, they achieved that," Archer said. "And they've made everything look like an ISIS terrorist attack. If anything's traceable, it's a safe bet it'll originate from Bahrain or somewhere else in the Middle East—not from here."

"But *why?*" Max asked. "Why target the Naval Academy and kill those kids?"

"They're midshipmen," Archer answered. "Sailors. And don't forget, they killed the SUPE and his wife too. They exploited all the vulnerabilities on that campus perfectly."

"To what end?" Max asked.

"As we close in on their organization, this creates a diversion for them," Archer explained. "It's whipping the entire country into a frenzy—of the likes we haven't seen since 9-11. It creates a public rationale for them to take extreme measures in the face of a domestic terror threat."

Jack stood up with a file in hand and placed it in front of Archer. "I found this internal memorandum in the State Department archives, recently signed by Special Representative Brian Hooker. He's the State Department's Office of Commercial and Business Affairs."

Archer scanned the memo:

The United States Department of Energy, the U.S. Principal Party in Interest and Authorized Agent of the United States, hereby authorizes V-TEC, Incorporated, to organize and conduct business under the laws of

Iran, and to have an office and place of business in
Tehran, Iran. The Department of State authorizes
VTEC, Inc. to act as the sole authorized agent for export
control for nuclear power generation plants, nuclear
waste facilities, and nuclear/radiological technology,
and to perform any other act that may be required by
law or regulation in connection with the exportation
or transportation of any goods shipped or consigned
by or to the USPPI, and to receive or ship any goods on
behalf of the USPPI....

Jack handed Archer four other similar memoranda. "Baghdad,
Iraq...Manama, Bahrain...Kuwait City, Kuwait...Amman, Jordan."

"This may be the smoking gun," Archer said finally, after
reviewing each memorandum. "Taken together, these memos provide
a window into their long-term agenda, and their motive—they've been
sole-sourced to construct nuclear power plants and waste facilities
throughout the Middle East."

"What does staging an Islamic terror attack accomplish for them,
aside from acting as a diversion?" Shen asked.

Archer shrugged. "Well, one thing it does, is that it mobilizes our
country to intensify its campaign against ISIS, to create at least some
stability so the reactors can be built with minimum public opposition,
not to mention terrorist subversion."

Jack shook his head. "I'd think the public would go ape shit if
they found out we were exporting nuke reactors to the Middle East."

"NIMBY," Max replied.

"What?" Shen asked, confused.

"Not-in-my-back-yard," Archer translated. "That's part of the
justification they'll use. No one wants a 3 Mile Island next door, in
Hometown USA."

Max nodded. "They'll show how the revenue from abroad
translates to urban renewal projects, balanced budgets, and good will,
peace and security They'll sign international treaties to fast track their
construction. We'll be the largest exporter of nuclear power in the world.

Right now it's Russia, and France isn't far behind."

"But they can't do it unless those countries are more stable than they are now," Archer explained. "More U.S. and NATO troops forward deployed, and you have the stability you need to build. Theoretically."

"Theoretically," Shen agreed.

Max considered for a moment. "Okay. Let's say that's their thought process. But why target the three Supremes?"

Shen handed Max a single page paper, with the headline:

U.S. Supreme Court

VTEC Yankee Nuclear Power Corp. v. NRDC, 475 U.S. 3519

VTEC Yankee Nuclear Power Corp.

v.

Natural Resources Defense Council, Inc.

Shen continued, looking over at Archer. "This is what Thorne revealed to us under duress, I believe. All three of the associate justices targeted had previously ruled in favor of the Natural Resources Defense Council in other cases they'd heard, prior to being appointed to the Supreme Court. This case is scheduled to be heard in two months, and it'll decide whether the nuclear power plant in Maine can be rebuilt by V-TEC, or not. It will also influence future reactor projects in other States to include the Cold Mountain Storage Site. So, chances are, they're hedging their bets."

"That means they're still at risk," Archer concluded.

Shen nodded. "If you look at each of the Supremes they targeted, they don't exactly share a political philosophy—Stein is conservative, Wainwright is liberal, and Thompson is a moderate."

"It's all profit-based, then?" Max suggested.

Archer nodded. "I think it's time we paid Dr. Robert Craine a visit."

Dag was holding something akin to a men's toilet kit, and placed it on the table in front of Archer.

"I'm almost afraid to ask," Archer said. "What's this?"

"It's a Dagger Disguise Kit," Dag answered. "As good as Hollywood! Completely alters your appearance with no makeup."

"Why do I need this?"

"You're on the FBI's 'Most Wanted' list, remember?"

Archer was well-accustomed to altering his appearance and his identity from past operations—but in the midst of everything now underway, he hadn't even considered disguising himself—until Dag had forced the issue as more of a *fait accompli*, than a formal request.

Jack Condon reinforced the need for caution. "We know we've removed threats. SU's leadership knows it too. We've gotta factor that into everything we do, or we'll get hurt."

"Try out the Charlie Chaplin look. It just might work for you," Laura said from the doorway, walking over to him as the others left the room.

"You're here! I didn't expect you," Archer said, pushing the disguise kit away. "Bogart is all that ever worked for me. Becky made me go to Halloween party once, and I think I looked pretty damn good as him. At least after a few drinks."

"Ah, the problem with the world, you know, is that everyone is a few drinks behind," Laura quoted. "Humphrey Bogart, *The Maltese Falcon*."

"I could use a drink right now," Archer answered, paused and looked up at Laura. "You know, I'd feel a lot better if you were out of Headquarters. These folks are turning out to be far more capable and dangerous than I ever thought they'd be."

Laura shook her head. "I'm fine, Archer. Really. No need to worry about me."

"Yeah, well, I do worry," Archer replied.

"We need the information," Laura said. "And this is the only way we're going to get it."

Archer stood up and looking into Laura's eyes, knowing it was futile to argue with her. "Things are never so bad they can't be made worse," Archer replied wryly, trying on a baseball cap. He looked up at her in resignation. "Just be safe, Okay?"

Chapter 29

"LIEUTENANT COLONEL ARCHER WAS RUNNING along a well-established 12 mile course when I passed him at the corner of Mabry Road and On-the-Line Road, on the evening of September 12th. We call it 'The Mabry Loop.' It was mapped out by 5th Special Forces Group, and many of us enjoy running and ruck-marching on it because it's circular and provides for a good long distance run or trek—you cross the Kentucky and Tennessee State lines while doing it," Zachary Hastings said from his seat at the conference table. A stenographer typed silently at the end of the table.

"Did you have any other interaction with the defendant during your run?" asked Sandra Wilkes, Archer's Defense Attorney.

"It was dark by that time, as I recall, but I do remember Lieutenant Colonel Archer casually saluted as we passed, and commented that he was also running the Loop."

"Do you recall what time you passed each other, Colonel Hastings? Sandra Wilkes asked.

"It was 8:16PM," Hastings answered. "I remember checking my watch."

Sandra Wilkes nodded. "Thank you, no further questions."

Archer awoke in his Airstream trailer with a start, in a cold, hard sweat. He hadn't thought about the Article 32 hearing following Becky's murder all these years—until now, and those memories were flooding back to him in his sleep. Vivid, detailed images, replete with sounds of the courtroom and voices of those participating.

Archer glanced at the clock. It was 5:15AM. He picked up the phone and dialed.

After several rings, Sandra Wilkes answered. "Luke Archer? Is that you?"

"Sorry, I didn't mean to wake you," Archer said apologetically.

"I was gonna leave you a message."

"No, it's okay," Sandy replied groggily, trying her best to compose herself. "It's good to hear from you. You're in the news, you know."

"I need your help," Archer said matter-of-factly. "I'm in a bit of a situation."

"I've noticed. The first step is to turn yourself in," Sandy said. "Or it'll just get worse. But you already know that."

"I can't do that right now," Archer replied.

"There's not much I can do for you until you do," Sandy replied.

"If I do, it gets much worse. There is something you can do for me though. I need a copy of the full court file and the investigation of Becky's murder."

"I'll have to go through my boxes in storage," Sandy answered. "That was fifteen years ago. Why do you need them?"

"Do you remember Zachary Hasting's testimony during the deposition?"

"Vaguely, yes," Sandy answered. "His testimony cleared you in the Article 32 hearing, preventing a court martial."

"He testified that he passed me on a run at the corner of Mabry Road and On-the-Line Road, on the Mabry Loop."

"Based on the coroner's report, her text to you, and the estimated time of your wife's murder, Hastings' testimony that he saw you on a 12 mile run proved your innocence," Sandy replied.

"Well, *that's* the problem," Archer said. "That intersection of Mabry Road and On the Line Road are at the halfway point of the Mabry Loop."

"I'm not sure what you're getting at," Sandy answered. "I'm sorry, it's 5:20 in the morning, and I'm not exactly coherent yet. Not until there's coffee."

"Yeah, that's the thing. I didn't pass Hastings where he said we passed. I was just starting my run, and he was finishing his. We passed one another at 52nd Street and Desert Storm Avenue. I remember because I received a pager message from Becky right after I passed him."

"The one where she said, 'I love you'?"

"Yes," Archer replied.

"How does that matter?" Sandy asked. "With Zachary Hastings' statement, you still have a solid alibi that proves you were several miles away when she was killed."

"Don't you see?" Archer exclaimed. "It's not about an alibi for me. It never was. Hastings wasn't clearing me, *he was clearing himself!*"

"That's hardly proof, Archer—without hard evidence, it's just conjecture."

"That's why I need the file," Archer explained. "Becky always told me Zack Hastings would often stop by our quarters to check on her while I was deployed, to make sure she was okay. She said he'd come by always after a run—said he was 'just passing by.' She was always curt, but polite to him, and yet it always caught her off-guard. I was grateful to Hastings when he testified on my behalf. But looking back now, his testimony was a deliberate, well-placed lie."

"Zachary Hastings is the Vice President-Elect," Sandy said. "At this point, he's practically untouchable."

"No one's untouchable," Archer replied. "Not in my world. Especially if he's the one who murdered my wife."

"Don't jump to any conclusions just yet. I'll find the file and overnight it to you," Sandy said. "Same P.O. Box in Maine, I assume?"

"Address it to the same name," Archer replied. "A.J. White."

Chapter 30

LAURA CHICONE DROVE INTO THE Watergate parking garage and parked her Jeep Grand Cherokee in its assigned space on the first floor. Stepping out, Laura was startled to see the large frame of Chris Stockman approaching her.

"Chris!" Laura exclaimed. "I didn't know you also lived in the Watergate."

Stockman shook his head and smiled. "I don't."

"Why are you here?" She asked, already suspecting the answer.

"Well, I think you know."

The realization that this was neither an accidental encounter or a social call caused her heart to pound. She frantically looked around for anyone else in the parking garage, and to look for any potential escape routes. She saw neither.

"No, I don't know. Why don't you enlighten me?"

Stockman nodded again. "Okay. We can play that game if you like. Or we can talk about how you poisoned Dan Thorne. He passed away last night."

Laura shook her head. "Oh my God! Dan's dead?" She asked, genuinely surprised. "I had no idea! How could you believe I killed him?"

"Well, if you didn't do it, Archer did."

"I have no idea what you're talking about—is this some kind of sick joke?" She made a move to walk around Stockman in apparent disgust, but he blocked her with an open hand. She backed away, or attempted to, but with a parked car behind her, there was nowhere for her to go.

With his other hand, Stockman pulled out a Colt 1911-style auto pistol in 9mm with a suppressor attached. "No joke. In fact, I can think of a lot of other places I'd rather be at two-in-the-morning. You know, I have to say I'm impressed with what you've achieved. You managed to infiltrate our organization, kill one of my operatives, and preempt one of our most important operations. So, Bravo!"

"I have no idea what—"

Stockman waved her off, and continued. "But what you failed to take into account was that you were the *only* other person who knew about the Supreme Court operation, and you knew the names of the justices targeted. No one else had access to all of that combined information. So when all three missions were stopped, it was immediately obvious to me who was responsible. And, of course, we know that was you."

Laura laughed uneasily. "Always the CI guy, aren't you, Chris? How does it feel to be a traitor to your country?" Laura asked rhetorically.

"Looking in, I guess I can understand how you feel that way," Stockman answered. "But as you might imagine, I look at it differently. Some of us saw our country going in a direction our Founders never anticipated, and we just decided to take action rather than talk about it."

"By killing Supreme Court Justices, journalists, slaughtering 18 and 19 year old Midshipmen, falsely accusing good men of crimes, and short-circuiting the entire Federal Government?" Laura said matter-of-factly. "You're a coward and a traitor. Nothing less."

"We're patriots who want to see our country win, and this is a revolution from within," Stockman countered. "While both political parties run our nation into the ground, we're righting the ship, beneath the decks. And we're almost there."

"How can you possibly believe that?" Laura asked weakly.

Stockman laughed. "You don't get it, do you? For a brief moment, I thought you knew much more than you do! When Zachary Hastings is President, that's when we'll be able to make a real difference. It's a shame, you know. I had such hopes for you."

Laura shook her head. "Hastings is the *Vice* President-Elect..." She caught herself. "Oh my God...you're planning on assassinating the President, aren't you?"

"We're well past that, fortunately," Stockman said, shaking his head. "He's very ill right now, and not expected to make it much past his inauguration."

"So who's the real poisoner here?" Laura mocked. "Why are you doing this?"

"Kennedy once said that 'Those who make peaceful revolution

impossible, make violent revolution inevitable.' That's where we are today." Stockman pursed his lips. "When all's said and done, I'll be the DCI under Hastings."

Laura laughed. "You've always been a bureaucrat, Chris. And that's the way you'll die—faceless, nameless, and disgraced bureaucrat. That's your destiny."

Laura heard the elevator and what she thought were voices. Stockman appeared to hear them as well. "I'm sorry, Laura. I really am…" He fired two shots into the center of Laura's chest, and watched her collapse to the ground on her back, the force of the fall rolling her to her side, facing away from him.

Chapter 31

```
LC  shot  2x  in  chest  at
Watergate  @  close  range.
Survived,  but  condition
critical.  Penetrated  her
chest wall and collapsed one
lung.  In  shock.  Ballistic
protection  vest  saved  her.
Admitted GWU Hospital.
```

Archer read Shen Lu's message twice before responding.

```
Need  her  out  of  hospital
soonest.  By  any  means,
regardless  of  condition.
Need plane at Berlin, NH in
1 hour —dest. BWI Signature.
```

His heart raced as he thought through all of the implications of Laura's shooting. Instinctively, though, he knew.

Hurriedly, Archer filled his tactical pack, throwing the items he knew he'd likely need to include several passports, credit cards, IDs and a change of clothes, along with an M4 Carbine, Springfield XD 5 Tactical pistol, ammunition, night vision goggles, flashlight, batteries, and a ballistic vest.

Laura had been somehow been compromised in the wake of the attacks in Washington, DC and Annapolis, and he knew he should have expected an intense search for anyone involved in compromising their plans. Nothing was more unsettling—or predictable—than a Washington, D.C. witch-hunt, and SU had given them a whole new, deadly dimension. Feeling responsible for putting her in that position, the anguish and fury was overwhelming for Archer. Instinctively, he knew Chris Stockman was either directly or indirectly responsible for the attempt on Laura's life, and that he would stop at nothing to finish the job, once he learned that she had survived.

Opening the door to the Airstream, he stopped to grab the disguise kit Dag had given to him and placed it into his pack as well.

Archer arrived at the Berlin Regional Airport in New Hampshire to find the same Challenger 350 waiting for him on the tarmac. The pilot greeted Archer again on behalf of the Tory Foundation, adding, *"Thank you for all you are doing, Colonel."*

When he emerged from the airplane at Signature-Baltimore wearing a blue Baltimore Ravens cap, a thick gray moustache, plaid flannel shirt, tan work boots, and black rimmed glasses, Archer looked like a distant, if vaguely familiar version of himself transformed into a Colorado-style wrangler.

Shen was waiting for him with a black Land Rover parked beside the plane. "You look like Mel Gibson after a night in jail."

"Not exactly the look I was going for, but it'll do," Archer answered. "How's Laura?"

"She'll make it," Shen replied. "Luckily, she was wearing a vest. The rounds penetrated skin and some bone, but stopped short of the heart. They put an ET tube into her lungs to help with breathing when they found her. The chest surgeon pulled out one of the bullets, but the other was too close to her heart. He was able to repair the damaged lung and get it reinflated."

Archer's shoulders sagged in grateful relief. "She was wearing a vest because she knew something wasn't right," he said, getting into Land Rover's passenger seat. "They'll finish the job if we don't get her out of there quickly."

Shen nodded. "Max and Dag are on it."

"Where did you say this happened?" Archer asked. "The Watergate?"

Shen nodded. "Their parking garage."

"Let's go there now."

Introducing himself as "Doctor Stefan Weiss—and Max, as transport nurse Katya Wachter—medical trauma staff members from "Critical Care Transport Services," Dag handed a physician's order to the chief medical officer, approving and directing the immediate transfer of patient Laura S. Chicone to The John's Hopkins Hospital in Baltimore via air ambulance.

The chief medical officer at George Washington University Hospital was a young female doctor of Indian descent. "This is highly irregular," the medical officer said shaking her head and checking her records. "And ill-advised, I must say. This patient just arrived with us this morning, and is in critical condition. She is not stable enough for transport of *any* kind, and we have not been notified."

"Doctor, while we apologize for any miscommunication between hospitals, please understand that we do not have any choice at this point, we understand there's a critical need for specialized care only available at Johns Hopkins," Dag said calmly. "We have a helicopter ambulance on the hospital roof now, and we have only ten minutes before it will be directed to lift off. It is fully equipped, and the patient will receive continuous monitoring of her ECG, BP, Oxygen Saturation, and End-Tidal CO2."

"She could easily die of cardiac arrest at this point, the two bullets were that close to her heart, and caused swelling and inflammation of the heart," the chief medical officer said. "She's on a ventilator and has an ET tube and chest tube. I must tell you, moving her now is very problematic, and will needlessly endanger her life."

"We'd like to get the ET and chest tubes out as quickly as possible," Dag replied automatically. "To eliminate complications, and prevent pneumonia, DVT and especially PE, given the damage to her lungs."

"It would be far better to wait at least twenty-four hours," the chief medical officer insisted obdurately.

"Madame, as a trauma surgeon myself, you should know transport medicine is our specialty, to include airway management, advanced cardiac life support and experience in critical care." Dag gestured to Max. "Our transport nurse is completely versed in heart-related intensive care procedures. Enroute, the patient will receive continuous central venous pressure monitoring."

"I need to contact the Hospital Operations Administrator for approval," the chief medical officer replied.

Dag handed her another paper. "He has already approved the transfer. We have our own transport trolley that is specially designed for the air ambulance. Upon arrival at Johns Hopkins, the patient will be admitted to our intensive care unit, and you can be assured that we will notify your Command Center and attending physician when the transfer is complete. Time is of the essence."

The chief medical officer inspected both of the papers, wrote "*Transfer AMA*" in large letters on the paper—an annotation Dag knew to mean "Against Medical Advice." The medical officer handed him back the paper, and said curtly, "This way."

In the room, Laura was semi-conscious, but her eyes opened wide with relief when she recognized both Max and Dag in medical garb.

"Good afternoon, Ms. Chicone," Dag said reassuringly in his heavily accented English, conducting a quick survey of the monitors, her record and checking her heartbeat with a stethoscope. "We'll be transporting you by helicopter to Johns Hopkins University Hospital immediately. Allow us to secure your monitors, pumps and oxygen on the trolley, and we'll be on our way. *Quickly*."

Laura grasped Dag's hand. He gently squeezed it, and whispered in her ear: "We need to get out of here before the hospital realizes what's happening. Bad guys on their way."

Laura returned the squeeze, then slipped back to unconsciousness.

Rolling the trolley out of the room, toward the large elevator, Max noticed the two men in dark suits who were approaching the front desk. "Get her on the chopper," Max told Dag, reaching for her suppressor and Glock 43. "If I'm not there when you get her on board, leave without me."

Surveying the floor, and noticing the same men standing no more than fifty feet away, Dag nodded.

Max returned to Laura's room. When the men entered, they closed the door, and found her in bed as the patient, wearing an Oxygen mask, apparently sleeping.

One of the men took out a box containing a syringe, opened it and prepared to inject Max; but before he could do so, Max lifted the silenced Glock from her side, still underneath the sheet, and shot them both in rapid succession.

Jumping off the bed, she quickly pulled the bodies of both men into the bathroom shower. Exiting the room, she walked to the stairwell, and ran up the stairs to the hospital helipad where the Tory Foundation helicopter was waiting with Dag and Laura already on board.

"Okay. Let's go," Max shouted above the rotor noise. "*Now.*"

Dag lifted off and once airborne, messaged his cleaning team about a new worksite that had a high probability of immediate compromise.

Walking through the first floor of the Watergate's parking garage, Shen pointed at the white Jeep Grand Cherokee. "There. That's Laura's."

Archer nodded, scanning the area surrounding the car. "Where was she shot?"

"Somewhere right around here, according to the witness statements in the police report."

"How did you get that?" Archer asked.

Shen looked over at Archer with a knowing *"Don't Ask"* glance.

"Okay," Archer replied. "Never mind. What else did it say?"

"Not much," Shen answered. "Two witnesses. Both heard voices, then two suppressed shots in quick succession. They found Laura still conscious on the ground right around here."

Archer knelt down and began searching underneath the cars. Shen did the same.

"The police have already been here," Shen said. "Doubt we'll find anything."

"Except this," Archer called out after several minutes of

searching.

Shen stood up to see Archer holding an expended cartridge case.

"What do you make of it?" Archer asked, handing the brass case to Shen.

Examining the markings underneath the casing, along the rim, Shen's eyebrows rose. "9mm + P, Glaser. Custom milled, probably subsonic. Not a normal round."

"Damn expensive too," Archer replied. He drew a deep, ragged breath. "Are you sure?"

Shen shrugged. "If we can get ahold of Laura's vest, it would help confirm."

Archer nodded. Noticing a tangled blue plastic fragment on the ground, he picked it up. "I think it may be time to pay Chris Stockman a visit."

Chapter 32

LUKE ARCHER AND SHEN LU were waiting for Laura at the Tory Foundation Operations Center when Dag and Max arrived. They had landed the helicopter on a nearby soccer field—a distance away from the Tory Operations Center, in order to conceal Laura's eventual destination. Transferring Laura to a nondescript Sprinter cargo van ground ambulance, driven by Jack Condon, Max and Dag continued to monitor Laura's condition enroute. The moment they approached the back of the strip mall, Archer rushed to the rear double doors and helped pull Laura's gurney out.

Inside the Tory Center, a full hospital room had been prepared for Laura, replicating what she had at George Washington University Hospital, with a full time trauma physician on staff.

Laura was wearing an oxygen mask, and her eyes were open. Archer noticed she was holding Max's hand. She seemed to smile through her mask when she saw Archer, and coughed, removing her mask momentarily. "Nice disguise, Bogart."

"Shen said I look like Mel Gibson in the rough," Archer said, smiling. The relief in his voice, palpable.

"Things are never so bad...they can't be made worse," she replied hoarsely. Her eyes were dilated and inflamed, raw against blanched skin. "I'm really sorry, Archer."

"No, no," Archer answered. "No apologies. Who did this to you?" Archer asked.

Laura struggled to speak, and when she did it came as a whisper. "Stockman. They're planning to...assassinate the President-elect."

"So Zachary Hastings can take his place?" Archer asked, already knowing the answer.

Laura nodded.

Archer squeezed her hand. "We have a room for you in here where you can heal. You'll have the best medical attention, from Dag and the Tory Foundation doctors. And you'll be safe here. I'll be back soon."

Laura nodded and returned the squeeze. "Archer?"

Archer bent down to her.

"Find my iPhone."

Luke Archer found Chris Stockman's cell phone number on his iPhone and dialed it from inside the Jeep. After a single ring, Stockman answered.

"By now you've realized that your attempt to kill Laura failed," Archer said calmly. "So, this is what's going to happen. You're going to either turn yourself into the police in one hour, or I'm going to kill you myself. You decide."

Archer heard Stockman laugh on the other end of the line. "You're not really giving me a choice, are you?"

"Your choice," Archer answered in a clipped tone. "But you have an hour to make it."

Stockman laughed again. "You know, it's almost comical—the #1 FBI's Most Wanted Criminal giving *me* an ultimatum. Here's your answer: *you* turn yourself in, right now, or we kill you and your entire team."

"I understand from Laura you plan to assassinate President-Elect Stone and install Zack Hastings?"

There was a long silence on the other end.

"Laura's delusional," Stockman finally answered. "Give yourself up, Archer. You're outgunned, outmanned, and outclassed. It's better for everyone if you just surrender yourself."

"By now, I would've thought you'd know me better than that." Archer paused, and exhaled. "I couldn't be more disappointed in you, Chris."

Chapter 33

55 MINUTES TICKED BY UNTIL Luke Archer saw the LCD screen of his secure radio transceiver light up.

"He's parking now. Accompanied by a four-man security detail," Max reported over the radio.

"Roger, Copy," Archer acknowledged.

"They're conducting an explosives check," Max reported. *"Stand by...he's going inside."*

From a small boathouse on the other side of the Potomac, wearing black watch caps and camouflage makeup, Archer and Shen watched Chris Stockman turn on the lights of the Wolf Street townhome in Old Towne, Alexandria. Through his binoculars, Archer could clearly see Stockman in his kitchen, talking on his cell phone.

"Okay," Archer said over his iPhone to Shen. "That's him. Let's go."

Behind the tripod-mounted Israeli LAHAT guided missile launcher, Shen took final aim at the fully lit kitchen.

Archer dialed Stockman's number from a second cell phone, and heard Stockman answer.

"You know your call's being actively tracked," Stockman said without preamble.

"Yeah, I'm routed through several international relays, so tracking me isn't going to be possible. Chris, I gave you the chance to make this right. But you had to take another route."

"Where are you?" The hint of panic in Stockman's voice was palpable and strident.

"A little cold out here, but still a good evening for fishing on the Potomac," Archer replied, seeking to keep Stockman in place for a few seconds. Watching through the binoculars, he saw Stockman rush toward the window.

Archer muted the connection to Stockman and ordered Shen to "Fire."

Shen fired the LAHAT missile toward the house. About three

seconds later, from the outside of the house, there was a brief flash of light and a muffled report, hardly noticeable given the ambient noise in the area. Archer thought it might have missed, when suddenly, the missile appeared to detonate silently in a dramatic, fiery burst of light that instantly reduced the top half of the house to ruins, illuminating the night sky in a dark red and orange. The deafening sound of the explosion, like a distant clap of thunder followed in a forceful wave a few seconds later. The sound of fire alarms and car alarms followed, traveling across the Potomac.

"Direct hit," Max reported over the radio.

Archer knew in advance the damage it would inflict, and so did Max, having used the same round on numerous occasions with the IDF in Lebanon and on the Golan Heights— the missile's warhead was capable of breaching more than eight inches of reinforced concrete, and was primary reason he'd decided to use it.

"Target destroyed," Archer replied. Dismantling the LAHAT, and loading it into a Chris Craft Commander, Archer started the engine and pushed the boat's throttle forward.

Chapter 34

KNOWING THAT A MASSIVE MANHUNT was already underway, Luke Archer advised the team to maintain as low a profile as possible, and travel by any means, to any place, unless absolutely necessary. Shen and Max elected to remain at the Tory Foundation Operations Center, while Dag committed himself full-time to assisting Laura in her recovery.

As an experienced Special Forces Medic, well-accustomed to delivering lifesaving aid to trauma victims on the battlefield, Dag was uniquely equipped to provide all of the medical care Laura needed to assist her in healing from her wounds.

"We'll continue her on antibiotics to prevent lung and wound infections, along with pain meds as required," Dag told Archer. "As soon as we can take her off the ventilator, we'll move her from a bed to a chair to prevent any possibility of pneumonia, DVT, and PE."

"I have no idea what you just said," Archer said.

"DVT is Deep Vein Thrombosis," Dag explained. "It occurs when a blood clot forms in one or more of the deep veins in your body, usually in your legs. PE is pulmonary embolus—when a leg clot breaks free and goes to the lungs. Both can kill you quickly...or slowly."

"How long of a recovery are we talking about?" Archer asked.

Dag shrugged. "Difficult to say. We'll begin respiratory therapy today, deep breathing exercises to help the lung stay inflated and heal more quickly, and then we'll progress to walking and strength building. Then we'll progress to hyperbaric chamber therapy." He paused and looked at Archer. "Laura's strong. She can do light office work in a week or two, and she'll be back to normal in three to four months."

"Okay," Archer nodded. Looking up at Dag, he pursed his lips, as if to reassess his response. "Take care of her, Doc."

Archer flipped through the library of photos on his iPad, stopping at those with Becky—some posed, but many spontaneous shots of a smile he remembered as both radiant and reassuring—often with her long waves of brunette hair blowing in the wind. One series of photos was taken in the same Airstream, parked in the very same spot in White Mountain National Forest. Gazing at those photos for an extended moment, Becky was beside him in bed, drinking a glass of Chardonnay, reading an old Anne Rice novel. She looked over at him, and catching his gaze, she smiled silently and wrapped her leg over his.

After a flipping through a few photos, the iPad's images became blurred as his tears began to hit the screen.

The memories that the images evoked were indelible. Emerging from deep within that vision of the past to where he was now was becoming more and more painful to endure. Wiping away the tears, he swallowed the remainder of the Woodford Reserve in his glass, and shoved his Browning Hi-Power away.

Another time. Another place.

Knowing he was now the government's primary target, Archer had decided to retreat back to his trailer in Maine, maintain a low profile, and use it as an opportunity to think, and at least try to make sense of everything.

A CNN report of Stockman's house—at least what was left of it, in flames— flashed on the screen. He unmuted the sound.

The high-profile, dramatic killing of a senior CIA official drew swift condemnation this morning from the CIA Director and President.

"With the murder of Christopher Stockman, one of the Central Intelligence Agency's senior leaders, our nation has come under direct attack by domestic terrorists," President Williamson said in prepared statement. "Be assured, we will find the perpetrators and prosecute them to the fullest extent."

And yet even as authorities vowed to investigate and apprehend whoever is responsible, terror experts pointed to the incident as a troubling sign that the activities of domestic militias within our borders are increasing in frequency and their attacks have reached an entirely new level of sophistication.

Stockman had been accompanied by bodyguards at the time of the killing, CIA Director Elliott Abraham told CNN.

No arrests have yet been made in the case, FBI Director Alan Fields said. "We have identified Luke Archer, a retired employee of the Central Intelligence Agency and retired Green Beret Colonel as a person of interest in this case."

A friend of Luke Archer's, who refused to be identified or appear in front of cameras spoke to us this morning. "If Luke Archer did this, he was definitely provoked. And that's all I'll say."

CIA Director Abraham rejected that view completely: "This is a stark reminder of the inherent risk and sweep of our global mission, as well as the bravery and integrity of those who perform it. There was no provocation."

Archer wasn't surprised by the report, but he found himself wondering who the vote of confidence in the narrative had come from. Whoever they were, he was grateful for their good instincts.

Archer already knew that two of the apparent top SU leaders were men with whom he had a long history. Chris Stockman was now dead, but Zachary Hastings remained alive. There were undoubtedly others, *but who were they?*

In addition to searching for, and trying to kill him and his team, SU was also doing their level best to frame him for his wife's murder.

On the television, a *Biography Channel* documentary was running on the life of Vice President-Elect Zachary Hastings. Watching the footage of Hastings as a young Army Captain holding and shooting various rifles and pistols in training, Archer found himself inexplicably keying in on the unique way Hastings both held and shot each of those weapons.

He shuffled through the papers on the table, remembering that among the mail items he'd picked up at the post office were the transcripts from the grand jury. A proceeding that ultimately found no evidence or grounds to try Archer for his wife's murder.

Chapter 35

LUKE ARCHER FOUND THE PACKAGE he had received from Sandra Wilkes, and began paging through the grand jury transcripts. When he came to the record of the coroner's testimony, he stopped.

> **Coroner**: *The wounds were localized to one area of the neck, which would signify that there was some limitation of movement. All five stab wounds were caused by extreme force with a single-edged knife indicated by the fact that each of the wounds have a blunt end and a sharp end. It is probable that the killer was positioned at the left side of the victim, holding her head with his right hand and inflicting the neck wounds with his left hand, producing right-to-left cuts and stabs.*
>
> **Defense (Wilkes):** *What you are saying then, Doctor, is that it is your opinion that the killer in this case was left handed?*
>
> **Coroner:** *Yes. That is my opinion, based on the wounds and the bloodstain pattern analysis conducted at the crime scene. To conduct these attacks right handed, the victim would have had to be held face down, with the attacker on top stabbing upwards. A very awkward and, if I may say, unlikely position for both victim and attacker.*
>
> **Defense (Wilkes):** *Was the victim found face up or face down, Doctor?*
>
> **Coroner:** *Face up.*
>
> **Defense (Wilkes):** *Thank you. I have no further questions.*

Archer stopped reading, and looked up at the TV set. As Hastings was answering questions in a sit-down interview, he was holding his reading glasses and gesturing for emphasis—all with his left hand.

Unnerved, Archer pulled out his copy of the yearbook from his last year at 5th Special Forces Group, and paged through the photos from that time. Photos of friends and comrades he hadn't seen for years. Some who had since passed away, to include an image he'd long forgotten of John Lee dressed up in a homemade Santa Claus outfit, while firing an M249 Light Machine Gun during a Taliban attack during one of their combat deployments in Afghanistan. In the front of the book, there was a posed photo of Colonel Zachary Hastings sitting down at his desk with a pen in his left hand.

Yet another photograph depicted Hastings visiting one of Archer's deployed teams in Afghanistan, shaking hands with the team leader. A large fabric bandage on the right side of Hastings' neck was visible in the photo. Turning the photograph over to the backside, he saw from the date that it was taken only two days after Becky's murder.

She fought....

He attempted to breathe deliberately, to no avail. For the moment, everything around Archer stood still. Now watching the coverage of Hastings on TV, and the images in the yearbook, he was more convinced than ever that Zachary Hastings was the one who killed his wife that night a decade and a half ago at Fort Campbell.

Chapter 36

```
            Would like to c u
            & Beau. Possible?

Yes! Today?

            3pm - Sunday River
            Covered  Bridge  -
            Newry
```

Luke Archer understood the risks associated with meeting Elena. Not only to himself, but to her as well. And yet, he felt his sanity slipping away, and if anyone could help him restore his perspective, he knew it was Elena. Before signing off, he typed one last text message to her:

```
            Careful   not   to
            be        followed.
            Take   back   roads
            wherever possible.
```

While he knew it was the safest course to follow, it was not the best path for his own long-term well being. From past experience, Archer knew well the effects of absolute isolation on his own mindset, and the ultimate outcome if he didn't make a change. And soon.

The last time he felt this kind of depression setting in was after Becky's murder. Like he was being swallowed up by the darkness, unfeeling, and strangely invulnerable.

Following her murder, he'd gone on a bourbon binge with no foreseeable end in sight, until John Lee had found him in the Maine wilderness, delusional and aimless.

At the time, it was a luxury for him not to care about himself or about others around him. The bourbon helped with that. Maybe too much. Soon, however, he found that he was not *able* to care about himself or others—and that downward spiral nearly destroyed him before John rescued him. Not by taking the bottle of bourbon away, but by drinking it with him, and imperceptibly weaning him off of it, until there wasn't another story to tell, or another tear to shed.

Ultimately, deploying abroad across many different high-threat theaters of war, under the operational control of the CIA, was what pulled him out. It gave him a renewed purpose, and even greater responsibilities. While they knew about Becky's murder, they didn't know about the drinking—and he'd never told them.

A year later, he was being held captive by Omar Mehsud Shah in Pakistan's Northwest Frontier Province—*Khyber Pakhtunkhwa*, bordering Afghanistan.

In reaching out to Elena, his hope was that she would help him re-center and draw him out of an increasingly dense fog before it was too late. All of the symptoms were there, and he recognized them like the friendly approach of an old troublemaking friend. He knew seeing Beau again would also help. Putting the bottle of Woodford Reserve away in the galley cabinet, he was grateful to Elena for still having faith in him.

After two of the V-Tec servers had suddenly become inoperative, V-Tec's IT Director received an immediate late-night call from V-Tec's authorized service provider informing him that while actively monitoring the V-Tec system, the provider's operative had noticed the servers had frozen, and that the likely cause was a dual hard drive failure. The IT Director was told that a team of technicians was on its way to replace the server drives that had failed, and to get V-Tec's system back up and running with minimal disruption.

It had not occurred to the IT Director that the repair team could also be responsible for the server failure.

Shen and Max flashed their contractor authorization badges at V-Tec's security desk and were waved through the turnstiles to a bank of elevators. After another round of security authentication inside the elevator, they descended to the basement, and were led to the V-Tec server room.

The disk drives that Shen and Max used to replace the two they had remotely sabotaged had some additional unique "add-on" capabilities that included autonomously and clandestinely transferring V-Tec's data back to the Tory Foundation Operations Center at a rate of 5 Gigabits/Second (GBps).

Before departing the server room, Max installed a "Leased Line" software program on the V-Tec phone network that would allow Dr. Robert Craine's office phone to be monitored remotely through the company's backbone network using the company's own fiber optic cables—sending data and audio at a range of 10MBps, allowing calls to be intercepted in real time– without alerting any of V-Tec's systems.

As a final measure, Shen installed several GSM Room Transmitters in the offices of Dr. Robert Craine, and the other C-Suite leaders of V-Tec. Unless V-Tec was actively searching for the installed technical surveillance systems, and knew precisely where to look, they were virtually undetectable.

Shen and Max walked out of V-Tec's corporate headquarters twenty minutes later, after informing a grateful and relieved corporate IT Director both servers had been replaced under full warranty.

Chapter 37

LUKE ARCHER COULD SEE Elena Campbell's red Jeep Grand Cherokee approaching from far down the road. Beau's head was hanging far outside the window, and he was barking excitedly. When the vehicle pulled into the parking lot, Beau caught sight of Archer standing by the covered bridge and leapt from the Jeep's window, rushing toward him. Elena shouted after Beau, shocked that the dog would actually jump from a moving vehicle.

Elena stepped out of the Jeep, watching the spectacle of Beau continually jumping up in the air and body slamming Archer. "I'd have jumped from the car too, but I was driving," she said, shaking her head.

"I'm glad both of you are here," Archer replied, trying to settle Beau down. "This bridge is the first stop on your tour."

"Nice bridge," Elena said, smiling, and obviously amused—she hadn't come for a tour, but Archer was providing it anyway.

"The locals call it 'The Artist's Bridge,'" Archer continued, pointing at the covered bridge, with its dark, weathered wood. "Built in 1811, washed out a couple times and rebuilt. This is the third attempt, built in 1872, and it stuck."

"I've always heard about it, but never had a chance to visit until now."

"It is off the beaten path," Archer said. "Understandable."

"It's as beautiful as people always said," Elena replied.

"They say it's one of the most photographed bridges in the country."

"Can I?" Elena asked, reaching into the Jeep. "Take photos?"

"Of course," Archer answered, walking with her as she aimed her camera toward the bridge. A mist was lifting off the water below. The forest around them was quiet. The air was still as in a church.

"It has a mystical feel to it, doesn't it?" Elena asked, looking briefly up at him. "This place?"

Archer nodded. "As you walk, always ask, 'Which is the stone that supports the bridge?'"

"Pardon me?"

Their feet echoed on the wooden surface.

Archer smiled, and looked over at Elena as they approached the center of the bridge. They could feel the mist and hear the roar of the water rushing below. "Kublai Khan said that to Marco Polo. For some reason, this place always reminded me of those two. Especially now."

Elena nodded, understanding. "Archer, I—"

"I owe you an explanation," Archer interrupted.

Elena shook her head slowly. "You don't owe me anything. I'm just worried about you."

"I appreciate you still having faith in me. Not many people would right now."

Elena leaned on the bridge's railing and looked down at the part-frozen river below. "'Sometimes, if you aren't sure about something, you just have to jump off the bridge and grow your wings on the way down.'"

"Marco Polo?"

She looked up at Archer, smiled at him and placed her arm in his as they walked. "Nope, Danielle Steel."

After a night of blessed rest, Elena joined Archer on the steps of his Airstream, overlooking the White Mountain National Forest campsite.

"It's easy to see why you come here," Elena said softly, looking up, shading her eyes against the morning sun reflecting on the snow. "It's beautiful."

Archer nodded, and handed her a cup of coffee. The forest of Balsam Fir stood around them, as if on guard.

"You were calling out your wife's name in your sleep last night, you know," Elena said.

"I'm sorry," Archer said. "Never knew I did that."

Elena took a sip of her coffee. A minute passed in silence, as birds chirped around them. "Can I ask you something?"

Archer looked over at her.

"Why are you fighting this battle?"

Archer didn't immediately answer, considering his response. Finally, he looked up, "Several decades ago, when I joined the Army, I raised my right hand and took an oath to protect and defend the Constitution of the United States. I've watched too many friends die living up to it."

"So is this your responsibility?"

Archer shrugged. "I'm not sure exactly. I've made a lot of mistakes in my life. All I can do is hope I'm not wrong."

"Your friends—Laura, Max, Jack, Shen,...they don't think you're wrong."

"After doing this for so long, I guess we look at the world differently than most. Maybe even think differently."

"In what way?"

Archer shrugged. His shoulders suddenly felt heavy. "Basic, fundamental ways, I suppose. Where you see a scenic valley, I see an ambush site and effective fields of fire. A shovel may seem like only a shovel to you, but to me it's a field expedient weapon. When you're looking at the menu, I'm looking at every face in the restaurant, looking at their hands, and finding the nearest exits. Does any of that make sense?"

Elena put her head on his shoulder and intertwined her arm in his. "Yes, but I'll probably never look at a dinner out with you quite the same way."

Archer laughed. "Sorry about that."

"How are your friends?" Elena asked, changing the subject. "I liked them very much."

Archer told her what had happened to Laura Chicone, omitting some of the details.

"Oh no! Laura?" Elena asked, genuinely concerned. "Is she going to be okay?"

Archer nodded. "She's lucky. I blame myself for what happened to her."

Elena ached for Archer, seeing the sadness in his eyes. "It's not your fault. You have to know that—"

Archer pointed up at the TV, where a CNN report came on with the Yankee Maine nuclear power plant in the background.

Fulfilling a campaign promise, President Elect William Stone today informed Congress of his plan to request that the U.S. Nuclear Regulatory Commission release operating licenses for new nuclear energy facilities in ten States, including a repair and renovation of this nuclear plant here in Maine, the Yankee Maine Plant.

President-Elect Stone's request from Congress for funds at the outset of his Presidency comes at a time when many other U.S. nuclear facilities are in the process of being prematurely retired due to financial pressures.

Another of President-Elect Stone's campaign promises was to begin exporting nuclear reactor technology to democratic countries worldwide, as he repeated in an appearance yesterday in Washington, D.C.:

"Nations around the world are seeking carbon-free energy options like nuclear power. The United States, has the strictest nuclear safety regulations, and we're missing an opportunity by not exporting our state-of-the-art expertise, and instead allowing Russia and China to freely export reactors that are far less safe, efficient or reliable."

V-Tec is a principal company that builds nuclear power plants in the United States and stands to benefit from President-Elect Stone's plan to export U.S. nuclear technology. Dr. Robert Craine, the CEO of V-Tec spoke recently at the Advanced Energy Conference in New York City:

"If we don't change our export policy, Russia and China will dominate the international nuclear energy market. But the United States can quickly close this gap, and we can play a key role in setting higher international industry standards for nuclear power safety and security. As Russia builds nuclear power plants for Iran, we should be assisting other nation-states in the Middle East— Bahrain, Kuwait, Saudi Arabia, Egypt and Jordan— in build their own state-of-the-art plants."

Yahima Shireman, Director of Nuclear Watch, testified at a recent Senate Energy and Natural Resources Committee meeting: "We are losing sight of the most important lesson from the Fukushima and Chernobyl catastrophes: that nuclear power is the most difficult and complex technology to manage, and that accidents can result that cause irreparable damage to the environment and human life.

Yankee Maine is the first of the Stone Administration's planned 500 nuclear reactors to be constructed in the United States over the next five years.

"This is at least part of what's driving their agenda," Archer commented.

"Making nuclear power available to the world?"

Archer nodded. "Making the United States a major energy exporter."

"But there's nothing illegal about that, is there?"

Archer motioned for Elena to sit down at the table and poured coffee for them both. "I have no problem with nuclear power, and I don't have a problem with the business end of it either. My issue is when they begin short circuiting the process, and killing the folks who stand in their way. Then you need to start asking *why*."

"Even if it gets *you* killed?"

"I believe it's a much larger issue than just nuclear power. This is just one of their funding mechanisms. If I allow them to continue, John's death will have been in vain."

"How can you possibly continue to fight them?" Elena asked. "When it's the *entire* government you're up against?"

Archer caught a glimpse of CNN's follow-on story about Vice President Elect Zachary Hastings. "By changing their internal calculus…" he replied.

"How do you do that?" Elena asked.

Archer frowned for a moment, then his brow cleared. Taking a sip of coffee, holding the cup with both hands on the table, he looked over at Elena and smiled. "By removing the stone that supports their bridge."

Chapter 38

DR. OTTO KLINGEMANN, Deputy Director General of the International Atomic Energy Agency, introduced himself to the couples sitting beside him at the V-Tec campaign donor's table in the middle of the Waldorf Astoria's Grand Ballroom.

Vice President-Elect Zachary Hastings was speaking at a podium on the stage, bordered by red and gold curtains, and large format LCD screens to the left and right. One American Sign Language interpreter below the dais signed as he spoke. The screens projected Hastings' image for maximum visibility to the audience, as Secret Service agents stood on watch below.

While Hastings outlined the ambitious energy agenda for the new administration, Klingemann noticed many of the wives and girlfriends in evening gowns, among others, were pretending to be interested in the speech, while covertly checking their Facebook and Instagram pages, and sending text messages throughout.

Dressed in a white tuxedo jacket and black pants, Klingemann pushed his slate gray, shoulder-length hair to the side. He placed his iPhone on the table beside another. Initiating the pairing operation was relatively simple and consisted of two separate steps: installing a roving bug, effectively turning the iPhone into a bugging device—enabling the microphones of the cell phone to be turned on and transmit conversations in-progress, even when switched off. In the second step, the neighboring phone was silently pinged to pair with the Unique IMEI Number—allowing the data from all incoming and outgoing communications and text messages to be remotely accessed.

Hastings finished his speech, and opened the floor up to questions from the audience. Placing his iPhone into his pocket, Klingemann stood first, and was handed a microphone from one of the event attendants.

"Mr. Vice President," Klingemann began in a high-pitched, heavy German accent.

"Not Vice President yet!" Hastings interjected to laughter from the audience.

"Of course. Mr. Vice President-*Elect*," Klingemann emphasized in his sing-song intonation, smiling and adjusting his round tortoise-framed eyeglasses, all to more laughter. "I believe I speak for everyone assembled here, to include my V-Tec hosts here, in congratulating you and President Stone on your election—"

Applause erupted across the ballroom and up the two tiers of filled-to-capacity balconies and boxes. Klingemann saw two television cameras now pointed in his direction, and his image was projected prominently on the LCD screens above. All those who had been texting, he noticed, had quickly put their iPhones aside.

Klingemann nervously cleared his throat and continued. "Sir, I am told you have always been a very accomplished athlete and long-distance runner. When you were the Commander of 5th Special Forces Group, I understand you went on many late-night long-distance runs. And during your runs, you would often check on the welfare of the spouses whose husbands were deployed. Very commendable; however, I must say, some would say you cared 'too much'—"

"Excuse me, Sir," Hastings interrupted, standing up straight, measuring. "Who are you, may I ask?"

"Oh, my sincere apologies, *Herr General*! I am Dr. Otto Klingemann."

There was an audible stir of interest among the crowd.

"And do you have a specific question, Doctor?" Hastings looked pale, but composed.

"Oh yes, of course, my question!" Klingemann replied absently, appearing somewhat scattered and confused. "My question, very simply, is whether you honestly believe it is possible for you to continue to run as you always have, while you are being relentlessly pursued by former comrades whom you now classify as terrorists."

Booing erupted from the audience, and Klingemann noticed event security officers were rapidly approaching him from across the room. Klingemann's unassuming, absent-minded demeanor suddenly changed. Pushing back the disheveled hair from his face, he continued without any trace of accent. "And finally, Colonel Hastings, because you were a Colonel then—did you honestly believe you could escape retribution for your brazen and horrific crimes, to include the murder of Becky Louise Archer?"

The Grand Ballroom erupted in booing and shouts of *"Fake!"* and *"Get him out of here!"*

Glancing up at the stage and on the oversized LCD screens above, Archer could see a leaden, rigid pallor slowly emerge on the face of Vice President-Elect Zachary Hastings. He laughed unconvincingly with malevolent eyes. It was the kind of apoplectic expression Archer had seen many times before when they had worked together, and when Hastings' stress was high.

It was the only acknowledgement he needed—the rest would soon follow.

As security struggled to forcefully extricate him from the V-Tec table and escort him from the ballroom, Archer stepped out of their grasp momentarily and approached the middle aged man dressed in a very expensive Kiton-K50 blue pinstripe suit whose place card read:

Dr. Robert Craine, CEO, V-Tec

Dumping a large plate of cheesecake on Craine's lap, Archer leaned down and whispered in his revived, contrived German accent: "And, *Herr Doktor*, you're dessert."

Catching a glimpse of their not-so-concealed Smith and Wesson .44 Magnum revolvers, Luke Archer realized the two men escorting him out of the Waldorf Astoria New York were not event security employees or even Secret Service, but privately contracted SU agents who had no intention of throwing him out on the street. Having bound his wrists to his front in flex cuffs, the men were leading him at a speed walk through the Waldorf Astoria, down flights of stairs, and doing their very best to avoid the luxury hotel's high-traffic areas.

As they moved swiftly downstairs toward the basement of the hotel, Archer continued to speak conversationally to both men in his faux German accent.

"Ver are you taking me, gentlemen? Vy do ve go to ze basement?"

"Please I ask you not to grip so tightly!"

"I did not mean to spill ze cheezecake on ze doktor!"

"My car is not in ze parking garage, why are ve going here?"

Seeing the large black Denali SUV directly in front of them, Archer realized their full intent, and knew that the moment had come to either interrupt their plans, or follow through with them to see where they led.

Unknowingly, his escorts had made a crucial error of omission in not formally handcuffing him, but rather flex cuffing him with his hands positioned to the front.

Archer stopped with his hands held out together, in a praying position. He pleaded with his escort-captors to his front. *"Gentlemen, I must kindly beg you to release me!"*

Pulling his arms forcefully and rapidly to his chest in a well-practiced, lightning-fast maneuver, Archer snapped the flex cuffs, freeing his hands. Keeping both men to his front, Archer kicked the man furthest away in the groin, and punched the other man in the solar plexus. Staying in constant motion, Archer delivered rapid, forceful kicks to both men's knees, causing both men to fall to the ground, writhing in pain. Seeing the man furthest to his right reach for his Smith & Wesson, Archer kicked his hand away as if he were kicking a field goal, and followed up by bending his knee into the man's nose, crushing it.

Archer heard the screech of tires, and looked up at the black Land Rover with Max at the wheel.

"Need a ride, *Herr Doktor*?" She asked, casually.

"Yeah, I do," Archer said, stepping into the passenger seat. Removing his earpiece receiver, glasses, wig, and the remaining elements of his disguise, he asked with a tone of contrived annoyance, "What took you so long?"

"Oh! Our apologies, *Herr Doktor*! We are *terribly* sorry for the very poor customer service!" Max commented dryly, looking over at him, and accelerating aggressively. "You see, we're ashamed to say that we did not immediately recognize the extreme urgency of your situation. Oh, and for future reference, may I say, it may be helpful for you to know…" She took the hairpin turn at full-speed, effortlessly and without warning, throwing Archer forcefully against the passenger door's window. With the exit visible, she further accelerated and raced through the Waldorf Astoria motor court, deftly weaving past a white Rolls Royce Ghost and a red Lamborghini Centenario, emerging onto 50th Street in a full sliding right turn—ostensibly without checking for oncoming traffic. Once in traffic, she concluded, "…that your transmitter is not optimized for hotel basements and parking garages!"

Chapter 39

LUKE ARCHER PICKED UP THE TELEPHONE inside the Tory Foundation Operations Center and heard Zachary Hastings' voice answer.

"Congratulations, Zack," Archer said. "Vice President of the United States! You're only a heartbeat away from the Presidency. Of course, you already knew that, didn't you?"

Hastings didn't immediately respond, but when he did his tone was icy and distant. "Archer, it took me awhile to realize that was you back there at the Waldorf Astoria. It's been awhile."

"You're right," Archer replied. "It's taken this long for me to realize that you were the one who killed my wife."

"*Goddammit, Archer!* After everything I did for you!" Hastings exclaimed. "I testify on your behalf, allow you to finish out your command with the highest honors, give you all the time you need to get your head straight, and help you to retire from the Army, and you accuse *me* of killing Becky? You're desperate. I understand that, but at this point you're also delusional, and you really do need to turn yourself in."

"You haven't seen me desperate," Archer said. "And as far as being delusional, I thought so too, until I read the coroner's report and the Grand Jury transcripts. Then it became obvious what happened that night, and how it happened."

"I'm sorry you feel that way," Hastings replied. "I really am. Reconstructing the past is never perfect—you know that better than most. Trying to do it from courtroom transcripts? Almost impossible. People die, memories fade, and facts are distorted by the passage of time, personal grudges and agendas. Now, Goddammit! Listen to me! If you don't turn yourself in, you *know* this won't end well for you."

"You testified that we passed one another halfway through our runs that night, but we both know that we passed one another at the beginning of our runs. You knew I wouldn't be home for another hour, and that gave you all the time you needed to go to our house, tie up, strangle, and stab her to death. Becky was killed by someone who was large, powerful, and left handed. Despite that, she fought against her killer, and I have pictures of you bandaged up immediately after she clawed your neck. In fact, you were in the house when I arrived, weren't you?"

"Interesting theory," Hastings answered. "But ridiculous, and a desperate attempt to deflect blame."

"Yeah, it is interesting," Archer continued. "I wondered 'Why now?' But the answer to that was right in front of me all along. Vice Presidential candidates have got to be thoroughly vetted even before their name is floated to the press—you go through a background check that would make Langley's close-up look like child's play. Of course, you passed with flying colors. As the youngest four star general in the history of our country, you're like a Boy Scout. That law firm you told everyone you were being hired onto? It was the same big lie you told everyone just to get them to be a good reference for you. But even those lawyers and investigators couldn't find any dirty laundry on you, could they?" Archer paused, and listened to Hastings' breathing on the other end of the line. "Still, you knew there was only one person who could ever come out of the woodwork to spoil it all. Well, here I am. Just a little late to the party."

"Turn yourself in, Archer." Hastings repeated in agitation.

"Now, I'm sure you've realized by now that your DNA is still on file with the Department of Defense's DNA Registry. And while you were attacking Becky, we both know she got a large piece of you. Only a fragment needs to be tested to prove you murdered her in cold blood. How you've avoided that all these years, I just don't know. ...Actually, on second thought, I do know. Those stars you wore? They helped. And now you're soon to be the Vice President. A big fish, yessir. But get ready, General—because when we're done you're gonna be no bigger than a minnow in the grass outside of a fishin' pond, with flies running across your eyeballs."

"Archer, I'm telling you, your days are numbered," Hastings hissed. "Your biggest mistake was escaping from Omar Shah. It would've saved you from all of this, you know. Shah was more than happy to execute you, and you would've died a hero. I had your nomination for the Medal of Honor ready to submit. Instead, you'll die in disgrace, as a wife killer."

Archer heard the line disconnect.

It took a moment for Hastings' comment to fully sink in; and when it did, it sparked a level of fury Archer hadn't experienced in years. The effort to eliminate Archer as a potential witness had *not*, in fact, just begun—it had been in progress for years.

Zachary Hastings had personally orchestrated his capture by Omar Shah more than a decade ago.

Chapter 40

LUKE ARCHER'S WORLD SEEMED to spin around him. He held his head with both hands in an attempt to make everything stand still, even for a moment...just to make sense of it all. Then he checked his phone to see that he'd recorded the whole conversation. Seeing the "save" function still spooling, he watched and waited until it stopped and then turned off the phone.

"Not the conversation you were hoping for?"

Archer looked behind him, and he saw Laura Chicone sitting in a wheelchair. Her voice was still hoarse, and she appeared weak, but the color in her complexion had returned.

Archer stood abruptly and moved to her side, placing his hand on her shoulder. "No, actually, it's the conversation I just captured," he said dismissively. "Now why are you out here? You should be resting!"

Laura shook her head and smiled. "I'm fine," she insisted, her voice hoarse. "The question is, how are *you*?"

"I think I just lost control of my conversation with Zachary Hastings," Archer replied.

"I doubt that."

"I should've anticipated Hastings' response," Archer answered.

"It's just a telephone call."

Archer shook his head slowly. "No, I meant I should have known what he was up to a long time ago. All the signs were there, and I ignored them."

"Signs?" Laura asked, coughing. "What signs?"

Archer reviewed all of the evidence he'd uncovered that led him to the conclusion that Hastings had, in fact, murdered his wife. Laura listened intently to Archer go on to describe his new belief that Hastings had been responsible for his capture, imprisonment and torture by Omar Shah.

"Hastings was the J3 running the Special Reconnaissance Mission targeting Shah. He knew I was OPCON to Langley, and convinced the Director of Central Intelligence to request me—by name—to conduct

191

the mission without any U.S. support on the ground. It was all scripted out from the very beginning."

"But you escaped," Laura replied calmly.

Archer nodded. "Yeah, that obviously wasn't supposed to happen."

"Are you saying—?"

"Omar Shah's assassination was directed in order to see me removed and so to cover up Hastings' involvement in my wife's murder," Archer said, finishing her thought.

"Well, we were all very well played, weren't we?"

"Obviously. It's why he wants me out of the picture so badly now," Archer continued. "I'm the only one who's in a position to identify him as Becky's murderer, and keep him from becoming Vice President."

"And POTUS," Laura said, pulling her iPhone out of her bathrobe pocket, and setting it on the table. She flipped the phone on with her thumb, and pushed the icon for the Voice Memos app. Locating the last voice memo she recorded, she pressed *Play*. At first, Archer only heard the sound of footsteps, Laura's voice, and then a voice he immediately recognized as Chris Stockman's:

> *"Chris! I didn't know you also lived in the Watergate."*
> *"I don't, Laura."*
> *"Why are you here?"*
> ....
> *"...You're a coward and a traitor. Nothing less."*
> *"We're patriots who want to see our country win, and this is a revolution from within. While both political parties run our nation into the ground, we're righting the ship, beneath the decks. And we're almost there."*
> *"How can you possibly believe that?"*
> *"You don't get it, do you? For a brief moment, I thought you knew much more than you do! When Zachary Hastings is President, that's when we'll be able to make a real difference. It's a shame, you know. I had such hopes*

for you."

"Hastings is the Vice President-Elect...Oh my God...you're planning on assassinating the President, aren't you?"

"We're past that, fortunately. He's very ill right now, and not expected to make it much past his inauguration."

"So who's the real poisoner here? Why are you doing this?"

Kennedy once said that 'Those who make peaceful revolution impossible, make violent revolution inevitable.' That's where we are today.

"When all's said and done, I'll be the DCI under Hastings."

You've always been a bureaucrat, Chris. And you'll die a nameless, disgraced bureaucrat."

"I'm sorry, Laura. I really am..."

Archer heard the distinct sound of two gunshots echo on the recording, followed by a crashing sound, and the fading sound of footsteps.

"He won't be causing you any more problems," Archer said.

"MmmHmm, I heard," Laura said. "I also heard someone launched a missile from the Potomac into his kitchen window. Any ideas who might have done that?"

"No idea."

"Quite a statement. But hardly a proportional response."

"Proportionality has never been my strong suit."

"Dan Thorne's dead," Laura announced abruptly. "His organs just stopped working."

Archer nodded, but didn't respond.

"Did we have anything to do with that?"

Laura asked, peering thoughtfully at him.

Archer looked over at Laura without answering.

Laura shook her head, and wiped away a tear.

"Are we God? Because it sure seems we've been playing him lately."

"He killed John," Archer answered simply.

"He also had a family," Laura replied emotionally.

"We're not on an even playin' field, if you haven't noticed. This is the only way to fight back." Archer said, and paused for a moment.

"When they come after my friends, they make that choice. Not me."

"Revenge, rivalry, hatred" Laura sighed. "Such a basic impulses. Unsophisticated. Not really interesting, and they don't make us any better than them."

"Alternatives? Archer asked. "Do you have any?"

Laura shrugged. "Forgiveness...connection...empathy. Far more complex and harder to come by. Harder in practice, too." After a long silence, she looked over at Archer. "Okay. How do we go about stopping a presidential assassination when they'll insist it's us who's behind it?"

"I have a few ideas," Archer said. "Can you play that for me again?"

As he walked on a deserted National Mall, Archer re-played Laura's recording of her confrontation with Chris Stockman. The recording was clear, and the conversational exchange between Laura and Chris Stockman belied the now foregone conclusion.

Stockman's response, when Laura realized they planned to assassinate the President-Elect, was what caught Archer's attention: *"We're past that, unfortunately. Kennedy once said that 'Those who make peaceful revolution impossible, make violent revolution inevitable.' That's where we are today...."*

What did he mean exactly when he told her, *"We're past that...""*?

The only logical explanation for his comment was that the President-Elect's assassination was either already underway, or had already occurred—albeit with a delayed result.

"Those who make peaceful revolution impossible, make violent

194

revolution inevitable.' That's where we are today....''

If there was any direct statement about the ultimate objectives of the SU organization, violent revolution from within appeared to be their goal. He backed the recording up, and played it again:

"That's where we are today...."

Looking up, Archer realized he was standing in front of the Lincoln Memorial. He climbed the granite stairs, and saw the statue of a stoic and wise President bathed in light directly in front of him. Turning around, in a direct line down the Mall, he saw the Washington Monument, and behind it, the dome of the United States Capitol.

With a presidential assassination apparently now in progress, Archer searched his contacts for Jim Swanson, the Director of the United States Secret Service.

Chapter 41

"LUKE ARCHER?" JIM SWANSON exclaimed. "Is that you?"

"It's me," Archer answered. "Sorry to call you so late."

"Quite alright," Swanson replied. "You know there's an outstanding Federal warrant out for you?"

"I'm aware," Archer said. "But anyone with any common sense can see it's bogus."

"Regardless—" Swanson stopped himself.

"It's been fourteen or fifteen years since I came to you with Omar Shah's threat against the president. You corroborated it and were able to intercept the cell in New York" Archer reminded him. "What I have to tell you now is far more dangerous and wide-reaching." He paused. "And I didn't kill my wife."

Swanson exhaled. "Alright, what can I do for you?"

"We need to meet," Archer said. "No one else. Just you and me."

Swanson didn't immediately answer. "Archer, you know I—"

"I wouldn't be calling you if it wasn't important, Jim." Archer interjected. "You know that."

"I do know that," Swanson said. "Okay. Where? When?"

"At the Ulysses S. Grant Memorial, in front of the Capitol," Archer replied, and checked his watch. "Midnight."

Luke Archer watched the tall silhouette of a man turn the corner of the monument. Recognizing him, he stepped out of the shadows.

"It's my favorite monument, for a lot of reasons," Archer said quietly, only loud enough for Swanson to hear him.

"Funny," Jim Swanson said. "All these years, and I've never paid much attention to it."

"At the time, it was the largest ever commissioned by Congress," Archer explained. "It was started in 1902. The sculptor was Henry Shrady. He spent twenty years of his life working on it, and then died stressed and overworked, two weeks before it was dedicated in 1922."

"Well, *there's* a lesson for all of us," Swanson replied with a tinge of sarcasm. "It's late. And unless I'm arresting you, I shouldn't even be here right now."

"You wouldn't be here right now if you also didn't know something very wrong was happening inside our government," Archer replied.

"I've never been one for conspiracy theories. So, unless you have facts to back it up, it's just paranoia." Swanson replied. "Nothing more."

"I think you know me better than that," Archer said, motioning for them to sit at an adjacent park bench.

Swanson exhaled deeply, sat down, and looked at Archer. "Alright, I'm listening."

"You heard about Laura Chicone being shot a few days ago at the Watergate?"

"Didn't she get transferred from the GW Hospital?"

Archer nodded. "We pulled her out before they could get to her. She's recovering."

"Let me guess—" Swanson interjected. "At an undisclosed location."

Archer nodded. "Something like that. Yeah. Chris Stockman was the one who shot her."

"Why are you assuming someone was trying to kill her in the hospital?"

"The two-man kill team in the hospital was a prime indicator for starters, and it's even more revealing that you don't know about it." Archer pulled out his iPhone, gave Swanson his earphones, and played Laura's recording.

"That's Chris Stockman?" Swanson exclaimed disbelievingly. "He was the one killed in Old Town with an anti-tank missile, wasn't he?"

"Yep."

"Were you responsible for that?" Swanson asked.

Archer pointed up at the statue of Ulysses S. Grant above them. "You know, this is exactly how his Soldiers would describe Grant as he would observe a battlefield. Shiloh, Vicksburg, Chattanooga or Appomattox—it didn't matter—he'd sit there on his Kentucky thoroughbred completely motionless while the battle raged in front of him—without a sword, shoulders low, wearing a wide-brimmed hat low over his head. The Confederates who saw him in the distance described him as the "Angel of Death."

Archer pointed to Grant's right. "And you see, over here is the Cavalry—seven horsemen stampeding onto the battlefield, about to crush a fallen Soldier who's one of their own." He pointed to the left. "Over there, are Artillery Soldiers trying to get a cannon in position. But the lead horse rears up with a broken bridle, causing the rest of the team to lunge and twist. Everyone else is in motion. Grant just sits there and observes."

Archer continued as Swanson looked over at him.

"What this is meant to show us is how individual Soldiers sacrifice for a noble purpose, as they fight for their country. I heard some congressmen and senators advocating for this statue to be torn down, because they say it glorifies war." Archer stopped and looked directly at Swanson, abruptly changing the subject. "Stockman deserved that and much more after what he did. You heard the last part of the conversation before he shot Laura. That's why I'm here—to help you stop Zack Hastings and the rest of his organization from killing our next President."

"Can you send that recording to me?" Swanson asked.

Archer touched a few buttons on his iPhone and watched the recording send via SMS to Swanson's Blackberry. "Okay. You have it."

"I have heard some things from my guys assigned to both William Stone and Zachary Hastings," Swanson admitted. "But it's all hearsay, so I haven't paid much attention to it."

"Like what?"

"President-Elect Stone has had doctors coming in and out of his mansion in New York far more often than what any of us would regard as normal. He's been complaining of muscle weakness, and it looks like his hair is thinning out, so they've cut his travel schedule down quite a bit so he can be at full strength at next week's inauguration."

"I think they're poisoning him, Jim," Archer said.

"Poisoning?" Swanson asked skeptically. "How? What makes you think that?"

"Because they've done it once already, to one of my friends who stumbled on to their operation in the North Carolina mountains. Several weeks later, he was dead. Have his doctors check for Polonium. It's hard to come by, but as an assassin's tool, it's perfect—unless you're looking for it, you'll never detect it, and if anything you'll confuse it for something else, like rat poison."

"It's starting to make sense now," Swanson commented.

"What do you mean?"

"Today, the President-Elect came to the White House and the moment he stepped in the West Wing doorway with his team, the alpha radiation detectors went off full blast. It was pretty embarrassing. We thought the system was malfunctioning because the normal detectors didn't go off at all. Obviously, that wasn't the case."

"Normal radiation detectors can't detect Polonium. My guess is that he's being given very low doses—probably topical at this point. On his clothing, or in his bed. But once he ingests it, even a few micrograms will be fatal for him."

"Jesus Christ…" Swanson exclaimed. "This is insane."

"What's your detail covering Hastings had to say?"

"Not much," Swanson shrugged. "Some old German guy asked him a question at the Waldorf Astoria up in New York yesterday, and he absolutely flipped out off-stage, screaming at our guys over and over to go after the German and arrest him…."

The phone rang, and Archer jumped from a deep sleep, expecting a call back from Jim Swanson. But it wasn't Swanson. It was Elena Campbell's voice on the other end.

"Was that you in New York, harassing Zachary Hastings?" she asked, slightly amused. "It's all over the news."

"May be better for you not to know," Archer replied with a wry tone, regaining his senses. "But whoever did it, I'm sure it was worth it for 'em."

"Nice disguise."

"Bold never gets old," Archer replied, looking down at his "Old Bay" coffee cup, with the same motto.

"My Dad was an Army helicopter pilot in Vietnam," Elena replied. "He used to tell me, 'There are *old* pilots, and there are *bold* pilots, but there are no *old, bold* pilots. When do we get to see you again?"

"I'm not sure hanging out with me is a good idea for you," Archer said abruptly.

There was a prolonged silence on the other end. "What exactly are you telling me?"

"Obviously you've seen the news," Archer replied. "I'm hotter than a burning stump right now, and they could easily come after you just to get to me."

"I've got Beau right here," Elena said reassuringly. "I'll be just fine."

"You've got a lot of stars in your crown," Archer said. "You know that?"

"I just believe in you, Luke Archer," Elena answered. "And your friends."

"We should hang up for now," Archer warned. "They're doin' their level best to track me."

Chapter 42

LUKE ARCHER HAD MET Congressman Daniel "Danno" Tory while both Archer and Robin were working for the CIA. At the outset of Robin's career, she had been assigned a deep cover role in Moscow based on her fluency in both Russian and Lithuanian. Together with Daniel Tory, they had almost single-handedly prevented a Russian invasion of the Baltic States as he was just beginning his Congressional career.

Although Robin did not work directly for Archer at the time, he had been her mentor throughout her time in the Agency, and had steadfastly supported her when political forces were rallying against both her and Congressman Tory. After Russian FSB-contracted assassins had killed the Tory Foundation leadership in Switzerland, Daniel and Robin made a deliberate decision to pursue the killers and preempt the Kremlin's plans to invade the Baltic States of Lithuania, Latvia and Estonia. In so doing, they also made a deliberate decision to ignore White House directives to cease what was referred to as "unmitigated interference in the President's constitutional authority to conduct the international affairs of the United States."

Upon their return to the United States, Congressman Tory was accused of violating the Logan Act of 1799—Conducting Foreign Relations Without Authority. However, during a set of Congressional hearings, and fully assisted by expert counsel who reminded Congress that "in the history of the United States, there had never been a prosecution under the Logan Act," both he and Robin were credited by the mass media for stopping the planned Russian invasion of the Baltics and, in the process, saving the NATO alliance.

With Robin's cover compromised as a result of that operation, she submitted her resignation from the CIA, and married Danno Tory.

As Congressman Tory's wife, Robin took over as the Executive Director of the Tory Foundation. The philanthropic activities of the Tory Foundation were well documented. Its focus was both broad and global, ranging from promoting open and ethical government, fair and competitive elections, and independent judiciaries, to high quality journalism, government institutions and practices that were accountable to the people.

Privately, Robin also led the intelligence arm of the Tory Foundation that informed all of their public efforts to support democracy around the world.

"I don't get over here as often as I'd like," Danno Tory said, shutting the door of the conference room behind him.

Archer stood up and shook hands with Danno, who brought him into a quick, but warm embrace. "It's good to see you, Congressman."

"Call me Danno," he insisted, shaking his head. "I've never been into titles. You know that."

Archer nodded. "It's been too long. Thank you and Robin for all you've done for us."

"It's not what we've done for you," Danno said, sitting down beside Archer at the long table. "It's what you're doing for all of *us*. I also appreciate you supporting Robin after our experience in the Baltics. If we hadn't known you so well, we likely wouldn't be here."

"Thanks," Archer replied. "A lot of folks would've thrown us to the wolves."

"Behind this veil of secrecy, and all of the attacks, it's clear to both Robin and me that our Republic is under siege," Danno said. "While no one wants to admit it, let alone prove it, you've finally begun to blow the lid off of it."

"And we've experienced absolute proof of what happens when you actively oppose them."

"The ground is shifting beneath our feet—the attacks on the Supreme Court justices and the massacre at the Naval Academy are clear indicators that they'll stop at nothing to achieve their objectives."

"Zachary Hastings is also involved."

Danno shook his head. "And he was supposed to be the *'New Eisenhower,'* the candidate *'beyond reproach.'* Why am I not surprised?"

"We believe they have a plot underway right now to kill President-Elect Stone.

"And as Vice President, Hastings would take his place," Danno said. "Do you have any proof?"

Archer placed his iPhone on the table and played the full content of Laura's recording.

"Jesus!" Danno exclaimed. "She's lucky to be alive."

Archer nodded.

"Has anyone warned the Secret Service?"

"I met with Jim Swanson last night," Archer said. "He seems to get it."

"Can you trust him?"

Archer nodded. "I've known Jim a long time. I think so. But the Secret Service and individual members of it can be corrupted or compromised as easily as with any other department or agency."

"What can I do to help you?" Danno asked.

"You already are." Archer pointed to the massive, glowing screens in the operations center beyond the glass walls of the conference room. "But I'd like to have our team provide you and your folks with their analysis. It'll give you an idea of what we're up against."

Archer sat to the right of Daniel Tory, and started the informal presentation. "Congressman, "If we're going to stop SU, we have to know what they are, what they want, and have a basic understanding of their strategy." Archer began. All three screens began flashing images of newspaper clippings and video footage of the Supreme Court assassination attempts, the killing of Sam Owen, and the Naval Academy massacre as background. "This organization is well-established, their reach is wide and deep, and their capabilities are formidable."

Photos of the Cold Mountain Nuclear Waste Repository and John Lee followed. "We believe they're currently funded through sole-sourced government contracting of nuclear power generation and waste storage, high-level hacking and phishing schemes, and they're now finalizing an import-export mechanism for nuclear power that will provide billions in revenue."

"In short," Archer continued, flipping to a sketch depicting four black and white columns, and a single red column in the center background, "We believe SU represents a 'Fifth Column' organization established within our government that aims to conduct a silent coup, and control the United States from within."

Danno interrupted. "That term, *'Fifth Column,'* it was used quite a bit in the 1930s during the Spanish Civil War as the Republicans, Communists, Socialists and Fascists were fighting for control of the government of Spain. Back then, the Fifth Column was considered a group of guerrillas, activists...and intellectuals who were trying to undermine a nation either in the open, or clandestinely," he said. "Is that what we have here? Or is this something different?"

"It's a similar concept, but it's not socialist or fascist, as near as we can tell. Nor is it Republican or Democrat, Liberal or Conservative. SU is a broad-spectrum threat, with people motivated primarily by power and money, rather than any specific ideology."

"Think Bernie Madoff, with bombing authority," Max interjected.

Archer pointed up at a hand-written slide, with photos beside each name. "What we're going to look at now is the team's best cut at anticipating SUs most likely organization and course of action –they're most likely is also their most dangerous."

Confirmed SU Members
Zachary Hastings (VPOTUS-E)
Dr. Robert Craine (Registered Democrat/significant democratic donor)
Senator Horace Bend (R, NC)
Congressman Ted McCormick (R, WY)
Governor Mike McKaren (D, PA)
Dr. John Langdon (registered democrat/IRS Commissioner)
Governor Peter Preston (R, VA)
Howard Holcroft (Federal Reserve Vice Chairman)
OMB Director Jack Bernan
Christopher Stockman (Independent) - Deceased CIA
Dan Thorne - Deceased CIA
Bethany Baxter, Attorney General Designee

Jacqueline Forrester, Secretary of Energy

"These are just the SU members we've been able to identify—they're the proverbial 'Tip of the Iceberg'," Archer said, transitioning to the next slide entitled, "Suspected SU Members," with more than 25 additional names across government and industry. "Here are others we have good reason to believe are on the SU rolls."

"*Christ!*" Danno exclaimed, under his breath. After a moment, he turned to Archer. "I know many of them—honestly, I'd never have guessed."

Archer nodded. "There are more. Likely many more, based on suspect financial holdings and transactions over the past six months that we've been able to trace, as well as email and telephonic communications we've intercepted during the last few days. The one thing we seem to have in our favor is that the leaders appear to be independent actors who have prominent positions within US Government departments and agencies, and there are probably hundreds of underlings that support them. They order, coordinate and conduct operations in loose, ad-hoc organizations, but it's not an interagency-run operation. So orders and instructions travel slowly down the chain. Likewise, actions or reactions from the field travel slowly up the chain as well."

Danno reviewed the slide silently, checked an app on his iPhone and then turned to Archer. "The Congressmen on this list may come from different parties, but they all have one thing in common," he said, showing them the Congressional Voting Record. "They all voted to export the construction of V-Tec nuclear power plants to Bahrain, Oman and Kuwait."

Archer nodded. "If we can get a list of the others who voted "YES," that may help give us a better window into SU's membership."

"At least on the Congressional side of things." Danno touched "SEND" on the iPhone's app. "You have it. Also, get a list of everyone who's on Hastings' transition team—they're all card carrying members, no doubt."

Shen stood. "The best way an organization can assume control of a country with a democratic form of government is to take actions

205

that are imperceptible, and appear to be Constitutionally-based. Gaining control over the key posts of government surreptitiously, not showing their true colors until it is too late to stop them—— the leadership of Congress, the Supreme Court, ultimately even the Presidency, and as many of the States as they can draw in with Governorships potentially creates an adequate foundation to gain control of the government and the nation."

"Suborning and redefining the rule of law to favor their perspective has to be part of that foundation," Danno observed, his brows quirked in interest.

"In this case, that's exactly what they've managed to do, from the top down," Shen answered. "By taking control of the government's enforcement mechanisms: the Attorney General, the FBI, IRS, and CFPB among others, a group can ultimately have complete freedom of maneuver, and be able to act with impunity. We've seen that the IRS has the full ability to stonewall Congress if it chooses."

"It's a smart strategy," Danno said. He invited the team to sit and walked around the circular bench below the LCD screens. "From the looks of it, it's a fairly phased operation. We believe Putin used some of the same methods, equally as deftly, to consolidate his power in Russia and to take over parts of the former Soviet Union when he felt the need," Danno explained. "Take over industrial capability to fund your plan, then gain control of all elements of national power, instill fear—and then enter the scene like the proverbial white knight reestablishing law and order in the midst of chaos, so you can gain the trust of the people...."

"All while inciting more violence," Archer added.

"Exactly," Danno replied. "They're not too far from their goal, and we don't yet know the full extent of their network." He paused and pointed up at the slide. "You mentioned it here. If they're going to have any hope of controlling dissent, a major target for them will be print and broadcast media."

"They've already killed Sam Owen," Archer said. "Right in front of me. They won't hesitate to kill more."

Danno nodded. "I can't overstate the importance of what each of you are doing." Gesturing to the LCD screens above, he continued. "You know, in 1933, a wealthy group of industrialists and bankers, including Prescott Bush—President George H.W. Bush's father, and George W. Bush's grandfather—were implicated in an attempt to overthrow the entire United States Government and implement Adolf Hitler's policies in a grand plan to overcome the Great Depression. Bush was joined by other big names—Heinz, Colgate and General Motors. They called themselves the 'American Liberty League.' They asked a Marine two-star General—at the time, the highest rank in the Marine Corps, to command a 500,000 man rogue army of veterans in a coup to remove FDR from office. The Marine General's name was Smedley Butler, who was also the most decorated Marine in U.S. history at the time. Butler played along with them to determine who was involved, and then reported their plan in testimony to Congress."

"What happened to them?" Laura asked, from the back of the room—having slipped in unnoticed during the middle of the briefing, wearing hospital pajamas.

Danno shook his head. "Congress refused to question any of the plotters and General Butler's testimony was omitted from the record. The media blackballed the story."

"They were all in on it," Archer said.

Danno nodded. "It's a lesson for all of us. First identify everyone involved in this conspiracy, then let the hammer down on the entire damned lot of 'em at the same time."

"Just as important," Archer said, "we need to identify whom we can trust. Right now, all I've got are a motley crew of émigrés from Israel, Taiwan, and Norway. Today, they wouldn't be allowed in the country!"

The entire team laughed.

"If you have to know, we're here because Colonel Archer asked us to be here," Dag announced.

"Yeah, I'm not sure what that'll buy you," Archer smiled. "But I'm grateful."

"We're also here because we're afraid of what will happen to our countries without the United States leading the way as a true democratic republic, If you can't survive, ours can't either…," Dag finished.

Danno smiled, stood, and faced all members of the assembled group. "If it's any consolation or comfort, know that attempts at revolution throughout our history have all ended badly for the revolutionaries." He checked his watch. "The House is holding a late night budget vote that could shut down the government, so I've gotta go," he explained. "Let me know how I can help you."

Archer stopped him as he began to walk away. "Congressman, there is one more thing you can do for us."

Danno turned to Archer expectantly.

"Be careful, and lean on us," Archer said, simply. "You and Robin—we need you both. Without honest people at the helm, nothing we do will make any difference."

Chapter 43

LUKE ARCHER LANDED IN New Hampshire, and drove to the isolated campsite that now represented his only respite from all the chaos. He missed his cabin in Camden, he missed Beau, and Elena—the two steadying influences he had remaining in his life. And yet, increasingly, he began to view every other place external to White Mountain National Forest as "the outside world." This had always been a sort of cocoon for him, and it was even moreso now.

Sitting in his Airstream with a fresh brew of French Press, the heat of the coffee warmed Archer's hands through the ceramic cup. He opened the thick legal-sized envelope, he'd picked up at his P.O. Box along the way in to the State Park. A yellow sticky with Sandy Wilkes's handwriting was attached to the clipped reports:

> Here's a copy of the police report, and the lab results from the crime scene. I've highlighted some of the more notable conclusions. Call me to discuss. Sandy

Archer paged through the multitude of reports—Bloodstain Pattern Analysis, Forensic Biology, Body Fluid Identification, DNA Interpretation, Fibers Analysis, Toolmarks Identification—many others, with complex charts, forensic medical analysis, and technical terminology like *Peak Height Ratio, Stochastic Threshold, DNA-STR profile, Random Match Probability...*terms he didn't fully understand.

He stopped at the report entitled "Body Fluid Identification," and studied the section Sandy had highlighted in yellow.

Victim U4127A

Item	**Fluid**	**Conclusion**

Item 1 - Four swabs with 100μl of semen

Blood:	Negative
Semen:	Positive/ Indicative
Saliva:	Negative
Other	

Archer distinctly remembered that he'd returned from a week-long classified mission in Africa the previous day, and Becky complained of feeling ill. For that reason, he recalled, they had not had intercourse at any time prior to her murder—that fact was confirmed in a separately highlighted section of the report that asked:

> Based on results obtained from DNA analysis, could the Suspect (Luke Archer) be a contributor to the questioned stains (Item 1 & 2)?
> ### Participant UA (Luke Archer/Suspect)
>
> Item 1: **No**
> Item 2: **No**

Although the lab result alone was exculpatory, it meant much more to Archer, and he wondered why he hadn't seen it until now. Sandy did not ask the question outright, she didn't need to—the conclusion that was left to draw was obvious:

Becky's murderer had also raped her....

The Bloodstain Pattern Analysis reported *Angle of Impact Determination* and *Pattern Descriptions* that included *Cast-off Pattern*, *Impact Pattern* and *Drip Pattern* for each bloodstain on the walls and floor of their Fort Campbell, Kentucky home. In one of the photographs, marked "Crime Scene," a yellow number had been placed by what appeared to be a smaller, narrow sneaker print in the blood on the floor. A white tape on the bottom read:

Unmatched/Inconsistent Shoeprint in Blood at Bedside.
Probable Inadvertent CID Forensics Team Contamination. No action taken. Not advanced.

Archer searched for the transcript of the Coroner's testimony, and re-read his statement at the deposition:

> **Defense (Wilkes):** *What you are saying then, Doctor, is that it is your opinion that the killer in this case was left handed?*
> **Coroner:** *Yes. That is my opinion, based on the wounds and the bloodstain pattern analysis conducted at the crime scene….*

In the report entitled "DNA Interpretation," Sandra Wilkes had highlighted the concluding question and answer:

> **Based on the examination of the DNA profiles, could the Victim (Item 1) and/or the Suspect (Item 2) be included as a possible contributor to the bloodstained tile (Item 3) and sink (Item 4) in the bathroom of the residence in question?**
>
>> According to the interpretation guidelines implemented in our laboratory, and according to Y-STR typing result, *neither* the victim (Item 1) or the suspect (Item 2) are possible DNA contributors attributed to Item 3 and 4.

Archer picked up his iPhone and pressed his speed dial for Sandra Wilkes. After a few rings, he heard her voice, slightly out of breath.

"I received the police report and lab results," Archer said without preamble. "Thanks."

"Just a second, Archer. You caught me on a run," Wilkes answered. "You read the parts I highlighted?"

"I did," Archer replied. "Do they mean what I think they mean?"

"Well, it means I can clear you once and for all, remotely, without you being present," Wilkes said.

"It also means Hastings raped Becky," Archer said. "Why wasn't I ever told?"

"There's a lot we weren't told," Wilkes replied. "Army CID deliberately covered this up, the question is *why?*"

"Well the answer to that is obvious," Archer said. "Colonel *Promotable* Zachary Hastings had his hands in the investigation throughout. People were scared to death of him. Everyone knew he was going to wear four stars someday."

"There's something else that was covered up...."

"What else?" Archer asked.

"I'm so sorry to have to tell you—I didn't know until I read the full autopsy report," Wilkes said, hesitating.

"What is it?" Archer insisted.

"Luke, Becky was pregnant...one month."

Chapter 44

LUKE ARCHER SAT IN BED, stomach clenched, lacking the will to rise. The bottle of Woodford Reserve shattered against the bedroom wall of the Airstream, placing a large dent in the smooth aluminum. His head pounded and his body ached, but he could not sleep.

The trailer reeked of alcohol.

He knew that in his state of sheer exhaustion, and in the wake of Sandy Wilkes's discovery, he was not thinking clearly. But he no longer gave a damn. His thoughts returned unwillingly to that evening, and even if he couldn't fathom it being any worse, for the first time he now realized the full extent of what had been taken from him.

Not only had Zachary Hastings murdered his wife, he'd also raped her—and he'd taken his unborn child away from them....

Locked in a state of rage and indignant rebuttal, Archer knew that of all the emotions across the full spectrum that were available to him, apathy was the most dangerous—but he didn't give a damn about that either. No matter what he did to move on with his life, to get himself back on track, it seemed like Zack Hastings had him on a long leash and would only allow him go so far before reeling him back in.

Elena Campbell seemed like the one person who understood him, outwardly, if not intuitively. Archer was grateful for her friendship, and since meeting her, he'd allowed himself to go as far as he'd ever gone in a relationship after Becky's passing. There was no rush for either of them. Nothing was forced, and everything was mutual. She still had no real appreciation of his tormented past...or at least its full extent, and he was painfully aware that could well drive her away for good. So he was in no hurry for her to learn of it.

But after his conversation with Sandy, assisted by too many glasses of bourbon, the indifference he thought he'd purged had returned. With a vengeance.

A dense fog, complete with a blanket of snow, had settled in throughout New England, extending up through Maine. Archer opened the trailer's door into the cloud enveloping it. The air was heavy with further impending snowfall.

He hadn't changed his clothes since he'd arrived, and the trailer now reeked of his own unwashed scent, as well as Kentuckey Bourbon.

FOX News blared on the TV set, with constant coverage on the transition of Presidential administrations, and the countdown to Inauguration Day—now only five days to go.

Seeing Vice President-Elect Zachary Hastings and his family smiling and waving at crowds quickly sobered him, and drew him out of his self-imposed depression.

A text from Laura popped into WhatsApp on his iPhone.

```
You Okay?
```

Intuitively, Archer knew that while he was currently in a safe location, away from civilization, he would not be able to do anything of real value unless he was back in Washington.

```
                    Fine here. Need to get
                         back. Plane?

      Low Ceilings from NY to Canada. No
flights for two days.

                              Train?

      Can U get to Boston? Take AMTRAK to
Union Station.

                                   Yes

      Ticket is waiting 4U at station. Use
identity #2.
```

Archer opened the box labeled simply "2," that Dag had given him at the operations center.

Packed inside was a passport, driver's license, and several credit cards, along with a thinly assembled disguise—wire-rimmed glasses, hairpiece, moustache and an Orioles' baseball hat.

Prior to boarding the Acela Express from Boston to Washington, D.C.'s Union Station, Archer stopped at Starbucks and picked up the day's *Washington Post*. Standing in line to purchase a cup of coffee and pay, he read the front-page headline and lead story:

A Nation on Edge as Stone Presidency Nears
By MAUREEN GRIMES JAN. 15

WASHINGTON — President Williamson and President-elect William Stone met today to discuss the upcoming changing of administrations. Both acknowledged the precarious situation facing the United States at home and abroad.

As Mr. Stone's inaugural draws near, the nation remains deeply divided, unsteady and on edge, as targeted violence racks the Capitol and across the country, with an intensity not seen since September 11th, 2001.

Washington and its suburbs are largely populated by political and policy professionals who work for the federal government. As a national capital, Washington remains a vibrant and wealthy economy in its own rite. Recently, however, the stability that has characterized Washington as America's capital and the surrounding region have been shaken to the core by terror attacks directed against three Supreme Court Justices and The United States Naval Academy.

President-Elect Stone and his Vice President-Elect, Zachary Hastings, have both pledged to return stability and economic growth to the country. Meanwhile, Washington is replete with preparations for Georgetown and Kalorama inaugural parties that bely the city's unease.

Archer fell asleep reading the article, momentarily waking during stops along the way—then falling back into deep sleep. Six hours later, the train stopped at Baltimore's Penn Station. As passengers unloaded and more boarded around him, his iPhone suddenly lit up with messages and news alerts.

The train departed and rapidly picked up speed toward Washington, DC.

Even a cursory glance at the headlines revealed the nightmare that was unfolding up and down the East Coast. The first messages were from Laura:

```
WashPost HQs leveled by truck bomb...K St
                       NW, DC is bedlam
          NYT also just hit by truck bomb
                     Coordinated attacks
               ISIS claiming responsibility
                               B Careful
```

Before Archer could open any of the news links reporting on the attacks, he heard an explosion and the deafening screech of steel tearing, as if the conductor had suddenly slammed the brakes. The train seemed to shake and decelerate, skipping upwards and then everything around him tilted to the side in a ghastly slow motion swirl. Archer felt himself suddenly airborne, being thrown violently across the rail car into the bathroom's bulkhead. Everything went black. When he came to, he found himself lying underneath a seat marked for the disabled.

The cacophony seemed to go on for hours, and then, at once, was transformed into still, complete silence. For a moment, he thought he

216

was dead. Then, just as abruptly, panic set in all around him, and strident cries for help and groaning filled the car. Miraculously, Archer was able to stand, but could feel blood dripping down his forehead and face, and into his eyes, obstructing his vision.

Looking around, he could see the lifeless body of the lady who had been sitting opposite him, impaled through the chest by a metal table rod. He stepped over her body, trying to make his way to the door. The car began filling with smoke and fumes. The survivors became more panicked—screaming and shouting. Archer looked around, trying to orient himself—avoiding several hot power cables that were hanging down and sparking ominously around them. After another moment, he realized the car was laying on its side, and the emergency windows were now positioned directly above him.

Archer asked a high school-aged boy to help him find large suitcases and stack them as high as he could manage. All the while, Archer reassured those who were still alive around him, telling them repeatedly, *"Everything will be okay," "We're going to get you out," "Help's on the way!"*

Standing on top of the pile of suitcases, Archer stretched his torso painfully upward, as far as he could reach, to a red emergency handle on one of the windows. He gripped it and pulled the glass forcefully inward. Encouraging the survivors, he and the boy boosted the injured passengers out of the emergency window one by one. Archer asked each of them for their name, and when an elderly lady asked him for his name, he told her simply that he was "Luke," and not to worry—everyone was going to get off the train, and be just fine.

Inhaling and exhaling like a winded horse, moving painfully with every breath, Archer asked the boy to help those survivors outside the train until help arrived. Meanwhile, he continued to go back inside the train with a cloth over his mouth to avoid inhaling more smoke, and remove those passengers who were still alive. Miraculously, he found his iPhone—the screen somewhat shattered, but functional— in the vicinity of the bulkhead he'd been thrown into during the derailment.

Baltimore firemen arrived *en masse*, and immediately began cutting steel, breaking through the top of the train in multiple spots on each car, and peeling the steel effortlessly back as if they were opening a tin can. Archer directed the firemen to the areas inside the cars where he knew survivors had concentrated in order to escape the billowing smoke.

As soon as Archer saw the police arrive, and satisfied that the firemen were in a far better position to help, he withdrew inconspicuously from the scene and disappeared into the nearby tangle of woods.

Chapter 45

"I NEED SOMEONE TO PICK ME up at the BWI-Amtrak station," Archer said through the damaged iPhone to Shen. "My train just derailed about two miles from here."

"We're already in your area—the minute we heard about the wreck, we left to try and find you," Shen said through a wave of static. "Are you okay?"

"Been better," Archer replied roughly. "If you can, bring me a change of clothes. The ones I have on are a mess."

"Archer, I haven't seen anything like this since 9-11," Shen said. "The attacks in DC, New York, the AMTRAK train....the whole world's exploding...."

"Look, folks are starting to stare. I'll meet you in parking garage number 2, top deck. And I need a new iPhone…"

Enroute to Tysons Corner, Archer changed clothes in the back seat of the Land Rover, while Shen and Max briefed him on the chaos that was engulfing the nation only a few days in advance of the inauguration. Shen handed him a new iPhone 8, already encased in a Mophie charging case.

"I cloned your sim card. Turn off your old phone and give it to me. Both the Washington Post and New York Times' Headquarters were hit by coordinated attacks five minutes apart," Shen said. "More than a thousand dead, and several thousand other casualties. Hospitals are full. Roads are closed in DC and New York City. I'm surprised you were able to reach us on your cell phone."

"The Acela's derailment came a minute after those attacks," Archer said in a hoarse, deep voice. "None of this was a coincidence— the Acela doesn't just randomly jump its tracks. And I don't think it had anything to do with ISIS."

Archer's iPhone vibrated, and he saw a text from Jim Swanson:

Need 2 CU—
where can we meet?

It was 4:30pm, and they were already on the Baltimore Washington Parkway, approaching the city limits of Washington, D.C. Archer replied:

National Arboretum,
Capitol Columns - 4pm

Sitting on the steps surrounded by the twenty-two Corinthian columns, Archer read the news articles on his iPhone, covering the chaos that was now engulfing the nation.

Archer looked up to see Jim Swanson walking past the reflecting pool, up the steps.

"This is the Arboretum's Ellipse Meadow," Archer said, as Swanson approached. "And these are the original Capitol Columns— the same ones that stood when Abraham Lincoln was sworn in as President."

"The country was in quite a mess then as well."

"Lincoln was an obscure Illinois politician when he won that election," Archer explained. "By all accounts, he wasn't supposed to win. But he defeated three other major-party candidates to become president."

Swanson nodded. "He led the country through its darkest days."

"And here we are."

Sitting down, Swanson saw the large cut on Archer's forehead. "Jesus, you *were* on that train, weren't you?"

Archer nodded, dabbing the still-bleeding wound with his cloth rag. "Yeah. How'd you know?"

"We got a report from the FBI that witnesses saw you on the scene evacuating people from the wreckage, and a helicopter news crew also have footage of you continually going back into the burning railcars. But then you disappeared."

"It was a deliberate attack, wasn't it?"

Swanson nodded. "Looks like whole sections of the tracks were cut by det cord, and judging from the way the train derailed, it was probably command detonated just before the train approached."

"ISIS doesn't have the capability to do that."

"I'd have to agree with you," Swanson said.

"You have an inauguration in a little over 24 hours from now," Archer said, looking at his watch.

Swanson nodded. "We've tried to convince the President-Elect to cancel the public ceremony, given the events of today, but he's refusing to even consider it. Says it would show weakness, and give the terrorists exactly what they want. But between you and me, he doesn't look well, at all. No one's talking about it, but there's growing speculation that he's very sick."

"We've talked about this," Archer said. "The threat's coming from within."

"It's been a pretty tightly held secret that in the aftermath of the several high viz crises that went south, President Williamson set up a voice activated recording system throughout the White House, including in the Oval Office, Cabinet Room, and Vice President's Office. His attorney general told him his cabinet members were saying one thing to him in his presence and then something completely different when he was out of the room, so he bugged the room, and listened to the meetings in private to get the full story so he could make informed decisions."

"By tomorrow, we had intended to disable it in preparation for the Stone Administration's arrival—but the thing is, Stone's senior staff arrived yesterday and have been claiming and occupying their desks and offices as if it were the first day of school." Swanson exhaled. "They've been using the VP's Ceremonial Office as a transition office. I heard some wild accounts of the conversations my guys had overheard, and so I got a copy of the recordings of the conversations between the Vice President-Elect and his folks."

He took several folded sheets of paper and passed them to Archer. "For your reading pleasure."

"Reader's Digest version?" Archer asked.

"A lot of their conversation consists of some kind of internal military code, which is interesting by itself," Swanson said. "But it appears someone's planning a natural gas disaster in north central Texas, in 'The Barnett Shale Fields,' whatever that is."

Archer nodded. "Yeah, it's one of the largest onshore natural gas fields in the country, or in the world for that matter," Archer said, searching on the internet for more information. He laid the iPhone with the Wikipedia page in front of Swanson. "It was one of the pieces of critical infrastructure we trained to protect two decades ago. Timing?"

Swanson shook his head. "Soon. That's all we have."

Archer nodded. "Okay, well, that's helpful."

"But why would they do *that?*" Swanson asked.

Archer shrugged. "I'm not sure, but because money is SU's overwhelming objective, my guess is that it's a subterfuge."

"What kind of subterfuge?"

"The kind where you create a national natural gas crisis of biblical proportions that stirs up tons of long-term political opposition to natural gas as a viable source of energy, and generates support for nuclear power, all so they can sell more of their reactors."

"There's one more thing that will become obvious as you read those transcripts," Swanson added.

"What's that?" Archer asked.

Swanson stood and faced Archer. "Apparently, you're now 'Public Enemy #1' for Vice President-Elect Zachary Hastings."

"Well, then, that's progress," Archer answered.

Chapter 46

LUKE ARCHER SAT IN THE CONFERENCE ROOM of the Tory Foundation Operations Center with Jack Condon, and read the transcript that Jim Swanson had given to him a few hours earlier.

Conversation No. 18-52
Date: 18 January
Time: 4:11 pm - 5:20 pm
Location: Office of the Vice President Elect

The Vice President-Elect met with Jonathan Krogh, Bethany Baxter, Jacqueline Forrester, and Alan Fields.

VPOTUS-ELECT: Say, are you tracking our friend, Archer?

KROGH: We think we may have a bead on him. Our source tells us he's in Boston, about to get on the Acela to DC.

VPOTUS-E: I shouldn't have to remind you how important it is to eliminate him. He's a threat.

KROGH: We're tracking him, and we have a team on the ground to deal with him whether he's here or in Camden.

VPOTUS-E: So what are we doing about it? I shouldn't have to tell you, Archer's a cancer on every plan we've made so far, and he breached our network. Right now, we'd be moving into this administration with a majority of friendly Supreme Court nominations ahead of us - just in time to stack the court to protect our necessary measures. Instead, because of him, we still have goddamned gridlock.

FORRESTER [Unintelligible]

KROGH: Well [unintelligible] that's a temporary problem.

VPOTUS-E: He's managed to kill and remove ten or so of your best men and women. Don't call this fucking temporary. I know him—he won't stop.

FIELDS: Fine, Mr. Vice President.

VPOTUS-E: Okay. Where are we with Barnett Shale?

FORRESTER: Kinda want to be careful what we say around this building.

VPOTUS-E: That reminds me, we're gonna need a whole new security classification to keep all of this to an absolute minimum—TS, with a SPECAT designator only for this group. Do you understand?

FIELDS: Yes, Sir. We have a team heading to Fort Worth. They have a plan to blow the four wells and the storage well they have there. The well alone stores gas carried by pipelines from the Barnett Shale Fields, Louisiana, the Midwest, and the Rocky Mountains.

FORRESTER: Once that's done, they have one of the worst environmental disasters of the century.

KROGH: It'll make the BP oil spill look like child's play.

VPOTUS-E: It needs to look like an accident. Is that clear?

FIELDS: Natural gas won't be seen to be a "cleaner" energy source anymore. This'll show it's as dirty as oil and coal.

FORRESTER: Nothing like the putrid smell of 5,000 metric tons of methane leaking per day to ruin the environment around a city.

VPOTUS-E: And make a lot of people sick. What's our plan to put Humpty Dumpty back together again?

[Laughter]

KROGH: Working on that. We'll pump heavy fluids and drilling mud into the wells to stop the flow of gas. Once it's been stopped, we'll pump cement into the well to permanently seal them. Could take six months.

VPOTUS-E: I want us to be ready. Have a plan, and come to the rescue quickly, but not too quickly. Once it's done, we'll shut them down as a competitor to V-Tec, and Craine can thank us later.

BAXTER: Fine, Mr. Vice President.

"What's this about Fort Worth?" Condon asked.

"They're planning to blow the gas wells there," Archer replied. "It'll make the entire city uninhabitable—and create a global disaster while they're at it. Shen, Dag and Max need to get down there now."

Chapter 47

UNDER THE CLEAR, STARLIT North Texas sky, the black-clad team of eight moved quickly and deliberately, breaching the fence at the southeast corner of Fort Worth's Willard Road. The traffic noise from the Loop 820 Access Road helped to mask their advance over the flattened landscape toward the drill site. In the distance, a 200 foot red and white derrick loomed, fully illuminated by floodlights. Surrounding the tower, massive, articulated 18-wheel service trucks lumbered across the access road in clouds of dust, hauling in more fracking fluid to the containment tanks, and removing wastewater from the containment ponds. As the team drew closer to its target, the acrid scent of exhaust, methane, benzene and toluene became more and more pungent.

On the site, floor hands and engineers of a working crew in white and orange helmets communicated through megaphones over the noise. Assisted by a constant mix of water and chemicals, the crew deployed the massive, articulated drill and its tungsten carbide steel bit deep underground at a 90-degree angle, boring beneath 5,000 residential homes and across 1,700 acres in Fort Worth's Rosedale subdivision. Smashing through tightly bound layers of shale, the bit had reached into the Barnett Field within the last four hours—the largest known reserve of methane in the United States.

The team leader stopped the group and viewed the surrounding landscape through his binoculars. The derrick and surrounding array of condensate tanks, compressor stations, pipelines, and open wastewater pits interrupted the otherwise beautiful backdrop of Lake Arlington in the distance. The team knew that the ground they were walking on was a volatile mix of shale and leaking methane. Even a slight spark underground could ignite the methane in the soil, and be very difficult—if not impossible—to extinguish. Ever—in perpetuity.

The team approached the barbed wire fence some distance away from the work site that contained the target—an operational natural gas wellhead that had been placed into operation two weeks prior. Cutting through the fence, the team climbed the short set of stairs and began dismantling the casing head and "Christmas Tree" of valves at the top of the apparatus. Once the casing head was removed, another operator wearing a welding mask, rubber apron and heavy rubber gloves strung a long line of magnesium ribbon down the shaft of the well. Two other men in welding masks poured premixed 35 lb. tubes of iron oxide, aluminum powder, barium nitrate, sulfur and dextrin down the well shaft, covering the magnesium ribbon.

Max tucked the butt of the custom .308 Larue OBR into her shoulder. Searching the green, ghostly image of her AN/PVS-27, she saw another man approach the wellhead with a cylindrical device that Max recognized as an ALSG814 "Incendiary" Thermite grenade.

"They've poured what looks to be four or five hundred pounds of some kind of powder into the well-head," Max reported through her whisper mike. "I don't know what it is, but it looks like a thermite grenade they're about to throw down the shaft. If we're going to preempt, we need to act now."

When detonated, a thermite grenade produces molten iron and can burn at temperatures up to 4,000 degrees Fahrenheit, and is capable of melting through a truck's engine block in seconds.

Dag was positioned beside Max, and having positioned a set of wind meters and a laser range finding night telescope connected to a small computer, Dag provided Max with regular range and windage readings to the targets they observed at the wellhead to their front. These readings, in turn, were indexed on a small screen in Max's line of vision in her riflescope, reducing the need for verbal communication between spotter and sniper. It was similar to the rig Max had used to eliminate Omar Mehsud Shah.

Shen, observing from a distant location, covering an access road at a proper vantage point, had cleared the area around them for any human, optical or digital surveillance presence.

"We're clear now," he said. "You can engage at will. I'd suggest the guy holding the grenade be first, and then the entire group."

"WILCO," Max said. "Standing by."

Dag adjusted the crosshairs onto the designated target and whispered, "Go."

From her position on the 200 foot tower, Max squeezed the trigger and saw the man carrying the thermite grenade fall to the ground a split second later. Very quickly, guided by information appearing on her scope, she adjusted her aim to the other three men around the wellhead. Max fired in rapid succession, her suppressed weapon making appreciable noise in the dark, but masked by the noise of the complex around them— killing all three. Another man appeared to race toward the wellhead with another thermite grenade, but Max cut him down with a shot to the center of his chest. The other men ran across the flattened earth, devoid of any cover or concealment. Dag precisely reported the location of each. One-by-one, Max engaged and dropped each of them in their tracks.

"8 EKIA," Dag reported to Shen.

"Roger," Shen answered. "Let the law enforcement folks handle the rest. Get out of there *now*."

A short while later, the team intercepted communications from an emergency crew at the wellhead.

"*Good God*...the grenade was only the detonator—they've created a massive improvised thermite bomb in this wellhead. It's filled with rust and aluminum powder. God knows what else—it smells like sulfur," the site foreman reported from the target site.

"If they'd lit this, it would've set the entire Barnett Field on fire and killed thousands of folks, *including us*...."

After several rings, Archer heard Zachary Hastings answer his home phone. "Well, you'll be disappointed to hear that both of your operations failed," Archer said flatly. "Blowing up the Barnett Shale Field in Fort Worth. After all those years we spent protecting it, you thought you could destroy it. Tell you what, I'll give you a 'C' for creativity."

"I don't know what you're talking about, Archer. You're fucking delusional," Hastings said, unable to conceal his anger.

"Delusional?" Archer said. "You have eight dead mercenaries in Fort Worth who are about to be connected to you."

"You're done, Archer," Hastings replied. "Do you understand me?"

"After all that *you've* done," Archer said evenly, "I promise you that the last face you'll see on this Earth will be mine—and that won't be a delusion. It'll be a reality."

Chapter 48

LUKE ARCHER ARRIVED IN New Hampshire via a late private flight, checked his surveillance devices remotely to ensure his camp had not been disturbed, and drove to his Airstream parked in the White Mountain National Forest. Lying on the bed, he flipped the channels of the television mounted on the wall, and stopped when he saw the ABC news anchor reporting with the headline: `"Texas Natural Gas Field Terror Attack Thwarted"`

`ABCNEWS has learned of a major terrorist assault planned on a natural gas field in Fort Worth, Texas.`

`According to FBI sources, a terror attack was planned on a portion of the Barnett Shale Field that contains over 5,000 residential homes in Fort Worth's Rosedale subdivision— the largest natural gas source in the United States.`

`The attack was prevented last night when, according to FBI sources, eight men of Middle Eastern descent were killed as they were about to set the natural gas pipeline on fire.`

`The FBI however, has not released further details of this plot because of its potential to impact on oil and natural gas prices, ABCNEWS has learned.`

`News about the planned attack in Fort Worth came amid heightened fears that ISIS` *agents had successfully infiltrated across the Mexican border, and had plans to target other "softer" targets in the United States.*

Following the incident, all oil and natural gas companies have been placed on a nationwide terror alert.

Natural gas is vital to Texas' economy. More than 450,000 Texans (3.9 percent of the state's workforce) were employed by the oil and natural gas industry. The industry accounts for 15.2 percent of Texas' gross state product.

The Natural Gas operation here in Fort Worth's Rosedale Subdivision represents the first effort to conduct natural gas drilling in a large city area, and if successful, would likely be a model for further residential drilling throughout the United States.

Speaking to reporters in Washington today, Vice President-Elect Zachary Hastings said the intercepted Fort Worth terror plot is an indicator of how well developed the FBI's intelligence capability has become when it comes to intercepting threats on U.S. soil.

"It does appear that our enemy is now among us, and is trying to frighten and kill freedom-loving people. This is a reminder of how dangerous the ISIS threat is to all Americans if we do not act now, proactively and forcefully."

Secretary of Energy Jacqueline Forrester further commented, "This reinforces our belief that fossil fuels like Natural Gas present an enduring danger to communities throughout the nation due to their volatility. We are actively exploring the expansion of nuclear power with enhanced safety measures installed."

"Are you watching this?" Archer said over the phone to Jack Condon. "These guys must think they're Teflon. They execute an attack and then take credit for stopping it when it doesn't work out for 'em."

"We need a good journalist who can see through all of this, and won't run when they find out what they're up against," Jack replied.

"It won't take long before they realize it's a death sentence," Archer said. "They killed Sam Owen, and they just bombed *The Washington Post* and *New York Times*."

"There are still some pretty fearless reporters out there."

"We need smart, honest, *and* fearless."

"Jan Rayburn."

"Excuse me?"

"You may remember her," Jack answered. "The freelance journalist who covered your captivity and escape from Omar Shah, former *60 Minutes* producer, war reporter," Jack said.

Archer remembered the interview he had with Jan Rayburn in the headquarters of 5th Special Forces Group, at Fort Campbell. It seemed so long ago. He remembered her to be fair, incisive and impartial, as much as she was intuitive and engaging. "I remember her. You know her?

"For years. She's a friend, and she's the best there is."

"Would she be willing to risk everything for this?"

"She lives on a lake in Connecticut. Semi-retired. I'll arrange a meeting," Jack said. "One more thing—Congressman Tory asked if he could meet you tomorrow evening at 7:30pm."

"Sure," Archer replied. "Where?"

"At the National Archives Museum," Jack said. "On Constitution

Avenue. Two hours after they close. Enter at the side entrance. They'll be expecting you under the name 'Patrick Janeck'—it's one of the identities the Tory Foundation issued to you. I've arranged for a plane to bring you back tomorrow afternoon."

Chapter 49

LUKE ARCHER APPROACHED THE GATE *through Dumbarton Oaks Park. Once in a location that had sufficient cover and concealment, he climbed over the tall iron fence, and lowered himself to the grounds of the U.S. Naval Observatory.*

Wearing black, and using the shadow of the trees to mask his advance, he moved quickly and soundlessly toward the illuminated house at Number One Observatory Circle. Passing the swimming pool, he walked through the gazebo up to the Veranda. He found the door to the Reception Hall open. To his immediate right, inside the doorway to the Living Room, a Secret Service agent sat, facing away from him on the sofa, reading a magazine. Archer approached him from behind, and swiftly wrapped his arm around the man's neck, clasping his hands and applying upward pressure to his carotid arteries. With the agent's blood flow restricted, he was rendered unconscious in seconds. Disarming the agent and removing his radio, Archer flex-cuffed his ankles and cuffed his wrists behind him, turned him to his side and placed a nasal mask saturated with Halothane over the agent's mouth and nose, ensuring unconsciousness. He placed a pillow under the side of the agent's head to show whomever might find him that the agent had not been a target.

Proceeding to the Reception Hall staircase, Archer ascended to the Master Bedroom and silently entered the large room. Moving slowly and deliberately to the king-sized bed, Archer placed his silenced Browning Hi-Power to the Vice President's chest, and watched Zachary Hastings wake with a start, eyes wide with shock. Hastings' wife shifted in her sleep beside him. For Hastings, there was no doubt who he was staring at in the darkened room.

"This is for Becky...." Archer whispered, staring directly into Hastings' eyes.

Firing a single round into Hastings' chest, Archer retreated from the house and ran across the lawn of the Vice President's Residence. As he moved swiftly through the trees, he looked up to see an infrared security camera pointing down, facing in his direction....

Archer awoke, wide-eyed, but it was the final moment in his dream that provided the revelation that he hadn't yet considered. He reached for his iPhone and speed dialed the number for the operations center. Jack Condon answered.

"Have we gotten anything back from the National DNA Registry on Hastings?"

"Yeah, we did hear back from them," Jack answered. "They have no DNA sample for him."

"They obviously destroyed it," Archer said.

"That'd be my guess."

"Well, I just had another thought," Archer said. "After he killed Becky, he had to escape the scene. There were no surveillance cameras around the housing area at Fort Campbell where we lived—they didn't feel it was warranted for Lieutenant Colonels and Majors, but I'll bet they had it for the Colonels' and Generals' housing area."

"I'll check it out," Jack answered. "If they had cameras there, and if footage is still on hand....all big *'Ifs'*."

Archer thanked him, as Jack continued speaking.

"I got ahold of Jan Rayburn, my journalist friend. She's willing to meet you anywhere, anytime you want."

"Okay," Archer said. "Tomorrow morning at 8:00am, Arlington National Cemetery, Section 7A."

"Your plane will be waiting for you at noon today, with a two hour slide. Same airport," Jack reminded Archer.

"Got it."

"Arch?" Jack asked, as if an afterthought.

"Yeah?"

"I have something else to show you when I see you."

"What is it?"

"I'd rather do it in person, if that's okay."

"Okay, see you tomorrow then."

Jack Condon had always enjoyed spending time on Friday

evenings at the Georgetown Four Seasons' Lounge. Whether he was sitting at the outdoor fire pit or in a leather armchair savoring a Tom Collins, gazing at the Asian frescoes, oil lamps and fixtures suspended from the leather ceilings, the Lounge at Bourbon Steak had always been a place for him to unwind and relax since his days as a Georgetown University undergraduate. It was also a place where he could easily stumble to his home located only a few blocks away—on the intersection of 28th and Dumbarton Streets.

Tonight, he needed the medicinal, low-intensity effects that he knew a few drinks could provide—a release from the total level of corruption he'd only just realized in paging through the volumes of surveillance transcripts, and monitoring the hours of conversations obtained from the listening devices inside V-Tec's headquarters that Shen and Max had just installed. One name kept appearing in all of those conversations, but it was the offshore bank account and the astronomical balance that confirmed his growing suspicions.

Archer should know….soonest.

"And what do we do now, Boss?" He muttered out loud, to himself, almost as a rehearsal for what expected to be a confrontation.

Making up his mind, he reached into his pocket to send a text message, but his phone was not there. In a Tom Collins-induced fog, he struggled to recall where he'd left it...where he'd used it last.

He signaled the bartender, and asked her if she happened to have seen an iPhone. When she replied she hadn't, he elected to pay his tab.

The front doors to the Four Seasons opened wide for him as he stumbled slightly into the frigid cold.

Even in Wintertime, midnights on Friday nights in Georgetown were bustling. By any measure, it was a social epicenter of Washington's nightlife. And even at this hour, Jack was always amazed at how many people were still searching for parking... making their way to the many other restaurants and bars that populated Georgetown's main artery on M Street.

The snowflakes began as light flurries when he was crossing Olive Street. But by the time he'd reached N Street, it was clear that it was a major snowstorm in the making.

He was dimly aware of the footsteps behind him that had softened in the rapidly accumulating snow.

A gust of wind blew him forward slightly, aided by the influence of gin in his system. He looked back, and thought he could make out the figure of a woman in a red-hooded winter coat veering off into the street. She seemed intent on passing him by, enroute to her parked car on Dumbarton Street, he thought. When she stopped mid-stride and faced him, he was confused at first, until she pointed a suppressed automatic pistol in his direction.

He stood in place...frozen...transfixed. And in a state of self-imposed denial. *No! This isn't happening...here...now.*

Across the street, he could see Scheele's Market —the oldest corner store in Georgetown—where he shopped throughout the week for the tradition, as much as its sheer convenience.

Two shots fired in quick succession, muted by the blowing wind and the thickening bed of snow on the ground.

The lights inside the small corner store illuminated the large flakes of snow falling steadily outside, creating a canopy of white over parked cars, the newspaper box, the streets and the corner street signs.

The perpendicular features of Sheele's storefront...the rectangular frame of the first floor window, and the two residential windows above, were Jack Condon's final images as his life's blood slowly drained into a red pool, framed in white by the snow around him.

Chapter 50

LUKE ARCHER TOOK THE D.C. METRO yellow line to the National Archives, Navy Memorial and Penn Quarter stop. He walked quickly through the blowing snowstorm, and entered the National Archives building on Constitution Avenue. As instructed, he introduced himself to the attendant as Patrick Janeck.

The attendant nodded and ushered him down to a large vault, with two armed guards standing by. The vault door was open. Inside, Congressman Daniel Tory was waiting for him.

"Good to see you, Archer," Danno said, shaking his hand. He waved him inside the vault. "This may be the most secure building in the world—more so than even Fort Knox."

"They just let you down here?" Archer asked, unable to conceal his surprise.

"The Archivist and I are good friends," Danno said. "I run the Committee on Homeland Security and Governmental Affairs. We oversee the National Archives, so he gives me free run of the place." Danno led Archer inside the vault where two other guards and a tall middle aged woman in a white lab jacket stood by a steel wall with a complex array of mechanical slats and electrical cords that had the appearance of the inside of an alien spaceship. He introduced the lady as Adrienne Simon, Deputy Archivist of the United States—she greeted Archer with a smile.

"From time to time, I come down here just to remind myself what's really important." Danno nodded at Adrienne who proceeded to press a series of commands on the computerized panel that she was standing alongside. At once, a metallic roar of gears in motion filled the vault. Part of the floor seemed to collapse in front of them. Simultaneously, the corresponding part of the ceiling slowly lowered in front of them, gradually revealing the encasements—large, deep gold plated titanium and aluminum historical picture frames containing the Declaration of Independence, the Constitution, and the Bill of Rights—which had only moments ago been on full display in the Rotunda.

238

Archer was stunned at the display in front of him. He looked over at Danno Tory and began walking beside each of the casements, surveying the documents closely. The effect on him was profound.

"Not many people get to see this procedure every evening—securing our nation's foundational documents," Daniel explained. "It's one of those activities that happens well behind the scenes, outside the public eye. But I thought you'd appreciate it."

Archer turned to face Danno, understanding both the meaning and symbolism. "I do."

Danno nodded. "I've asked Adrienne to show us something else that the Archives just received on loan."

Adrienne led both men to another part of the vault. She pulled a set of white gloves over her hands, and issued a set to both men. She pulled out a large metal drawer in one of the walls and lifted a document out of a glass case, setting it on the counter in front of them. The document was a letter on old parchment, with elaborate handwriting throughout.

Philadelphia June 18th 1775.

My Dearest,

I am now set down to write to you on a subject which fills me with inexpressable concern—and this concern is greatly aggravated and Increased when I reflect on the uneasiness I know it will give you—It has been determined in Congress, that the whole Army raised for the defence of the American Cause shall be put under my care, and that it is necessary for me to proceed immediately to Boston to take upon me the Command of it. You may believe me my dear Patcy, when I assure you, in the most solemn manner, that, so far from seeking this appointment I have used every endeavour in my power to avoid it, not only from my unwillingness to part with you and the

Family, but from a consciousness of its being a trust too great for my Capacity and that I should enjoy more real happiness and felicity in one month with you, at home, than I have the most distant prospect of reaping abroad, if my stay was to be Seven times Seven years. But, as it has been a kind of destiny that has thrown me upon this Service, I shall hope that my undertaking of it, is designd to answer some good purpose—You might, and I suppose did perceive, from the Tenor of my letters, that I was apprehensive I could not avoid this appointment, as I did not even pretend (t)o intimate when I should return—that was the case—it was utterly out of my power to refuse this appointment without exposing my Character to such censures as would have reflected dishonour upon myself, and given pain to my friends—this I am sure could not, and ought not to be pleasing to you, & must have lessend me considerably in my own esteem….

The letter was signed: *Geo. Washington*

"This is one of the only letters that George Washington wrote to his wife, Martha, that has survived," Adrienne said. "After the President died, she burned all of their letters. This was found alone in a desk drawer."

"I believe it's one of the most significant communications in our nation's history," Danno said. "Because it reflects the mindset of Washington at the time, as he considered the implications of becoming our nation's Commander in Chief in its war to separate from Britain— its parent. His decision to accept command would place him over the development of our Constitution and later lead to him becoming our first, and by many accounts, our finest President. The candor of the letter is reinforced by the fact that he wrote it to his wife. The whole sentiment—it's definitely genuine."

"Did Martha mean for this to be discovered?" Archer asked Adrienne. "Is that why it was found, by itself?"

Adrienne smiled, and straightened up. "No one can say for sure. Martha Washington was a very private person. She, perhaps even more than her husband, understood his legacy before it was fully formed."

"What do you think though? Archer asked, genuinely interested.

"As an archivist and historian, I would be skeptical that it was anything more than an unintentional omission," Adrienne replied, and then pointed at the letter. "But as a woman, you know, I must say, you don't just forget a letter like this from the love of your life."

Archer nodded, grateful for her insights. "He was obviously a reluctant warrior."

"That's why I wanted you to see this," Danno replied. He thanked Adrienne, and turned to Archer. "Walk with me."

Another encasement was being lowered to their level, Danno pointed at it. "The *Magna Carta,*" he said. "Written more than 500 years before the founding of The United States, it was the original model for our Constitution and Bill of Rights. There were several original copies made at its drafting, and the United States received one as an honorarium from the United Kingdom for the U.S saving the Brit and French bacon in World War One."

"All of this. Not just one simple document." Archer said. "It puts things in perspective, doesn't it?"

Danno led them up to the Rotunda of the Archives. Archer looked up and saw the elaborate murals by Barry Faulkner depicting Thomas Jefferson's presentation of the Declaration of Independence to John Hancock in 1776, and a presentation of the Constitution to George Washington by Madison in 1787.

Danno stopped and looked at Archer. "I've been asked confidentially to run for Speaker of the House."

"What happened to the current Speaker?" Archer asked.

"Someone's threatening to release some compromising information on him if he doesn't resign next week," Danno said. "Beyond that I just don't know."

"Why you?"

"That was my question—*Why me?*" Danno replied. "I'm only on my fourth term in Congress. Had it not been for the adventure Robin and

I had in the Baltics against the Kremlin, I wouldn't be a committee chair right now, and I doubt I'd be considered for this position."

"Who made the request?" Archer asked.

"Two senior Congressmen whom I trust," Danno said. "They're worried about other candidates on the short list for consideration. But I don't believe in coincidences anymore."

"You may be all that stands between our Democracy becoming a complete Kleptocracy," Archer said. "You know you'll be putting a bull's-eye on yourself, if you sign up for that? Not a figurative one, but a real one."

Danno nodded, continuing to walk past the Emancipation Proclamation that had also just been lowered to the vault. "Before I ran for any office, I wanted to make a difference, but I didn't really know why, until I learned about my family's past in Lithuania, and how they fought against the Nazis in World War II—and then against the Soviets during the Cold War. Their sacrifices became my reason *Why*. Living up to their example is what drives me now."

"It's a personal decision, Congressman," Archer said. "I don't have to remind you what you'll be up against."

"All of this," Danno exhaled. "It's Orwellian."

"No, it's worse," Archer replied. "These people stand for nothing. They'll do anything and say anything to achieve their objectives, however twisted. Stripping away the vestiges of our history is vital to that effort." Archer gestured at the walls around them, and the soaring ceiling above. "This place...it's as much a threat to their agenda as you or me."

Danno looked up. "Can I ask you a question, Archer?"

Archer stopped and looked at Danno.

"What drives *you*?"

Archer looked down at the ground. "The memory of the men and women I served with who aren't with us anymore," he answered directly, then pausing. "And those who are. They keep me going."

Whatever your decision on this, you should know we're your greatest supporters."

Danno nodded. "Thank you."

Archer shook Danno's hand, and looked intently in his eyes.

"Always."

Chapter 51

"I FOUND SOMETHING YOU NEED TO SEE," Sandy Wilkes said over the phone. "Check your email account."

Archer asked Laura to access his email account on the operations center server. She quickly located Sandy's email and opened the video labeled:

FORT CAMPBELL, KY

CRIMINAL INVESTIGATION DIVISION

SECURITY CAMERA ARCHIVES

Cole Park Golf Course

220720052330Z

Archer recognized the date-time group on the email as the same date Becky was murdered.

July 22, 2005....

It was a date forever seared into his memory. The digital video that appeared on the screen appeared to show a static night time display of a golf course, which Archer quickly recognized from his years on Fort Campbell as "Cole Park."

After only a few moments, the video showed a man running through the golf course, holding his hand to his neck. At an intersection surrounded by forest, he recognized as "Creek Road," the man stopped behind a tree and removed his T-Shirt. Bunching it up, he placed it in a plastic grocery bag, and threw the bag into a culvert before continuing to run off the screen toward what Archer knew to be the General Officer and Colonel's housing area.

Despite the somewhat degraded, grainy quality of the picture, Archer instantly recognized the man—from his frame and loping gait alone, but also from the oblong shape of his head and his long, straight nose.

"That's Hastings," Archer said conclusively.

"We believe it is," Sandy replied. "Right when I saw this, I sent a private investigator to that location to do a search. We found his shirt in that very same culvert."

"But it's been almost a decade and a half," Archer said.

"Wrapped up in a plastic grocery bag," Sandy replied. "It's been degraded by the elements, but we're getting a DNA test now. There's a chance it may deliver results. Hastings' biggest mistake was placing it in a plastic bag and tying it up. That act alone went a long way in protecting the integrity of the DNA on the shirt. Regardless, the tape is also compelling in itself."

"He was bleeding like a stuck pig," Archer commented. "Becky definitely fought back."

"This is a step forward," Sandy explained. "But I can't overemphasize the importance of being cautious and deliberate with every step we take. We don't have any DNA sample for Zachary Hastings, and you can be sure the White House will fight this to the bitter end with an army of attorneys. Chain of custody will be primary among their arguments. We're talking about a murder charge."

"We'll be careful," Archer replied. "But I also want us to move quickly, before this bastard can hurt anyone else." Then, considering what he had just said, added, "Before he can hurt any more of our team and friends."

"We have to not only stop him, but discredit him in such a way that his organization is neutralized and removed." Laura said.

"So someone reputable can take his position as Vice President," Sandy added, from the speaker phone.

Archer turned to Laura. "I'd like to get hold of Jim Swanson, tomorrow if possible."

"He was relieved from his position today, as Director of the Secret Service."

"Why?" Archer asked.

"'Loss of confidence,' is what I'm hearing from a friend at the

Post."

Archer nodded. "Okay. I'll call him," he replied, returning to the call with Sandy Wilkes. "Sandy, I think I have a good way to get what we need on Hastings, but I need you to meet someone here in D.C.—can you fly in tomorrow?"

Archer replayed the digital video of Zachary Hastings over and over, until Laura came up behind him and whispered, "How can we shift your attention?"

Archer looked up at her, pointed at the screen, and attempted keeping his voice steady. "At the time...when all this happened...I never even considered that Hastings was Becky's murderer."

"Do you think you have him now?" Laura asked.

"He's done a fairly good job of setting me up."

"How do you feel now?"

Archer shrugged. "It's strange. I always thought I'd want to exact revenge on whomever killed Becky. For years, that's all I thought about. But now, I don't feel much of anything."

"Right now, killing him might be the merciful thing to do."

"Yeah, well," Archer said slowly. "I'm not feeling very merciful either."

Laura paused, and turned to him. "Is this worth the struggle?"

Archer shrugged. "Honestly, I never considered it wasn't."

"Sometimes I feel like we're operating in a huge vacuum, with no real context of the larger picture."

"Dead Americans...friends," Archer replied. "I can't stand by and see my country torn asunder. If you've got to know, that's all the context I need."

"And now you're 'Public Enemy #1."

"It's a personal decision on how you justify it. It always is, in any fight."

"How do you do it?" Laura asked directly.

"What do you mean?" Archer asked, unsure of purpose of the

246

question.

"How do you hold up in the midst of all this?"

Archer shrugged. "The same way you did after being shot point blank at the Watergate. It's what we do."

"I'd rather not repeat that if it's okay with you," Laura said.

"You were wearing a vest," Archer said. "You *knew* something wasn't right, didn't you?"

Laura hesitated before answering. "Someone had searched my desk, car and my apartment the day before. They were careful, but left a few unmistakable indicators—so I asked Robin Tory if they had a vest I could borrow."

"Why didn't you tell me?"

"You would've pulled me out," she replied, mildly indignant.

"Yeah." Archer nodded. "I would have."

"I still had work to do," Laura said. "We wouldn't have known SU's full plan now if I'd just given up."

"It came at a helluva price. You're no use to me, or any of us, if you're dead."

Laura nodded. "The same goes for you."

Archer nodded, and sipped his coffee. "Where's Jack? I haven't seen him lately."

"He hasn't been in," Laura said. "At least I haven't seen him. I'll check on him."

Shen entered the room and handed a file to Archer.

"Don't forget your meeting tomorrow morning with Jan Rayburn."

"At Arlington Cemetery," Archer said, holding up the file. He turned to Laura. "Want to come?"

Laura nodded. "I could use the fresh air."

Archer walked with Laura through the road lined with white gravestones. In the frigid early morning mist, Archer lost himself in the names on the stones, looking reflexively at those with names of friends he'd served with through the years, and whose funerals and burials he'd attended.

"John Lee is going to be buried there, on that hill," Archer said, pointing. "He'll be right beside the last surviving American veteran of World War I, Frank Buckles."

"He always did manage to keep the most interesting company," Laura replied.

The quietude of the cemetery at that early hour was striking in its ability to reflect the souls placed to rest amidst the trees and monuments, as far as they eye could see. At the base of a hill, they stopped in the middle of Section 7-A, in front of a large stone, engraved in grey rustic cut granite—in large block letters, "ARCHER." Below, in smaller letters, two names:

James	Katherine
May 2, 1932 - June 30, 2016	October 6, 1936 - July 5, 2016

Laura stared for a moment at the stone, and looked up at him.

"My parents," Archer replied, without being asked.

"Oh Archer, I didn't—"

Archer shook his head gently. The lines of his face relaxed. "They both passed away within days of one another. They loved one another more than any two people I've met, then or since."

"Your Dad—he was a general?" Laura asked, pointing at the four large stars on top of the memorial stone, above the name.

"An Admiral," Archer replied. "You wouldn't know it if he was out of uniform, and you were just meeting him. Even his gravestone doesn't say 'Admiral.' Four stars and that's it. Very unassuming, and humble."

"Like his son," Laura commented.

Archer shook his head. "I'll never be the man he was. He had a way of making sense of chaos. Me? I tend to get all caught up in it."

"And your mom?"

"She supported him, and raised us," Archer replied, smiling. "It was a full time job."

Laura smiled. "I'll bet."

"But she was my most formative influence. When I was in grade school, I once told her while she was doing laundry, I didn't think I could ever match Dad's achievements. She placed the laundry basket down, stopped everything she was doing, and looked me in the eyes. *'Luke Archer, you can do anything and be anything you want to be, and don't let anyone tell you otherwise.'*"

"She was right."

"I could use both of them right about now," Archer said. "After Becky was killed, I was in an abyss. Both of them...and John...they pulled me out of it. They found Beau for me."

Laura nodded, choosing to remain silent and listen.

"I don't know why," Archer continued. "But this is the only place I feel like I can hear them talking to me...or at least remember what they once said. I can actually recall their voices, what they sounded like."

"What would they be telling you now?" Laura asked.

Archer took two oblong white stones from his coat pocket and placed them on top of the gravestone, and stepped back.

"Do what's right."

Archer pointed at the large dark granite stone beside them. "Joe Lewis—one of the greatest heavyweights of all time is buried right there. Beside him is Lee Marvin—an Academy Award winner."

He pointed at several other graves to her front. "ABC newsman Frank Reynolds is right there.

Archer guided Laura up the walkway to the gravesite of John F. Kennedy and his family. The bright orange and red eternal flame pierced through the Arlington National Cemetery's veil of fog. "There's someone I want you to meet."

A middle aged, heavy set woman in a quilted overcoat stood in the plaza of the Kennedy gravesite, bounded by the low granite wall, inscribed with quotations from President Kennedy's inaugural address and other speeches. The woman turned to face them, and smiled at Archer.

"Laura—" Archer began, in an attempt to introduce them. But before he could finish, the woman extended her hand.

249

"I'm Jan Rayburn," the woman said smiling. Her hair was short—a mix of light brown and gray.

"Thanks for meeting us on such a cold morning."

"It's not often I get to meet the FBI's Most Wanted."

"In a cemetery, no less," Laura added.

"I figured it would be the last place they'd look." Archer replied dryly. He pointed at Robert F. Kennedy's grave. "The last time our nation was in such turmoil was when he and Martin Luther King were assassinated within three months of each other, in 1968. No one ever thought we'd be experiencing the same turbulence again."

"In many ways, it feels even more dangerous," Laura commented.

"Are you wearing comfortable shoes?" Archer asked.

Jan nodded. "I am."

"Okay," Archer said to both women. "We'll walk then. I have a story for you."

Exiting Arlington National Cemetery with Laura Chicone, Archer looked over at the rolled up copy of the *Washington Post* on the park bench. Walking over, he picked it up, and read the headline, and the story below it:

Daniel Tory elected House Speaker
First Independent in History to be Speaker of the House

By Maureen Grimes, Washington Post Congressional Reporter
Updated 5:17 AM ET, Thu January 18

The vote was a seminal moment and first-ever event after House Republicans nominated Daniel Tory, a registered Independent from Illinois, for the position of House Speaker on Wednesday. Tory had been in the initial stages of running for Governor of Illinois.

But both liberals and conservatives who did not support former Speaker Holloway for re-election said that after weeks of infighting, they were eager to move on with the virtually unprecedented election of an Independent as Speaker of the House, and give Tory the space to craft a real bipartisan legislative agenda for the first time in history.
After he was sworn in as Speaker, Tory praised former Speaker Holloway, calling him "one of our great Speakers," and urged members from both sides to come together.

Tory attempted to get members to turn the page saying "we have a lot to work on together. So if you ever pray, pray for me—and let's pray for each other — regardless of our party affiliation."

After a standing ovation Tory joked, "And that doesn't mean you should pray for me to become either a Democrat or a Republican."

He took the oath on his own copy of the *New American Bible* and kept the gavel he wielded as Chairman of the Homeland Security committee.

Tory will face 'monumental obstacles' as speaker.

The 42-year-old Illinois Independent first worked in Washington as a White House Fellow, as a Special Assistant to the White House Chief of Staff. He worked on Capitol Hill as a legislative aide and won his House seat when he was 35.

Before officially handing him the gavel, Jeff Holloway congratulated him and noted his path to the speakership went from serving as a young aide to the Mayor of the small town of Lake Forest, Illinois, to Congress.

Even before his tenure in the House began, Tory and his wife, Robin, attracted national attention for their efforts in halting Russia's planned invasion of the Baltic States. Tory was nearly killed on several occasions throughout a harrowing ordeal in Russia and Lithuania.

With the speaker's title, Tory takes on a national profile and the difficult challenge of corralling what has been an unruly and divided House.

In his first speech, he said the ongoing division and polarization ran counter to what had always before been characterized as American values, and pledged to work on both sides of the aisle to bring reasonable members of Congress closer together.

"We can be part of the solution, or part of the problem," Tory said. "We won't always agree — and that's fine. But we need to approach our problems honestly, openly and ethically. There is no more important prerequisite for progress."

In an odd, seemingly out-of-place moment of his maiden speech, Tory concluded by saying, "President Eisenhower once warned all of us, 'The potential for the disastrous rise of misplaced power exists and will persist.'"

After delivering his speech, Tory walked down to shake hands with his colleagues, even with those who voted against him, still holding the Bible he placed his hand on to take the oath of office.

Archer texted Danno Tory via WhatsApp, and received an immediate series of responses.

Congratulations on the new job, Mr. Speaker

Condolences maybe?

Will help U in any way

Thx. Feels like a ton of bricks just landed on me. Will vet all Committee Chairmen & remove all tainted by SU. #1 Priority.

& ID the Incorruptibles...

Counting on U.

Anytime/place. B careful. Remember UR now a big target

Chapter 52

LUKE ARCHER WALKED WITH SANDRA WILKES, and approached a tall man leaning on the balcony overlooking the Reading Room of the Library of Congress.

"Sandy," Archer said introducing her. "This is Jim Swanson, Director of the Secret Service."

"Former Director," Swanson corrected, shaking her hand. "As of yesterday. You heard?"

Archer nodded. "Jim played a leading role in preempting the attack in Texas, and in keeping us informed throughout."

"Although I wasn't given a reason, that was likely why I was fired," Swanson said. "Believing I was behind the leak."

"One day soon, being fired by these folks will be a badge of honor," Archer replied.

"Sooner likely, than later," Sandy added.

"Thanks for meeting me." Attempting to change the subject, Archer gestured at the library below. "As public spaces go, it's one of my favorites in this town—quiet, with plenty of places to disappear. Temporarily at least."

"It's a beautiful space," Sandra agreed, looking down at the desks, antique wooden chairs and lamps that formed concentric circles in the room around a central book issuing station. Statues stood by on the periphery of the room providing overwatch. Overhead, the muralled dome was every bit as impressive as the Capitol Rotunda's.

Archer nodded. "I wanted you both to meet, because each of you are in a position to make a difference in stopping these people—Zachary Hastings, among them."

"You have my complete support," Swanson replied. "But now that I'm officially retired from the Secret Service, I'm afraid I'm no better than a used banana peel."

Sandy smiled. "You're more of an asset now than ever, if you're willing."

"Hastings—he's as corrupt as the day is long," Swanson replied directly. "So I'll help in any way I can."

"Part of our challenge is knowing who has—and who hasn't—been tainted by SU," Archer said. "Identifying the 'Incorruptibles.'"

"We know you're one of those we can trust," Sandy added.

"I'll do whatever I can," Swanson said. He pulled out a folded envelope and handed it to Archer. "This may be a good start."

Archer took the envelope, looking at Swanson with curiosity.

"More transcripts," Swanson said. "I still have folks on the inside who are talking to me and want to help. But I'm afraid I don't have the actual recordings. It's the best I could do."

Archer nodded. "We'll review all of it."

"There's one thing in there I believe will be of interest," Swanson continued, gesturing toward the envelop now in Archer's hand. "There's a continual reference to a residence in Kalorama. Keeps coming up."

"We'll take a look at it," Archer said nodding. He turned to Sandy. "We'd like to review some additional evidence with you."

"What kind of evidence?" Swanson asked.

Sandy looked up at Swanson, and over at Archer. "The kind that proves Zachary Hastings killed Becky Archer."

Swanson looked over at Archer with surprise.

Archer nodded as if reading his mind. "My wife."

Inside the Operations Center, Luke Archer handed the transcript to Dag—who read it with eyes raised throughout.

Hastings: I don't need to remind you what we're up against with Archer. The fact that he's still out there is the most dangerous threat all of us face.

Fields: Understand. But he's proven elusive, to say the least.

Hastings: I warned you about him! Of course he's elusive. I've known the bastard a long time. He'll also kill you as soon as look at you. And he'll do it in your sleep.

Fields: We've got him on all of the Terrorist Watch Lists, and he's #1 on the FBI's Most Wanted. We've also issued an Interpol Red Notice for him.

Hastings: You just don't get it. None of that matters. What matters is mobilizing every asset we've got—not to capture him. But to kill him.

Fields: Yes, Sir. Understand. Our operations center at Fessenden is actively working to find him and his team.

Hastings: I don't think you do understand. Tell Abraham I want to talk to him.

"Nice to know you're appreciated," Dag said, handing the transcript back to Archer. "That's Alan Fields he's talking to? The FBI Director?"

"Yeah."

"Hastings doesn't like you very much, does he?"

"He's a victim of the 'Hundred Battles Syndrome'," Archer replied.

"The Hundred Battles Syndrome?" Dag asked. "What's that?"

"It's one of Sun Tzu's maxims— 'If you know the enemy and know yourself you need not fear the results of a hundred battles,'" Archer replied. "He doesn't know himself, and he definitely doesn't know me as well as he thinks he does."

"Ahh!" Dag exclaimed. "I've always been more Clausewitz than Sun Tzu."

Archer smiled. "What do we know about this operations center in Fessenden?"

Dag pointed up at the screen, providing a narrative for each photo of an 18th-century style neoclassical brick and limestone mansion. "It's three miles south of Kalorama. 3107 Fessenden Street, Northwest in

Forest Hills. Samuel Lehrman—the Giant Food supermarket heir—built the house in 1994. 20,000 square feet. Designed by Leon Chatelain of Chatelain Architects, and built by Gibson Builders. Seven bedrooms, fourteen baths, private staff quarters, wine cellar, and an elevator. Outside, it's all custom brick and limestone facade, terraces, lap pool, pool house, English gardens, a sports court, lawns, motor court entrance—all on an acre of parkland—which is unusually large for Kalorama.

"Who owns it now?" Archer asked.

Dag held up his index finger. "That's interesting, because we don't really know for certain. All we do know is that several years ago it sold to an 'undisclosed international buyer' for $18 Million—the largest sum for a residential purchase in D.C. at the time, until Jeff Bezos moved in next door."

Archer nodded at Dag, Max and Shen. "Okay. Let's find out what's inside."

Paging through *The Washington Post*, he stopped suddenly. Clenching his eyes shut, he leaned back in his chair, head facing the ceiling in anguish.

As the others left, Shen had seen Archer's reaction and remained behind in the Operations Center's conference room and approached Archer.

"You okay, Boss?"

Archer turned in his chair to face Shen, handing him the "Metro" section of *The Washington Post*. Below-the-fold, the headline read:

D.C. Police Identify Man Fatally Shot on Residential Georgetown Street

Jack Condon was 45 Year Old former National Security Council Senior Director

"Oh Jesus, not Jack…."

"What kind of heartless lunatic guns someone down in front of his home?" Archer asked.

Shen exhaled. "That's the enemy we're facing. They destroy anything that stands in their way."

"Jack Condon was never a physical threat to them. He was a goddamn Intel analyst for Christ's sake!"

Shen sat down in front of Archer. "Don't sell him short. You and I both know he was one of the best in the business—he'd done it all—Counterintelligence, Counterterrorism, Analytics, Paramilitary Operations.... You can't find guys like Jack anymore. He could do it all, and he was pointing us in the right directions so we all *could* be a bigger threat to them."

"Jack pinpointed the government's gambit with V-Tec, and he played a principal role stopping that attack in Texas. He helped save a lot of lives. No one knows that."

"Someday they will. He knew the risks, and he'd do it all over again. He didn't deserve that kind of ambush. What can I do?"

Archer nodded. "For now, we all just need to remember what he died for."

"He was a good friend...a huge loss—not only for us, but for the country."

"If we make it through this, we need to ensure he has a star on the wall at Langley." Archer paused and exhaled. "I need to call his parents. He had two labs didn't he?"

Shen nodded solemnly. "He loved those dogs. I'll see if I can find 'em."

Chapter 53

"I BELIEVE THEY MADE their initial appearance today, in a very interesting way," Danno Tory said over the phone to Luke Archer.

"How so?" Archer asked.

"Almost imperceptibly, if it weren't so obvious," Danno answered. "In a routine in-brief—they've devised a completely legal, enhanced 401(k)—a 407(b) pension account that's open only to Committee Chairs and select members. It allows them to contribute 100% of their salary, up to $350,000 per year. The employer matches 70% of their contributions."

"*$350,000?*" Archer asked with obvious surprise. "*70%?*"

"All based on seniority," Danno answered. "Their stated purpose is to compensate congressional leaders for their prohibition against board memberships, international and domestic travel, maintaining dual residences, and repayment of campaign expenses."

"Sounds like a damn good plan," Archer replied. "Where can I sign up?"

"Yeah, and it's as illegal as Bathtub Gin."

"Not if you're the one who makes the rules," Archer said. "What did you leave them with?"

"I said I'd get back to them," Danno said. "And I asked to see a list of who was currently on the plan."

Archer nodded. "Wouldn't tell them 'No' just yet. We need to draw them out."

"I never thought I'd see this level of corruption, and so widespread in this country...in our own government."

"They've managed to build quite a machine," Archer said. "Now we have to bring it down."

When he hung up the phone, Archer looked up to see Shen sitting beside him. Without speaking, Shen placed a large sealed envelope on the table in front of Archer.

"What's this?"

"They didn't have any CCTV coverage of the area where Jack was killed, but they do have an ANPR camera looking at license plates from the roof of The Four Seasons. Every license plate that passes by, coming and going is recorded. Not sure it'll help, but I ran a copy of their feed for that night."

Archer nodded. "I'll take a look at it. Maybe Jim Swanson's guys can run the numbers." Pausing, holding onto the thick envelope with both hands, he looked up at Shen. "Jack was the one who told me about John dying, you know. It occurred to me, we wouldn't be together again, doing any of this if it weren't for him."

"I think I may have found a way into the Fessenden House," Dag said to the assembled team. "But I'm afraid Shen isn't going to like it."

"Well, then, I like it already," Max replied, smiling.

"What do we have to do?" Shen asked. "Scale the walls? I have no objection to that."

"No," Dag answered. "You'll need to wear a tux."

"Absolutely not," Shen said. "I'd rather use breaching charges or close air support."

"Why tuxes?" Archer asked, ignoring the howls of laughter.

"Because Dr. Robert Craine happens to be hosting an inauguration party there tomorrow evening in honor of Zachary Hastings," Dag said. "With eight hundred of their closest friends."

"How did we find out about that?" Archer asked. "It's not on any of the official inaugural lists."

"Through the listening devices and viruses we installed at V-Tec," Dag answered. "I've taken the liberty of RSVP'ing to the reception for the three of you."

"The three of us?" Archer asked. "Last I counted there were four of us."

"Shen and Max, me," Dag answered. "Not you."

"Why can't I go?"

Dag pressed a button on his computer and pointed to the screen, where three color photos of Archer were displayed on an "FBI Most Wanted" poster, with his name in bold red type. "You're a celebrity. And

Zachary Hastings is on the invitation list. That's why."

Archer nodded. "Okay," he said. "What's the plan then? If Hastings is attending, security will be heavier 'n a dead preacher."

Dag smiled at Archer's expression. "Thanks for that visual. I have it covered," he said, bringing up a set of blueprints and overhead image of the house on the screen above.

Dag used a laser pointer to review the interior and exterior layout of the mansion. He continued: "The house is located in the wealthy Forest Hills neighborhood of Washington—about four miles, or fifteen minutes, from the White House. There are two gated entrances, terraces and a sweeping curved staircase that overlooks fountains, English gardens, a patio, lap pool, pool house and a half-court basketball court, as well as private staff quarters. The house itself has four levels, and is constructed of concrete, steel, and limestone. With seven bedrooms, nine full bathrooms and five half-bathrooms, the house has an elevator that leads down to a billiard room and a temperature-controlled wine cellar and tasting room."

"We're attending as guests?" Shen asked.

Dag nodded. "We're now officially inaugural party crashers. We'll be on the updated invite list. Craine is doing the party in honor of Hastings. Whenever you're talking to someone, be sure to ask if they're friends of Craine's or Hastings'. When they ask you, just claim the opposite one. Spend the time to get to know the bar staff. Tip them generously. Make friends at the bar, order a round of shots on you for whoever's in the vicinity. Target V-Tec employees, and any senior government officials—they're most likely SU. Remember their names."

"The key is to blend in, so nobody doubts your reason for being there," Archer added.

"No weapons," Dag said. "They'll be screening and searching everyone. Wireless earpieces worn by each of you. Transmitters will be concealed in Max's purse."

Archer turned to them. "Operate together. Rotate searching, and surveillance. Any questions?"

"Yeah, I have one," Max said. "Will Shen dance with me?"
Everyone laughed, knowing well dancing was completely out of

character for Shen.

"That would be a true act of despair," Shen replied deadpan.

"What exactly are we looking for?" Max asked.

"Documents, electronic files, photos, recordings, video footage…" Dag answered, "Anything that strengthens our case against the members of the SU organization, and helps us learn more about them. Who they are, what they're planning—where and when."

"The transcript mentioned an 'operations center at Fessenden'," Archer said. "If it exists, we need to know about it."

"And gain access?" Max asked.

"Only if it can be done without being noticed," Dag replied. "We can't take any unnecessary risks while we're in there."

"Any other questions?" Archer asked, looking at each member of the team.

Laura edged into the room in her hospital pajamas, and everyone greeted her enthusiastically. "I feel like I'm the third wheel around here lately. Sorry I've been so useless."

"We're just glad you're still with us," Shen replied.

"Good to have you on this side of the grass," Max added.

Laura laughed. "You can't get rid of me that easily!"

Archer nodded. "Okay, look, everyone just be damn careful. And Dag?"

Dag looked up expectantly.

"I just got a call from Oslo, and learned your wife is almost nine months pregnant—were you planning on telling us at some point?"

"Ah!" Dag exclaimed, amidst the group's cheers. "I can have no secrets with you, *Colonel*! I didn't want to be a distraction for the group."

"Okay," Archer replied, holding up a faxed sonogram with the 4-D image of a baby *in utero*. "Well, evidently Margit's delivery date has been moved up a week, so we need to talk."

Chapter 54

Congressman Daniel Tory Takes Stand Against Presidential Directive 20

Claims Abolishes Posse Comitatus and gives President "Dictatorial Powers"

Today, on the eve of his Inauguration, President-Elect Stone said that tomorrow, immediately following his oath of office, he will sign a classified Presidential order, called "Presidential Directive 20," outlining imminent conditions under which the Posse Comitatus Act of 1878, that prohibits the use of the US military for police actions on American soil, will no longer apply. With the newly outlined policy, under a range of loosely defined "exceptional" conditions, the Department of Defense and CIA will be authorized to conduct unrestrained operations within the United States without Congressional approval or oversight."

Presidential Directive 20 states that "in emergency extraordinary circumstances, including contingencies that constitute unlawful obstruction or rebellion against the authority of the United States, the Department of Defense and CIA shall be fully empowered to carry out, activities that are necessary to quell large-scale, unexpected civil disturbances, as well as lethal operations against terror threats.

Speaker of the House Daniel Tory (I, IL) took strong exception to the President-Elect's planned actions, taking the floor on Sunday night with unscripted remarks, captured by C-Span: "Without any consultation with or involvement by the legislative and judicial branches, Presidential Directive

20 authorizes the military to use lethal force domestically, and effectively abolishes the Posse Comitatus Act."

Attorney General-Designee Bethany Baxter stated: "As a policy matter, law enforcement authorities in this country provide the best means for incapacitating terrorist threats; however, in extraordinary circumstances it may be necessary and appropriate for the President to authorize the military and CIA to use lethal force and apply intelligence assets within United States territory if required, in order to protect the homeland."

Congressman Tory's lone two-hour scathing critique of the President-Elect and Attorney General-Designee on the House floor Sunday night, only hours prior to the Presidential Inauguration, was virtually unprecedented by a member of Congress:

"With the stroke of a pen, the President will place the military and CIA in charge of security within the borders of the United States. This unlawful and unconstitutional order has been drafted without any consultation with Congress or judicial review, and in direct contravention to Posse Comitatus. If signed, and allowed to stand, PD 20 tips the balance of our government fully to the gates of 1600 Pennsylvania Avenue, giving the President what amount to dictatorial powers."

Attorney General-Designee Baxter dismissed Tory's concerns outright. "Any thought that the President-Elect could abuse this power is really nothing more than hysteria."

Hearing of Congressman Tory's spontaneous opposition, the President-Elect made a rare unannounced appearance

Sunday night at Blair House, stating, "In the end, if the people cannot trust their government to do the job for which it exists — to protect them and to promote their common welfare — all else is lost."

When asked about the President Elect's remarks, during a late night interview in the parking lot of the U.S. Capitol, Congressman Tory shook his head, and said: "Sadly, we will no longer be a government of the people, by the people, for the people. The question every American citizen needs to ask themselves today is, 'Is that acceptable?'"

Sitting in the Pavilion Cafe, overlooking the National Gallery of Art Sculpture Garden Ice Rink, Archer set his coffee down, impressed that Danno Tory had learned about Presidential Directive 20, and spontaneously decided to take a stand, unscripted—speaking for two consecutive hours without any break.

The Washington Post, continuing to operate out of rented office space in the wake of the bombing of its headquarters, had been so impressed with the issue and Danno's performance that they published a full transcript of his speech in a special section of the paper. The *Post's* decision to print a dedicated insert was both rare and an almost unprecedented statement of solidarity and support for the whole Separation of Powers principle, and system of checks and balances as outlined in the Constitution.

Archer glanced up to see Jim Swanson and Sandy Wilkes approaching. As she sat down, Sandy handed Archer a manila envelope from her purse.

As Archer read, his eyebrows raised in surprise. He looked up at both Sandy and Jim with an expression of genuine shock. "How in the world did you get Hastings to agree to provide a DNA sample?"

Swanson shook his head. "He didn't, and he doesn't yet know he provided one. I asked a member of the White House Mess to hold onto his water glass after lunch, and had it tested," he said. He took a sip of coffee. "Good to still have friends inside the 18 Acres."

Archer continued to read the lab report. "It's conclusive then?"

"His DNA matches the blood on the T-Shirt with 1 in 113 billion accuracy," Sandy said. "So does Becky's."

Archer looked down. "Next steps?"

Sandy nodded. "We need to have everything prepared to present to a Federal judge and grand jury," she said. "It's not a slam dunk. These results won't hold up in court, but they're enough to issue a warrant for a formal re-test. We can also base the petition on the disappearance of his records from the military DNA database. In other words, we're close."

"They'll come after all of us with everything they've got," Archer replied. "To include the kinetic variety. We need to be ready for them."

"Do we have a media strategy?" Swanson asked.

Archer nodded. "Jan Rayburn's on board," he replied. "She's a freelance journalist who's come out of retirement to focus only on this. She's working on an expose—print and TV. I spent time with her a few days ago, and will continue to feed her information."

"She's one of the very best," Sandy agreed. "You know her?"

"She interviewed me once, a long time ago," Archer replied. "But Jack Condon reconnected us. It may be the reason he was killed."

"I'm so sorry," Sandy said. "There's still a lot we need to do before we can completely hand this off to her. We've got a lot of information that creates a compelling case, but now we need to piece it all together."

"And identify the gaps and seams," Swanson added. "There are still plenty."

Archer nodded. "After tonight, there's a good possibility we'll know much more."

"What's happening tonight?" Sandy asked.

"We're crashing an inaugural party," Archer answered.

"Sounds fun," Sandy quipped. "Can I go?"

"I always hated those parties," Swanson injected. "Glad I don't have to go to any more."

Sandy smiled, and pointed out at the ice rink. "Sitting here, people are skating and completely oblivious to the fact that we're on the verge of uncovering the largest criminal scandal in our nation's history."

"Surrounded by sculptures by Louise Bourgeois, Alexander

Calder, and Roy Lichtenstein," Swanson said, pointing at each of them.

"What's to come will likely make Watergate look like *Alice in Wonderland*," Sandy said.

"It'll have an immediate global impact," Swanson added. "And you'll be a household name—like Woodward and Bernstein."

"I'd like to avoid that, if possible," Archer said. "You all can be the public face of this, not me."

"Not likely," Sandy said. "It'll all come with clearing your good name. Better to be famous than infamous."

Archer held up the lab findings. "Can I keep these?"

Sandy nodded. "They're copies."

"There's something else you should know," Swanson said. "The President-elect's health is declining quickly, and they've confirmed he was likely poisoned with polonium."

"What does that mean?" Archer asked. "The inauguration's tomorrow."

"They're keeping it all very close hold," Swanson said. "They don't want the media to find out. I'm told he's accepted the inevitable, and they're trying to get him the oath of office, just for the sake of his own legacy."

"According to Section 3 of the 20th Amendment, if a winning Presidential candidate dies or becomes incapacitated between the counting of electoral votes in Congress and the inauguration, the Vice President-elect becomes President."

"So Hastings would take over as president, regardless," Archer concluded.

"Making an impeachment inevitable," Sandy interjected.

"Unless we move quickly," Swanson said.

Archer nodded. "So that's what we'll do."

Walking past the long line of black official cars in the driveway of the Fessenden Mansion to stand in line, a hostess approached Max and Shen with an iPad.

"Your names and IDs please?"

"Zhang and Rebecca Wei," Max replied, arm-in-arm with Shen, handing her their IDs. "And this is Bjørn Larsen," she said, referring to Dag.

The hostess surveyed her list, checked their names, and returned their IDs. The team proceeded through a Secret Service security station consisting of walk-thru metal detectors and X-Ray scanners with conveyor belts checking purses, wallets and containers full of keys and loose change. Emerging from the security gauntlet, Max intertwined arms with Shen and Dag and stepped through the massive double-doors, complete with lion door knockers. A stately center hallway led to grand formal rooms, already crowded with people in tuxedos and evening gowns sipping from glasses of champagne, and sampling hors d'oeuvres. Classical music filled the large room.

"Bach," Max commented to Shen. "Gavotte en Rondeau."

"I wouldn't know Bach from Mozart," Shen replied.

A middle aged lady dressed elegantly in a beaded chiffon evening dress stopped beside Max and pointed at the source of the music. "They're the Marine Corps Chamber Orchestra," she said. "The President's Own."

"Very impressive," Shen said. "Believe this is Bach's Gavotte en Rondeau, if I'm not mistaken. A beautiful piece of music."

"Indeed it is," the lady replied, obviously impressed.

Max shook her head slightly, and coughed to prevent laughing out loud. "Exquisite!"

"I'm Linda Craine," the lady said, extending her hand to Max and Shen.

"I'm Rebecca and this is Zhang," Max answered, shaking her hand. "I love your dress! Versace?"

"Oh, thank you!" Linda Craine replied. "Yes! I told Donatella that I needed a dress for tonight, so she created this herself—it's an original."

"Absolutely stunning," Max said with a charming smile, perfectly in command of herself. "And so is your home!"

"Feel free to look around!" she exclaimed. "It's an 18th century-inspired design, like the Dumfries House in Scotland, among others."

"We'd love to see more of it, if that's okay?" Max replied.

"By all means," Linda Craine replied. "Feel free to walk around."

As they were walking away from Linda Craine, Max whispered to Shen. "You see what happens when you compliment a woman on her dress?."

"Well played," Shen whispered back to Max.

"Recommend you all make full use of your hall passes quickly," Archer transmitted to the team over their earpieces. "Dag, you'll find a package at the southwest fence for you."

"Got it," Dag replied. "I'll distribute."

"I'm in the elevator," Max reported. "The basement has two levels— 'B1' and 'B2.'" Requires a keycard to access the B2 level."

"Assume that's where their operations center is located," Archer replied. Examining the house blueprints, he sent another transmission. "There's another entrance in the back stairwell. They don't build these with a single entrance and exit point, but you'll need to get your hands on a key card for entry."

"I'll try," Shen whispered back. "But I'll need some help."

"I found the other entryway," Shen reported to the team. "Two levels down. There's a door in the basement. It requires a special key card."

"I believe Max may be able to help us," Shen said quietly.

"How's she managing that?" Archer asked.

"Well, presently, she's slow dancing with our host, Dr. Craine," Shen said, deadpan. "And it appears she's managed to pick his pocket— quite deftly, in fact."

"Chinaman," Max commented into her microphone a few moments later. "You owe me that dance."

There were no alarms when Max and Shen entered. The room was filled with rows of computer monitors and flat screen televisions mounted on the walls, each broadcasting different news channels.

An athletic African-American man wearing glasses, khaki pants and a sweater approached them. "May I help you?"

"We're on a self-guided tour of the mansion!" Shen exclaimed, doing his best to appear lightly intoxicated. "Linda told us we could walk around and see their beautiful home!"

Now standing in front of Shen and Max, the man further surveyed them in their formal attire. "Can I see your identification?"

"Oh, yes! Of course!" Shen said absently reaching for his wallet. "We're part of the party upstairs, and I thought I'd just show my friend around, if that's okay?"

"I don't believe I've seen you here before," the man answered, increasingly suspicious. "Are you even authorized—?"

The question was interrupted with Max stumbling into them both, also feigning intoxication, and without warning—thrust a side hammer fist to his throat, simultaneously injecting his jugular, causing him to crumple to the floor in a heap.

Shen stood wide eyed at the man, and then at Max.

"Pilates," Max replied simply.

"Yeah, right," Shen replied. "And what's keeping him down?"

"Methohexital," Max said, looking up at Shen. "It's a barbiturate—fast acting, but short lived, so we don't have a lot of time. He'll never know who--or what--hit him."

Shen looked over at Max. "Okay. I'd be very happy to dance with you."

Max shook her head with a slight smile, and pointed to the lone computer screen that was lit up. "Looks like he's already logged into their system." She pulled out a USB flash drive from her pocket and inserted it into the back of the computer screen. "This shouldn't take long."

"Okay," Shen said. "I'm going to take a look around."

Max proceeded to scan passwords stored into the computer, downloaded all of the files on the network's hard drive, and generated a backdoor override. After several minutes into the file download, she noticed the "nsc.eop.gov" domain names.

"Jesus, they have a backdoor into all of the White House's

classified and unclassified servers for the National Security Council!"

"Max, you need to move quickly," Archer transmitted, increasingly concerned.

"Oh my God…" Max exclaimed. She looked up to see Shen standing in front of her, holding a file.

"What is it?" Shen asked, distracted.

"They're going to kill them too," Max replied. "Tonight!"

"*Who?* Who are they killing?" Shen exclaimed. "What are you talking about?"

Max placed the file on the desk. It was marked "TOP SECRET." The names on the file read:

DANIEL / ROBIN TORY

Chapter 55

"MR. SPEAKER, I NEED TO SEE YOU," Luke Archer said flatly over the secure phone.

"Okay," Danno Tory replied groggily. He glanced at the digital clock on his bedside table. "It's one-thirty in the morning! It can't wait?"

"Afraid not," Archer replied. "You and Robin are in grave danger."

"Meet me at my house," Danno replied. "We'll let my security detail know we're expecting company."

"Already on the way. We'll be there in twenty minutes," Archer said. "Lock all your doors. If you have guns handy, you'll want 'em locked and loaded.

"Aren't we overreacting here just a—" Danno stopped in mid sentence, looking out the window onto the street in front of their Capitol Hill townhouse. Something on the street caught his eye. "Archer?"

"Mr. Speaker?"

"I don't see our security detail."

Archer inhaled. "Wake Robin now."

The sound of glass breaking downstairs preceded the house alarm that was now blaring. Robin shot up and spun out of bed. "Who was on the phone?" She asked, pulling the .45 Automatic out of the bed glove.

"Archer," Danno replied. "He said we're in danger."

Chambering a round in the handgun, she passed it to her husband. "It's loaded," she whispered, and then pulled a Benelli M4 Tactical Shotgun from its storage position under the bed and loaded a shell into the chamber. Simultaneously, she spilled the 12 gauge shotgun shells onto the floor behind the bed.

Danno started to turn the bedroom lights on, but Robin stopped him. "No!" She whispered. "Our best defensive position is right here." She pulled the thick table desk down onto its side, positioning it adjacent

272

to the doorway. She then looked around and opened two windows and punched out the screens. She looked intently at Danno, pointing at both windows. "If necessary, we'll escape over the roof."

"Why not do that now?"

"Because we don't know what's waiting for us out there," Robin replied calmly, insistently.

Danno nodded. At once, in a deafening cacophony, loud shots erupted into the walls and glass of the bedroom, causing both Danno and Robin to throw themselves to the ground. Robin stood up and advanced toward the door, firing the three shells through the doorway in quick succession. Hugging the walls while thumbing shells into the Benelli, she moved down the hallway, crouching, shotgun at the ready, surveying the downstairs foyer. A shadow appeared on the staircase, and Robin fired five shots before watching the dark figure crumple to the ground. Robin retreated back into the bedroom and reloaded the shotgun. The phone was ringing incessantly, and outside, sirens sounded in the distance, growing louder and louder.

"Answer it!" Robin shouted above the piercing alarm, peaking around the corner downstairs, sweeping the barrel of the shotgun toward the foyer.

Danno picked up the phone and didn't wait for a voice. "We need the police here now," he said in a calm, but firm voice—doing his best to remain calm.

Robin shouted. "WINDOW!"

A man in black tactical gear was on the roof, standing at their bedroom window. Both Danno and Robin fired simultaneously. "Jesus! They're *inside* our house!"

Robin moved into the hallway, firing the shotgun rapidly, deliberately sweeping at targets she could not see below the balcony into the foyer. A large blast sounded, accompanied by a blinding light. Automatic gunfire erupted below, followed by silence, and a series of shouts exclaiming, *"Clear!"*

"Robin! Mr. Speaker!"

Danno recognized Archer's voice.

"All clear down here! You both safe?"

Danno and Robin walked down the stairway, surveying the scene. Five bodies, of men dressed in black, lay strewn around the foyer at their feet.

"Mr. Speaker, Robin, we need to get you away from here now," Archer said in a low, voice over the house alarm, holding the grip of an M4 Carbine by his side.

"Where?" Danno asked.

"To the Operations Center for now," Archer replied. "This is a coup attempt, any way you view it."

"It's a Kill List," Luke Archer said matter-of-factly, handing the file to Daniel and Robin Tory. "And you both were at the top of it."

"Why?" Danno asked. "Who would want to kill us?"

"Mr. Speaker," Archer began. "You are the third in the line of succession to the Presidency. As an Independent, you also represent the only real obstacle to Vice President Hastings if he were to become POTUS."

"They want to install their own Speaker," Robin said.

"Not only that," Archer answered. "Judging from the way they've targeted Supreme Court Justices and they're trying to install a whole new government—*their own*."

"Under crisis conditions, they'd have a free hand to do whatever they want, and they've certainly established those conditions," Danno said. "There's one good thing about that list, though."

Danno shot a skeptical glance at Archer. "What could possibly be good about a Kill List?"

Robin nodded, looking up at the video monitor of names and headshots of those on the list. "Because they're the Incorruptibles."

"The *Who?*" Danno asked.

"The 'Incorruptibles,'" Robin repeated. "They're the ones who haven't been tainted. The ones we know we can trust."

Danno nodded. "Once we clean this up, they would be the first we'd go to in filling the positions that end up vacated by SU conspirators."

"Whom we try for Insurrection and Treason," Robin replied icily.

Archer held out a hand. "Look, before we can end this, we need to know where it begins."

"Don't we know that already?" Robin asked.

"We have a good idea," Archer answered. "But someone—or something—is funding this effort. It goes well beyond any single corporation, and involves not just millions, but *billions* of dollars. And it may originate outside our borders."

"Where exactly?" Robin asked.

Archer shrugged. "Russia...China...who knows? It's something we ought to be considering."

"Wasn't that polonium they used against John Lee?" Robin asked.

Archer nodded. "The FSB used it to kill Alexander Litvinenko. It's one of their signature weapons of assassination. Indications were the polonium used to kill John Lee came from Argonne National Laboratory, but since that information came from a government source, it can't be trusted — yet."

"We need the media's support," Danno said. "Now's the time to get them involved."

"Will they believe any of this?" Archer asked.

"The good ones will," Danno replied. "I know a few—freelancers mostly."

Robin shook her head. "Well, we can start by giving them a tour of our bullet-riddled home before the FBI can intervene."

Archer picked up a 3x5 card on the desk in front of him, and wrote out Jan Rayburn's name and phone number. "Jan's already helping us with the investigation into Zachary Hastings. She's a great reporter. You can trust her."

"I know her," Danno said, taking the card. "You believe all of this is connected?"

Archer nodded. "I do. So, I'd like to send Max and Dag along with you for protection."

Chapter 56

"WHO ARE THEY, ARCHER?" Danno Tory asked. "Republicans or Democrats?"

"Liberals or Conservatives...Nationalists or Globalists?" Archer shrugged. "Neither, and both," he answered. "But not just one. As tempting as it may be, depending on your own politics, you can't put a label on them. And if we do it we're making a big mistake."

"What do they want?" Danno asked. "What's their agenda? Can we at least define that?"

Archer nodded. "Part of it, at least. The common denominators are there. They want to secure the reigns of the entire U.S. Government. They're driven by power and money. And while they say publicly that the Constitution is their guide, in reality, they don't give a damn about it."

"You may have just described half of America," Robin replied.

"And all of K Street," Danno added.

"That's why they're so elusive. And dangerous. They can blend in."

"More than half the country will go along with them just out of blind loyalty, I'm afraid. It's a pandemic-like disease."

"How do you eradicate it?"

Archer shook his head. "I don't know, Mr. Speaker. That's going to be up to you. But I have a good idea of where to start."

Archer's cell phone rang. Answering, he recognized Laura's voice, strident in its urgency. "We just intercepted this conversation between Hastings and his aide. Listen."

Of the disembodied set of recorded voices, Archer recognized one of them as Hastings':

> *"They got in the way at the Tory house, so [Unintelligible]. Listen—let's have someone pay a visit to the Vet up in Maine...Camden, is it?"*
>
> *"White Mountain National Forest... Okay, send me the*

276

coordinates.. I'll send a team up there now."
"Don't kill her. At least not yet. We'll use her as leverage."

"I think they're going after Elena," Laura said, with a tone of urgency.

"I sent her and Beau to my trailer, just to be safe," Archer replied. "Somehow they found her location. I need to get up there now."

"Okay. Give me ten minutes, and I'll have transportation for you," Laura replied. "Start driving to Signature at BWI. By the time you get there, you'll have a plane waiting for you."

"It needs to be stocked with an 'A' Bag of equipment and ammunition," Archer replied. "Just in case."

"Archer?"

"Yeah," Archer answered, distracted and concerned.

"It'll be okay," Laura reassured him. "They don't know where she's at. Beau's with Elena. He'll protect her until you arrive."

Chapter 57

BY PRIVATE JET FROM BWI'S Signature Air to New Hampshire, Luke Archer boarded a Sikorsky S76C, and forty minutes later, landed in a clearing within White Mountain National Forest in close proximity to his campsite. All the while, he tried desperately to call Elena, but received no response. Archer checked his watch—and saw the time: 4:46am. Archer stepped off before the wheels hit the ground, at a full sprint and fully armed. Elena's Jeep Grand Cherokee was on the trail, and the door to the trailer was open—which he knew to be an ominous indicator. Whether it was her house or the trailer, he remembered Elena always insisted on closing doors.

Something was wrong.

Inside the trailer, Archer shouted for Elena loudly. Faint light streamed out into the darkened hallway.

"Beau?" he called out.

Nothing.

Just inside the trailer's shower, Beau was lying on the ground, bleeding profusely—shot twice in his chest and leg. Somehow, miraculously, he was still alive. He reached down to touch Beau, while stepping over him, and found the sleeping quarters empty and torn asunder. His pottery lamp lay shattered on the ground, papers strewn around the bed.

"Elena!" Archer shouted again.

No response.

He heard the helicopter outside in the nearby clearing, rotors still turning, waiting for him.

Stepping back to Beau, he sat beside him against the wall and held his head and kissed him. In lifting him up, Archer looked down and saw several sections of black shirts and pants—all torn and bloodied. "You got a piece of 'em, didn't you?"

Beau whimpered. Archer nodded, knowing he was dying, in a great deal of pain, and beyond any hope of recovery.

Archer lifted him up, and set him down outside, beside the trailer beside the firepit.

He pulled out his silenced Hi-Power, and caressed his big, beautiful dark head.

"Thank you for protecting her—I'll find her, and bring her home…." Looking into Beau's dark eyes, tears flowed down Archer's face.

"Laura, they got Elena just before I could reach her," Archer shouted over his cell phone. "I need to locate her now."

"Got it," Laura replied. "We'll get to work on finding her."

"Target Portland airport, and all the smaller ones with airstrips that can accommodate a Learjet or Gulfstream."

"Where are you?" Laura asked.

"Over Route 302, heading Southeast toward Portland," Archer replied. "Let me know what you find out."

Archer dialed again and heard Jim Swanson answer. "Jim, I need the cell phone and home numbers for Zachary Hastings," Archer said. "They've taken a good friend of mine hostage, and they killed my dog."

"Stand by," Swanson replied. "Let me know what else I can do."

Archer saw Laura Chicone's number dialing in, and answered.

"Archer, they're taking a seaplane!" Laura exclaimed over the phone. "Labrador Seaplane Base, in Naples—only 30 miles from you. It flies out of Sebago Lake. It's registered to the Path Corporation, a CIA front company."

"Okay, we're turning around," Archer replied. "We'll try to intercept it. Need to know their flight plan."

"Got it. They're transferring to a Gulf Stream V at Signature Air at BWI. Tail number is N44982. Archer—" Laura replied "It's the Guantanamo Bay Express."

Luke Archer pointed at the navy blue and white single-engine seaplane plowing across Sebago Lake. Through binoculars, he was able to confirm the tail number as the plane that was carrying Elena: N44982.

"We gotta keep that plane from taking off," Archer told the pilot. "By any means."

"The max weight for a seaplane that size is about 2800 pounds," the pilot said. "Our best bet is to first slow it down so they can't reach their liftoff speed, then weigh it down, and alter their center of gravity so they can't take off."

Archer nodded. "Get on top of 'em," he directed.

The pilot nodded, and put the helicopter into a rapid, deep dive, attempting to cross the plane's flight path.

But the seaplane was accelerating too quickly and too far in front of them down the lake.

"They're going too fast and their lift is too much for us to stop 'em," the pilot reported.

From a distance, through the plane's side window, he could see Elena. She appeared to have a hood over her head and her hands were bound and tied to a bar on the plane's ceiling above her.

"I'm sorry, Sir," the pilot's voice came overhead. "When they've picked up that kind of speed and that kind of head start, we don't have much of a chance."

"Thanks for trying," Archer answered, watching the plane fly off in the distance. A feeling of guilt and helplessness overwhelmed him, to the extent that he hadn't experienced since Becky had been killed, and when he'd found her body.

"If it's any help, our on-board radar has them flying due south," the pilot continued. "Toward Washington."

"Do you have enough fuel to get me back to DC, direct?"

"Yes, Sir," the pilot replied. "We'll file a flight plan enroute, and have you back in less than 3 hours.

Chapter 58

Luke Archer received the text message on his cell phone as the helicopter was landing at The National Presbyterian Church heliport.

"Colonel Archer, we called ahead for a vehicle," the pilot said over the intercom system. "American University is right over there. Good luck, Sir."

Archer thanked the pilot. It was approaching dusk. The image of Elena, bound and tied, with a hood over her head was what haunted him as he stepped off the helicopter into its rotor wash. The text message was equally disconcerting—he knew well what it would involve, but he was also troubled that it had been sent to him at all.

How had they obtained his cell phone number?

The car they had sent was a white Land Rover, and he saw Laura standing there beside it. As Archer approached, Laura hugged him. The helicopter's rotor wash picked up in intensity as it lifted off.

"I'm so sorry, Archer," Laura said, opening the car door for him. "We'll find Elena. I promise."

Once inside, Archer handed her his cell phone in silence so she could read the text message he'd just received.

"Don't go," she answered emphatically, handing him back his phone.

Archer shook his head slowly. "This time, I've got to."

"No!" Laura replied. "They'll kill you!"

"And they'll kill her if I don't show up," Archer said quietly. "I don't have much of a choice."

"You have plenty of choice!" Laura exclaimed. "It's why you have us."

"He killed Becky," Archer said. "I'm not going to let him kill Elena too."

"Please don't," Laura answered. "We're all here to help you get her back. All of us."

"I appreciate the offer, but I've gotta do this alone."

"So just stand by on the sidelines and watch them kill you? Is that it?"

Archer shook his head, checking the ammunition in his Browning Hi-Power. "Hopefully, it won't come to that."

"You and I both know what they're capable of," Laura answered. "Couldn't you try to negotiate with them?"

Archer looked at her for a long moment before replying. "How do you negotiate with fanatics?"

"I don't know," Laura replied. "Tell them you'll back off in exchange for Elena, and for dropping the charges they've leveled against you. The only reason they're going after you is because you represent their sole obstacle."

"And that's why you need to leave this be," Archer said, slowly shaking his head— "As a friend, I'm asking you to understand."

"Well, I don't understand."

Archer nodded. "Listen, if hadn't gone out on a run that evening, Becky would still be here. But I left her. I'm not leaving Elena."

"What if you don't come back?" Laura asked, eyes welling with tears. "What if they kill you?"

"Regardless if I come back or not, someone needs to see all of this through—Zachary Hastings and SU can't be allowed to succeed. This is bigger than all of us. It's about the country. Our democracy."

Laura shook her head emphatically. "So tell me, what is this really? A personal vendetta? A crusade? What is it for you?"

Archer turned to face Laura. "I thought you, more than any other, would understand. It's what we've always done. You and I have never been on the sidelines, we've been on the frontlines. We haven't tried to parse or rationalize what we do, or why we do it. Them taking Elena doesn't change that."

"Okay, I got it." Laura replied, a look of wariness closing over her features. She handed back his cell phone. "You have a death wish. I'll hold your coat then."

"Pray for all of us," Archer replied. "That's what you can do."

"Archer?"

Archer looked into her eyes. Tears were rolling down her cheeks. She wiped the tears away with her hand. "Come back."

Luke Archer parked the Land Rover on the top level, in the far northeastern corner of Union Station's parking deck. It was a crisp, clear night. The illuminated view of the United States Capitol was unobstructed, and served as a reminder to Archer why he'd undertaken this effort.

> *"I, Luke Beckett Archer, do solemnly swear that I will support and defend the Constitution of the United States against all enemies, foreign and domestic; that I will bear true faith and allegiance to the same..."*

Archer recalled his father in front of him in his dress blue uniform with four-star shoulder boards, both of their right arms raised, delivering the oath to him. He repeated it, word for word, and then at its conclusion, his father grasped his hand tightly. *"That oath,"* his father said, eyes locked in his. *"It never expires."*

Behind him, he heard the sound of vehicles ascending the ramp. Turning around, he saw a line of three black SUVs approach. When they stopped, their headlights were focused on Archer. He shielded his eyes. Two men in black tactical SWAT gear exited each of the three vehicles and pointed M4 Carbines in his direction.

One of the men opened the door of the far right SUV, and Elena stepped out. She ran toward Archer and fell into his arms.

"Luke!" Elena exclaimed, sobbing. "My God! What's happening?"

"Are you okay?" Archer asked softly, confidently—holding her tightly.

Elena nodded. *"Why are they doing this?"*

"They knew they could get to me through you," Archer said, smiling reassuringly at her.

"It'll all be okay. This is my fault. Now listen to me—you need to get in this vehicle and drive toward the Lincoln Monument. There's a cell phone in the console. My team will call you. Do what they say, and you'll be fine. *Do you understand?"*

Elena's small, petite body jerked in his embrace. She stepped back with an expression of heavy incomprehension.

Her eyes were wide, terrified. Pleading.

"But what about *you*?"

"I'll be fine," Archer insisted gently, but firmly. "You have to go now, and let me handle this."

"*No!* You can't give yourself up to them!"

Archer shook his head, and pointed at the men surrounding them. "If you don't go now, both of us'll be killed," Archer said evenly. "We have no choice—I have to do this. Now go. *Please*."

Elena shook her head, swallowed, and wiped her tears. She kissed him, and fixed her eyes on him. "Come back to me."

One of the men—tall, bald and dressed in black tactical gear—stepped forward, motioned for him to put his hands behind his back, and handcuffed him tightly in hinged steel cuffs that offered no flexibility or movement. As the man was handcuffing him, he noticed the chunks of skin and puncture marks on his right arm.

The one who shot Beau....

"You met my dog, I see," Archer commented.

The man looked up at him with contempt, tightening the handcuffs so they pinched his skin.

Archer watched Elena get into the Land Rover and drive away. As it disappeared down the ramp of the parking garage, he was led to the black SUV that she had just emerged from.

The sound of the door shutting indicated that it was an armored vehicle. The windshield and windows were heavily tinted, and the front partition was raised, preventing him from seeing the front seat or the windshield view ahead.

The doors locked with a jarring finality, the locking mechanisms activating in unison. A few seconds later the electric partition lowered. The occupant of the passenger seat turned around, and at first he believed he was hallucinating.

"Hello, Archer," Laura said directly. "I was so hoping it wouldn't come to this."

Chapter 59

"LAURA?" LUKE ARCHER ASKED in disbelief. *"Why?*

Laura shook her head. She was wearing a tailored charcoal suit, dangling pearl earrings, and a dark blue Hermès scarf. Her eyes were dark with mascara and resignation, and something behind them had changed.

"Don't judge me, Archer. I wouldn't expect you to understand. I took over this movement to lead our country back from a very dangerous precipice, and we're doing that. I thought you, of all people, would come to see that clearly. But you became another obstacle, and I couldn't talk you out of it. We can't turn back now."

"You started this?" Archer replied, breathing shallowly.

"Rather amazing what you can do when you remain anonymous," Laura replied blankly.

"I don't get it," Archer replied. "Chris Stockman shot you! He tried to kill you!"

Laura laughed slightly. "He did—at least he thought he did. It was staged for the security cameras and the audio recording you heard."

"And you let me kill him?"

Laura shook her head. "He made the mistake of venturing off on his own separate agenda, over time he'd become a liability, and a threat to the cause—and he really did intend to kill me."

"And me?" Archer asked. "So now I'm a liability to you?"

"I had hoped you would find a way to join us," Laura answered. "But now I know that's not possible."

"How did I misjudge you so completely?"

"For starters, you didn't think to check and see if Dr. Robert Craine had a sister."

Archer's eyes widened and he fought the urge to cough violently. "He's your *brother*?"

"He's a good man, and together we've built SU into an organization with real values, principles and honorable people our Founders would be proud of."

286

"Yeah, the Kremlin's maybe, but not ours," Archer replied sardonically.

"Actually, we're all that stands between the extreme left or right taking over this country and destroying it."

"Ah, I see. You're centrists," Archer replied, his voice thick with sarcasm. "So killing Midshipmen, the Speaker of the House, Supreme Court Justices and an entire Texas township are all reasonable goals in your scheme."

"If we're to start over...to have a fresh start," Laura replied irritably. "Their sacrifice was...is necessary."

"Let me guess," Archer said, hardly concealing his disgust. "Your brother will be Zachary Hastings' Vice President?"

Laura nodded. "Bob's a recognized global business leader who understands energy and international relationships. He'll be a great Vice President—and eventually a great president."

"And you?" Archer asked. "You'll be Oz, behind the curtain? Is that it?"

"It's worked so far," Laura replied. "Honestly, I prefer to operate behind the scenes."

"Well, there are a few real problems with that."

Laura smiled, amused. "What might those be?"

"First, you're not elected. And foremost, it's treason," Archer answered. "Tell me, after serving your country honorably for two decades, how does it feel to be a run-of-the mill traitor?"

"I don't view it like that at all," Laura answered, shaking her head. "In the grand scheme of things, our actions will be proven to be a salvation to this country"

"That's the problem with your brand of heroics," Archer replied. "You need dragons to slay in order to establish your bona fides. What you forget is that even once you believe you have those credentials in place, they have no foundation. They're all written in sand."

"We're revolutionaries, and that makes us heroic," Laura replied. "Of all people, I thought you would understand."

"Sorry to disappoint you." Archer looked out the window and saw the mansions of Kalorama passing by. A few minutes later, the car pulled into the driveway of the Fessenden mansion. Archer exhaled. "Ah, home sweet home."

Chapter 60

LUKE ARCHER WAS LED into the foyer of the house by men who were dressed like United States Secret Service agents. "I should've known how you knew this place so well," he remarked to Laura.

"It was graciously donated to us by the government of Russia," Laura said. "For a worthy cause."

"Of course," Archer replied, his voice thick with sarcasm. "Every insurrection needs one, doesn't it?"

Laura stopped and turned around to face Archer. "There's much you don't quite grasp yet. While I understand your anger and perceived sense of betrayal, world peace and stability both come at a high price—and that's what we're achieving here."

"To include at the cost of friendships and trust."

Laura shrugged. "If necessary, yes."

"And killing your former teammates?" Archer asked. "That's easy for you?"

"They made a decision to get in our way," Laura replied. "They were all warned, to include you. You were the one who decided to kill Dan Thorne. Had you not done that, we probably could have avoided all of this. After you killed Dan, I knew you wouldn't hesitate to kill me."

"Well you know, my Dad always said, 'crow and corn can't grow in the same field.' Guess he was right."

"I have no idea what you're talking about," Laura said dismissively.

Archer looked directly into Laura's eyes. "John, Sam, Jack...all those midshipmen you slaughtered...every one of them made a decision to defend our nation against the likes of you, your brother, and Zachary Hastings. They are heroes. You? You're traitors—the enemy."

Laura laughed. "As a nation, we've always prided ourselves on being revolutionaries. Our Founders, risked their lives against a colonial power. Now we are doing precisely the same thing in resisting the corruption of our current entrenched government. You may not like it, or you may just disagree, but we're justified in our rebellion, and we're just as patriotic as you think you are."

Archer looked around the elaborate living room. "Why have you brought me here? There are easier places to execute your enemies."

Laura smiled, and pressed the button on a remote control, causing the large mirror in the living room to transform itself into a television screen. She motioned to him to sit on the sofa. "Now, I'd like to show you why your efforts are misguided."

She pressed another button on the remote and the video played— an obviously very professionally produced documentary in a *Frontline*-like format, narrated by a former network news anchor who Archer recognized by face, but not name. Graphic images and media footage flashed on the screen, of rioting in the streets of Baltimore, Dallas and Chicago...cities engulfed in flames, the aftermath of domestic and international terror attacks, inner city gang killings, impoverished single-parent families in West Virginia, heroin overdose victims, homeless people in Washington, D.C., celebrities and musicians protesting on the national mall.

> *Two and a half centuries ago, our Founding Fathers signed the Declaration of Independence, and took up arms to create a new kind of government that, as Alexander Hamilton said, was to be formed through reflection and choice, rather than by accident and force. A self-proclaimed group of revolutionaries, our Founders' worldview centered on three revolutionary ideas. "Unalienable Rights"— Life, Liberty and the pursuit of Happiness. For them, the most powerful of these ideas was an unquenchable thirst for liberty. Freedom from oppression. Those freedoms and rights, traditionally seen as indispensable and absolute, are today being systematically eroded by a central government rife with corruption that has systematically used its power to attack its opponents, and our Constitution, to degrade our borders, and which has refused to enforce our laws designed to preserve the safety and well-being of all Americans.*

"What is this? Some kind of self-justification?" Archer interrupted, without any attempt to disguise his contempt. "Please spare me."

Laura sighed and shook her head. "It's only meant to show you why we're here, and what you're up against. It's much larger than you or me at this point."

Archer shook his head and laughed. "Save it, Laura— I could care less how you choose to rationalize yourselves."

The Soldiers of the Union grew from the ideals espoused by our Founders. With the recognition that if the federal government became too powerful and overstepped its authority, the framers of our Constitution saw the requirement for people to develop plans of resistance and resort to arms to reset the rule of law and restore balance. This time has finally come to all responsible citizens to protect themselves against the government's tyranny, to take up arms, to resist and restore our Founders' vision, and to adapt and revise the Constitution to the modern day realities of our nation and our people....

"Brilliant," Archer scoffed, hearing enough. "'Government tyranny.' 'Responsible citizens.'..."

Laura shrugged. "Benjamin Franklin once remarked that 'We need a revolution after every two centuries, because all governments become stale and corrupt after 200 years.'"

"As he left Independence Hall on the final day of the Constitutional Convention of 1787, someone asked Benjamin Franklin, 'Well, Doctor, what have we got—a Republic or a Monarchy?'"

Archer stopped there. Feigning amusement, Laura couldn't resist.

"What was his response?"

"A Republic, if you can keep it."

"Thanks for that vignette," Laura replied. "That's our aim, and this revolution is long overdue."

"Yeah, that's where your argument is so flawed," Archer answered flatly. "Fatally so."

"How might that be?"

"It can only be done by the consent of the governed. It's written in the Declaration of Independence," Archer pointed at the mirrored TV screen. "And if you do it, you can't do it with the intent to overthrow the Constitution—it can only be directed against those who pervert it. Clearly, that's what you're trying to do."

"We're not the enemy, Archer" Laura replied. "Someone needs to make the difficult decisions. Unfortunately, it's too late for you to learn that, after all these years you never saw the big picture, even then."

"What exactly are you talking about? Archer asked.

Laura nodded. "It's a bit sad actually. We had high hopes for you."

"I'm not following...at all."

Laura laughed. "That's been the common lament of yours for years now. You never really figured any of this out."

"Figured *what* out?"

"First you thought it was just bad luck Omar Mehsud Shah's militia captured you. Years later, you blame General Zachary Hastings for compromising you. But you never stopped to think someone else might have been involved, did you?"

"Who?" Archer shot back. "*You?* You were behind that?"

"The capture, the torture," Laura answered matter-of-factly. "And they were supposed to kill you too, but instead you went ahead and escaped."

"Why?" Archer cried. His stomach recoiled. His nerves felt like they were disintegrating. "Jesus...*Why?*"

"I was younger then, you know," Laura answered, sitting down in front of Archer. "Call it a fawning crush—the kind you never quite get over. But, as I discovered, it was the unrequited variety, because you were married."

"That's ridiculous," Archer scoffed, feeling himself losing his composure.

Laura nodded, and she spoke softly. "That was the problem. Because it was ridiculous to you, but not for me."

"I was married for God's sake!"

Laura nodded slowly. "And Becky was in the way."

"She was your *friend*!" Archer shouted in disbelief.

Laura shook her head. "I pretended to be her friend. Eventually, she figured it out. She figured everything out—being the psychiatrist she was. She said she was going to tell you, so I asked Zachary to accompany me on a visit with her that night."

Archer shook his head. "What? *What night?*"

"At first she didn't know why we were both at your front door, you know," Laura continued. "She saw Zack, and something happened to you during your run—that you'd been in an accident. She let us inside, but it didn't take long for her to become suspicious. She asked us to leave, and when we wouldn't, she tried to call the MPs. Zachary pulled the phone out of its socket. And then she fought. I told Zachary to do what he wanted with her, so both of us got what we came for."

"You are batshit crazy," Archer seethed, finally understanding her twisted narrative. "*You were there too?*"

"Zachary told me he'd always had an attraction for Becky," Laura replied. "So I used that to my own advantage."

"How was killing my wife *possibly* to your advantage?"

"Simple strategy of substitution," Laura replied. "With Becky gone, I could comfort you and have you to myself."

"Well, it didn't quite work out that way, did it?"

Laura shook her head. "No, and that's the great tragedy in all of this. But eventually, we all need to just move on don't we?"

"So fifteen years later, you decide to kill me?" Archer seethed. "And then what?"

"We have a new technology for disposing of nuclear waste, you know. We place concentrated plutonium into the walls of a mountain, seal it up, and let the heat generated by the radioactivity build up to the point where it literally melts the surrounding rock, dissolving the radioactive wastes in a molten mass that eventually cools down and crystallizes, actually incorporating the radioactive material into the rock."

"Rock melting," Archer said. "I saw you're doing it on Cold Mountain. The only problem, as I understand it, is that it's not safe, because with all that material, and all that heat, you get so much energy and pressure, you'll turn the whole mountain into a radioactive volcano."

Laura glanced at her watch and looked up with a sidelong smile.

"Turns out, it works with human remains just as efficiently."

"How creative. I'm just garbage to you now...something to dispose of," Archer said evenly. "Is that it? First Becky. Now me?"

Laura shook her head, and her footsteps crossed the parquet floor. "You know, I stayed in the house—in your office—to watch your reaction when you came back that night," Laura continued, ignoring Archer's last comment. "Becky was in your arms. I knew then that I couldn't ever have you. So I left."

Archer remembered the excerpt from the police report he didn't understand at the time:

Unmatched/Inconsistent Shoeprint in Blood at Bedside.
Probable Inadvertent CID Forensics Team Contamination. No action taken. Not advanced.

"That was *your* shoe print in the crime scene photo, wasn't it?" The realization left Archer practically breathless, his flesh crawling. At once, he recalled seeing her unlock her iPhone with her left thumb. "That was *you* in the house I heard? Jesus, I've heard enough," Archer said through gritted teeth, standing up in a sudden, violent motion, heaving his wide shoulders forward.

Two men, to include the bald bodybuilder who had handcuffed Archer, immediately rushed to his side and pushed him down, forcefully.

"If you're not gonna kill me this minute, d'ya suppose I could use your bathroom? You do have twelve of 'em in this house, as I recall."

Laura hesitated a moment, then nodded her approval to the men. "Cuff his hands to the front. Escort him to the bathroom in the foyer. Make sure you keep an eye on him, guns drawn."

"Thanks for the freedom," Archer said, his tone thick with sarcasm.

"When you come back, you're going to make a small video of your own."

"Funny, that's the last thing Omar Shah said to me on my last visit with him."

Stepping into the bathroom, he turned and shouted out, "I'll be just a minute."

At the moment the door shut, a deafening explosion sounded around him, and the blast wave knocked Archer down to the sink and toilet.

The mansion's sprinkler system kicked in immediately.

Archer forced the door open to find the entire first floor littered with fragments of marble and plaster, and immersed in dust and water from the sprinkler. Both of his guards were sprawled on the floor, dead. He picked up one of their Beretta automatic handguns, and made his way, gun at the ready, into what had previously been the living room.

Laura Chicone was on the floor, badly burnt, and clearly dying. Her eyes fluttered.

"What...happened?" Laura asked tremulously.

"That inauguration party we crashed?" Archer asked. "While you were skipping out of the festivities, I had Dag rig the entire first floor of this place with listening devices and explosives. Thanks to your blueprints of the house, I knew the bathroom was constructed out of steel and reinforced concreted— a good, solid safe room. I told Dag to detonate once he knew I was inside. The code phrase to approve the detonation was "Thanks for the Freedom," and the execution command was 'I'll be just a minute.'"

"You knew?"

Archer nodded. "Not about you being there with Becky. But the rest of it, I figured out over time. It was the little things: covering up the origin of the polonium, trying to pass it off as Russian—that was my first indicator. And you were spoon-feeding me information I already knew. The final indicator was a transcript of a conversation that confirmed I was taking the train from Boston to D.C.—you were the only one who knew that, Laura. The train wreck was no coincidence. And that round Chris Stockman used to shoot you was a Glaser Safety Slug—used by Air Marshals and other special mission units to minimize penetration. You switched the bullets in his pistol with those. Any other round would've killed you. Shen got a copy of the ANPR surveillance in Georgetown on the evening of Jack Condon's murder, and it proved you were there. We checked your Jeep and found Glaser rounds in your glove compartment— the same kind you had Chris shoot you with. Finally, I asked Jim Swanson for your FBI and Secret Service files, and that revealed your family history—which I now realize I should've done at the outset. Max and Dag followed you to your visits here, to this big house."

"I'm sorry for hurting you, Archer," Laura said, struggling to utter the words.

"No one's more sorry than me," Archer said with resignation. "All so unnecessary. I always regarded you as one of my closest friends."

"You told me to always do the right thing," Laura said in a strangled tone. "I thought I was doing the right thing for us—"

Archer shook his head, and looked away. "You took everything from me, you know. You made me believe happiness was transitory— and that may be. But through all of this, I've learned that the bad times… they're transitory too. So now I live in the present. You failed, Laura."

Laura swallowed. "Now…is all we have," she gasped, and her stare turned frozen and opaque.

They were her last words.

Archer's ears were ringing loudly. His eyes squinted in a vain attempt to see through the smoke and dust from the massive explosion. To his right, he looked over and could see the red strobe lights each of his team members were wearing, as they entered the ruins of the Fessenden mansion. He heard the faint scream of sirens approaching in the distance. Out of the corner of his eye, he saw a group of three figures in black tactical gear entering from the balcony.

"Get down, Archer!"

Archer recognized Max's voice, and looked up to see each of them collapse to the ground. He looked over to see Max and Shen continuing to fire at each target with their suppressed M4's. A moment later, he saw red laser dots doing a surreal dance around the house, searching for additional targets.

Shen handed Archer a .45 Automatic. "It's locked and loaded."

"We've gotta go!" Max shouted. *"Now!"*

"Just a second," Archer said, returning to the reinforced bathroom that had protected him from the blast. Lying beside it was the bald bodybuilder who was still alive, struggling to move toward an M4 Carbine that had landed several feet away.

Archer kicked the M4 away and pointed his .45 at the man, looking him in the eyes. "You didn't have to kill my dog."

One shot rang out, and Archer maneuvered through the wreckage to rejoin his team members.

Epilogue

"IT'S WHERE HE LOVED TO BE," Elena said, suggesting that Archer bury Beau in the woods behind her house. "We'd go on hikes in those woods whenever I had the time. After what he did for me, I'd love to have him there."

When he had finished with the burial, Archer sat beside Elena on a log, and said simply, "I'm sorry for all of this."

Elena shook her head slowly. "It's not your fault."

"None of this would've happened if they hadn't connected you to me."

Elena turned to Archer and looked directly into his eyes. "Look, there's obviously a lot I still don't know about you, Archer. I can wait for that. But I do believe in you."

"A lot of times these days, I'm not sure I believe in myself," Archer said. After an extended silence between them, he turned to her, "I never intended any of this for you. I understand completely if you don't want any part."

Elena smiled and shook her head. "That's the last thing I want. You and your friends are the only ones who can stop this nightmare."

"Get ready, then."

"For what?"

Archer looked over at her. "As a young lieutenant, I was stationed at Fort Sill, Oklahoma. When I got down there in May. The weather was beautiful. A week later, I looked up in the sky and saw my first tornado right in front of me. That was the first of two dozen over the next two months." He handed her a copy of the *New York Times*. "Oklahoma's tornado season— that's the best way I can describe what's ahead."

Congress Impeaches and Convicts Vice President Hastings for Treason
Ailing President Consults On Successor

By Jan Rayburn
Special to The New York Times

Washington, January 30—Only ten days following the inauguration, Zachary Hastings has been convicted and removed from office as Vice President of the United States today. This action followed. He was charged with high treason and impeached for overt actions to influence the presidential election prior to and during his assumption of the Vice Presidency.

The stunning development, ending a Federal grand jury investigation of General Hastings in Baltimore and terminating his political career, shocked his closest associates and precipitated an immediate search by an ailing President Stone for a successor.

"I categorically deny these charges and denounce these proceedings," General Hastings declared in a formal statement. Both the notice of impeachment and his conviction were delivered at 12:00 P.M. to Secretary of State Tracy Faulkner as provided in the Succession Act of 1792.

Minutes later, General Hastings stood before United States District Judge John R. Jones in a Baltimore courtroom, and read from a statement in which he pleaded "Not Guilty" to Government charges that he had led an active campaign of subversion and sabotage against the U.S. Government.

Tells Court Innocent of all Charges

"I categorically deny all charges against me, and will prove my innocence in court," the nation's 50th Vice President told the stilled courtroom.

In his dramatic courtroom statement, General Hastings declared that he was innocent of any other wrongdoing.

In a failed attempt to preempt the impeachment proceedings, General Hastings sent a letter to President Stone saying that he was resigning.

The impeachment automatically set in motion, for the second time since the resignation of Vice President Spiro Agnew, the provisions of the 25th Amendment to the Constitution, under which the President must nominate a successor who will be subject to confirmation by a majority vote in both houses of Congress. Until a successor is confirmed and sworn in, the Speaker of the House, Daniel Tory, Independent of Illinois, will be first in line of succession to the Presidency.

General Hastings' sudden impeachment came only 11 days after he made an emotional declaration to a Miami audience: "I will not resign if indicted! I will not resign if indicted!"

It marked the first time in the nation's history that the Vice-Presidency was vacated by impeachment, and the third time by resignation. The first resignation of a Vice President was in 1832, when John C.

Calhoun stepped down after he was chosen to fill a Senate seat from South Carolina. The second time was in 1973, when Spiro T. Agnew resigned following an admission of federal tax evasion.

One stunned Hastings associate remarked this morning, "None of us understand it. We are flabbergasted."

The shock of the announcement of General Hastings' impeachment had barely worn off when the White House and leaders in Congress began deliberating about both the politics and the mechanics of Vice Presidential succession.

President Stone was said to have begun consultation with leaders "both within and outside the Administration" on the nominee to succeed General Hastings.

The Senate majority leader has assembled bipartisan Congressional officials to discuss the selection process and prepare for hearings to assess the qualifications of the nominee.

Speculation About Successor

The White House has repeatedly denied that it had a "contingency" list of potential successors. Published reports, and renewed speculation today, centered on the possibility that President Stone would nominate Speaker of the House and Illinois Independent Daniel O. Tory. Because Speaker Tory was born in Lithuania, and came to the United States as a young boy, an effort has been underway to amend Article II of the Constitution to allow his appointment to Vice President of the United States. In

only one week, and with broad bipartisan
support, the amendment has received the
required super-majorities in both houses
of Congress, and quickly proceeded to a
state-by-state vote, where forty-one states
approved the amendment, making it part of
the U. S. Constitution. Since the nation's
founding, several thousand amendments have
been proposed in Congress, but only thirty-
four have been sent to the states--with the
passage of this amendment, twenty-eight
of those have been formally added to the
Constitution.

General Hastings, whose career ended at
the age of 56 years, disappeared from public
view this afternoon as the limousine in which
he was riding pulled away from the Baltimore
courthouse and the former Vice President
waved to spectators. Simultaneously, in a
sign that the level of corruption runs far
deeper than originally believed, the FBI
raided the offices of Senator Horace Bend,
Congressman Ted McCormick, and Governor Mike
McKaren.

"Archer, with the line of succession and with the President's
condition, they tell me I'm likely going to be President," Danno Tory
said.

"You'll be a fine President, Mr. Speaker," Archer replied, looking
over the Washington Mall from the Capitol Rotunda balcony. The noises
of the city were muted by the recent snowfall. Upon entering the rotunda,
he couldn't help but feel out of place in his blue jeans, flannel shirt and
leather jacket, amidst everyone else wearing suits and business attire.

"You know, my Uncle Jonas, who fought against the Nazis and

the Soviets during World War II, used to always tell me, 'Danno! You will be President!', but I never believed it, or expected it. Especially this way. It doesn't seem right."

"It doesn't take much of a fortune teller to tell you these aren't ordinary times," Archer said, handing him a copy of *The Washington Post*.

Danno looked down at the newspaper's headline:

Nuclear Energy Conglomerate Shut Down by FBI and Homeland Security:
CEO Commits Suicide

Following FBI and DHS raids in three States, V-Tec CEO Dr. Robert Craine commits suicide in prison.

Danno nodded, setting the newspaper down. "No they aren't." Looking closer, he saw the accompanying photos of the VMAX Storage Facility at Cold Mountain, crediting Luke Archer as the photographer.

"You took these photos?" Danno asked.

Archer nodded. "*Qui audet adipiscitur*," Archer replied, blowing smoke from his cigar.

"I have a hard enough time with English," Danno replied, smiling.

"Who Dares Wins," Archer replied. "The British SAS's motto. A good friend of mine who commanded that regiment reminds me of that from time to time."

"Mark Lyons?"

Archer nodded, visibly surprised. "You know Mark?"

"My father introduced me to him," Danno replied. "He defused the entire Balkans fiasco a few years back."

"Small world."

Danno blew a large cloud of smoke from his cigar, and looked at it. "Cuban? Are these legal yet?"

Archer shrugged, exhaling smoke. "I prefer to think of it as burning their crops."

Danno laughed. "Al Haig?"

"Or Kinky Friedman," Archer smiled. "Not sure who said it first. Gets to perspective though. How you view the world."

"Have you ever doubted whether you were up to a certain task?"

Archer nodded. "Every day. But you always have two choices— to stay in the fight, or withdraw. My dad used to tell me you only really lose if you quit."

"Well, I'm not gonna quit," Danno answered.

"I know you're not. They say a blind mule doesn't fall when he follows the bit," Archer replied, pouring from John Lee's bottle '26 Macallan's into Danno's glass. "If your bit is the Constitution, you won't fall, because you'll have the country's support."

"So, then." Archer raised his glass to Danno. "To the Constitution."

"To the Constitution," Danno replied, taking a sip and savoring it, then glancing at the setting sun. "Would you consider a position in the White House? Maybe National Security Advisor?"

Archer shook his head. "I'm going back to teaching fifth graders."

"Safer than what you've been doing lately, isn't it?"

"Safer, less risky maybe. But no less challenging, to be honest."

"So I can't convince you to reconsider?"

"I think you'd be much better served if I were available to you behind the scenes."

Danno nodded. He took another swallow, not waiting for the taste of it. "I understand."

"You know I'm always here. Anytime. Anyplace."

Danno nodded, eyes on his glass, sipped the bourbon, and held it in his mouth a while before swallowing. "I know that. It's the one thing that gives me confidence."

"We all have plenty of reason to be confident now, but also cautious," Archer said tactfully, setting his glass down on the concrete balcony.

"Blind mule, eh?" Danno asked, grinning amiably.

"As stubborn as you are," Archer answered, chuckling. "Another thing about blind mules, you know—they ain't afraid of the dark."

Zachary Hastings attempted to conceal his surprise, entering his home and seeing Luke Archer sitting down at his kitchen table pointing a suppressed Browning Hi-Power at him. His wide eyes revealed a visceral rage that was impossible to hide.

"Tell me, how were your impeachment hearings, Zack?" Archer asked bluntly. "And your introduction to criminal court?"

"I have a security team outside the house, Archer," Hastings said with a slightly quavering voice.

"I think they're there to make sure you don't escape. Not protect you."

If you plan to kill me, you'll never get away with it."

"That was my plan," Archer replied. "Has been for a while now. I even dreamt about it. But someone made me realize there are better ways to handle it. That if I were to kill you, I'd probably feel better for a while, but then I'd realized I'd only be joining you in wading in your slop."

Hastings shook his head and laughed. "So if you're not going to kill me, what's your plan exactly?"

Archer's brows drew together in contrived thought. He pointed toward the television above the kitchen counter. The color screen had been paused in place, and a date-time stamp was visible in the right corner. "Take a look at this. I think you'll probably recognize it."

"What are you talking about?" Hastings asked, smirking.

Archer pressed "PLAY" on the remote, and the unmistakable image of Hastings running from the back door of a home in a bloodstained shirt came into clear focus. "You'll recognize our home at Fort Campbell on this video, and of course, that's obviously you running away from it after raping and killing Becky."

A cold shadow fell over Hastings as he watched.

As the video continued to play, Hastings abruptly looked away. Whatever he'd expected, it wasn't this. "That's ridiculous," he said with contempt and a trace of fear. "That's not me!"

"Oh, actually, it is you," Archer answered firmly. "We found some CCTV footage of you in grainy black and white, that could have been open to some interpretation, I suppose. But that also served a purpose, because it led us to your shirt that was covered in Becky's blood, that you dumped in a plastic commissary bag in the culvert by your old house. Believe it or not, the shirt was still there, and it was well-preserved by the bag. None of us expected the Fort Campbell MP detachment would notify us that they'd only installed new high-resolution color CCTV cameras two weeks prior to this!"

Hastings' face tightened into abject coldness and his eyes went flat. "I should have had Omar Shah kill you when he had you."

Archer nodded in resignation. "You and Laura—you probably should have. But of course, when he had the chance, he didn't."

Hastings seemed genuinely surprised to hear Archer's awareness of Laura's role in collaboration with his. "A missed opportunity."

"And I have you both to thank for that 'vacation.' The spa treatments—being covered in your own shit...the odd brand of Pilates they practice—binding your arms together behind your back and raising you up until your hands were in front of your face? It was lovely. Thanks for that."

"You deserved that and more, Archer," Hastings hissed. "You and your people have been the one obstacle we faced in rebuilding our country, and restoring our place in the world."

"Well, we've never been a kleptocracy-of-the-few and I'm pretty sure our Founders never envisioned that form of government for us," Archer said quietly. "Come to think of it, they warned us against it. But I have to hand it to you. You came damn close to achieving it. I was wondering how Omar Shah was suddenly found, out of the blue. The reality is that he was going to tell everyone about your collaboration, wasn't he? But you had to identify him, and I was the only one who could do it."

"You're the traitor, Colonel, not me."

"We'll just let God and the courts be the judge of that, *Major*," Archer replied, letting it sink in.

Hastings betrayed a confused expression.

Archer answered. "Oh, you didn't hear, did you? The Secretary of Defense just confirmed you'll be demoted to the last rank that you served in honorably. There's a question! When exactly *did* you go completely off the rails?"

Breathing deeply, Hastings made a derogatory noise, staring at Archer with disdain and fear.

Archer pointed at the video showing Hastings on the run, now hiding the bag containing his bloodstained T-Shirt. "This is your personal copy. The original, along with the T-Shirt, chain of custody report, and independently verified DNA results have been delivered to Jim Swanson, the newly appointed FBI Director. We've also provided the Department of Treasury with the account numbers of all your foreign bank accounts, and the U.S. Marshals Service has just confiscated Dr. Craine's private jet you planned to take to the Caymans. That convinced the judge that you are indeed, a flight risk. Your FBI detail should be arriving any minute now to escort you to your new home."

Hastings stole a quick glance at Archer, and then looked away again, visibly shaken. "You think you've won, don't you?"

"Answering that is like guessing at the direction of a rat hole underground," Archer replied slowly. "So no, I don't."

"Because you've only scratched the surface of a foundation that's been built over years," Hastings said evenly. "We're interconnected, compartmented, and global, and we can't be stopped by a few amateurs like you. All of us have sworn an oath to readily sacrifice ourselves, if necessary."

"Well, I'd say it's a right good start then." Archer stood up, his eyes narrowed. "All of the justice in the world isn't fastened up in the courthouse. And none of us are under any illusions that righting this ship will be simple after all the damage you've caused."

Archer heard the sound of multiple car doors closing outside the house, and nodded. "That would be the FBI—I'll leave you to it then."

THE FIFTH COLUMN

President Succumbs to Radiation Poisoning at the Hands of own Vice President
Speaker of the House Daniel Tory Assumes the Presidency

By JAN RAYBURN
Special to THE NEW YORK TIMES

Washington, D.C., January 30—President Stone has died three weeks after drinking red wine laced with polonium 210 — a rare substance that is only available through government nuclear reactors. Mr. Stone consumed the poisoned wine at the home of Dr. Robert Craine, CEO of V-TEC, and a significant contributor to his campaign. In a previously prepared statement President Stone accused his own running mate and Vice President, Zachary Hastings, of his own murder.

Speaker of the House Daniel O. Tory was sworn in as the 56th President of the United States 60 minutes after Mr. Stone's death.

Mr. Tory is 42 years old; Mr. Stone was 56.

Scientists were alarmed at the use of the rare and hard-to-produce substance, Polonium 210, which is dangerous when breathed, injected or ingested. The substance was used to poison former KGB agent, Alexander Litvinenko, in 2006 in London.

President' Stone's family, citing what they called a statement dictated by the dying President Stone, accused Vice President Hastings of a "barbaric and ruthless" murder — a charge Hastings' attorney promptly rejected.

JOHN FENZEL & TOM RENDALL

President Stone died from the effects of radiation poisoning at 12:30 P.M., Eastern Standard Time. He was pronounced dead at 1 P.M.

Priests Administer Last Rites

Mrs. Stone was in the hospital near her husband when he died. Two priests administered last rites to Mr. Stone, a Roman Catholic. They were the Rev. Christopher Pelayo and the Rev. Basil Lender. When the body was taken from the hospital in a bronze coffin about 2 P.M., Mrs. Stone walked beside it. Her face was sorrowful. She looked steadily at the floor. Her hand rested lightly on her husband's coffin as it was taken to a waiting hearse. She was then escorted by the Secret Service back to the White House for Mr. Tory's swearing in.

Mr. Tory was sworn in as President by Supreme Court Chief Justice Ana Schonfeld. Schonfeld was appointed as Chief Justice in October.

The ceremony, delayed about five minutes for Mrs. Stone's arrival, took place in the East Room of the White House, and was attended by White House Staff and Congressional leaders.

Mrs. Stone stood stoically at the left of Mr. Tory. Mrs. Tory, wore a light blue dress, stood at her husband's right.

As Chief Justice Schonfeld read the brief oath of office, Mr. Tory's hands rested on a black, leather-bound Bible as Chief Justice Schonfeld read and Tory repeated: "I do solemnly swear that I will perform the duties of the President of the United

309

States to the best of my ability and defend, protect and preserve the Constitution of the United States."

Those 34 words made Daniel O. Tory, one-time Mayor of Lake Forest, Illinois, the President of the United States.

Tory Embraces Mrs. Stone.

Mr. Tory embraced Mrs. Stone and she held his hand for a long moment. He also embraced Mrs. Tory and Mrs. Evelyn Kennedy, Mr. Stone's private secretary.

Mr. Stone's staff members appeared stunned and bewildered. Lawrence F. O'Connell, the Congressional liaison officer, and P. Kenneth O'Brien, the appointment secretary, both long associates of Mr. Stone, appeared stricken by sorrow. None had any comments.

Other staff members believed to be in the room for the swearing-in included Katrina Franks, the White House receptionist; Miss Pamela Turner, Mrs. Stone's press secretary, and Ryan Costa, the assistant White House press secretary.

Mr. Costa announced the President's death, with choked voice and red-rimmed eyes, at about 1:16 P.M.

"President Stone died at approximately 1 o'clock Eastern Standard Time today here at Walter Reed," Mr. Costa said at the hospital. "He died of radiation poisoning. I have no other details regarding the assassination of the President."

The FBI's investigation of President Stone's poisoning and assassination this week uncovered an established criminal network of senior administration officials, congressional members and staff who were actively attempting to assume control of all elements of U.S. power. The series of dramatic events that followed, culminated yesterday in the impeachment and conviction of Vice President Zachary Hastings.

Vice President Hastings Arrested at Home

Shortly after the assassination, Vice President Zachary Hastings, 56 years old, who had risen to the rank of 4-Star General in the United States Army and selected by Mr. Stone to be his running mate, was arrested by the FBI at his home, and charged with the killing.

President Tory's First Statements and Actions

Daniel Tory was the nation's first Independent Congressman to be elected Speaker of the House, and he's be the first President of the United States since Millard Fillmore who was not a member of a major political party. "I am an American first, and an Independent second," Tory repeated yesterday. "My first priority, during these turbulent times, is to protect and defend the Constitution of the United States. I take that oath very seriously. My immediate goal is to begin the work of healing our nation."

Daniel Tory's assumption of the Presidency represents the first time a Speaker of the House has risen to the position as President. With no Vice President appointed to become President, the 1947 Succession Act directs that the line of presidential succession begins with the Speaker of the House followed by the President pro tempore of the Senate (the longest serving senator).

Mr. Tory's first act as the incoming President was to request the resignations of all political appointees, effective immediately.

Turning on the ignition of the Sabre 66 Dirigo Express Cruiser, Archer glanced quickly at the other articles that appeared below the fold:

Lawmakers Abolishing Consumer Financial Protection Bureau

Powerful Republicans and Democrats sponsoring a bill that would abolish the CFPB.

By JAN RAYBURN, Associated Press
WASHINGTON (AP) — In an unprecedented display of unity, four powerful Republicans and Democrats have introduced legislation in the House and Senate to abolish the Consumer Financial Protection Bureau (CFPB).

President Daniel Tory's proposed budget also targeted the CFPB for elimination.

"The lack of congressional oversight over the CFPB's $1 Billion budget and operations, to funding illicit and clandestine government sponsored operations aimed at subverting opposition groups, the agency continues to grow in power and magnitude without any accountability to Congress and the people,"

President Tory stated in his national television address last night.

The president can fire the director only for cause, and Mr. Tory did exactly that last evening, just prior to his television address. President Tory also noted that Congress doesn't set the budget for the CFPB, which is funded through transfers from the Federal Reserve.

Fifty-seven congressmen and seventy-five senators have signed on to bills that target the CFPB for elimination.

"Right now, it is a combination of regulator, judge, jury, and executioner. And it's unconstitutional," Mr. Tory stated.

Supreme Court rejects Renewal of Nuclear Plant in Maine

By JAN RAYBURN, Associated Press
Washington | The U.S. Supreme Court has declined to hear V-Tec's challenge of an appeals court ruling that overturned State approval of a plan to build two nuclear reactors in Maine.

Setting aside the newspaper, Archer looked over at Elena sitting beside him at the helm of the boat, as it cut effortlessly through the water.

After all that had transpired, he was glad she had agreed to accompany him on this trip.

After several minutes, Archer pointed in the distance at Isle au Haut's harbor in the distance. "That's Duck Harbor," he said quietly. It's also part of Acadia National Park. Not many people come out here though."

He looked around, seeing a massive sunset over the bow of the ship, and then shut the 900-horsepower Volvo engines down and dropped the anchor. Turning to Elena, Archer said simply, "She'd like it here, I think."

Elena nodded, understanding Archer's intent, but feeling suddenly like an outsider.

Archer pulled out the box holding Becky's ashes, and as he'd done so many times since her passing, rubbed his hands over the top and sides. "I'll come back here to visit you."

Stepping out onto the main deck, he heard the pattering of paws racing toward him, and looked back to see the Rottweiler-Mastiff mix puppy Elena had rescued, charging toward him.

"Sorry," Elena said mildly, shaking her head. "She doesn't quite understand boat etiquette just yet."

"We'll just have to teach her," Archer replied.

"You haven't even named her yet," Elena laughed.

Archer smiled, then looked at Elena. "Are you okay with this?"

"I should be asking you if you're okay with me being here?" Elena answered delicately.

"I'd prefer it, if it's okay with you?"

Elena nodded. Solemn. "Of course."

Archer nodded and led them along the gunwale to the bow of the ship.

Leaning against the stainless steel railing, he took an envelope from his pocket, with an old card inside. "Becky gave this to me on our tenth anniversary. I didn't understand the message at the time, because we were in the prime of our lives. Now, somehow, it all makes sense."

Archer handed it to Elena. "Will you read it for me?"

Elena nodded, took the envelope, removed the card, and opened it. Reading it silently at first, she began to cry. "Oh, Archer, are you sure—?"

Archer nodded, holding the box tightly in his hands.

Elena read the message reverently, out loud:

"When all may end, don't be sad because I've gone. Smile for all that goes on. Open your eyes wide, and see all that still endures, and hear the laughter to remind you—of the love and life we shared."

When Elena finished reading the inscription in the card, Archer quietly opened the box and removed the top seal. Holding his arms out, he allowed the ashes to be carried off over the water, into the wind.

"Thank you," Archer said, closing the box, and taking a deep breath as the last of the ashes disappeared into the waves.

He looked down on his new pup, tugging on his pant leg.

"Let's name her *Belle*," Elena said, smiling tearfully.

"You're beautiful," he whispered, leaning over, kissing the side of her head, he felt tears come to his eyes, and an accompanying sense of infinite peace.

Brightened at once, she lifted her hands to his head and looked deeply into his eyes, smiled—then kissed him back. "So are you."

Looking out at the horizon, she pointed at another boat approaching them in the distance. "Expecting anyone?"

A loud siren cut across the water...followed by repeated blasts of a foghorn.

Archer lifted a pair of binoculars to his head. After a moment, he shook his head and smiled.

"Who is it?" Elena asked.

"Pirates," Archer replied, shaking his head in disbelief. "A damn motley crew of 'em...."

It was a tugboat to be exact—with a red and black hull, and tire fenders. Through the binoculars, Archer recognized Shen, Dag, and Max hanging off the rails of the tug's bow, shouting and laughing with bottles in hand.

"...And they're all three sheets to the wind."

As they drew closer, Elena also recognized the group. Breaking out into a broad smile, she waved at them. Archer was also smiling, still shaking his head.

"*Colonel!* Elena!" Max shouted, raising an old bottle of Chateau Latour. "Mind if we join you!"

Once on board, Archer filled glasses with the wine for everyone on board. Archer raised his glass.

"To fallen comrades...until we meet again."